Praise for *The Piano Teacher* by Janice Lee

"Sleek, spare prose...*The Piano Teacher* is laced with intrigue."
—*The New York Times Book Review*

"Immensely satisfying debut."
—*People* (4 stars)

"This season's *Atonement*...The riveting narrative follows Claire, a conventional, middle-class British girl, as she moves to Hong Kong in the 1950s with her civil servant husband and is transformed, E. M. Forster style, by the freedom of the exotic place. The book has an incredibly escapist pull....Reading *The Piano Teacher* is the perfect vicarious voyage." —*Elle*

"Sensual and gripping."
—*Good Housekeeping*

"Evocative, poignant and skillfully crafted, *The Piano Teacher* is more than an epic tale of war and a tangled, tortured love story. It is the kind of novel one consumes in great, greedy gulps, pausing (grudgingly) only when absolutely necessary....If we measure the skill of a fiction writer by her ability to create characters and atmosphere so effortlessly real, so alive on the page, that the reader feels a sense of participatory anxiety—as if the act of reading gives one the power to somehow influence the outcome of purely imaginary events—then Lee should be counted among the very best in recent memory."
—*Chicago Tribune*

"War, love, betrayal—an exquisite fugue of a first novel...Intensely readable debut novel."
—*O, The Oprah Magazine*

"Lee tells two engrossing love stories....Just hide your phone before cracking this one open—or risk calling your ex."
—*Marie Claire*

"East meets West, and peace meets war, in a compelling debut novel."
—*Body & Soul*

"Lee is at her best when describing the horrors of the blood-soaked occupation. She paints a compelling portrait of the devastating choices people make in order to survive."
—*TimeOut New York*

"Janice Y. K. Lee delivers a standout debut."
—*The Boston Globe*

"The novel is sustained by elegant prose and a terrific sense of place. As Graham Greene evoked Vietnam in *The Quiet American*, Lee, born and raised in Hong Kong long after the war, captures the city as it was during World War II, its glittering veneer barely masking the panic and corruption beneath."
—*The Miami Herald*

"Lee delivers a standout debut.... The rippling of past actions through to the present lends the narrative layers of intrigue and more than a few unexpected twists. Lee covers a little-known time in Chinese history without melodrama, and deconstructs without judgment the choices people make in order to live one more day under torturous circumstances."
—*Publishers Weekly* (starred review)

"A lush examination of East-West relations."
—*Kirkus Reviews*

"Lee has created the sort of interesting, complex characters, especially in Trudy, that drive a rich and intimate look at what happens to people under extraordinary circumstances."
—*Booklist*

"Rarely does one encounter a debut work as beguiling and assured as Janice Lee's *The Piano Teacher*. Rich with intrigue, romance, and betrayal, this wonderfully written, utterly captivating novel dazzles with its sharp-eyed renderings of beau monde Hong Kong as it is plunged into the crucible of war. With its fascinating interplay of East and West and wide cast of effervescent characters, especially the singularly haunting Trudy Liang, this is a truly transporting—and indeed irresistible—work of fiction."
—Chang-rae Lee

"This is rare and exquisite story. It does exactly what a great novel should do—transports you out of time, out of place, into a world you can feel on your very skin."
—Elizabeth Gilbert, author of *Eat, Pray, Love*

"One of the most insightful, elegant, and atmospheric novels I've read in a long time. Janice Lee is nothing short of brilliant and her novel is impossible to put down."
—Gary Shteyngart

"Compelling... A persuasive re-creation of a time and place."
—Penelope Lively

PENGUIN BOOKS

THE PIANO TEACHER

Janice Y. K. Lee was born and raised in Hong Kong and graduated from Harvard College. A former editor at *Elle* magazine, she currently lives in Hong Kong with her husband and children. *The Piano Teacher* is her first book.

The Piano Teacher

A NOVEL

Janice Y. K. Lee

PENGUIN BOOKS

PENGUIN BOOKS

Published by the Penguin Group

Penguin Group (USA) Inc., 375 Hudson Street,
New York, New York 10014, U.S.A.

Penguin Group (Canada), 90 Eglinton Avenue East, Suite 700, Toronto,
Ontario, Canada M4P 2Y3 (a division of Pearson Penguin Canada Inc.)

Penguin Books Ltd, 80 Strand, London WC2R 0RL, England

Penguin Ireland, 25 St Stephen's Green, Dublin 2, Ireland (a division of Penguin Books Ltd)

Penguin Group (Australia), 250 Camberwell Road, Camberwell,
Victoria 3124, Australia (a division of Pearson Australia Group Pty Ltd)

Penguin Books India Pvt Ltd, 11 Community Centre,
Panchsheel Park, New Delhi – 110 017, India

Penguin Group (NZ), 67 Apollo Drive, Rosedale, North Shore 0632,
New Zealand (a division of Pearson New Zealand Ltd)

Penguin Books (South Africa) (Pty) Ltd, 24 Sturdee Avenue,
Rosebank, Johannesburg 2196, South Africa

Penguin Books Ltd, Registered Offices:
80 Strand, London WC2R 0RL, England

First published in the United States of America by Viking Penguin,
a member of Penguin Group (USA) Inc. 2008
Published in Penguin Books 2009

1   3   5   7   9   10   8   6   4   2

THE LIBRARY OF CONGRESS HAS CATALOGED THE HARDCOVER EDITION AS FOLLOWS:
Lee, Janice Y. K.
The Piano Teacher / Janice Y. K. Lee
p. cm.
ISBN 978-0-670-02048-5 (hc.)
ISBN 978-0-14-311653-0 (pbk.)
1. Piano teachers—Fiction.   2. Married women—Fiction.   3. English—China—Hong Kong—
Fiction.   4. Hong Kong (China)—Fiction.   5. Nineteen fifties—Fiction.   I. Title.
PS3612.E34295P56 2009
813'.6—dc22   2008027449

Printed in the United States of America
Set in Dante
Designed by Francesca Belanger

For my parents

❖ Part I ❖

May 1952

IT STARTED as an accident. The small Herend rabbit had fallen into Claire's purse. It had been on the piano and she had been gathering up the sheet music at the end of the lesson when she knocked it off. It fell off the doily (a doily! on the Steinway!) and into her large leather bag. What had happened after that was perplexing, even to her. Locket had been staring down at the keyboard and hadn't noticed. And then, Claire had just... left. It wasn't until she was downstairs and waiting for the bus that she grasped what she had done. And then it had been too late. She went home and buried the expensive porcelain figurine under her sweaters.

Claire and her husband had moved to Hong Kong nine months ago, transferred by the government, which had posted Martin at the Department of Water Services. Churchill had ended rationing and things were starting to return to normal when they had received news of the posting. She had never dreamed of leaving England before.

Martin was an engineer, overseeing the building of the Tai Lam Cheung reservoir, so that there wouldn't need to be so much rationing when the rains ebbed, as they did every several years. It was to hold four and a half billion gallons of water when full. Claire almost couldn't imagine such a number, but Martin said it was barely enough for the people of Hong Kong, and he was sure that by the time they were finished, they'd have to build another. "More work for me," he said cheerfully. He was analyzing the topography of the hills so that they could install catchwaters for when the rain came. The English government did so much for the colonies, Claire knew.

They made the locals' lives much better but they rarely appreciated it. Her mother had warned her about the Chinese before she left—an unscrupulous, conniving people who would surely try to take advantage of her innocence and goodwill.

Coming over, she had noticed it for days, the increasing wetness in the air, even more than usual. The sea breezes were stronger and the sunrays more powerful when they broke through cloud. When the *P&O Canton* finally pulled into Hong Kong harbor in August, she really felt she was in the tropics, hair frizzing up in curls, face always slightly damp and oily, the constant moisture under her arms and knees. When she stepped from her cabin outside, the heat assailed her like a physical blow, until she managed to find shade and fan herself.

There had been seven stops along the month-long journey, but after a few grimy hours spent in Algiers and Port Said, Claire had decided to stay onboard rather than encounter more frightening peoples and customs. She had never imagined such sights. In Algiers, she had seen a man kiss a donkey and she couldn't discern whether the high odor was coming from one or the other, and in Egypt, the markets were the very definition of unhygienic—a fishmonger gutting a fish had licked the knife clean with his tongue. She had inquired as to whether the ship's provisions were procured locally, at these markets, and the answer had been most unsatisfactory. An uncle had died from food poisoning in India, making her cautious. She kept to herself and sustained herself mostly on the beef tea they dispensed in the late morning on the sun deck. The menus that were distributed every day were mundane: turnips, potatoes, things that could be stored in the hold, with meat and salads the first few days after port. Martin promenaded on the deck every morning for exercise and tried to get her to join him, to no avail. She preferred to sit in a deck chair with a large brimmed hat and wrap herself in one of the scratchy wool ship blankets, face shaded from the omnipresent sun.

There had been a scandal on the ship. A woman, going to meet her fiancé in Hong Kong, had spent one too many moonlit nights on the deck with another gentleman and had disembarked in the Philippines with her new man, leaving only a letter for her intended. Liesel, the girlfriend to whom the woman had entrusted the letter, grew visibly more nervous as the date of arrival drew near. Men joked that she could take Sarah's place, but she wasn't having any of that. Liesel was a serious young woman who was joining her sister and brother-in-law in Hong Kong, where she intended to educate Unfortunate Chinese Girls in Art: when she held forth on it, it was always with capital letters in Claire's mind.

Before disembarking, Claire separated out all of her thin cotton dresses and skirts; she could tell that was all she would be wearing for a while. They had arrived to a big party on the dock, with paper streamers and loud, shouting vendors selling fresh fruit juice and soy milk drinks and garish flower arrangements to the people waiting. Groups of revelers had already broken out the champagne and were toasting the arrival of their friends and family.

"We pop them as soon as we see the boat on the horizon," a man explained to his girl as he escorted her off the boat. "It's a big party. We've been here for hours." Claire watched Liesel go down the gangplank, looking very nervous, and then she disappeared into the throng. Claire and Martin went down next, treading on the soft, humid wood, luggage behind them carried by two scantily clad young Chinese boys who had materialized out of nowhere.

Martin had an old school friend, John, who worked at Dodwell's, one of the trading firms, who had promised to greet the ship. He came with two friends and offered the new arrivals freshly squeezed guava drinks. Claire pretended to sip at hers, as her mother had warned her about the cholera that was rampant in these parts. The men were bachelors and very pleasant. John, Nigel, Leslie. They explained that they all lived together in a mess—there were many, known by their companies, Dodwell's Mess, Jardine's Mess, et cetera, and they assured Claire and Martin that Dodwell's threw the best parties around.

They accompanied them to the government-approved hotel in Tsim Sha Tsui, where a Chinese man with a long queue, dirty white tunic, and shockingly long fingernails showed them to their room. They made an arrangement to meet for tiffin the next day and the men departed, leaving Martin and Claire sitting on the bed, exhausted and staring at one another. They didn't know each other that well. They had been married barely four months.

She had accepted Martin's proposal to escape the dark interior of her house, her bitter mother railing against everything, getting worse, it seemed, with her advancing age, and an uninspiring job as a filing girl at an insurance company. Martin was older, in his forties, and had never had luck with women. The first time he kissed her, she had to stifle the urge to wipe her mouth. He was like a cow, slow and steady. And kind. She knew this. She was grateful for it.

She had not had many chances with men. Her parents stayed home all the time, and so she had as well. When she had started seeing Martin—he was the older brother of one of the girls at work—she had eaten dinner at restaurants, drunk a cocktail at a hotel bar, and seen other young women and men talking, laughing with an assurance she could not fathom. They had opinions about politics; they had read books she had never heard of and seen foreign films and talked about them with such confidence. She was enthralled and not a little intimidated. And then Martin had come to her, serious, his job was taking him to the Orient, and would she come with him? She was not so attracted to him, but who was she to be picky, she thought, hearing the voice of her mother. She let him kiss her and nodded yes.

Claire had started to draw a bath in their hotel room when another knock on the door revealed a small Chinese woman, an amah, she was called, who started to unpack their suitcases until Martin shooed her off.

And that was how they arrived in Hong Kong, which was like nothing Claire had imagined. Apart from the usual colonial haunts— all hush and genteel potted palms and polished wood in white-washed buildings—it was loud and crowded and dirty and bustling. The buildings were right next to one another and often had clothing hung out to dry on bamboo poles. There were garish vertical signs hung on every one, and they advertised massage parlors and pubs and hair salons. Someone had told her that opium dens still existed in back-alley buildings. There was often refuse on the street, some-times even human refuse, and there was a pungent, peppery odor in town that was oddly clingy, attaching itself to your very skin until you went home for a good scrub. There were all sorts of people. The local women carried their babies in a sort of back sling. Sikhs served as uniformed security guards—you saw them dozing off on wooden stools outside the banks, turbaned heads hanging heavily off their chests, rifles held loosely between their knees. The Indians had been brought over by the British, of course. Pakistanis ran carpet stores, Portuguese were doctors, and Jews ran the dairy farms and other large businesses. There were English businessmen and American bankers, White Russian aristocrats, and Peruvian entrepreneurs— all peculiarly well traveled and sophisticated—and, of course, there were the Chinese, quite different in Hong Kong from the ones in China, she was told.

To her surprise, she didn't detest Hong Kong, as her mother had told her she would—she found the streets busy and distracting, so very different from Croydon, and filled with people and shops and goods she had never seen before. She liked to sample the local bakery goods, the pineapple buns and yellow egg tarts, and some-times wandered outside Central, where she would quickly find herself in unfamiliar surroundings, where she might be the only non-Chinese around. The fruit stalls were heaped with not only oranges and bananas, still luxuries in postwar England, but spiky, strange-looking fruits she came to try and like: star fruit, durian, lychee. She would buy a dollar's worth and be handed a small, waxy brown bag and she would eat the fruit slowly as she walked. There were small stalls made of crudely nailed wood and corrugated tin, which housed specialty shops: this one sold chops, the stone stamps the Chinese used in place of signatures; this one made only keys; this one had a chair that was rented for half-days by a street dentist and a barber. The locals ate on the street in tiny little restaurants called *daipaidong,* and she had seen three worker men in dirty singlets and trousers crouched over a plate containing a whole fish, spitting out the bones at their feet. One had seen her watching them, and deliberately picked up the fish's eyeball with his chopsticks and raised it up to her, smiling, before he ate it.

Claire hadn't met many Chinese people before, but the ones she had seen in the big towns in England were serving you in restaurants or ironing clothes. There were many of those types in Hong Kong, of course, but what had been eye-opening was the sight of the affluent Chinese, the ones who seemed English in all but their skin color. It had been quite something to see a Chinese step out of a Rolls-Royce, as she had one day when she was waiting on the steps of the Gloucester Hotel, or in business suits, eating lunch with other Englishmen who talked to them as if they were the same. She hadn't known that such worlds existed. And then with Locket, she was thrust into their world.

After a few months settling in, finding a flat and setting it up, Claire had put the word out that she was looking for a job teaching the piano, somewhat as a lark, she put it—something to fill the day—but the truth was, they could really use the extra money. She had played the piano most of her life and was primarily self-taught. Amelia, an acquaintance she had met at a sewing circle, said she would ask around.

She rang a few days later.

"There's a Chinese family, the Chens. They run everything in town. Apparently, they're looking for a piano teacher for their daughter, and they'd prefer an Englishwoman. What do you think?"

"A Chinese family?" Claire said. "I hadn't thought about that possibility. Aren't there any English families looking?"

"No," Amelia said. "Not that I've been able to ascertain."

"I just don't know . . ." Claire demurred. "Wouldn't it be odd?" She couldn't imagine teaching a Chinese girl. "Does she speak English?"

"Probably better than you or me," Amelia said impatiently. "They're offering very adequate compensation." She named a large sum.

"Well," Claire said slowly, "I suppose it couldn't do any harm to meet them."

Victor and Melody Chen lived in the Mid-Levels, in an enormous white two-story house on May Road. There was a driveway, with potted plants lining the sides. Inside, there was the quiet, efficient buzz of a household staffed with plentiful servants. Claire had taken a bus, and when she arrived, she was perspiring after the walk from the road to the house. The amah had led her to a sitting room, where she found a fan blowing blessedly cool air. A houseboy adjusted the drapes so that she was properly shaded. Her blue linen skirt, just delivered from the tailor, was wrinkled, and she had on a white voile blouse that was splotched with moisture. She hoped the Chens would allow her some time to compose herself. She shifted, feeling a drop of perspiration trickle down her thigh.

No such luck. Mrs. Chen swooped through the door, a vision in cool pink, holding a tray of drinks. A small, exquisite woman, with hair cut just so, so that it swung in precise, geometric movements. Her shoulders were fragile and exposed in her sleeveless shift, her face a tiny oval.

"Hello!" Mrs. Chen trilled. "Lovely to meet you. I'm Melody. Locket's just on her way."

"Locket?" Claire said, uncertain.

"My daughter. She's just back from school and getting changed into something more comfortable. Isn't the heat dreadful?" She set down the tray, which held long glasses of iced tea. "Have something cool, please."

"Your English is remarkably good," Claire said as she took a glass.

"Oh, is it?" Melody said casually. "Four years at Wellesley will do that for you, I suppose."

"You were at university in America?" Claire asked. She hadn't known that Chinese went to university in America.

"Loved every minute," she said. "Except for the horrible, horrible food. Americans think a grilled cheese sandwich is a meal! And as you know, we Chinese take food very seriously."

"Is Locket going to be schooled in America?"

"We haven't decided, but really, I'd rather talk to you about your schooling," Mrs. Chen said.

"Oh." Claire was taken aback.

"You know," she continued pleasantly. "Where you studied music, and all that."

Claire settled back in her seat.

"I was a serious student for a number of years. I studied with Mrs. Eloise Pollock and was about to apply for a position at the Royal Conservatory when my family situation changed."

Mrs. Chen sat, waiting, head tilted, with one birdlike ankle crossed over the other, her knees slanted to one side.

"And so, I was unable to continue," Claire said. Was she supposed to explain it in detail to this stranger? Her father had been let go from the printing company and it had been a black couple of months before he found a new job as an insurance salesman. His pay had been erratic at best—he was not a natural salesman—and luxuries like piano lessons were unthinkable. Mrs. Pollock, a very kind woman, had offered to continue her instruction at a much-reduced fee, but her mother, sensitive and pointlessly proud, had refused to even entertain the idea.

"And what level of studies did you achieve?"

"I was studying for my seventh grade examinations."

"Locket is a beginning student but I want her to be taught seriously, by a serious musician," Mrs. Chen said. "She should pass all her examinations with distinction."

"Well, I'm certainly serious about music, and as for passing with distinction, that will be up to Locket," Claire said. "I did very well on my examinations."

Locket entered the room, or rather, she bumbled into it. Where her mother was small and fine, Locket was chubby, all rounded limbs and padded cheeks. She was wider than her mother already, and had glossy hair tied in a thick ponytail.

"Hallo," she said. She had a very distinct English accent.

"Locket, this is Mrs. Pendleton," Melody said, stroking her daughter's cheek. "She's come to see if she'll be your piano teacher so you must be very polite."

"Do you like the piano, Locket?" Claire said, too slowly, she realized, for a ten-year-old child. She had no experience with children.

"I dunno," Locket said. "I suppose so."

"Locket!" her mother cried. "You said you wanted to learn. That's why we bought you the new Steinway."

"Locket's a pretty name," Claire said. "How did you come about it?"

"Dunno," said Locket. She reached for a glass of iced tea and drank. A small trickle wended its way down her chin. Her mother took a napkin off the silver tray and dabbed at her daughter's chin.

"Will Mr. Chen be arriving soon?" Claire asked.

"Oh, Victor!" Melody laughed. "He's far too busy for these household matters. He's always working."

"I see," Claire said. She was uncertain as to what came next.

"Would you play us something?" Melody asked. "We just got the piano and it would be lovely to hear it played professionally."

"Of course," Claire said, because she didn't know what else to say. She felt as if she were being made to perform like a common entertainer—something in Melody's tone—but she couldn't think of a gracious way to demur.

She played a simple étude, which Melody seemed to enjoy and Locket squirmed through.

"I think this will be fine," Mrs. Chen said. "Are you available on Thursdays?"

Claire hesitated. She didn't know whether she was going to take the job.

"It would have to be Thursdays because Locket has lessons the other days," Mrs. Chen said.

"Fine," said Claire. "I accept."

Locket's mother was of a Hong Kong type. Claire saw women like her lunching at the Chez Henri, laughing and gossiping with one another. They were called *taitais* and you could spot them at the smart-clothing boutiques, trying on the latest fashions or climbing into their chauffeur-driven cars. Sometimes Mrs. Chen would come home and put a slim, perfumed hand on Locket's shoulder and comment liltingly on the music. And then, Claire couldn't help it, she really couldn't, she would think to herself, You people drown your daughters! Her mother had told her that, about how the Chinese were just a little above animals and that they would drown their daughters because they preferred sons. Once, Mrs. Chen had mentioned a function at the Jockey Club that she and her husband were going to. She had been all dressed up in diamonds, a black flowing dress, and red, red lipstick. She had not looked like an animal. Bruce Comstock, the head of the Water office, had taken Martin and Claire to the club once, with his wife, and they drank pink gin while watching the horse races, and the stands had been filled with shouting gamblers.

The week before the figurine fell into Claire's purse, she had been leaving the lesson when Victor and Melody Chen came in. It had rung five on the ornate mahogany grandfather clock that had mother-of-pearl Chinese characters inlaid all down the front of it and she had been putting her things away when they walked into the room. They were a tiny couple and they looked like porcelain dolls, with their shiny skin and coal eyes.

"Out the door already?" Mr. Chen said drily. He was dressed nattily in a navy blue pin-striped suit with a burgundy pocket square peeping out just so. "It's five on the dot!" He spoke English with the faintest hint of a Chinese accent.

Claire flushed.

"I was here early. Ten minutes before four, I believe," she said. She took pride in her punctuality.

"Oh, don't be silly," Mrs. Chen said. "Victor is just teasing you. Stop it!" She swatted her husband with her little hand.

"You English are so serious all the time," he said.

"Well," Claire said uncertainly. "Locket and I had a productive hour together." Locket slipped off the piano bench and under her father's arm.

"Hello, Daddy," she said shyly. She looked younger than her ten years. He patted her shoulder.

"How's my little Rachmaninoff?" he said. Locket giggled delightedly.

Mrs. Chen was clattering around in her high heels.

"Mrs. Pendleton," she asked, "would you like to join us for a drink?" She had on a suit that looked like it came out of the fashion magazines. It was almost certainly a Paris original. The jacket was made of a golden silk and buttoned smartly up the front, and there was a shimmery yellow skirt underneath that flowed and draped like gossamer.

"Oh, no," she answered. "It's very kind of you, but I should go home and start supper."

"I insist," Mr. Chen said. "I must hear about my little genius." His voice didn't allow for any disagreement. "Run along now, Locket. The adults are having a conversation."

There was a large velvet divan in the living room, and several chairs, upholstered in red silk, along with two matching black lacquered tables. Claire sat down in an armchair that was far more slippery than it looked. She sank too deeply into it, then had to move forward in an ungainly manner until she was perched precariously on the edge. She steadied herself with her arms.

"How are you finding Hong Kong?" Mr. Chen said. Melody had gone into the kitchen to ask the amah to bring them drinks.

"Quite well," she said. "It's certainly different, but it's an adventure." She smiled at him. He was a well-groomed man, in his well-pressed suit and red and black silk tie. Above him, there was an oil of a Chinese man dressed in Chinese robes and a black skullcap. "What an interesting painting," she remarked.

He looked up.

"Oh, that," he said. "That's Melody's grandfather, who had a large dye factory in Shanghai. He was quite famous."

"Dyes?" she said. "How fascinating."

"Yes, and her father started the First Bank of Shanghai, and did very well indeed." He smiled. "Melody comes from a family of entrepreneurs. Her family was all educated in the West—England and America."

Mrs. Chen came back into the room. She had taken off her jacket to reveal a pearly blouse underneath.

"Claire," she said. "What will you have?"

"Just soda water for me, please," she said.

"And I'll have a sherry," Mr. Chen said.

"I know!" Mrs. Chen said. She left again.

"And your husband," he said. "He's at a bank?"

"He's at the Department of Water Services," she said. "Working on the new reservoir." She paused. "He's heading it up."

"Oh, very good," Mr. Chen said carelessly. "Water's certainly important. And the English do a fair job making sure it's in the taps when we need it." He sat back and crossed one leg over the other. "I miss England," he said suddenly.

"Oh, did you spend time there?" Claire inquired politely.

"I was at Balliol," he said, flapping his tie, now obviously a college tie, at her. Claire felt as if he had been waiting to tell her this fact. "And Melody went to Wellesley, so we're a product of two different systems. I defend England, and Melody just loves the United States."

"Indeed," Claire murmured. Mrs. Chen came back into the room and sat down next to her husband. The amah came in next and offered Claire a napkin. It had blue cornflowers on it.

"These are lovely," she said, inspecting the embroidered linen.

"They're from Ireland!" Mrs. Chen said. "I just got them!"

"I just bought some lovely Chinese tablecloths at the China Emporium," Claire said. "Beautiful lace cutwork."

"You can't compare them with the Irish ones, though," Mrs. Chen said. "Very crude."

Mr. Chen viewed his wife with amusement.

"Women!" he said to Claire. Another amah brought in a tray of drinks.

Claire sipped at her drink and felt the gassy bubbles in her mouth. Victor Chen looked at her expectantly.

"The Communists are a great threat," she said. This is what she had heard again and again at gatherings.

Mr. Chen laughed.

"Of course! And what will you and Melody do about them?"

"Shut up, darling. Don't tease," said his wife. She took a sip of her drink. Victor watched her.

"What's that you're drinking, love?"

"A little cocktail," she said. "I've had a long day." She sounded defensive.

There was a pause.

"Locket is a good student," Claire said, "but she needs to practice more."

"It's not her fault," Mrs. Chen said breezily. "I'm not here to oversee her practice enough."

Mr. Chen laughed. "Oh, she'll be fine," he said. "I'm sure she knows what she's doing."

Claire nodded. Parents were all the same. When she had children, she would be sure not to indulge them. She set her drink down.

"I should be going," she said. "It's harder to get a seat on the bus after five."

"Are you sure?" Mrs. Chen said. "Pai was getting us some biscuits."

"Oh, no," she demurred. "I really should be leaving."

"We'll have Truesdale drive you home," Mr. Chen offered.

"Oh, no," Claire said. "I couldn't put you out."

"Do you know him?" Mr. Chen asked. "He's English."

"I haven't had the pleasure," Claire said.

"Hong Kong is very small," Mr. Chen said. "It's tiresome that way."

"It's no trouble at all for Truesdale," Mrs. Chen said. "He'll be going home anyway. Where do you live?"

"Happy Valley," answered Claire, feeling put on the spot.

"Oh, that's near where he lives!" Mrs. Chen cried, delighted at the coincidence. "So, it's settled." She called for Pai in Cantonese and told her to call the driver.

"Chinese is such an intriguing language," Claire said. "I hope to pick some up during our time here."

Mr. Chen raised an eyebrow.

"*Cantonese,*" he said, "is very difficult. There are some nine different tones for one sound. It's much more difficult than English. I picked up rudimentary English in a year, but I'm sure I wouldn't have been able to learn Cantonese or Mandarin or Shanghainese in twice that."

"Well," she said brightly, "one always hopes."

Pai walked in and spoke. Mrs. Chen nodded.

"I'm terribly sorry," she said, "but the driver seems to have left already."

"I'll be fine taking the bus," Claire said. Mr. Chen stood up as she picked up her things.

"It was very nice to meet you," he said.

"And you," she said, and walked out, feeling their eyes on her back.

At home, Martin had arrived already.

"Hullo," he said. "You're late today." He was in an undershirt and his weekend trousers, which were stained and shiny at the knees. He had a drink in his hand.

She took off her jacket and put on a pot of water to boil.

"I was at the Chens' house today," she said. "Her parents asked me to stay for a drink."

"Victor Chen, is it?" he asked, impressed. "He's rather a big deal here."

"I gathered," she said. "He was quite something. Not at all like a Chinaman."

"You shouldn't use that word, Claire," Martin said. "It's very old-fashioned and a bit insulting."

Claire colored.

"I've just never..." She trailed off. "I've never seen Chinese people like this."

"You are in Hong Kong," Martin said, not unkindly. "There are all types of Chinese."

"Where is the amah?" she asked, wanting to change the subject.

Yu Ling came from the back when Claire called.

"Can you help with dinner?" Claire said. "I bought some meat at the market."

Yu Ling looked at her impassively. She had a way of making Claire feel uncomfortable, but she couldn't bring herself to sack her. She wondered how the other wives did it—they appeared to handle the help with an easy aplomb that seemed unfamiliar and unattainable to Claire. Some even joked with them and treated them like family members, but she'd heard that was more the American influence. Her friend Cecilia had her amah brush her hair for her before she went to bed, while she sat at her dressing table and put on cold cream. Claire handed Yu Ling the meat she had bought on the way home.

Amah put to work, she went and lay down on the bed with a cold compress over her eyes. How had she gotten here, to this small flat on the other side of the world? She remembered her quiet childhood in Croydon, an only child sitting at her mother's side while she mended clothes, listening to her talk. Her mother had been bitter at what life had handed her, a hand-to-mouth existence, especially after the war, and her father drank too much, maybe because of it. Claire had never imagined life being much more than that. But marrying Martin had thrown everything up in the air and changed it all.

But this was the thing: she, herself, had changed in Hong Kong. Something about the tropical clime had ripened her appearance, brought everything into harmony. Where the other Englishwomen looked as if they were about to wilt in the heat, she thrived, like a hothouse flower. Her hair had lightened in the tropical sun until it was veritably gold. She perspired lightly so that her skin looked dewy, not drenched. She lost weight so that her body hung together compactly and her eyes sparkled, cornflower blue. Martin had remarked on it, how the heat seemed to suit her. When she was at the Gripps or at a dinner party, she saw that men looked at her longer than necessary, came over to talk to her, let their hands linger on her back. She was learning how to speak to people at parties, order in a restaurant with confidence. She felt as if she were finally becoming a woman, not the girl she had been when she had left England. She felt as if she were a woman coming into her own.

And then the next week, after Locket's lesson, the porcelain rabbit had fallen into her purse.

The week after, the phone rang and Locket leaped up to answer it, eager for any excuse to stop mangling the prelude she had been playing, and while she had been chattering away to a schoolmate, Claire saw a silk scarf lying on a chair. It was a beautiful, printed scarf, the kind women tied around their necks. She put it in her bag. A wonderful sense of calm came over her. And when Locket came back into the room with only a mumbled "Sorry, Mrs. Pendleton," Claire smiled instead of giving the little girl a piece of her mind. When she got home, she went into the bedroom, locked the door, and pulled out the scarf. It was an Hermès scarf, from Paris, and had pictures of zebras and lions in vivid oranges and browns. She practiced tying it around her neck, and over her head, like an adventurous heiress on safari. She felt very glamorous.

The next month, after a conversation where Mrs. Chen told her she sent all her fine washing to Singapore, because "the girls here don't know how to do it properly, and, of course, that means I have to have triple the amount of linens, what a bother," Claire found herself walking out with two of those wonderful Irish napkins in her skirt pocket. She had Yu Ling hand wash and iron them so that she and Martin could use them with dinner. She pocketed three French cloisonné turtles while Locket had abruptly gone to the bathroom—as if the child couldn't take care of nature's business before Claire arrived! A pair of sterling salt and pepper shakers found their way into her purse as she was passing through the dining room, and an exquisite Murano perfume bottle left out in the living room, as if Melody Chen had dashed some scent on as she was breezing her way through the foyer on her way to a gala event, was palmed and discreetly tucked into Claire's skirt pocket.

Another afternoon, she was leaving when she heard Victor Chen in his study. He was talking loudly into the telephone and had left his door slightly ajar.

"It's the bloody British," he said, before lapsing into Cantonese. Then, "can't let them," and then some more incomprehensible language that sounded very much like swearing. "They want to create unrest, digging up skeletons that should be left in the closet, and all for their own purposes. The Crown Collection didn't belong to them in the first place. It's all our history, our artifacts, that they just took for their own. How'd they like it if Chinese explorers came to their country years ago and made off with all their treasures? It's outrageous. Downing Street's behind all of this, I can assure you. There's no need for this right now." He was very agitated and Claire found herself waiting outside, breath held, to see if she couldn't hear anything more. She stood there until Pai came along and looked at her questioningly. She pretended she had been looking at the brush painting in the hallway, but she could feel Pai's eyes on her as she walked toward the door. She let herself out and went home.

Two weeks later, when Claire went for her lesson, she found Pai gone and a new girl opening the door.

"This is Su Mei," Locket told her when they entered the room. "She's from China, from a farm. She just arrived. Do you want something to drink?"

The new girl was small and dark and would have been pretty if it hadn't been for a large black birthmark on her right cheek. She never looked up from the floor.

"Her family didn't want her because the mark on her face would make her hard to marry off. It's supposedly very bad luck."

"Did your mother tell you that?" Claire asked.

"Yes," Locket said. She hesitated, "Well, I heard her say it on the telephone, and she said she got her very cheap because of it. Su Mei doesn't know anything! She tried to go to the bathroom in the bushes outside and Ah Wing beat her and told her she was like an animal. She's never used a faucet before or had running water!"

"I'd like a bitter lemon, please, if you have it," Claire said, wanting to change the subject.

Locket spoke to the girl quickly. She left the room silently.

"Pai was stealing from us," Locket said, eyes wide with the scandal. "So Mummy had to let her go. Pai cried and cried, and then she beat the floor with her fists. Mummy said she was hysterical and she slapped her in the face to stop her crying. They had to get Mr. Wong to carry Pai out. He put her over his shoulder like a sack of potatoes and she was hitting his back with her fists."

"Oh!" Claire said before she could stifle the cry.

Locket looked at her curiously.

"Mummy says all servants steal."

"Does she, now?" Claire asked. "How terrible. But you know, Locket, I'm not sure that's true." She remembered the way Pai had looked at her when she came upon her in the hallway and her chest felt tight.

"Where did she go, do you know?" she asked Locket.

"No idea," the girl said cheerfully. "Good riddance, I say."

Claire looked at the placid face of the girl, unruffled by conscience.

"There must be shelters or places for people like her." Claire's voice quivered. "She's not on the street, is she? Does she have family in Hong Kong?"

"Haven't a clue."

"How can you not know? She lived with you!"

"She was a maid, Mrs. Pendleton." Locket looked at her curiously. "Do you know anything about your servants?"

Claire was shamed into silence. The blood rose in her cheeks.

"Well," she said. "I suppose that's enough of that. Did you practice the scales?"

Locket pounded on the piano keys as Claire looked hard at the girl's chubby fingers, trying not to blink so that the tears would not fall.

June 1941

IT BEGINS like that. Her lilting laugh at a consular party. A spilled drink. A wet dress and a handkerchief hastily proffered. She is a sleek greyhound among the others—plump, braying women of a certain class. He doesn't want to meet her—he is suspicious of her kind, all chiffon and champagne, nothing underneath, but she has knocked his glass down her silk shift ("There I go again," she says. "I'm the clumsiest person in all Hong Kong") and then commandeers him to escort her to the bathroom where she daubs at herself while peppering him with questions.

She is famous, born of a well-known couple, the mother a Portuguese beauty, the father a Shanghai millionaire with fortunes in trading and money lending.

"Finally, someone new! We can tell right away, you know. I've been stuck with those old bags for ages. We're very good at sniffing out new blood since the community is so wretchedly small and we're all so dreadfully sick of each other. We practically wait at the docks to drag the new people off the ships. Just arrived, yes? Have a job yet?" she asks, having sat him on the edge of the tub while she reapplies her lipstick. "Is it for fun or funds?"

"I'm at Asiatic Petrol," he says, wary of being cast as the amusing newcomer. "And it's most certainly for funds." Although that's not the truth. A mother with money.

"How delightful!" she says. "I'm so sick of meeting all these stuffy people. They don't have the slightest knowledge or ambition."

"Those without expectations have been known to lack both of those qualities," he says.

"Aren't you a grumpy grump?" she says. "But stupidity is much more forgivable in the poor, don't you think?" She pauses, as if to let him think about that. "Your name? And how do you know the Trotters?"

"I'm Will Truesdale, and I play cricket with Hugh. He knows some of my family, through my mother's side," he says. "I'm new to Hong Kong and he's been very decent to me."

"Hmmm," she says. "I've known Hugh for a decade and I've never ever thought of him as decent. And do you like Hong Kong?"

"It'll do for now," he says. "I came off the ship, decided to stay, rustled up something to do in the meantime. Seems pleasant enough here."

"An adventurer, how fascinating," she says, without the slightest bit of interest. Then she finishes up her ablutions, snaps her evening bag shut, and, firmly taking him by the wrist, waltzes—there is no other verb; music seems to accompany her—out of the powder room.

Conscious of being steered around the room like a pet poodle, her momentary diversion, he excuses himself to go smoke in the garden. But peace is not to be his. She finds him out there, has him light her cigarette, and leans confidentially toward him.

"Tell me," she says. "Why do your women get so fat after marriage? If I were an Englishman I'd be quite put out when the comely young lass I proposed to exploded after a few months of marriage or after popping out a child. You know what I'm talking about?" She blows smoke up to the dark sky.

"Not at all," he says, amused despite himself.

"I'm not as flighty as you think," she says. "I do like you so very much. I'll ring you tomorrow, and we'll make a plan." And then she is gone, wafting smoke and glamour as she trips her way into the resolutely nonsmoking house of their hosts—Hugh loathes the smell. He sees her in the next hour, flitting from group to group, chattering away. The women are dimmed by her, the men bedazzled.

● ● ●

The phone rings at his office the next day. He had been telling Simonds about the party.

"She's Eurasian, is she?" Simonds says. "Watch out there. It's not as bad as dating a Chinese, but the higher-ups don't like it if you fraternize too much with the locals."

"That is an outrageous statement," Will says. He had liked Simonds up to that point.

"You know how it is," Simonds says. "At Hong Kong Bank, you get asked to leave if you marry a Chinese. But this girl sounds different, she sounds rather more than a local girl. It's not like she's running a noodle shop."

"Yes, she is different," he says. "Not that it matters," he adds as he answers the phone. "I'm not marrying her."

"Darling, it's Trudy Liang," she says. "Who aren't you marrying?"

"Nobody." He laughs.

"That would have been quick work."

"Even for you?"

"Wasn't it shocking how many women there were at the party yesterday?" she says, ignoring him. The women in the colony are supposed to be gone, evacuated to safer areas, while the war is simmering, threatening to boil over into their small corner of the world. "I'm essential, you know. I'm a nurse with the Auxiliary Nursing Service!" The only way women had been allowed to stay was to sign up as an essential occupation.

"None of the nurses I've ever had looked like you," he says.

"If you were injured, you wouldn't want me as a nurse, believe me." She pauses. "Listen, I'll be at the races at the Wongs' box this afternoon. Do you care to join us?"

"The Wongs?" he asks.

"Yes, they're my godparents," she says impatiently. "Are you coming or not?"

"All right," he says. This is the first in a long line of acquiescences.

•   •   •

Will muddles his way through the club and into the upper tier, where the boxes are filled with chattering people in jackets and silky dresses. He comes through the door of number 28 and Trudy spies him right away, pounces on him, and introduces him to everybody. There are Chinese from Peru, Polish by way of Tokyo, a Frenchman married to Russian royalty. English is spoken.

Trudy pulls him to one side.

"Oh, dear," she says. "You're just as handsome as I remember. I think I might be in trouble. You've never had any issues with women, I'm sure. Or perhaps you've had too many." She pauses and takes a theatrical breath. "I'll give you the lay of the land here. That's my cousin, Dommie." She points out an elegant, slim Chinese man with a gold pocket watch in his hand. "He's my best friend and very protective, so you better watch out. And avoid her, by any means," she says, pointing to a slight European woman with spectacles. "Awful. She's just spent twenty minutes telling me the most extraordinary and yet incredibly boring story about barking deer on Lamma Island."

"Really?" he says, looking at her oval face, her large golden-green eyes.

"And he," she says, pointing to an owlish Englishman, "is a bore. Some sort of art historian, keeps talking about the Crown Collection, which is apparently something most colonies have. They either acquire it locally or have pieces shipped from England for the public buildings—important paintings and statues and things like that. Hong Kong's is very impressive, apparently, and he's very worried about what will happen once the war breaks loose." She makes a face. "Also a bigot."

She searches the room for others and her eyes narrow.

"There's my other cousin, or cousin by marriage." She points out a stocky Chinese man in a double-breasted suit. "Victor Chen. He thinks he's very important indeed. But I just find him tedious. He's married to my cousin, Melody, who used to be nice until she met him." She pauses. "Now she's . . ." Her voice trails off.

"Well, here you are," she says, "and what a gossip I'm being," and drags him to the front where she has claimed the two best seats. They watch the races. She wins a thousand dollars and shrieks with pleasure. She insists on giving it all away, to the waiters, to the bathroom attendants, to a little girl they pass on the way out. "Really," she says disapprovingly, "this is no place for children, don't you think?" Later she tells him she practically grew up at the track.

Her real name is Prudence. "Trudy" came later, when it became apparent that her given name was wholly unsuitable for the little sprite who terrorized her amahs and charmed all the waiters into bringing her forbidden fizzy drinks and sugar cubes.

"You can call me Prudence, though," she says. Her long arms are draped around his shoulders and her jasmine scent is overwhelming him.

"I think I won't," he says.

"I'm terribly strong," she whispers. "I hope I don't destroy you."

He laughs.

"Don't worry about that," he says. But later, he wonders.

They spend most weekends at her father's large house in Shek O, where wizened servants bring them buckets of ice and lemonade, which they mix with Plymouth gin, and plates of salty shrimp crackers. Trudy lies in the sun wearing an enormous floppy hat, saying she thinks tans are vulgar, no matter what that Coco Chanel says.

"But I do so enjoy the feel of the sun on me," she says, reaching for a kiss.

The Liangs' house is spread out on a promontory where it overlooks a placid sea. They keep chickens for fresh eggs—the hen house far away, of course, because of the odor—and a slightly fraying but still belligerent peacock roams the ground, asserting himself to any intruders, except the groundskeeper's Great Dane, with whom it has a mutual treaty. Trudy's father is never there; mostly he is in Macau, where he is said to have the largest house on the Praia Grande and a Chinese mistress. Why he doesn't marry her, nobody knows. Trudy's mother disappeared when she was eight—a famous case that is still unsolved. The last anyone had seen of her she had been spotted stepping into a car outside the Gloucester Hotel. This is what he likes most about Trudy. Having so many questions in her life, she never asks questions about his.

Trudy has a body like a child—all slim hips and tiny feet. She is as flat as a board, her breasts not even buds. Her arms are as slender as her wrists, her hair a sleek-smoky brown, her eyes wide and Western, with the lid-fold. She wears form-fitting sheaths, sometimes the *qipao,* slim tunics, narrow pants, always flat silk slippers. She wears gold or brown lipstick, wears her hair shoulder-length, straight, and has black, kohl-lined eyes. She looks nothing like any of the other women at events—with their blowsy, flowing floral skirts, carefully permanent-waved hair, red lipstick. She hates compliments—when people tell her she's beautiful, she says instantly, "But I have a mustache!" And she does, a faint golden one you can see only in the sun. She is always in the papers, although, she explains, it's more because of her father than that she is beautiful. "Hong Kong is very practical that way," she says. "Wealth can make a woman beautiful." She is often the only Chinese at a party, although she says she's not really Chinese—she's not really anything, she says. She's everything, invited everywhere. Cercle Sportif Français, the American Country Club, the Deutscher Garten Club, she is welcome, an honorary member to everything.

Her best friend is her second cousin, Dommie, Dominick Wong, the man from the races. They meet every Sunday night for dinner at the Gripps and gossip over what has transpired at the parties over the weekend. They grew up together. Her father and his mother are cousins. Will is starting to see that everyone in Hong Kong is related in one way or another, everyone who matters, that is. Victor Chen, Trudy's other cousin, is always in the papers for his business dealings, or he and his wife, Melody, are smiling out from photographs in the society pages.

Dominick is a fine-chiseled boy-man, a bit effeminate, with a long string of lissome, dissatisfied girlfriends. Will is never invited to Trudy's dinners with Dommie. "Don't be cross. You wouldn't have fun," she says, trailing a cool finger over his cheek. "We chatter away in Shanghainese and it would be so tedious to have to explain everything to you. And Dommie's just about a girl anyways."

"I don't want to go," he says, trying to keep his dignity.

"Of course you don't, darling," she laughs. She pulls him close. "I'll tell you a secret."

"What?" Her jasmine smell brings to mind that waxy yellow flower, her skin as smooth, as impermeable.

"Dommie was born with eleven fingers. Six on the left hand. His family had it removed when he was a baby, but it keeps growing back! Isn't that the most extraordinary thing? I tell him it's the devil inside. You can keep pruning it, but it'll always come back." She whispers. "Don't tell a soul. You're the first person I've ever told! And Dominick would have my head if he knew! He's quite ashamed of it!"

Hong Kong is a small village. At the RAF ball, Dr. Richards was found in the linen room of the Gloucester with a chambermaid; at the Sewells' dinner party, Blanca Morehouse had too much to drink and started to take off her blouse—you know about her past, don't you? Trudy, his very opinionated and biased guide to society, finds the English stuffy, the Americans tiresomely earnest, the French boring and self-satisfied, the Japanese quirky. He wonders aloud how she can stand him. "Well, you're a bit of a mongrel," she says. "You don't belong anywhere, just like me." He had arrived in Hong

Kong with just a letter of introduction to an old family friend, and has found himself defined, before he did anything to define himself, by a chance meeting with a woman who asks nothing of him except to be with her.

People talk about Trudy all the time—she is always scandalizing someone or other. They talk about her in front of him, to him, as if daring him to say something. He never gives them anything about her. She came down from Shanghai, where she spent her early twenties in Noel Coward's old suite at the Cathay, and threw lavish parties on the roof terrace. She is rumored to have fled an affair there, an affair with a top gangster who became obsessed with her, rumored to have spent far too much time in the casinos, rumored to have friends who are singsong girls, rumored to have sold herself for a night to amuse herself, rumored to be an opium addict. She is a Lesbian. She is a Radical. She assures him that almost none of these rumors is true. She says Shanghai is the place to be, that Hong Kong is dreadfully suburban. She speaks fluent Shanghainese, Cantonese, Mandarin, English, conversational French, and a smattering of Portuguese. In Shanghai, she says, the day starts at four in the afternoon with tea, then drinks at the Cathay or someone's party, then dinner of hairy crab and rice wine if you're inclined to the local, then more drinks and dancing, and you go and go, the night is so long, until it's time for breakfast—eggs and fried tomatoes at the Del Monte. Then you sleep until three, have noodles in broth for the hangover, and get dressed for another go around. So fun. She's going to go back one of these days, she says, as soon as her father will let her.

The Biddles hire a cabana at the Lido in Repulse Bay and invite them for a day at the beach. There, they all smoke like mad and drink gimlets while Angeline complains about her life. Angeline Biddle is an old friend of Trudy's, a small and physically unappealing Chinese woman whom she's known since they were at primary school together. She married a very clever British businessman whom she rules with an iron fist, and they have a son away at school. They live in grand style on the Peak, where Angeline's presence causes some discomfort as Chinese are supposed to have permission to live there, except for one family who is so unfathomably rich they are exempt from the rules. There is a feeling, Trudy explains to Will later, that Angeline has somehow got one over on the British who live there, and she is resented for it, although Trudy admits that Angeline is hardly the most likable of people to begin with. In the sun, Trudy takes off her top and sunbathes, her small breasts glowing pale in contrast to the rest of her.

"I thought you thought tans were vulgar," he says.

"Shut up," she says.

He hears her talking to Angeline. "I'm just wild about him," she says. "He's the most stern, solid person I've ever met." He supposes she is talking about him. People are not as scandalized as one might think. Simonds admits he was wrong about her. Although the Englishwomen in the colony are disappointed. Another bachelor taken off the market. Whispered: "she did swoop down and grab him before anyone even knew he was in town."

For him, there have been others, of course—the missionary's daughter in town in New Delhi, always ill and wan, though beautiful; the clever, hopeful spinster on the boat over from Penang—the women who say they're looking for adventure but who are really looking for husbands. He's managed to avoid the inconvenience of love for quite some time, but it seems to have found him in this unlikely place.

Women don't like Trudy. "Isn't that always the case, darling?" she says when he, indiscreetly, asks her about it. "And aren't you a strange one for bringing it up?" She chucks him under the chin and continues making a pitcher of gin and lemonade. "No one likes me," she says. "Chinese don't because I don't act Chinese enough,

Europeans don't because I don't look at all European, and my father doesn't like me because I'm not very filial. Do you like me?"

He assures her he does.

"I wonder," she says. "I can tell why people like you. Besides the fact that you're a handsome bachelor with mysterious prospects, of course. They read into you everything they want you to be. They read into me all that they don't like." She dips her finger in the mix and brings it out to taste. Her face puckers. "Perfect," she says. She likes them sour.

Little secrets begin to spill out of Trudy. A temple fortune-teller told her the mole on her forehead signifies death to a future husband. She's been engaged before, but it ended mysteriously. She tells him these secrets then refuses to elaborate, saying he'll leave her. She seems serious.

Trudy has two amahs. They have "tied their hair up together," she explains. Two women decide not to marry and let a space in the newspaper, like vows, declaring they will live together forever. Ah Lok and Mei Sing are old now, almost sixty, but they live in a small room together with twin beds ("so get that out of your mind right now," Trudy says lazily, "although Chinese are very blasé about that sort of thing and who cares, really") and are a happy couple, excepting that they are both women. "It's the best thing," Trudy says. "Lots of women know they'll never get married so this is just as good. So civilized, don't you think? All you need is a companion. That sex thing gets in the way after a while. A sisterhood thing. I'm thinking about doing it myself." She pays them each twenty-five cents a week and they will do anything for her. Once, he came into the living room to find Mei Sing massaging lotion onto Trudy's hands while she was asleep on the sofa.

He never grows used to them. They completely ignore him, always talking to Trudy about him, in front of him. They tell her he has a big nose, that he smells funny, that his hands and feet are grotesque. He is beginning to understand a little of what they say, but their disapproving intonation needs no translation. Ah Lok cooks—salty, oily dishes he finds unappealing. Trudy eats them with relish—it's the food she grew up with. She claims Mei Sing cleans, but he finds dust balls everywhere. The old woman also collects rubbish—used beer bottles, empty jars of cold cream, discarded toothbrushes—and stores it underneath her bed in anticipation of some apocalyptic event. All three of the women are messy. Trudy has the utter disregard for her surroundings that belongs to those who have been waited on since birth. She never cleans up, never lifts a finger, but neither do the amahs. They have picked up her habits—a peculiar symbiosis. Trudy defends them with the ferocity of a child defending her parents. "They're old," she says. "Leave them alone. I can't bear people who poke at their servants."

She pokes at them though. She argues with them when the flower man comes and Ah Lok wants to give him fifty cents and Trudy says to give him what he wants. The flower man is called Fa Wong, king of flowers, and he comes around to the neighborhood once a week, giant woven baskets slung around his brown, wiry shoulders filled with masses of flowers. He calls out, "fa yuen, fa yuen," a low, monotonous pitch for his wares, and people wave him up to their flats from the window. He and the amahs love to spar and they go at it for ages, shouting and gesticulating, until Trudy comes to break it up and give the man his money. Then Ah Lok gets angry and scolds Trudy for giving in too easily, and the old lady and the lovely young woman, their arms filled with flowers, go into the kitchen, where the blooms will be distributed into vases and scattered around the house. He watches them from his chair, his book spread out over his lap, his eyes hooded as if in sleep—he watches her.

He is almost never alone these days, always with her. It is something different for him. He used to like solitude, aloneness, but now he craves her presence all the time. He's gone without this drug for so long, he's forgotten how compelling it is. When he is at the office, pecking away at the typewriter, he thinks of her laughing, drinking tea, smoking, the rings puffing up in front of her face. "Why do you work?" she asks. "It's so dreary."

Discipline, he thinks, don't fall down that rabbit hole. But it's useless. She's always there, ringing him on the phone, ready with plans for the evening. When he looks at her, he feels weak and happy. Is that so bad?

They are eating brunch at the Repulse Bay and reading the Sunday paper when Trudy looks up.

"Why do they let these awful companies have advertisements?" she asks. "Listen to this one—'Why suffer from agonizing piles?' Is there a need for that? Can't they be a bit more oblique?" She shakes the newspaper at him. "There's an illustration of a man suffering from piles! Is that really necessary?"

"My heart," he says. "I don't know. I just don't know." A displaced Russian in a dinner jacket plays the piano behind him.

"Oh," she says, as if it's an afterthought. "My father wants to meet you. He wants to meet the man I've been spending so much time with." She is nonchalant, too much so. "Are you free tonight?"

"Of course," he says.

They go for dinner at the Gloucester, where Trudy tells him the story of her parents' meeting while they're waiting at the bar. She is drinking brandy, unusual for her, which makes him think she might be more nervous than she is letting on. She swirls it around the snifter, takes a delicate whiff, sips.

"My mother was a great Portuguese beauty—her family had been in Macau for ages. They met there. My father was not as successful then, although he came from a well-to-do family. He had just started up a business selling widgets or something. He's very clever, my father. Don't know why I turned out to be such a dim bulb." Her face lights up. "Here he is!" She leaps off the stool and rushes over to give her father a kiss. Will had expected a big, confident man with the aura of power. Instead, Mr. Liang is small and diffident, with an ill-cut suit and a sweet air. He seems to be overwhelmed by the vitality of his daughter. He lets Trudy wash over him, like a force of nature, much like everyone else in Hong Kong, Will thinks. The maître d' seats them with much hovering and solicitous hand waving, which neither Trudy nor her father seems to notice. They speak to each other in Cantonese, which makes Trudy seem like a different person entirely.

They do not order. Their food is brought to them, as if preordained. "Should we order?" he ventures and their faces are astonished. "You only eat certain dishes here," they say. Trudy calls for champagne. "This is a momentous occasion," she declares. "My father's not met many of my beaus. You've passed the first gauntlet."

Wan Kee Liang does not ask Will about his life or his work. Instead, they exchange pleasantries, talk about the horse races and the war. When Trudy excuses herself to go to the powder room, her father motions for Will to come closer.

"You are not a rich man," he says.

"Not like you, but I do all right." How odd to assume.

"Trudy very spoiled girl, and wants many things." The man's face betrays nothing.

"Yes," Will says.

"Not good for woman to pay for anything."

Trudy's father hands him an envelope.

"Here is money for you to take Trudy out. Will cover expenses for a long time. Not good for Trudy to be paying all the time."

Will is utterly bemused.

"I can't take that," he says. "I'm not going to take your money. I've never let Trudy pay for a meal."

"Doesn't matter." The man waves his hand. "Good for your relationship."

Will refuses and puts the envelope on the table, where it sits until they see Trudy approaching. Trudy's father puts it back in his suit jacket.

"Not meant to be insult," he says. "I want best for Trudy. So best for her means best for you. This means little to me, but might make difference for you two."

"I appreciate the thought," Will says. "But I can't." He lets it go at that.

The next week, Will receives letters in the post from restaurants and clubs around town informing him that his accounts have been opened and are ready for use. One has a note scribbled in the margin, "Just come in, you won't even need to sign. We look forward to seeing you." The tone: apologetic to a good customer, but deferring to the wishes of their best.

He is a little irritated, but not so much, more bemused than anything. He puts the letters in a drawer. He supposes that to Wan Kee Liang everyone looks like a pauper, looking for handouts. The Chinese are wise, he thinks. Or maybe it's just Trudy's family.

Trudy loves the Parisian Grill, is great friends with the owner, a Greek married to a local Portuguese who sees no irony in the fact that he serves the froggiest of foods. She refuses absolutely to go to a Chinese restaurant with Will, will only go with Chinese people, who she says are the only ones who appreciate the food the way it should be.

The Greek who runs the Parisian Grill, his name is now Henri, changed from God knows what, loves Trudy, views her as a daughter, and his wife, Elsbieta, treats Trudy like a sister. She goes there for first drinks almost every night, often ends evenings there as well. Henri and Elsbieta are polite to him, but with a certain reserve. He thinks they have seen too many of Trudy's beaus. He wants to protest that he is the one in danger, protest over the red vinyl banquettes, the smoky white candles burned down to smudgy lumps, but he never does.

They meet everyone at the Parisian Grill. It is the sort of place one goes to when one is new in town, or old, or bored. Hong Kong is small, and eventually everyone ends up there. One night, they have drinks at the bar with a group of visiting Americans and then are invited to dinner with them.

Trudy tells their new friends that she loves Americans, their open-handed extravagance, their loud talk and braying confidence. When someone brings up the war, she pretends not to hear, ignoring them and instead going on about the qualities she feels all Americans have. They have a sense of the world being incomparably large, she says, and a sense that they are able to, not colonize, but spread through all countries, spending their money like water, without guilt or too much consciousness. She loves that. The men are tall and rangy, with long faces and quick decisions, and the women let them be, isn't that wonderful, because they're so busy with their own committees and plans. They invite all and sundry to their events, and they serve marvelous items like potato salads and ham and cheese sandwiches. And, unless there is a very special type of Englishman present (she tips her head toward Will), they tend to diminish the other men in the room. It's very odd, but she's seen it. Haven't you noticed that? If she had it all to do over, she says to the dinner table, she would come back as an American. Barring that possibility, she's going to marry one. Or maybe just move there, if someone objects to her marrying an American, said with eyes cast demurely down as a joke. Will thinks back to when she complained that they were tiresomely earnest and just smiles. She has free will, he says simply. He would never do anything to stop her from doing what she wanted. The Americans applaud. An enlightened man, says a woman with red lips and an orange dress.

• • •

Life is easy. At the office, he is expected in at nine-thirty, then a two-hour lunch is not uncommon, and they knock off at five for drinks. He can go out every night, play all weekend, do whatever he wants. Trudy's friends move to London and want someone responsible to take care of their flat, so Will moves to May Road and pays the ludicrous rent of two hundred Hong Kong dollars, and this only after much wrangling to get her friends, Sudie and Frank Chen, to take anything at all. They all go out for dinner, and it's very civil.

"You're doing us a favor!" they cry, as they pour more champagne.

"You really are, Will," Trudy says. "No one in all Hong Kong would agree to do anything so nice for the Chens, you know. They've awful reputations around here, that's why they're leaving."

"Be that as it may," Will says, "I have to pay something."

"We'll talk about it later," the Chens say, but they never do. Instead they drink four splits of champagne and end up going to the beach at midnight to hunt for crabs by candlelight.

May Road is different from Happy Valley, his old neighborhood. Filled with expatriates and housewives and their servants, it is a bourgeois suburb of England, or how he'd always imagined them to be. Children walk obediently next to their amahs, matrons climb into the backs of their chauffeured cars, it's much more quiet than the chattering bustle of his old haunt. He misses Happy Valley, the vitality of it, the loud, rude locals, the lively shops.

But then there is Trudy. Trudy has a large place not five minutes from him. He walks the winding road to her flat every day after picking up new clothes after work.

"Isn't this nice?" she says, lavishing him with kisses at the door. "Isn't it delicious that you're so close and not in that dreadful Happy Valley? I do think the only time I'd go there before I met you was when I needed plimsolls for the beach. There's this wonderful shop there..."

And then she's on to something else, crying out to Ah Lok that the flowers are browning, or that there's a puddle in the foyer. At Trudy's, there's no talk of war, no fighting except squabbling with the servants, no real troubles. There's only ease and her sweet, lilting laugh. He slips gratefully into her world.

June 1952

CLAIRE HAD BEEN WAKING at the same time every night. Twenty-two minutes after three. By now, she knew it without even looking at the clock. And every night, after she started awake, she would look over at the hulking shape of her husband as he slept, and she would be calmed from the shock of consciousness. His chest rose and fell evenly as his nose reverberated with a gentle snore. He always slept heavily, aided by the several beers he had every evening. She sat up, clapped twice loudly, her hands stiff, the sound like two bullets in the night. Martin shifted at the noise, then breathed freely. That trick was one of the few that her mother had imparted about married life. The clock now showed 3:23.

She tried to go back to sleep. She had done it once or twice before, fallen back asleep before her body got too awake. Breathing softly, she lay flat on her back and felt the damp linen sheet beneath and the light weight of the cotton quilt on top. It was so humid she could wear only a thin cotton nightdress to bed, and even that grew sticky after a day or two. She must buy a new fan. The old one had sputtered to a stop last week, caked with mossy mold. A fan, and also some more electric cord. And lightbulbs. She mustn't forget lightbulbs. She breathed lightly, over the slight rumble of Martin starting up again. Should she write the things down? She would remember, she tried to tell herself. But she knew she would get up and write it down, so as not to forget, so as not to obsess about forgetting, and then she would be up, and unable to go back to sleep. It was settled. She got up softly and felt her way out of the mosquito netting, disturbing a resting mosquito that buzzed angrily in her ear before flying away. The pad was lying next to the bed on a table, and she penciled in her list.

Then, the real reason. She reached into the depths of the bureau and felt around carefully for the bag. It was a cloth bag, one she had got for free at a bazaar, and it was large and full. She pulled it out, quietly.

Going into the bathroom, she switched on the light. The tub sat full of water. There hadn't been rain for several months now, and the government was starting to ration. Yu Ling drew the tub full every evening, between five and seven o' clock, when the water was on, for their use during the day.

Claire set the bag down and dipped a bucket in the water and wet a washcloth to wipe her face. Then she sat on the cool tile floor and pulled her nightdress up so that she could place the bag between her legs.

She dumped the contents out.

There were more than thirty items glittering up at her. More than thirty costly necklaces, scarves, ornaments, perfume bottles. They looked almost tawdry, jumbled together in the harsh bathroom light, against the white tile, so Claire laid down a towel and separated them, so that each had a few inches of space, a cushion against the floor. There, now they looked like the expensive items they were. Here was a ring, thick, beautifully worked gold, with what looked like turquoise. She slipped it on her finger. And here was a handkerchief, so sheer she could see the pale pink of her palm underneath it. She sprayed it with perfume, a small round bottle of it, called Jazz. On the bottle there was a drawing of two women dancing in flapper dresses. She waved the scented handkerchief around. Jasmine scent. Too heavy. She groomed her hair with the tortoiseshell comb, rubbed French hand lotion around her fingers, then carefully applied lipstick to her mouth. Then she clipped on heavy gold earrings and tied a scarf around her head. She stood in front of the mirror. The woman who looked back was sophisticated and groomed, a woman who traveled the world and knew about art and books and yachts.

• • •

She wanted to be someone else. The old Claire seemed provincial, ignorant. She had been to a party at Government House, sipped champagne at the Gripps while women she knew twirled around in silky dresses. She had her nose pressed up against the glass and was watching a different world, one she hadn't known existed. She could not name it but she felt as if she were about to be revealed, as if there were another Claire inside, waiting to come out. In these few hours in the morning, dressed in someone else's finery, she could pretend she was part of it, that she had lived in Colombo, eaten frog's legs in France, or ridden an elephant in Delhi with a maharaja by her side.

At seven in the morning, after she had brewed herself a cup of tea and eaten some buttered toast, she made her way to the bedroom. She stood over her sleeping husband.

"Wake up," she said quietly.

He stirred, then rolled over to face her.

"Cuckoo," she said a little louder.

"Happy birthday, darling," he said sleepily. He propped himself up on one elbow to offer a kiss. His breath was sour but not unpleasant.

Claire was twenty-eight today.

It was Saturday, and the beginning of summer. Not too hot yet, the mornings had a breeze and a little bit of cool before the sun warmed up the afternoons and the hats and fans had to come out. Martin worked half-days on Saturdays but then there was a party at the Arbogasts', on the Peak. Reginald Arbogast was a very successful businessman and made a point of inviting every English person in the colony to his parties, which were famous for his unstinting hand and lavish foods.

"I'll meet you at the funicular at one," Martin told her.

At one, Claire was at the tram station waiting. She had on a new dress the tailor had delivered just the day before, a white poplin based on a Paris original. She had found a Mr. Hao, an inexpensive man in Causeway Bay who would come and measure her at home and charge eight Hong Kong dollars a dress. It had turned out quite well. She had sprayed on a bit of Jazz although she still found it strong. She dabbed it on, then rubbed water on it to dilute the smell. At ten past one, Martin came through the station doors, and gave her a kiss.

"You look nice," he said. "New dress?"

"Mm-hmm," she said.

They took the tram up the mountain, a steep ride that seemed almost vertical at times. They held on to the rail, leaned forward, and looked outside, where they could see into people's homes in the Mid-Levels, with curtains pushed to one side, and newspapers and dirty glasses strewn on tables.

"I would think," Claire said, "if I knew that people would be looking in my house all day from the tram, I'd make a point of leaving it tidy, wouldn't you?"

At the top, they found that the Arbogasts had hired rickshaws to take their guests to the house from the station. Claire climbed in.

"I always feel for the men," she said quietly to Martin. "Isn't this why we have mules or horses? It's one of these queer Hong Kong customs, isn't it?"

"It's a fact that human labor here often costs less," Martin said. Claire stifled her irritation. Martin was always so literal.

The man lifted up the harness with a grunt. They started to roll along and Claire settled into the uncomfortable seat. Around them the green was overwhelming, tropical trees bursting with leaves that dripped when scratched, bougainvillea and every other type of flowering bush springing forth from the hillsides. Sometimes she got the feeling that Hong Kong was too alive. It seemed unable to restrain itself. There were insects crawling everywhere, wild dogs on the hills, mosquitoes breeding furiously. They had made roads in the hillsides and buildings sprouted out of the ground, but nature

strained at her boundaries—there were always sweaty, shirtless
worker men chopping away at the greenery that seemed to grow
overnight. It wasn't India, she supposed, but it certainly wasn't England. The man in front of her strained and sweated. His shirt was
thin and gray.

"The Arbogasts apparently had this place undergo a massive
cleaning after the war," Martin said. "Smythson was telling me
about it, how it had been gutted by the Japanese and all that was
left was walls, and not much of those at that. It used to belong to
the Bayer representative out here, Thorpe, and he never came back
after he was repatriated after the war. He sold it for a song. He'd had
enough."

"The way people lived out here before the war," Claire said. "It
was very gracious."

"Arbogast lost his hand during the war as well. He has a hook
now. They say he's quite sensitive about it so try not to look at it."

"Of course," Claire said.

When they walked in, the party was in full swing. Doors opened
onto a large receiving room which led into a large drawing room
with windowed doors open onto a lawn with a wide, stunning view
of the harbor far below. A violinist sawed away at his instrument
while a pianist accompanied him. The house was decorated in the
way the English did their houses in the Orient, with Persian carpets
and the occasional wooden Chinese table topped with Burmese
silver bowls and other exotic curiosities. Women in light cotton
dresses swayed toward one another while men in safari suits or blaz-
ers stood with their hands in their pockets. Swiftly moving servants
balanced trays of Pimm's and champagne.

"Why does he do this?" Claire asked Martin. "Invite the world, I
mean."

"He's done well for himself here, and he didn't have much before,
and wants to do something good for the community. What I've
heard, anyway."

"Hello hello," said Mrs. Arbogast from the foyer, where she was greeting guests—a thin, elegant woman with a sharp face. Sparkly earrings jangled from her ears.

"Lovely of you to have us," said Martin. "A real honor."

"Don't know you, but perhaps we shall have the pleasure later." She turned aside and looked for the next guest. They had been dismissed.

"Drink?" Martin said.

"Please," said Claire.

She saw an acquaintance, Amelia, and walked over. Too late, she saw that Mrs. Pinter was in the circle, partially hidden by a potted plant. They all tried to avoid Mrs. Pinter. Claire had been cornered by her before and had spent an excruciating thirty minutes listening to the old woman talk about ant colonies. She wanted to be kind to older people but she had her limits. Mrs. Pinter was now obsessed with starting up an Esperanto society and would reel unwitting newcomers into her ever more complicated and idiotic plans. She was convinced that a universal language would have saved them all from the war.

"I've been thinking about getting a butler," Mrs. Pinter was saying. "One of those Chinese fellows would do all right with a bit of training."

"Are you going to teach him Esperanto?" Amelia asked, teasing.

"We have to teach everyone but the Communists," Mrs. Pinter said placidly.

"Isn't the refugee problem alarming?" Marjorie Winter said, ignoring all of them. She was fanning herself with a napkin. She was a fat, kind woman, with very small sausagelike curls around her face.

"They're coming in by the thousands, I hear," Claire said.

"I'm starting a new league," said Marjorie. "To help the refugees. Those poor Chinese streaming across the border like herded animals, running away from that dreadful government. They live in the most frightful conditions. You must volunteer! I've let space for an office and everything."

"You remember in 1950," Amelia said, "some of the locals practically ran hotels, taking care of all their family and friends who had fled. And these were the well-off ones, who were able to book passage. It was quite something."

"Why are they leaving?" Claire said. "Where do they expect to go from here?"

"Well, that's the thing, dear," Marjorie said. "They don't have anywhere to go, imagine that. That's why my league is so important."

Amelia sat down. "The Chinese come down during war, they go back up, then come down again. It's dizzying. They are just these giant waves of displacement. And their different dialects. I do think Mandarin is the ugliest, with its *wer* and its *er* and those strange noises." She fanned herself. "It's far too hot to talk about a league," she said. "Your energy always astounds me, Marjorie."

"Amelia," Marjorie said unsympathetically. "You're always hot."

Amelia was always hot, or cold, or vaguely out of sorts. She was not physically suited to life outside of England, which was ironic since she had not lived there for some three decades. She needed her creature comforts and suffered mightily, and not silently, without them. They had been in Hong Kong since before the war. Her husband, Angus, had brought her from India, which she had loathed, over to Hong Kong in 1938 when he had become undersecretary to the Department of Finance. She was opinionated, railing against what she saw as the unbearable English ladies who wanted to become Chinese, who wore their hair in chignons with ivory chopsticks and wore too-tight cheongsams to every event and employed local tutors so they could speak to the help in their atrocious Cantonese. She did not understand such women and constantly warned Claire against becoming one of such a breed.

Amelia had taken Claire under her wing, introducing her to people, inviting her to lunch, but Claire was often uncomfortable around her and her sharp observations and often biting innuendo. Still, she clung to her as someone who could help her navigate the strange new world she found herself in. She knew her mother would approve of someone like Amelia, even be impressed that Claire knew such people.

Outside, the thwack of a tennis ball punctuated the low buzz and tinkle of conversation and cocktails. Claire's group migrated toward a large tent pitched next to the courtyard.

"People come and play tennis?" Claire asked.

"Yes, in this weather, can you believe it?"

"I can't believe they have a tennis court," said Claire with wonder.

"And I can't believe what you can't believe," Amelia said archly.

Claire blushed. "I've just never . . ."

"I know, darling," Amelia said. "Just a village girl." She winked to take the sting out of her comment.

"You know what Penelope Davies did the other day?" Marjorie interrupted. "She went to the temple at Wong Tai Sin with an interpreter, and got her fortune told. She said it was just remarkable how much this old woman knew!"

"What fun," Amelia said. "I'll bring Wing and try it out too. Claire, we should go!"

"Sounds fun," Claire said.

"Did you hear about the child in Malaya who had the hiccups for three months?" Marjorie was asking Martin, who had joined them with drinks in hand. "The Briggs' child. His father's the head of the electric over there. His mother almost went mad. They tried a witch doctor but no results. They didn't know whether to bring him back to England or just trust in fate."

"Can you imagine having the hiccups for more than an hour?" Claire said. "I'd go mad! That poor child."

Martin knelt down to play with a small boy who had wandered over.

"Hallo," he said. "Who are you?"

"Martin wants children," Claire said, sotto voce, to Amelia. She often found herself confiding in Amelia despite herself. She had no one else to talk to.

"All men do, darling," Amelia said. "You have to negotiate the number before you start popping them out or else the men will want to keep going. I got Angus down to two before we started."

"Oh," Claire said, startled. "That seems so . . . unromantic."

"What do you think married life is?" Amelia said. She cocked an eyebrow at Claire. Claire blushed and excused herself to go to the powder room.

When she returned, Amelia had drifted away and was talking to a tall man Claire had never seen before. She waved her over. He was a man of around forty with a crude cane that looked as if it had been whittled by a child out of pine. He had sharp, handsome features and a shock of black hair, run through with strands of gray, ungroomed.

"Have you met Will Truesdale?" Amelia said.

"I haven't," she said, as she put out her hand.

"Pleased to meet you," he said. His hand was dry and cool, almost as if it were made of paper.

"He's been in Hong Kong for ages," Amelia said. "An old-timer, like us."

"Quite the experts, we are," he said.

He suddenly looked alert.

"I like your scent," he said. "Jasmine, is it?"

"Yes. Thank you."

"Newly arrived?"

"Yes, just a month."

"Like it?"

"I never imagined living in the Orient but here I am."

"Oh, Claire, you should have had more imagination," Amelia said, gesturing to a waiter for another drink.

Claire colored again. Amelia was in rare form today.

"I'm delighted to meet someone who's not so jaded," Will said. "All you women are so worldly it quite tires me out."

Amelia had turned away to get her drink and hadn't heard him. There was a pause, but Claire didn't mind it.

"It's Claire's birthday," Amelia told Will, turning back around. She smiled, brittle; red lipstick stained her front tooth. "She's just a baby."

"How nice," he said. "We need more babies around these parts."

He suddenly reached out his hand and slowly tucked a strand of hair behind Claire's ear. A possessive gesture, as if he had known her for a long time.

"Excuse me," he said. Amelia had not seen; she had been scanning the crowd.

"Excuse you for what?" Amelia asked, turning back, distracted.

"Nothing," they both said. Claire looked down at the floor. They were joined in their collusive denial; it suddenly seemed overwhelmingly intimate.

"What?" Amelia said impatiently. "I can't hear a damn thing above this din."

"I'm twenty-eight today," Claire said, not knowing why.

"I'm forty-three." He nodded. "Very old."

Claire couldn't tell if he was joking.

"I remember the celebration we had for you at Stanley," Amelia said. "What a fete."

"Wasn't it, though?"

"You're still with Melody and Victor?" Amelia inquired of Will.

"Yes," he said. "It suits me for now."

"I'm sure it suits Victor just fine to have an Englishman chauffeuring him around," she replied slyly.

"It seems to work for everyone involved," Will said, not taking the bait.

Amelia leaned toward him confidentially. "I hear there's been chatter about the Crown Collection and its disappearance during the war. Angus says it's starting to come to a boil. People have noticed. Have you heard anything?"

"I have," he said.

"They want to ferret out the collaborators."

"A bit late, don't you think?"

After a pause, when it became apparent that nothing more was forthcoming from Will, she spoke again. "I hope the Chens are treating you well?"

"I cannot complain," he said.

"A bit odd, isn't it? You working over there."

"Amelia," he said. "You're boring Claire."

"Oh, no," Claire protested. "I'm just . . ."

"Well, you're boring me," he said. "And life is too short to be bored. Claire, have you been to the different corners of our fair colony? Which is your favorite?"

"Well, I have been exploring a bit. Sheung Wan is lovely—I do like the markets—and I've been over to Kowloon, Tsim Sha Tsui on the Star Ferry of course, and seen all the shops there. It's very lively, isn't it?"

"See, Amelia," Will said. "An Englishwoman who ventures outside of Central and the Peak. You would do well to learn from this newcomer."

Amelia rolled her eyes. "She'll grow tired of it soon enough. I've seen so many of these bright-eyed new arrivals, and they all end up having tea with me at the Helena May and complaining about their amahs."

"Well, don't let Amelia's rosy attitude affect you too much, Claire," Will said. "At any rate, it was a pleasure to meet you. Best of luck in Hong Kong." He nodded to them politely and left. She felt the heat of his body as he passed by.

Claire felt bereft. He had assumed they would not meet again.

"Odd man?" she said. It was more of a statement.

"You've no idea, dear," Amelia said.

Claire peeked after him. He had floated over to the side of the tennis court, although he had some sort of limp, and was watching Peter Wickham and his son hit the ball at each other.

"He's also very serious now," Amelia said. "Can't have a proper conversation with him. He was quite social before the war, you know, you saw him at all the parties, had the most glamorous girl in town, quite high up at Asiatic Petrol, but he never really recovered after the war. He's a chauffeur now." Her voice dropped. "For the Chens, actually. Do you know who they are?"

"Amelia!" Claire said. "I teach piano to their daughter! You helped me arrange it!"

"Oh, dear. The memory goes first, they say. You've never run into him there?"

"Never," Claire said. "Although the Chens suggested he might give me a lift one time."

"Poor Melody," said Amelia. "She's very *fragile*." The word said delicately.

"Indeed," Claire said, remembering the way Melody sipped her drink, quickly, urgently.

"The thing with Will is"—Amelia hesitated—"I'm quite certain he doesn't need to work at all."

"How do you mean?" Claire asked.

"I just know certain things," Amelia said mysteriously.

Claire didn't ask. She wouldn't give Amelia the satisfaction.

September 1941

TRUDY IS DRESSING for dinner while he watches from the bed. She has finished with her mysterious bathing ritual with its oils and unguents and now she smells marvelous, like a valley in spring. She is sitting at her dressing table in a long peach satin robe, wrapped silkily around her waist, applying fragrant creams to her face.

"Do you like this one?" She gets up and holds a long black dress in front of her.

"It's fine." He can't concentrate on the clothes when her face is so vibrant above it.

"Or this one?" A knee-length dress the color of orange sherbet.

"Fine."

She pouts. Her skin gleams.

"You're so unhelpful."

She tells him Manley Haverford is having a party, an end-of-summer party, at his country house this weekend and that she wants to go. Manley is an old bigot who used to have a radio talk show before he married a rich but ugly Portuguese woman who conveniently died two years later, whereupon he retired to live the life of a country squire in Sai Kung.

"Desperately," she says. "I want to go desperately."

"You loathe Manley," he says. "You told me so last week."

"I know," she says. "But his parties are fun and he's very generous with the drinks. Let's go and talk about how awful he is right in front of him. Can we go, can we? Can we? Can we?" She wears him down. They will go.

. . .

So Friday, late afternoon, he plays hooky from work and they spend the twilight hours bathing in the ocean by Manley's house. To get there, they drive narrow, winding roads carved right out of the green mountain, blue water on their right, verdant hillside on their left. His house is through a dilapidated wooden gate and at the end of a long driveway, and right by the sea, with a porch that juts out, and rough stone steps leading down to the beach. He's had coolers filled with ice and drinks and sandwiches brought down to the sandy inlet. The still-hot sun and water make them ravenous and they eat and eat and eat and curse their host for not bringing enough.

"Me?" Manley asks. "I assumed I had invited civilized people, who ate three meals a day."

Victor and Melody Chen, Trudy's cousins, wander down from the house, where they had been resting.

"What are we doing now?" Melody asks. Will likes her, thinks she's nice, when she's not around her husband.

A woman they have never met before, newly arrived from Singapore, suggests they play charades. They all moan but acquiesce.

Trudy is one team's leader, the Singapore woman the other. The groups huddle together, write words on scraps of damp paper. They put them all in the empty sandwich basket.

Trudy goes first. She looks at her paper, dimples.

"Easy peasy," she says encouragingly to her group. She makes the film sign, one hand rotating an imaginary camera lever.

"Film!" shouts an American.

She puts up four fingers, then suddenly ducks her head, puts her arms in front of her, and whooshes through the air.

"*Gone with the Wind,*" Will says. Trudy curtsies.

"Unfair," says someone from the other team. "Pet's advantage."

Trudy comes over and plants a kiss on his forehead.

"Clever boy," she says, and sinks down next to him.

Singapore gets up.

"She's your nemesis," Will tells Trudy.

"Don't worry," Trudy says. "She's idiotic."

The afternoon passes pleasantly, with them shouting insults and drinking and generally being stupid. Some people talk about the government and how it's organizing different Volunteer Corps.

"It's not volunteering," Will says. "It's mandatory. It's the Compulsory Service Act, for heaven's sake. They're quite opposite. Why don't they just call a spade a spade? Dowbiggin is being ridiculous about it."

"Don't be such a grump," Trudy says. "Do your duty."

"I guess so," he says. "Must fight the good fight, I suppose." He thinks the organization is being handled in an absurd fashion.

"Is there one for cricketers?" someone asks, as if to prove his point.

"Why not?" somebody else says. "You can make up one however you want."

"I hardly think that's true," Manley says. "But I'm joining one that's training out here on the weekends, on the club grounds. Policemen, I think, although I'd think they'd be rather busy if there was an attack."

"Aren't you too old, Manley?" Trudy asks. "Old and decrepit?"

"That's the wonderful thing, Trudy," he says, with a forced smile. "You can't fire a Volunteer. And at any rate, the one here at the club is convenient."

"I'm sending Melody to America," Victor Chen says suddenly. "I don't want her to be in any danger."

Melody smiles uneasily, doesn't say anything.

"The government is preparing," says Jamie Biggs. "They are storing food in warehouses in Tin Hau and securing British property."

"Like the Crown Collection?" Victor asks. "What are they going to do about that? That's part of English heritage."

"I'm sure all the arrangements have been made already," says Biggs.

"The food will go bad before anyone gets it," says another man.

"Cynic," says Trudy.

She lifts up gracefully and goes toward the ocean. All this talk of war bores her. She thinks it will never happen. They all watch her, rapt, as she plunges into the sea and comes up sleek and dripping—her slim body a vertical rebuke to the flatness of the horizon between the sky and sea. She walks up and shakes her wet hair at Will. Drops of water fall and sparkle. Then someone asks where the tennis rackets are. The spell is broken.

Over dinner, Trudy declares that she is going to be in charge of uniforms for the Volunteers. "And Will will be the fit model," she says. "Because he's a perfect male specimen."

John Thorpe, who heads up the American office of a large pharmaceutical company, looks doubtful. "Rather small and ugly, isn't he?" he says, although this is more a description of himself and not at all of Will.

"Will!" Trudy cries. "You've been insulted! Defend your honor!"

"I've better things to defend," he says. And the table falls silent. He is always saying the wrong thing, popping the gaiety. "Er, sorry," he says. But they are already on to the next thing.

Trudy is describing the tailor who is going to make the uniforms.

"He's been our family tailor for ages and he can whip out a copy of a Paris dress in two days, one if you beg!"

"What's his name?"

"Haven't the slightest," she says easily. "He's The Tailor. But I know where the shop is, or my driver does, rather, and we're the best of friends. Do you fellows prefer orange or a very bright pink as colors?"

They decide on olive green with orange stripes ("So boring," the women sigh and orange is given as a concession) and Trudy asks who is to measure the men.

They volunteer her.

She accepts ("Isn't there something about dressing left?" she asks innocently), then says Will will measure in her stead. Trudy's frivolity, Will has noticed, has boundaries.

• • •

Sophie Biggs is trying to get everyone interested in moonlight picnics. "They're ever so much fun," she says. "We take a steamboat out, with rowboats, and when we reach the islands we row everyone ashore with the provisions and a guitar or an accordion or something." Sophie is a large girl and Will wonders if she is a secret eater because she eats tiny portions when she is out. Right now, she is poking her spoon around the vichyssoise.

Trudy sighs. "It sounds like so much labor," she says. "Wouldn't it just be easier to have a picnic at Repulse Bay?"

Sophie looks at her reproachfully. "But it's not the same," she says. "It's the journey."

Sophie's husband claims to be in shipping, but Will thinks he's in Intelligence. When he tells Trudy this later she cries, "That big lout? He couldn't detect his way out of a paper bag!" But Jamie Biggs is always listening, never talking, and he has a watchful air about him. If he's that obvious, Will supposes he's not very good. After Milton Pottinger left last year, someone had told Will that he was Intelligence. He hadn't been able to believe it. Milton was a big, florid man who drank a lot and seemed the very soul of indiscretion.

Edwina Storch, a large Englishwoman who is the headmistress of the good school in town, has brought her constant companion, Mary Winkle, and they sit at the end of the table, eating quietly, talking to no one but each other. Will has seen them before. They are always around, but never say much.

Over dessert—trifle—Jamie says that all Japanese residents have been sent secret letters about what to do in case of an invasion, and that the Japanese barber chap in the Gloucester Hotel has been spying. The government is about to issue another edict that all wives and children are to be sent away without exception, but only the white British, those of pure European extraction, get passage on the ships. "Doesn't affect me," Trudy says, shrugging, although she holds a British passport. Will knows that if she wanted, she could get on the boat—her father always knows someone. "What would I do in Australia?" she asks. "I don't like anybody there. Besides, it's only for pure English—have you ever heard of anything so offensive?"

She changes the subject. "What would happen," she asks, "if two guns were pointed at each other and then the triggers were pulled at the same time. Do you think the two people would get hurt or would the bullets destroy each other?"

There is a lively discussion about this that Trudy becomes bored with very quickly. "For heaven's sake!" she cries. "Isn't there something else we can talk about?" The group, chastised, turns to yet other subjects. Trudy is a social dictator and not at all benevolent. She tells someone recently arrived from the Congo that she can't imagine why anyone would go to godforsaken places like that when there are perfectly pleasant destinations like London and Rome. The traveler actually looks chagrined. She tells Sophie Biggs's husband that he doesn't appreciate his wife, and then she tells Manley she loathes trifle. Yet, no one takes offense; everyone agrees with her. She is the most amiable rude person ever. People bask in her attention.

At the end of dinner, after coffee and liqueur, Manley's houseboy brings in a big bowl of nuts and raisins. Manley pours brandy over it with a flourish and Trudy lights a match and tosses it in. The bowl is ablaze instantly, all blue and white flame. They try to pick out the treats without burning their fingers, a game they call Snapdragon.

Going to the restroom later, Will glimpses Trudy and Victor talking heatedly in Cantonese in the drawing room. He hesitates, then continues on. When he returns, they are gone and Trudy is already back at the table, telling a bawdy joke.

After, they go to bed. Manley has given them a room next to his and they make love quietly. With Trudy, it is always as if she is drowning—she clutches at him and burrows her face into his shoulder with an intensity she would make fun of if she saw it. Sometimes, the shape of her fingers is etched into his skin for hours afterward. Later, Will wakes up to find Trudy whimpering, her face lumpy and alarming; he sees that her face is wet with tears.

"What's wrong?" he asks.

"Nothing." A reflex.

"Victor upset you?" he asks.

"No, no, he wants to . . ." She is blurry with sleep. "My father . . ." She goes back to sleep. When he throws the blanket over her, her shoulders are as cold and limp as water. In the morning, she remembers nothing, and mocks him for his concern.

In the following weeks, the war encroaches—wives and children, the ones who had ignored the previous evacuation, leave on ships bound for Australia, Singapore. Trudy is obliged to make an appearance at the hospitals to prove she is a nurse. She undergoes training, declares herself hopeless, and switches to supplies instead. She finds the stockpiling of goods too funny. "If I had to eat the food they're storing, I'd shoot myself," she says. "It's all veggie tins and bully beef and awful things like that."

The colony is filled with suddenly lonesome men without wives who gather at the Gripps, the Parisian Grill, clamor to be invited to dinner parties at the homes of those few whose wives remain. They form a club, the Bachelors' Club ("Why do the British so love to form clubs and societies?" Trudy asks. "No, wait, don't say, it's too grim") and petition the governor to have their wives returned. Others, more intrepid, turn up suddenly with adopted Chinese "daughters" or "wards," and they dine with them and drink champagne and get silly and flirtatious and then disappear into the night. Will finds it amusing, Trudy less so. "Wait until I get my hands on them," she cries while Will amuses himself with teasing her about which Chinese hostess would soon get her claws into him.

"You're like a leper, darling," she counters. "You British men are going out of fashion. I might have to find myself a Japanese or German beau now."

Will remembers this time well, how it was all so funny, how the war was so far away, yet talked about every day, how no one really thought about what might really happen.

September 1952

CLAIRE WAS WAITING for the bus after Locket's piano lesson when Will Truesdale drove up in the car.

"Would you like a lift?" he asked. "I'm just off work."

"Thank you, but I couldn't put you out," she said.

"Not at all," he said. "The Chens don't mind if I take the car home for the night. Most employers want their cars left at home and the chauffeur to take public transport home, so it's very convenient for me."

Claire hesitated, then got into the car. It smelled of cigarettes and polished leather.

"It's very kind of you."

"Did you have a good time at the Arbogasts' the other day?" he asked.

"It was a very nice party," she said. She had learned not to be so effusive, that it marked her as unsophisticated.

"Reggie's a good sort," he said. "It was nice to meet you there too. There are too many of those women who add to the din without adding anything else. You shouldn't lose that quality, that quality of seeing everything new, for what it is. All the women here..." he trailed off.

He drove well, she thought, steady on the steering wheel, his movements calm and unhurried.

"You're not wearing the perfume you had on the other day," he said.

"No," she said, wary. "That's for special occasions."

"I was surprised that you had it on. Not many English people wear it. It's more the fashionable Chinese women. They like its heaviness. Englishwomen like something lighter, more flowery."

"Oh, I wasn't aware." Claire's hand went unconsciously to her neck, where she usually dabbed it on.

"But it's lovely that you wear it," he said.

"You seem to know a lot about women's scents."

"I don't." He glanced over at her, his eyes dark. "I used to know someone who wore it."

They rode in silence until they arrived at her building.

"You teach the girl," he said as she was reaching for the door, his voice suddenly urgent.

"Yes, Locket," she said, taken aback.

"Is she a good student?" he asked. "Diligent?"

"It's hard to say," she said. "Her parents don't give her much of a reason to do anything so she doesn't. Very typical at that age. Still, she's a nice enough girl."

He nodded, his face unreadable in the dark interior of the car.

"Well, thank you very much for the ride," she said.

He nodded and drove off into the gathering dusk.

And then, a bun. A bun with sweetened chestnut paste. That was how they met again. She had been walking up Potter Street to where there was a bus stand, when it started to pour. The rain, big, startling plops of water, fell heavily and she was soaked through in a matter of seconds. Looking up at the sky, she saw it had turned a threatening gray. She ducked into a Chinese bakery to wait out the storm. Inside, she ordered a tea and a chestnut bun and, turning to sit at one of the small circular tables, spotted Will Truesdale, deliberately eating a red bean pastry, staring at her.

"Hullo," she said. "Caught in the rain too?"

"Would you like a seat?"

She sat down. In the damp, he smelled like cigarettes and tea. A newspaper was spread in front of him, the crossword half-finished. A fan blew at the pages so they ruffled upward.

"It's coming down like cats and dogs. And so sudden!"

"So, how are you?" he asked.

"Fine, thank you very much. Just coming from the Liggets', where I've borrowed some patterns. Do you know Jasper and Helen? He's in the police."

"Ligget the bigot?" He wrinkled his forehead.

She laughed, uncomfortable. His hand thrummed the table, though his body was in repose.

"Is that what you call him?" she asked.

"Why not?" he said.

He did the crossword as she ate her bun and sipped at her tea. She was aware of her mouth chewing, swallowing. She sat up straight in her chair.

He hummed a tune, looked up.

"Hong Kong suits you," he said.

She colored, started to say something about being impertinent but the words came out muddled.

"Don't be coy," he said. "I think..." he started, as if he were telling her life story. "I imagine you've always been pretty but you've never owned it, never used it to your advantage. You didn't know what to do about it and your mother never helped you. Perhaps she was jealous, perhaps she too was pretty in her youth but is bitter that beauty is so transient."

"I'm sure I haven't the slightest idea what you're talking about," she said.

"I've known girls like you for years. You come over from England and don't know what to do with yourselves. You could be different. You should take the opportunity to become something else."

She stared at him, then pushed the paper bun wrapper around on the table. It was slightly damp and stuck to the surface. She was aware of his gaze on her face.

"So," he said. "You must be very uncomfortable. My home is just up the way if you want to change into some dry things."

"I wouldn't want to..."

"Do you want my jacket?" He looked at her so intently she felt undressed. Was there anything more intimate than really being seen? She looked away.

"No, I..."

"No bother at all," he said quickly. "Come along." And she did, pulled along helplessly by his suggestion.

They climbed the steps, now damp and glistening, the heat already beginning to evaporate the moisture. Her clothes clung to her, her blouse sodden and uncomfortable against her shoulder blades. In the quiet after the rain, she could hear his breathing, slow and regular. He used his cane with expertise, hoisting himself up the stairs, whistling slightly under his breath.

"In good weather, there's a man who sells crickets made out of grass stalks here." He gestured to a corner on the street. "I've bought dozens. They're the most amazing things, but they crumble when they dry up, crumble into nothing."

"Sounds lovely," Claire said. "I'd like to see them."

They got to his building, and walked up some grungy, industrial stairs. He stopped in front of a door.

"I never lock my door," he said suddenly.

"I suppose it's safe enough around these parts," she said.

Inside, his flat was sparsely furnished. She could see only a sofa, a chair, and a table on bare floor. When they stepped in, he took off his soaking shoes.

"The boss says I can't wear shoes in the house."

Just then, a small, wiry woman of around forty came into the foyer. She was wearing the amah uniform of a black tunic over trousers.

"This is the boss, Ah Yik," he said. "Ah Yik, this is Mrs. Pendleton."

"So wet," the little woman cried. "Big rain."

"Yes," Will said. "Big, big rain." Then he spoke to her rapidly in Cantonese.

"Tea for missee?" Ah Yik said.

"Yes, thank you," he said.

The amah went into the kitchen.

They looked at each other, uncomfortable in their wet and rapidly cooling clothes.

"You are proficient in the local language," she said, more as a statement than a question.

"I've been here more than a decade," he said. "It would be a real embarrassment if I couldn't meet them halfway, don't you think?" He took a tea towel off the hook and rubbed at his head. "I imagine you'd like to dry off," he said.

"Yes, please."

She sat down as he left. There was something strange about the room, which she couldn't place until she realized there was absolutely nothing decorative in the entire flat. There were no paintings, no vases, no bric-a-brac. It was austere to the point of monkishness.

Will came back with a towel and a simple pink cotton dress.

"Is this appropriate?" he asked. "I've a few other things."

"I don't need to change," she said. "I'll just dry off and be on my way."

"Oh, I think you should change," he said. "It'll be uncomfortable otherwise."

"No, it's quite all right."

He started to leave the room.

"Fine," she said. "Where should I . . ."

"Oh, anywhere," he said. "Anywhere you won't scandalize the boss, that is."

"Of course." She took the dress from him. "Looks around the right size."

"And there's a phone out here if you want to ring your husband and let him know where you are," he said.

"Thank you," she said. "Martin's in Shanghai, actually." And she went into the bathroom.

The bathroom was small but clean, with a frosted-glass window high above the toilet. It was the wavy, pebbled kind, with chicken wire running through it. Next to that, there was a small fan set into the wall with a pull string attached. It was humid, with the rain splattering outside, and the musty feel of a bathroom that hadn't gotten quite aired out enough after baths. Next to the tub there was a low wooden stool with a porcelain basin on top. Claire leaned forward into the mirror. Her hair was mussed, fine blond strands awry, and her face was flushed, still, with the exertion of climbing up the hill. She looked surprisingly alive, her lips red and plump and wet, her skin glowing with the moisture. She undressed, dropping her soaked blouse to the floor, which sloped slightly to a drain in the middle. She toweled off and pulled the dress over her hips. It was snug, but manageable. Why did Will have a dress lying around? It was very good quality, with perfectly finished seams and careful needlework. She went out to where Will was sipping from a thermos of tea.

"Fits you well," he said neutrally.

"Yes, thank you very much."

All of a sudden, Claire couldn't bear it. She couldn't bear this man with his odd pauses and his slightly mocking tone.

"Something to eat, perhaps?" he said. "Ah Yik makes a very good bowl of fried rice."

"I think I'd better leave," she said.

"Oh," he said, taken aback. She took satisfaction in his surprise, as if she had won something. "Of course, if you'd rather."

She got up and left, putting her shoes on at the door while Will stayed in the living room. When she turned to say good-bye, she saw he was reading a book. This infuriated her.

"Well, good-bye, then," she said. "I'll have my amah return the dress. Thank you for your hospitality."

"Good-bye," he said. He didn't look up.

• • •

That night, after dinner, she couldn't relax. Her insides seemed too large for her outside, a queer sensation, as if all that she was feeling couldn't be contained inside her body. Martin was still away, so she put on her street clothes and got on the bus to town, bumping over the roads, elbow out the window, open to the warm night air. She disembarked in Wanchai, where there seemed to be the most activity. She wanted to be around people, not so alone. The wet market was still open, Chinese people buying their cabbages and fish, the pork hanging from hooks, sometimes a whole pig head, red and bloody, dripping onto the street. This was the peculiarity of Hong Kong. If she walked ten minutes toward Central, all would be civil, large, quiet buildings in the European classical style, and wide, empty streets, yet here, the frenetic activity, narrow alleys, and smoky stalls were another world. All around her, people called to one another loudly, advertising their wares, a smudge-faced child played in the street with a dirty bucket. A pregnant woman carrying vegetables under her arm jostled her and apologized, her movements heavy and clumsy. Claire stared after her, wondering what it would be like to have a child inside you, moving around. A young couple with linked arms sat down at a noodle stand and broke out loudly in laughter.

Next to her, a wizened elderly lady tugged at Claire's arm. Dressed in the gray cotton tunic and trousers most of the local older women seemed to favor, she had a small basket of tangerines on her arm.

"You buy," she said. She smelled like the white flower ointment the locals used to fend off everything from the common cold to cholera. One of her teeth was gray and chipped, the others antique yellow. The woman's brown face was a spider web of deeply etched lines.

"No, thank you," said Claire. Her voice rang out like a bell. It seemed as if her foreign voice stilled the bustle around her for a moment.

The woman grew more insistent.

"You buy! Very good. Fresh today." The woman pulled at Claire's arm again. Then she reached up and touched Claire's hair like a talisman. The local Chinese did that sometimes, and while it had been frightening the first time, Claire was used to it by now.

"Good fortune," said the old woman. "Golden."

"Thank you," said Claire.

"You buy!" the woman repeated.

"I'm not looking for anything today, but thank you very much." The hum around her resumed. Claire continued walking. The old woman followed her for a few yards, then shambled off to find more promising customers.

Why not buy a tangerine from an old lady, Claire thought suddenly. Why not? What would happen? She couldn't think of why she had declined, as if her old English self, with its defenses and prejudices, was dissolving in the humid, fetid environment around her.

She turned around but the woman had already disappeared. She breathed deeply. The smells of the wet market entered her, intense and earthy. Around her, Hong Kong thrummed.

And then, suddenly, he was everywhere. She saw Will Truesdale waiting for the bus, at Kayamally's, queuing up at the cinema. And though he never saw her, she always lowered her head, willing him not to notice. And then she'd peek up, to see if he had. He had a way of seeming completely contained within himself, even when he was in a crowd. He never looked around, never tapped his feet, never looked at his watch. It seemed he never saw her.

When she went for Locket's lesson on Thursdays, she found herself looking for Will Truesdale. She heard the amahs laughing at his jokes in the kitchen, and she saw his jacket hanging in the entry foyer, but his physical presence was elusive, as if he slipped in and out, avoiding her. She lingered at the end of her lesson, but she never saw him or the car.

Then they were at the beach the next weekend. She hardly knew how it had happened. She had come home. The phone rang. She picked it up.

"I've a friend with one of those municipal beach huts," he said. "Would you like to go bathing?" As if nothing had happened. As if she would know who it was by his voice.

"Bathing," she said. "Where?"

"On Big Wave Bay," he said. "It's a perk for the locals but they don't mind if we sign up as well. It's a lottery system and you get a cottage for the season. A group of us usually get together to do it and swap weekends. It's quite nice."

She shut her eyes and saw him, Will, the difficult man with his thin shoulders and gray eyes, his dark hair that fell untidily into his eyes, a man who stared at her so intently she felt quite transparent, a man who had just asked her to go bathing with him, unaccompanied. And she opened her eyes and said yes, she would join him at the beach that Sunday. Martin was away for three weeks and he had telegraphed from Shanghai to let her know he would be delayed for some time. He was taking a tour of major Chinese cities to see their water facilities, which he expected to be very primitive.

And so, it was water. She wondered why she hadn't thought of it before. How it rendered everything changed. She was a different woman in a different sphere. And Will! The way he plunged in, without a thought, his limp gone, dissolved into the current. He was a fish, darting here and there, swimming to the horizon, farther than she would ever go.

They were the only non-Chinese people at the beach. The water was still warm from the summer, the air just starting to crisp. The hut was a simple structure with wooden cupboards; inside were communal woven straw mats. The sand was fine and speckled with small, black withered leaves. Families picnicked around them, chattering loudly, small children scrambling messily in the sand. He wanted to go out to the floating diving docks, some two hundred yards out. When she said she couldn't, that it was too far, he said of course she could, and so she did. Out there, they climbed onto the rocking circle and sunned themselves like seals. He lay in the sun, eyes closed, as she surreptitiously watched, his ribs jutting out, his body pocked with unnamed scars of unknown origin. He wore short cotton trousers that were heavy with water. He wasn't the type to wear a bathing suit.

It was hot, hot. The sun hid behind clouds for brief moments and then blazed out again. There was no cover. She wished for a cold drink, a tree for shade, both of which seemed impossibly far away on the shore.

"We should have swum out with a thermos of water," she said.

"Next time," he said, eyes still shut.

"Tell me your story," she said, after allowing herself a minute to digest what that meant. She was still vibrating with the strangeness of the situation—that she was out at the beach with a man, intentions unknown.

"I was born in Tasmania, of Scottish stock," he said mockingly, as if he were starting his own autobiography. He sat up and crossed his legs—a swami.

"Why?" she said.

"My father was a missionary and we lived everywhere," he said. "I've only been to England once, and loathed it. My mother was a bit of a bohemian and she had some money from her family so we were set in that way."

Hong Kong was full of people like Will, wandering global voyagers who had never been to Piccadilly. Claire had been just once, and there had been an old man in tattered clothes who would shout "Fornicators!" at everyone who passed.

"And how did you learn?"

"School, you mean? Taught at home—good basic education of the Bible and the classics." He held up his hands so that they blocked the sky. "It's all you need, really, isn't it?" His voice was sarcastic. "Solid background for life."

"So how did you come to be a chauffeur?"

"A couple I knew before the war, I used to live in their flat while they were living abroad. They came back after, and found me this job with their cousins. I didn't know what else to do. No interest in going back to an office. And I've very few skills," he said. "But I do know Hong Kong like the back of my hand."

"And how did you end up in Hong Kong?"

"My parents were in Africa, and then in India. When they retired back to England, I stayed on as an assistant manager at a tea plantation, then got tired of that after three years and was on a ship to a variety of places and ended up in Hong Kong. Just picked it out of a hat, really. I came here like everyone else, not knowing anything, and sort of took it from there." He stopped. "Of course, that's the story I tell all the ladies."

She could not tell if he was joking or not.

"Oh?"

They were still lying on the too sunny floating dock, waves rocking them, sky an ethereal blue above them.

"How was India?" Claire asked.

"Very complicated."

"And Partition?"

"After I left, of course. They needed us out. But undoubtedly a mess in the interior. Trains carrying tens of thousands of corpses back and forth. Humans capable of doing the worst to each other."

Claire winced. "Why?" She had never heard anyone talk about historic events in such a personal way.

"Who knows."

"And life there before all that?"

"Rather incredible. We've carved out quite a world for ourselves, you know, still. Society's rather limited of course. Women—our women—were in short supply."

"You never married?"

"No," he said. "I never did."

There was silence.

"Is the inquisition over?" he asked.

"I haven't decided," she said.

He hadn't asked a single question about her life. They lay silently and let the sun beat down on them.

They went to eat, hot, salty chicken drumsticks from a Chinese vendor who sold them bottles of soy milk as well. There were little stalls clustered around the small village where you could buy a woven mat to lay on the sand, a bathing suit, a cold drink. Will watched her eat. A mangy dog ambled through the tables and chairs.

"I can't eat much," he said. "I'm all messed up inside from the war. I was a big chap before, if you can believe it."

Her stomach leaped inside of her as he moved closer.

He took her hand and guided it to his mouth and took a small bite. His grip was firm and sandy.

"It comes up again, sometimes," he said. "Like bile." He chewed slowly, made a grimace.

After they ate, they walked back to the car. He leaned over to open the door for her. His limp was apparent. Human again. She turned to him, back against the door, and he pushed her shoulder back and kissed her, a fluid movement that seemed inevitable. She was encircled in his arms, his hands on the car. A physical kiss, one she felt intensely, his lips pressing hard on hers—she felt like she was drowning.

She told herself: This is Hong Kong. I am a woman, displaced. A woman a world away from who I am supposed to be.

He stood up and looked at her. He traced her profile with his finger.

"Should we go?" he asked.

"Do you like me?" she asked on the car ride back, her hair full and thick from the sea salt. She didn't know where they were going.

"I haven't decided yet," he said.

"Be good to me," she said. It was a warning. She wanted to save herself.

"Of course," he said, but there was no conviction in his voice.

After a few moments, he asked, "Do you think you'll be teaching the girl for long?"

"I haven't any idea. She shows no enthusiasm but her parents seem keen on the idea of her learning to play."

"You like her, though?"

"Well enough. I have no affinity for children." She said this automatically, something her mother had always told her.

"You're too young. You're a child yourself," he said.

"You like children?"

"Some children," he said.

A few weeks later, she asked, "Why me?"

"Why anyone?" he answered. "Why is anyone with anyone?"

Desire, proximity, habit, chance. All these went through her mind, but she didn't say a word.

Then, the cruel.

"I don't like to love," he said. "You should be forewarned. I don't believe in it. And you shouldn't either."

She stared at him, the sting sharp, but she didn't change her expression. She knelt down and retrieved her clothes and went into the bathroom to dress. Claire often didn't speak around Will, never knowing what to say. She didn't want to give too much of herself when he gave so little, but when they were lying together in bed, she felt awful, sharing this intimacy with someone who didn't really seem to care. And then going home to Martin. With him, the private was mundane, a chore, some heavy breathing and shoving, not at all pleasurable or romantic. With Will, it was something else entirely: fraught and unexpected and excruciating. And like a drug. She had never known it could be like that. She closed her eyes and tried not to think of what her mother would say if she knew.

He would drive her home on Thursdays after the lesson. The amahs had started to talk, she knew it, from the way they would look at her and smirk. She ignored them, except for when she asked them for a cup of tea. She had resorted to taking one sip, and then asking for more sugar, or more milk, so they'd have to go back and fix her cup. It was petty, she knew, but the only way to redress the indignity of their sideways glances.

Today, Will opened the door with a flourish.

"Where to, madam?"

"Oh, shut up," she said, climbing in. "Let's go to your place."

"Let's go out, do something," he said. "What about dinner on the water? There's a sampan restaurant I go to sometimes. They row you out, cook you a fish?"

"I have to have dinner at home," she said. "Martin's home tonight so I haven't much time."

"Or let's go up to the Peak and look at the stars."

"Are you even listening to me?" she said, exasperated. "I don't know that I even have time to go to your flat today."

"Whatever you want, darling," he said. "I'll just drive you home, then, and you can go fix Martin a delicious meal."

"Stop the car," she said.

He drove up onto the side of the road and turned off the car.

"As directed," he said.

"Why do you," she said, suddenly furious. "You, you always do *whatever* I say to do, and then . . . it never seems like you're doing anything but what you want to do."

He looked at her with amusement.

"I haven't a clue what you're talking about," he said.

"You *do*," she said. "You know exactly what I'm talking about, but you're pretending…Oh, never mind." She raised her hands in surrender.

"Just take me home," she said. "You've ruined it."

There had been times when Claire felt that she could become a different person. She sensed it in herself, when someone made a comment at dinner, and she thought of the perfect, acerbic reply, or something even racy, and she felt her mouth opening, her lungs taking in air so that she could then push out the words, but they never came out. She swallowed her thought, and the person she could have become sank down again, weighted by the Claire that was already too evident in the world. She sensed it when she held a glass at a cocktail party and suddenly felt the urge to crush it in her hand. She never did. That hidden person had ballooned up and deflated so often, the elasticity of her possibility diminished over time.

But then came Will. She could say to him all the things she thought, as long as it didn't have anything to do with them, and he didn't find any of it surprising. He didn't have an idea of what she should be like. She was a new person—one who could have an affair, one who could be ribald, or sarcastic, or clever, and he was never surprised. She was out of context with him. She was a new person. Sometimes she felt that she was more in love with that new person she could be, that this affair was an affair with a new Claire, and that Will was just the enabler.

December 1941

THE HOLIDAYS are coming. Despite the rumblings of war, Hong
Kong decks itself out with Christmas lights and decorations. Lane
Crawford, store of a million gifts, advertises its genuine English crys-
tal as the perfect present, costume parties are planned, the Drama
Club puts on "Tea for Three." The air is crisp, the moisture sucked
out by the cool, and people walk briskly on the streets. The Wongs,
a famous merchant family, are having a Grand Diamond Jubilee
Party at the Gripps to celebrate their sixtieth anniversary.

"The new governor's coming, that Young fellow," Trudy says.
"And the governor of Macau, who's a great friend of father's. I've
three new dresses arriving today! A yellow silk chiffon to die for!
And a gray crêpe de chine, so elegant. Do you mind if I go with
Dommie instead of you? You hate these things anyway, don't you?"

Will shrugs. "Fine," he says. "Doesn't matter."

Her eyes narrow.

"Nothing does ever bother you, does it?" she says. "I used to like
that but now I'm not so sure. Well, anyways, my father gave me
something today. Something very special."

She motions him into her bedroom.

"He says he was going to give it to my mother for their tenth
anniversary, but then, you know..." Her voice trails off. Trudy has
always been quite unsentimental about her mother's disappearance,
but today, there's something caught in her voice.

"Darling Trudy," he says, and pulls her near.

"No, I'm going to show you something," she says. "No time
for hanky-panky." She opens a drawer and pulls out a small black
velvet box.

"Will you marry me?" she says jokingly as she opens the box and thrusts it toward him.

Inside is an enormous emerald. Will almost can't see the ring behind it. It glows and glows.

"Smokes," he says. "That's quite a stone."

"I love emeralds, although I should love jade, being Chinese," Trudy says. "Emeralds are so beautiful and so very fragile. Jade is so, hard. If I knocked this against a table—you know how clumsy I am—it might break. They're not durable like diamonds." She plucks the ring out of the box and then suddenly throws it up in the air. Will's heart leaps inside him like a small bird, and he wildly grabs for the jewel, catching it on its way down. He stares at the green gem in his hand, blood coursing wildly. It nestles in his palm like a cold insect.

"I knew you'd catch it," Trudy says dispassionately. "That's the best thing about you. You're . . . not dependable, exactly, but good in a fix, I suppose."

Will hands the ring back to Trudy, angry, and watches as she slips it on her slim finger.

"Beautiful, isn't it?" she says. "It's the nicest thing I own."

He walks out of the room.

On Saturday, there is another party, the Tin Hat Ball, to raise 160,000 pounds so that the people of Hong Kong can present a bomber squadron to England. Trudy begs him to go with her as, at the last one, the only dashing men were Americans and that "wasn't right." "You are fickle," he says, but she ignores him.

In the ballroom of the Peninsula, Trudy is much in demand, as usual. She is claimed three times in a row by a Canadian major. Will is at the Long Bar having a drink, talking idly to Angeline Biddle, when Trudy comes up behind him and interlocks her fingers in front of his eyes.

"Did you miss me?" she says.

"You were gone?" he asks. He knows how to talk to her.

"What are you drinking?" Trudy asks Angeline.

"Ox's Blood," she says. "It's champagne mixed with sparkling burgundy and maybe some brandy."

"Sounds dreadful," Trudy says, seizing Will's whiskey instead. She sips at it. "Don't the Canadians have the funniest names for their teams?"

"Regiments, Trudy," he corrects.

"What are they, the Royal Guns or something?" says Angeline.

"No, they're the Royal Rifles and the Winnipeg Grenadiers. They've just come from Newfoundland to help protect us. They love Hong Kong."

"I'll bet they do," he says. "I'm sure it seems like heaven."

She pouts.

"You're not going to be all dull and jealous, are you?" She adjusts the straps of her dress, distracted. "Anyway, I'm spoken for the next few dances. Angeline, you'll take care of my Will, won't you?"

Angeline and Will look at each other and shrug.

"Of course, darling," Angeline says.

As soon as Trudy leaves, they drift away from each other. Will finds Angus Enderby leaning against a wall. Trudy's cousin, Dominick, wanders by, gives them a curt nod.

"Strange fellow, that," says Angus. "Can't figure him out."

"Trudy says he's a girl."

"Something more than that, though. Less innocent." He pauses. "You know there are Fifth Columnists infiltrating. They're supporting that Wong Chang Wai chap, who the Japanese installed in China. I've heard Dominick has been seen with a lot of that crowd. And Victor Chen, of course, thick as thieves with whoever can help him. Rumor has it that he had the Japanese consulate over for dinner last week. Very hush-hush. Better watch himself. That's a dangerous game."

"He's a survivor."

"Yes." Angus shrugs. "Can't believe the war effort's been turned into a party. The new governor's a fool for coming."

A stout woman is at the bar, with a thinner lady, both sipping whiskey, watching the dancing impassively.

"Do you know Edwina Storch?" Angus asks Will, nodding toward the two.

"I've seen her around. Not met them formally."

"Headmistress of Essex, old-timer. Grim, formidable. Been around forever. Her partner, Mary Winkle."

Will and Angus walk over to the women. Edwina inclines her head regally, a queen holding court.

"Hello, Angus. Merry Christmas."

"Edwina, I wanted you to meet Will Truesdale, somewhat of a new arrival to these shores. And Will, this is Edwina Storch and Mary Winkle, Hong Kong institutions. They know where all the skeletons are buried."

"Pleased to meet you," says Will.

"I've seen you around," Edwina says. "You're with the Liang girl."

"Yes," Will says. He is not surprised by her bluntness. He has run into this type before: the unapologetic, rude English matron who fancies herself an adventuress and desires nothing more than to intimidate.

"That didn't take you long."

"No, it didn't, luckily," he says lightly. "She's been a wonderful introduction to Hong Kong."

Edwina Storch harrumphs.

"That's a skewed sense of Hong Kong you're getting!"

Mary Winkle lays a small, reproachful hand on Edwina's arm.

"Now, now," she whispers. "Trudy has always been lovely, if misunderstood. I do like her so very much."

Will smiles at her. "She is lovely, isn't she?"

Edwina sips noisily at her glass.

"What's that you're drinking?" she asks.

"Single malt."

"A man's drink. Since you're with Trudy, I thought you might be a champagne drinker."

"Are you friends with her?" he asks politely.

"Of course," she says. "In Hong Kong, everyone has to be friends or it's very unpleasant."

"Of course," he says agreeably to the women and bows to them before taking his leave. After a pause, Angus joins him back at the bar.

"Something about that woman turns me into a schoolboy about to wet his trousers," Angus says.

"And you keep going back for more," Will says drily.

"That one likes her creature comforts," Angus says. "Always after me about civil salaries and what an outrage they are. Never met a headmistress more interested in money."

The two men pull at their drinks.

"I heard the governor's told all the men in the Bachelors they were off their heads for wanting their wives back. His wife's still in Malaysia, no?"

"Yes, but I don't know that that's any safer, do you?" Will says. "How is Amelia?"

"Fine, but she's making noises about coming back. She's just in China, you know, refused absolutely to go to Australia. So, she's in Canton, and complaining mightily. I can hear the racket from here." Angus looked gloomily at the dance floor. "Might let her come back just so I can get some peace." He paused. "Though that seems rather counterintuitive, eh?"

"Everything to do with women seems counterintuitive."

"Trudy not leaving?" Angus asks.

"Refuses. Says there's nowhere to go. Which is sort of the truth for her, I think."

"Pity," says Angus. "A lot of places could use her right now."

"Yes, she could charm everyone," Will says.

"A formidable weapon, indeed," Angus says.

"Did you see the paper today? Roosevelt sent Hirohito a cable?"

"Yes. We'll see how effective that is. What are they having you do at the office?"

"They sent around a memorandum a few weeks ago saying that our Volunteer positions took precedence over company business, but we are supposed to register with them during fighting, if it breaks out. They've given us a number to call with our location. I don't know that they know what they're doing."

They watch Trudy twirl around the dance floor, laughing, ivory-white arms draped over her partner's shoulders. Afterward, breathless and happy, she tells Will that her partner was the "head of the whole thing. He's very important, and he seemed to like me very much, telling me all about the situation we're in. And it's terribly ironic," she says. "The dreariest of people are safe—the Germans, bless their stolid hearts, the Italians with their awful, funny ways. Hong Kong's going to be so dull, no parties worth going to at all."

"So you're interested when he tells you about the war, are you?"

"Of course, darling. He knows what he's talking about."

The orchestra is playing "The Best Things in Life Are Free," and Trudy is complaining. "He's horrible," she says about the accompanist. "I could get up right now and play better than that." But she isn't given a chance because a short man with a megaphone strides through the ballroom and gets up onstage. The orchestra grinds to a halt.

"All those men who are connected to the American Steamships Line are ordered to report aboard ship as soon as possible. I repeat, all those connected with American Steamships Line are required to report onboard right now."

There is a long silence, then on the dance floor, couples uncouple, at the bar, men stand up from their bar stools and pull down their shirt fronts. A few start to make their uncertain way to the door.

"I hate American accents," Trudy says. "They sound so stupid." She seems to have forgotten her great love for Americans.

"Trudy," Will says. "This is serious. Do you understand?"

"It'll be fine, darling," Trudy says. "Who would bother with our small pocket of the world? It's just the alarmists." She calls for more champagne.

Dominick comes by and whispers something in her ear. He stares at Will while he's doing it.

"Good evening, Dominick," he says.

"Hallo," is the laconic reply. Dominick is one of those queer Chinese who are more English than the English, yet has no great love for them. Educated in the most precious way in England, he has come back to Hong Kong and is affronted by everything that is in the least bit crass, which is to say, everything—the swill on the streets, the expectorating, illiterate throngs of coolies and fishmongers. A hothouse flower, he thrives only in the rarest of society circles, around damask napkins and clear, ringing crystal—Will would very much like to see him in a rubber apron ladling out soup to butchers and their ilk in a street-market noodle shop, the kind with the bare electrical bulb hanging dangerously on a filament.

"Terrible news, isn't it?" Will says.

"This too will pass." Dominick dismisses him with a slow wave of his marble-white palm. Will finds himself wondering if those hands have seen any labor more arduous than the writing of a thank-you note on cream bond or the lifting of a champagne bowl. He watches the two of them whispering together. They belong together (were it not for the accident of their family relations) but he supposes such a pairing would combust, their pale electricity extinguishing the other.

Dominick says suddenly, "It's not all bad for Trudy and me, you know. The Japanese are closer to us than the English. At least they're Orientals."

Will almost laughs and then realizes that Dominick is serious.

"But you're the least Oriental person I know," he says mildly.

Dominick narrows his eyes. "You've no idea what you're talking about," he says.

Trudy intervenes. "You're both talking nonsense. Don't talk about this beastly nationality matter—it makes me ill." She brushes Will's hair back from his face. "All I know is that the Japanese are a very peculiar people."

"You should not say such things," Dominick says. "You should not."

"Oh, bother!" Trudy says. "Have another drink and shut up."

It is the first time Will has seen Trudy get irritated with Dominick. She wants to go shortly thereafter and they leave, but not before she gives Dominick a quick kiss on the cheek to let him know he's been forgiven.

On Sunday they wake and go to town for dim sum. There is an odd tension in the air, and the wet markets are filled with grim shoppers filling their bags. They go home and listen to the radio and eat a simple dinner. The amahs are flitting about, chattering nonstop, and it's giving Will a headache. The office rings up and says that work is suspended until further notice. That night, he and Trudy slip and slide in their sleep, waking each other in their restlessness, breathing loudly.

Monday, December 8. The rude *brrring* of the telephone. Angeline wakes Trudy and Will with the news that her husband has just received word of a broadcast to all Japanese that war with Britain and the United States is imminent. The engineers have been ordered to blow all bridges leading into the territory. Then, as they digest the news still groggy from sleep, they hear the air-raid sirens, and then, terribly, from a distance, then closer, the whing and whine of aircraft and the dull thud of bombs. The phone rings again. All Volunteers are to be in place by three in the afternoon. They turn on the radio and Will gets dressed as Trudy watches him from the bed. She is pale and quiet.

"It's madness for you to go out in this," she says. "How are you going to get to the office?"

"I'll drive," he says.

"But you don't know what condition the roads are in. You might be hit by a bomb or someone might..."

"Trudy," he says. "I have to go. I can't just sit by."

"Nonsense," she says. "And I don't want to be alone."

"Let's not quarrel," he says gently. "Call Angeline. Then go over to her house. Have her send her boy to escort you. And I'll ring you there when I'm able. You should probably stock up on some food as well."

He kisses her cool cheek and leaves.

In town, he drives by the King's Theater. It still seems to be operating. *My Life with Caroline* is the feature and there are, astonishingly, a few people queuing up for tickets.

When he reports to HQ, it's abuzz with activity, men jostling for space and supplies, with a sense of urgency he has not seen before. Outside, it's eerily quiet but for the intermittent boom of bombs. He sits and waits for his assignment. There's a map over a desk with the colony marked out. A dotted line is drawn from Gin Drinkers Bay to Tide Cove with a fortress at Shing Mun—the first line of defense. There's been a concrete tunnel built south of the Jubilee Reservoir where soldiers can climb to pillboxes to fire. "This should keep us for a while," a man says, noticing Will studying the map. "It's fairly difficult to breach, I'd say." On the wall, someone has typed up excerpts from General Maltby's speech that morning: "It is obvious to you all that the test for which we have been placed here will come in the near future. I expect each and every member of my force to stick it out unflinchingly, and that my force will become a great example of high-hearted courage to all the rest of the British empire who are fighting to preserve truth, justice, and liberty for the world."

Suddenly, over the radio, they hear Roosevelt's voice. "Quiet, dammit," someone shouts. The volume is turned up. Roosevelt announces the bombing of Pearl Harbor and a quiet shock descends upon the office.

Roosevelt is done, and there is the buzzing of the radio before the announcer comes in. "And that was President Roosevelt of the United States..."

"That's good for us," a fellow says finally. "Means the Americans are in it now, whether they like it or not."

"It means the war has gotten much bigger," says another, quietly.

SHE WAS PARANOID. She always had been. When she pushed open a door or picked up a wineglass, she made a point of smudging the slight map that her oils, finger whorls, and dust had created—as if Scotland Yard were hot on her trail. She didn't want to be leaving clues, fragments, parts of herself, around. When she ran her fingers through her hair, she kept the strands that slid out, and disposed of them in a dustbin. Her fingernail parings were housed in a tissue and flushed down the toilet.

This paranoia was beneficial, it turned out. Martin, distracted with work, with the workings of water, never noticed that her comings and goings had suddenly taken on a much more deliberate air. Must get Darjeeling at the shop, must go visit at St. Stephen's Hospital every Thursday, must do a lunch with the girls every Wednesday. She limited their intimacy to the bare minimum. She could not think that she was that woman, that woman she had heard her mother and her friends talking about in the kitchen, that woman who went from man to man in a single day. The kind of woman who could be kicked out of the colony and sent home on a ship in disgrace.

The awful thing was, she didn't feel as badly as she thought she ought to. She had always thought of women who had lovers as immoral women who cared nothing about society and manners and the way things should be. And yet, here she was, carrying on with a man who didn't even particularly seem to like her. And Martin was good. This was the inescapable fact. And he was good to her. Whether he loved her, she didn't know. He was certainly pleased to have a wife and a home and all of that taken care of, but she didn't know how much of that had to do with her as a person. Sometimes she felt that he had married her, dropped her into a slot labeled "wife," and gotten on with his life. But she was sensible enough to see that she was the guilty one in this arrangement. Martin was guilty of nothing but benign neglect. She was taking advantage of a good man.

But any bad feeling she had about the situation was always drowned out by the sensation Will created in the pit of her stomach when he approached her, cut the space between them in half, and half again, coming at her with those hooded, sardonic eyes. It was narcotic, that feeling, and she couldn't go for long without it.

Claire was trying to become invisible, so that she would be all the more visible around Will. She spoke less and less, didn't meet with the other wives, never left the flat unless she had to. Her days revolved around him, when she could see him next, what she would say to him, how he would touch her. Sometimes he refused. She would come over and lie in bed, and he would roll over and go to sleep, saying he was tired, and she would be left alone, her hot breath coming in and out, her head spinning with frustration. She wanted to own him, for him to want to own her, but he tread lightly around her—he didn't want to leave a mark. She wanted to be branded, a red, raw wound.

At Will's she lay in bed and realized that someone in the flat above played the same song over and over again. It was a melancholy tune she didn't recognize, and the words were muffled through the ceiling. She never mentioned it to him, as if she wanted to keep it a secret, a knowledge that she had, only for her, as if it were something of his only she knew about.

When she bought him presents, it almost paralyzed her. She had wanted to buy Will a pair of slippers, but she thought the soles were rather slippery and so she had imagined an entire scene where he wore them, and then fell and cracked his head open, and she would be left, pale with regret and longing. So she didn't buy them, and bought him a new teapot instead. He handed it over to Ah Yik, barely noticing it.

Christmas was coming and she was filled with dread. This is what it's like to be Martin, she thought. Somewhat dim, simple, in love with someone who doesn't love you back. It made her miserable. Will wanted her to not call him during the holidays. It was a difficult time for him, he said. A lot of memories. So she called him during the day just to hear the phone ring. Sometimes he would answer, his voice tense and annoyed. Other times the phone would ring and ring and she would imagine the amah shaking her head, knowing, the way women know, who it was. Funny, how that transcended culture.

Martin's superior, Bruce Comstock, had asked him to their beach club in Shek O, where they had hired a cabana for Saturday, and so, that morning, they packed up towels and their bathing suits, rolled down the windows in the company Morris, and drove out to the end of the island.

The road was narrow and carved right out of the hills. On their left was a wall of lush green mountain, almost steaming from the heat, and on their right, a glorious view of blue sea and sky. White boats bobbed on the water, looking for all the world like toys in an enormous bathtub.

"It feels like we're on the Italian coast, or what I imagine it to be like," she said.

"Isn't it marvelous?" he said. She reached into her bag, pulled out Melody Chen's scarf, and tied it around her head.

"That new?" Martin asked.

"Yes," she said easily. "I bought it at one of those little carts on Upper Lascar Row. You know, that neighborhood with the curry shops and carpets."

"It looks good on you," he said. They drove on.

. . .

The bathing club was simple and well used. They met the Comstocks at the bar and had a drink before the ladies went to the locker room to change into their bathing costumes.

Minna Comstock was in her early fifties and formidable. She had two children away at university, and lived her life with vigorous energy. She played tennis twice a week and golf on Ladies' Day at Fanling. In the locker room, she stripped down to her underclothes without embarrassment. Her body was firm but wrinkles hung from her bosom, her arms, her stomach. It seemed as if she had too much skin for the body she had.

"I bought a nice bathing suit at Wing On," Claire ventured. "They have quite a lot of merchandise."

"Wear British," Mrs. Comstock barked. "The items here are cut for the Chinese frame and aren't suitable for us. Too small. I only buy at Marks and Spencer and I always bring back loads of things from home leave, good marmalade and proper knives and things like that. Have you seen what they call a knife around here? Barbaric implement called a chopper." She hoisted a well-muscled leg onto a bench and started to oil it. "Have some lotion," she said, handing the slippery bottle to Claire. "It'll protect you from too much sun." Mrs. Comstock was brown in the oddest places—on her calves between her sock line and where her short pants must have ended, and on her arms between her shirtsleeves and where her golf gloves began.

"Thank you," Claire said. She smoothed some cream on her face. She didn't enjoy the sun, thought the fashion of browning yourself like some animal on a spit was quite peculiar.

On the beach, the wooden cabanas were covered in white cotton broadcloth, large and airy with hooks for hanging up robes and compartments for bags.

"We're number twenty-three," Bruce said. "You can put your belongings there while we bathe." Inside, there were beach chairs and an ice box. Bruce surreptitiously made them gin and Schweppes ("Highway robbery, what they charge you at the bar," he whispered) and they sat down and sipped them.

"Isn't this nice," Claire said. "So relaxing."

With a jolt of recognition, she suddenly spotted Locket running toward the sea in a white-and-red polka-dot bathing suit. When she followed her path back, her eyes fell upon the Chens drinking cocktails on the club terrace with a group of people. Melody Chen had on a wide-brimmed straw hat and sunglasses and looked like a film star.

"If you'll excuse us," she said to the Comstocks. "I just see some people I should say hello to."

She brought Martin over to the Chens' table.

"Hello," Victor Chen said, as she stood over him. He squinted at her. "Oh, it's . . ." He paused. "These are the Silvas," he continued smoothly, gesturing to the couple sitting next to him. "Michael is Hong Kong's foremost obstetrician. And this is Dave Bradley, with the NBC. He's from the United States, so he and Melody have been getting on a little too well for my taste." He turned to the table. "And this is Locket's piano teacher." Claire nodded and smiled. Mrs. Chen gave out a little shriek. "Locket!" she cried, and was out of her chair and down to the beach where Locket was in danger of being enveloped by an enormous wave. The group watched her run down to her child.

"Victor," Claire said. "My husband, Martin Pendleton."

"Of course," he said immediately.

"Pleased to meet you," Martin said. He smiled, uncomfortable.

Melody Chen came back from scolding Locket. "I wish they'd let the help in the club. It's such a stupid rule," she said. "It's just exhausting not to have Pai around. Oh, I mean Francesca." She turned to Mrs. Silva with a confidential air. "Did I tell you what happened?" They started conversing in lowered tones. Claire couldn't decide whether to attend Martin's conversation with Victor Chen, or his wife's conversation with her friend.

"...here with Bruce Comstock..."

"...Austrian crystal figures my mother gave me..."

"...very good banker..."

"...everyone's trying out new girls from rural China but they're awful with meals, can't cook at all and their own food's inedible, you have to teach them every single thing... I gave her a new name, of course, Francesca, because I want to go to Italy soon..."

Claire stood there, caught in one of those moments where everybody is having a conversation and one is excluded. She felt ill at ease, as if she had been forgotten.

"What a beautiful head scarf," Mrs. Chen said to her suddenly. "I have one that's a bit like it." A strange expression glanced over her face.

"Thank you," Claire said, with a cool she hadn't known she possessed. She had forgotten about the scarf. She patted her head casually, trying not to panic. "Thank you very much."

"Is it Hermès?" Melody Chen asked. "I love the colors—orange and brown are my favorite—autumn, you know."

"Oh, no," Claire said. "I got it here, actually. It's just some inexpensive thing I got off a hawker. I can give you the exact location if you..."

"Well, it looks just as nice as the real thing," Melody Chen interrupted. "You tall women can pull anything off." She sipped at her martini.

"Well," Mr. Chen said in the ensuing lull. "It was certainly nice to see you."

Claire didn't sleep that night. She got up after Martin's breath deepened, and walked barefoot over to the window. Beneath her feet the lacquered wooden floor was smooth and cool, spotless from the mopping Yu Ling gave it every other day. Her body was still overheated from the sun she had received that day at the beach; her arms and legs felt as if the rays were still simmering beneath her skin. She cranked the window open slowly, the metal hinges creaking, and watched the pinpoints of light that were people with insomnia just like her. There was a breeze and the humid night air entered the room and cooled her body. Her head was abuzz. She hadn't been able to concentrate on anything since their encounter with the Chens. She was sure she had behaved quite queerly to the Comstocks, as she had seen Minna give a look to Bruce after she had knocked over her drink for the second time. She hadn't said anything to Martin because she hadn't the slightest idea what she would have said. "Darling, I've been stealing from the Chens and I'm afraid I've been found out. I've stopped, though, don't worry." He would think her quite mad. And perhaps she had been. She rested her head against the cool pane of the window. She didn't think Melody Chen had put two and two together. And she would never accuse Claire of stealing without concrete proof, would she? Claire looked out at the dark night and wondered if it looked the same back home in England.

❖ Part II ❖

December 9, 1941

So, THIS IS WAR. Before, he would have called it driving. He's taking a lorry full of cable drums to Causeway Bay, along with five or six Chinese workers squatting in the back. In the seat next to him is Kevin Evers, who apparently knows what to do with the cable, or what to tell the workers to do. It is now chaos back at HQ, phone and radio squawking endlessly. The airport was bombed just hours ago, with the loss of some twenty-five aircraft, and the tension is rising. Will has been told to deliver the drums and get back on the double. Evers is nervously jabbering away.

The roads at least are empty of vehicles, although there are plenty of people still on the streets. A woman beats a man with a large burlap bag, striking him with her small hands, screaming, as he shakes her off and runs. The looting has already begun.

And, hard to believe, a few days ago he was at a party in a dinner jacket, sipping champagne and exchanging barbed jokes with Trudy and her crowd.

In Causeway Bay, he finds the building where he's to drop off the drums and they're unloading the lorry when the siren wails again. Everyone scurries inside, the whiz of air and the loud reverberation of the explosion. The ground shudders. Evers breathes loudly next to him. When they ring back to HQ, they're told to stay as bombing will probably intensify, park the lorry in a safe place, and billet at a flat on Montgomery Street. With a stubby pencil he writes down the number on a grimy piece of paper smudged with oil: 140. It sounds familiar.

When they venture there, they ring the doorbell and find a frightened amah who lets them in and reaches into her tunic to unearth a wrinkled envelope. When they open it, they find a rather poignant note:

> *To Whoever You May Be,*
>
> *Welcome to our home. We hope you will make yourselves comfortable in this difficult time. We are an English couple who moved to Hong Kong some seven years ago and enjoy it immensely, so we hope this is not the last chapter. We have moved as directed upwards, and hope that our flat provides you with safe shelter. In the spirit of wartime, we ask that you be courteous to our amah, mind the furniture, and refrain from smoking.*
>
> *Sincerely, Edna and George Weatherly.*

"Aaah," says Will suddenly.

"What?" Evers asks, lighting up a cigarette and giving Will one as well, for good measure.

"Nothing." It is just that he knows them. He's met them before, and been here for a drink. This was when he first arrived, in the weeks before he met Trudy, before everything, as she would never know people like the Weatherlys. They were very good people, respectable, and coming to Hong Kong had been their great adventure. From a small village in the Cotswolds, they still had a wide-eyed wonder at the vastness of the world and marveled that they had ended up in the Far East. He had met them at a small English shop in Causeway Bay, buying tea, a few weeks after he had arrived, and after striking up a conversation, they had invited him over. Nice people. He never saw them after he started up with Trudy. Different speeds.

They toss a coin for the bed, and Will gets the floor.

"You could sleep in the old bird's bed." Evers nods toward the small room the amah has in the back.

"I'm not that hard up," Will says lightly. "She's had a rough time of it too, without me taking her room."

"Just thinking of you, mate." Evers shrugs. "Do you think she could rustle up some supper?"

Will rummages in his pack. Trudy, still Chinese enough to be obsessed with food, had made sure he had some tins in his rucksack although he had deemed it unnecessary. "I have bully beef and some carrots."

The amah is happy to have something to do. She holds up a cup of rice and cooks it with the meat and vegetable, and then they eat—she taking a bowl to her room, and the two men in the dining alcove, with the radio turned on, disembodied voice crackling on with news of the war.

"The bridges at the northern frontier have been blown up to prevent the advancement of Japanese troops...." Later, someone who was there will tell Will of the surreal scene—the British assiduously setting up their explosives in plain sight of the Japanese, who were just as diligently building another bridge to swing across once the destruction had happened, the two sides studiously ignoring each other, neither questioning the inevitability of what the other was doing, nor trying to stop it. "Doesn't that just sum it all up," this man, a policeman, said. "Thoroughly demented."

All through the night, the flat shudders and is lit with the fire of bombs. Will hears Evers, his rapid breath, neither of them asleep.

In the morning, Evers washes himself thoroughly.

"Don't know the next time I'll be able to do this," he says, toweling off with one of the Weatherlys' linens and tossing it in the corner. "Do you think breakfast is in the offing?"

"Do you think of anything else but food?"

"What else is there to think about, mate? Times like these, you get to the basics—what you eat, where you shit, finding a place to sleep. It's what keeps you sane."

They call HQ to see what to do next. Nobody knows a thing.

"Just stay there for now," a voice barks at them. They hear clattering and men shouting. The line clicks off.

"Good to know they're on top of the situation," Evers says.

"We're the civilians. I'm sure the top guys know what's going on."

"One would hope."

They decide to go out. Montgomery Street is empty, being primarily an enclave for European expatriates who have all fled to higher ground or to China. The few storefronts—a bakery, a shoe repair shop—are closed up and dark inside. The windows are already dirty from the soot and dirt kicked up by the bombs, but through one, Will can see a rotting egg tart, its glistening yellow surface slowly being invaded by green mold. A fly lands on top and starts making its way across the mold, twitching its antennae. An airplane whines overhead and Will flinches instinctively.

When they go back to the flat, the amah is gone, her room as clean as if she had never lived there.

"Nothing to do here," Evers says. "I think we should try to get back to HQ. It's going to drive me mad staying here doing nothing."

They gather their belongings and pick their way in the gathering dusk through the streets. Refuse has started to build up on the curbs and a low, persistent stench rises from the road. They see a car speed up as it approaches them, and in it a Chinese man averting his gaze. They are in sight of the lorry and Will remarks that the doors are open when they hear it. Evers's head cocks up to the whining sound, and Will watches him watch the first bomb come down and destroy a building not fifty feet away. It is as if it is in slow motion. Evers yells, "Watch out!" and dives for the ground. Will follows and he feels the earth open up and fall below them, his body dealt an enormous crushing blow, ears ringing and eyes stinging, and then in the next moment—the next moment of clarity—they are crawling toward the shelter of the lorry, the closest thing there is. In the back of his mind, as the ground is pounded and shaken by the intensifying chaos, Will notes the lorry has been picked clean.

The tires are missing and the open doors reveal a missing steering wheel. Evers is shouting something else, something about this being civilian territory and why are they bombing, but Will can't hear the rest because he is thinking that the tires are missing and that it is hard to move forward with the ground shaking like this, and then all is white.

December 15, 1941

WHEN HE WAKES UP, he is woozy and cold. Overhead, an enormous light is glaring down at him. The sheets are like ice on his swollen limbs. He is afraid to look at his own body.

But here is relief. He is not dead. Then he remembers. Evers. But he doesn't remember. Every part of his body hurts so much he feels as if his head is about to explode. He lifts the sheet. His left knee is swollen to the size of a small melon. Around the bandage bulges flesh colored purple, black, livid, angry.

Jane Lessig, whom he has met before at parties, comes by. She is dressed in white, and in his woozy state he thinks she looks like an angel.

"There you are," she says. "You had us worried, you know."

"Water?"

"No water for you right now. Doctor's orders."

He doesn't think he's ever felt quite so awful in his life.

"I'm so embarrassed," he tells her.

"What on earth for?" She cranks up his bed with a quizzical look.

"It was just a short experience," he tries to explain. "Nothing warlike about it."

"You're talking nonsense."

He sees she doesn't understand his meaning. He tries again.

"Evers?"

"Don't worry about him," she says, and walks quickly away.

He wanders in and out of consciousness.

He sees Trudy in a white dress, like a nurse, like a bride, like a shroud. She sponges his forehead. But her hair is blond now. She is not Trudy.

"Listen," whispers the wondrous Jane Lessig. "You were not in the Volunteers. You're a civilian who was walking down the street and hit by debris from a bomb." She doesn't want him to go to a POW camp. It's unclear who is going where but she thinks the civilians will be better off than the soldiers. He nods. He understands, then forgets. She says it to him every day, like an incantation that will save him.

Jane Lessig brings him a bowl of pudding.

When he gets up to look out the window, the first time he has been up, he is surprised to find that he has a limp.

"I've a limp!" he says to Jane Lessig.

"Yes, you have," she says. "And a fine one at that."

"I'm feeling much better," he says. "I think I could be discharged soon."

"Do you, now?" she says crisply. "We'll leave that to the doctors, shall we?"

But he does feel better and when Dr. Whitley comes around, Will is dressed and ready to go.

"I don't think I'm doing much good here, do you?" he asks.

"Will," Dr. Whitley says. "It's very different out there. Kowloon's besieged and we're trying to hold out here for as long as possible. There have been enormous casualties. Do you know where you could stay?"

"Could go to Trudy's?" he wonders.

"She's been here every day," the doctor says. "But I didn't let her come in. I thought it would be too upsetting for her. You're not at your most handsome. She said to tell you she's staying with Angeline and would be by later on today."

"Oh," Will says. "Then I'll stay until she comes."

The doctor gives him a peculiar look and nods. He's finished looking at Will's knee.

• • •

When Trudy comes, she is different. He can't tell why and then he sees—she has no lipstick on, no jewelry, her clothes are drab, no color of any sort. He mentions this to her, sort of an ice breaker to take away from the fact that he is injured, in a hospital, that the world is at war. It is odd to be shy with Trudy. He does not want to seem diminished in front of her.

"I don't want to attract any sort of attention," she says. "It's like walking on pins out there in case you run into a Jap. Father's gone to Macau. He wanted me to come, but I didn't want to." She walks over to the window. "He's worried about me," she says, looking down and fingering the cloth of her skirt. "If they win, they'll be brutal beyond belief."

"How did you get here?"

"I had Angeline's driver bring me. We're camping out at her place on the Peak, although the whole Peak is supposed to be evacuated by now. They think it's too exposed, but we've managed to stay undetected, and it's quiet up there. She has the dogs and her houseboy along with the amahs and the chauffeur so we have some protection."

The upper class always do what they want, he thinks, inappropriately.

"It's nerve-racking, like playing a game of poker," she says. "You never know when you're going to be stopped, and people are turning against each other. Old Enderby was roughed up by some Sikhs because they said he looked at them funny. That lovely old man." She stops suddenly. "How are you feeling? Here I am going on about the outside and you're all . . ." Her voice trails.

"Evers is dead," he says. "But you didn't know him. He was with me when the bomb got us."

Trudy looks at him, blank. "You're right," she says. "I don't know him."

"I want all the news," he says. "Do you have any?"

"Angeline says that we're not doing very well. Apparently they expected the Japs from the south, by the sea, but they came from the north instead and just breezed right through the defenses there. And it's really awful outside." Her voice hiccups. "I saw a dead baby on a pile of rubbish this morning as I came here. It's all around, the rubbish and the corpses, I mean, and they're burning it so it smells like what I imagine hell smells like. And I saw a woman being beaten with bamboo poles and then dragged off by her hair. She was half being dragged, half crawling along, and screaming like the end of the world. Her skin was coming off in ribbons. You're supposed to wear sanitary pads so that... you know... if a soldier tries to... Well, you know. The locals and the Japanese both are looting anything that's not locked down, and thieving and generally being impossible. They're all over the place in Kowloon, running amok. We're thinking about moving out to one of the hotels, just so we're more in the middle of things, and we can see people and get more information. The Gloucester is packed to the rafters but my old friend Delia Ho has a room at the Repulse Bay and says we can have it because she's leaving to go to China. We can share the room with Angeline, don't you think? And apparently, the American Club has cots out and people are staying there as well. They have a lot of supplies, I suppose. Americans always do. Everyone wants to be around other people."

"I suppose that's a good idea," Will says.

"Dommie says it's only a matter of time before the Japanese have the whole island, so he says it really doesn't matter."

"That's hopeful. Always the optimist."

"I don't think he really cares." Trudy laughs, a shrill sound. "He's just waiting to see what side he should join. He's learning Japanese at a fast clip."

"You know what a dangerous thing he's doing. It's not a matter for laughter."

"Oh, bother!" Trudy comes and sits down next to him. "Your injury has quite done away with your sense of humor. Dommie is a survivor, just like you and me, and he'll be fine. When can you leave?"

"I think soon. And they're eager to be rid of me. There are people with far more serious injuries, I imagine."

"But can you walk and all that?"

"I'll be fine," he says shortly. "Don't worry about me."

Dr. Whitley discharges him with reluctance.

"If it weren't for Trudy," he says, wrapping fresh bandages around Will's abdomen and knee, "I would never let you go. I know she'll take care of you."

Trudy is sitting at the foot of the bed.

"And the little fact that you have too few beds," she rejoins. "Will here is taking up valuable space. I'm on your side, Doctor. I was a nurse for two weeks. Remember?"

The doctor laughs. "Of course. How could I forget?" He turns serious. "Trudy, you must change the bandages daily, and you must cleanse the skin and the wounds with a solution of water and peroxide that I'll have the nurse make up for you. No matter if Will says he doesn't need it, you must do it without exception."

Trudy nods. "I'll be a model of reliability and efficiency," she says.

Once at Angeline's, she sets him up in bed although he feels fine. Their room is messy, with her clothes spilling out of a suitcase onto the floor and her toiletries scattered on the windowsills, the bathroom basin, the bed. There are model airplanes strung from the ceiling and a wooden desk piled high with schoolboy mysteries.

"Whose room is this?"

"It's Giles's—my godson, did you know him?"

"I've never met him."

"He's always away at school and now they're having him stay for the meantime with Frederick's family in England until this all settles down."

"Oh," he says. The room is streaked with dusty light from a window. "I'm not an invalid, you know," he says. "I could probably walk to Central and back."

"Don't be ridiculous," she says. "You're to take it easy."

But he is better, and she sees it, and soon they venture out, to see empty roads, closed storefronts, people scurrying from place to place, not looking anywhere but at the ground.

"There's been an incredible amount of looting," she says. "And the government is rationing rice. It's been rather amazing. I was walking down Gloucester Road and I saw police firing their guns in the air to disperse a crowd, and I wondered, where do those bullets go? When they come down, if they hit someone, can't they kill somebody that way?"

"Trudy, darling. You always think of what nobody else thinks about."

"And probably for good cause," she says. "I'm rather an idiot about everything."

They walk farther.

"It doesn't feel like our town anymore, does it?"

"It's too dreary."

They link arms and go home, where Angeline is crying in the cellar and the amahs have made a small meal of rice and Chinese vegetables dotted with salted pork. They eat and drink weak tea, feeling the invisible constraints of the reality around them.

The next few days are Spartan and regulated, lived as if they might be the last, heightened with the surreal. They eat to sustain themselves, listen to the radio for the latest news, and go to the distribution center for supplies, which are given out sporadically and randomly. One day it's bread and jam, another it's bananas, and then it's flashlights. They take what they can get and go to the black market for the rest as, between them, Trudy and Angeline have a lot of cash. At the black market in town, the atmosphere is tense, the buyers irate at the prices and shouting insults at the vendors, a few having the grace to look embarrassed behind their tables of random goods—the tins of potted meat, the small bags of sugar, the cooking utensils. The price of rice is at an all-time high, and it is as precious as gold. The ground shakes intermittently and the night is lit by fire. They see piles of dead bodies and weeping women beside them. Dominick stops by with provisions he's got ahold of somehow, and they have the delicacy not to ask. He tells them to stay at Angeline's for as long as possible. They have not been bothered and that is a good sign. There are a few other families holding fort at their homes as well. Will's injury makes it impossible for him to go anywhere too far. Angeline's driver manages to procure the newspaper most days, and the news is grim—the Japanese advancing inexorably and surprisingly fast.

"I can't believe they still get the paper out every day," Angeline says. She has not bathed in days and is starting to smell more than musty. She has not heard from her husband. He had last sent a message a week ago when he was fighting for the Volunteers on Mount Nicholson.

"Should we go to the Repulse Bay?" Trudy asks.

"I feel odd not doing anything," Will says. "I feel like other men are fighting and I'm sitting around doing nothing."

"You're injured, you imbecile," Trudy says. "You'd be more of a hindrance. You're slowing me down and I'm only putting up with it because you're a warm body to sleep next to at night. I assure you that others will not feel that way."

The next day they wake up to find the help vanished. Trudy is entirely unsurprised.

"A clean getaway. I'm surprised the dogs haven't deserted us." She starts washing the dishes that were left in the basin. He rises to help her. "You sit down," she orders. "They lasted longer than I thought. Angeline's always been a beastly employer although she pays twice the going rate."

"What happened to Ah Lok and Mei Sing?" Will asks, remembering them suddenly.

"I told them they should leave, and they wouldn't, and so I locked them out of the flat until they went away. There was lots of crying and wailing—you know them. They have relatives I'm sure they'd rather be with."

"You're their family, Trudy."

"But I'm not, really. And it's more dangerous for them to be with me. They're not going to be bothered once they're part of the crowd out there. I'm the one who's going to get attention, hanging about with all you foreigners."

"It must have been very hard to make them leave," he says, reaching for her hand.

She shakes him away.

"It's fine, Will. Please don't be sentimental right now. I couldn't stand it."

"What day is it?" he asks.

"Almost Christmas. The twentieth, I think." She looks wistful. "The parties should be in full swing by now." Then, "Will."

"Trudy."

"I've some things I've had to hide, but I want you to know where, because if something happens, you should go get them."

"Like?"

"I've a lot of money that my father gave me before he went to Macau, and my jewelry too. Altogether, it's worth a lot of money... more than enough to live on for ages."

"I'll take note but I don't need it, if that's what you're implying. I'll be fine with what I have."

"And I hired a box at the bank, the main one. And I've your name and Dominick's name down as people who can access it. But the thing is you have to both sign for it, unless one is dead, so you have to get along. Although I imagine things are different in wartime. There's a key. It's in the planter off my bedroom window in the flat.

I've brought it inside, and it's just filled with earth. It's on the bottom, so you'll have to dig it out. But if there's no key, you can still get to it—it will just take a bit longer. Legal things, you know."

"Noted," he says.

"You must remember," she says. "You really must."

Angeline emerges from her bedroom in a dressing gown and they explain about the missing servants. She collapses into a chair.

"I don't understand," she says again and again. "They've been with me for years." Quickly, she becomes practical. "Did they take anything?"

They hadn't thought to look. They go to the pantry and see their fast-dwindling supplies—rice, a few potatoes and onions, flour, sugar, a few soft apples—untouched.

"Servants get a raw deal," Will says. "They're always the last thanked and the first accused."

"This is survival," Angeline says. "I'm surprised they didn't take anything. I would have, and not had a single qualm."

"Let's all have a drink," Trudy says.

"That's the most sensible thing you've said all week," Will says.

He goes to get a bottle of scotch—they are not in danger of running out of liquor anytime soon. They pour glasses, turn on the radio, and the announcer is reading a message from Churchill. "The eyes of the world are upon you. We expect you to resist to the end. The honor of the empire is in your hands."

"We're being abandoned," Trudy says. "They're not doing anything to help us. What do Churchill and the goddamned British empire expect us to do?" Her eyes look hard and glassy but Will sees they are filmed with tears.

Every day leaflets fall from the sky, Japanese planes whirring overhead and letting loose propaganda, all over the colony, telling the Chinese and the Indians not to fight, to join with the Japanese in a "Greater Far Eastern Co-Prosperity Sphere." They've been collecting them as they fall on the ground, stacking them in piles, and Trudy wakes up on Christmas Day and declares a project, to make wallpaper out of them. In their dressing gowns, they put on Christmas carols, make hot toddies, and—in a fit of wild, Yuletide indulgence—use all the flour for pancakes, and paste the leaflets on the living room wall—a grimly ironic decoration. One has a drawing of a Chinese woman sitting on the lap of a fat Englishman, and says the English have been raping your women for years, stop it now, or something to that effect, in Chinese, or so Trudy says.

"Hmmm . . ." she says. "Isn't this a drawing of you and me?" She sits on his lap, puts her arms around his neck, and bats her eyes. "Please, sah, you buy drink for me?"

"It's of me and Frederick, you idiot," says Angeline. "Look at how fat the man is." It's the first time she's mentioned her husband in days.

Another leaflet has two Orientals facing each other and shaking hands. "Japanese and Chinese are brothers. Do not struggle and join our side," translates Angeline.

"They seem to have forgotten Nanking," Trudy says. "They weren't so fraternal then, were they?"

"I feel . . . oppressed," says Angeline. "I think we should turn Will in, don't you, darling?"

"I think that fellow is Dominick." Will points to one of the Chinese figures.

"Don't joke about that," Trudy pouts. "Why do you think we have so much food? Dommie's taking care of us, and I don't really care how at this point."

"Point taken but not agreed with," Will says. "Why are those damn leaflets so obvious and inflammatory?"

They hear a car motoring up the driveway and tense their shoulders. Trudy runs to the window and tentatively lifts up the drape.

"It's Dommie!" she shouts with relief and goes to open the door.

"Speak of the devil." Will sits down.

Dominick enters and unwraps a muffler from around his neck.

"Merry Christmas and all that," he says, languid even in the midst of war.

"And to you," Will says.

"I've brought a few provisions to make it feel extra holiday-ish." He brandishes a basket from which he extracts the *South China Morning Post*, a tin of pressed duck, a sack of rice, a loaf of bread, two jars of strawberry jam, and a fruitcake. The women clap their hands like pleased children. "Can you make anything with this, Trudy?" He sprawls into a chair, elegant limbs splayed out, the hunter having provided for his women.

"I'm hopeless in the kitchen, you know that." Trudy grabs the newspaper.

" 'Day of good cheer,' " she reads. "That's the headline. 'Hong Kong is observing the strangest and most sober Christmas in its century-old history.' "

"It's as if Hong Kong didn't exist before the English got here," Dominick interrupts.

"Shut up, I'm reading," Trudy says. " 'Such modest celebrations as are arranged today will be subdued.... There was a pleasant interlude at the Parisian Grill shortly before it closed last night when a Volunteer pianist, in for a spot of food before going back to his post, played some well-known favorites in which all present joined with gusto.' " She looks up. "People are at the Grill and I'm not? That's a travesty if I ever heard one. I've been isolated up here in the Peak and people have been going out? Have you been going out, Dommie? And how dare you not take me with you!"

"Trudy. It's not good for women to be out these days. You should be tucked away, safe, at home. Now, mend my trousers and make us some lunch."

She throws the paper at his head.

"What's the news?" Will asks.

"Not good for England," Dominick says easily. "They're outnumbered and outclassed. There are just so many Japanese and they've been properly trained. They're on the island already, swarming around everywhere. They landed the night of the eighteenth. The English are depending on soldiers who haven't been trained on the terrain and don't know what to do. The chain of command is not being well executed. And malaria's running rampant."

Will notices Dominick is careful not to say "we" or "our."

"So we're not doing well, it sounds."

"No," Dominick says evenly. "You are not doing well at all. I think it's only a matter of time. The governor's a fool, rejected an offer of cease-fire with some absurd British proclamation of superiority. Has his head in the sand. I've been getting news from our cousin Victor, who always knows what's going on with these things. He's still at home."

"Do you want pancakes?" Trudy interrupts.

"No, thanks," Dominick says. "I can't stay long."

"What are you doing with your time these days?" Angeline asks. "Besides taking care of us, I mean."

"You cannot believe what is going on," he says. "You're in a cozy little bunker here. It's horrific out there. I'm just trying to keep on top of the situation." His face is bland and smooth, eyes like black coals. Will wonders if it would be right to call a man beautiful.

"If we hear of a surrender, we'll leave, since I assume they'll be looting up here in the Peak first thing," Will says.

"And if you see any uniforms at all, you should be out of here like a shot."

"Is there anything else we should be doing?" Angeline asks.

"No, not really. You have money, I assume. If it gets really bad, I suppose a hospital is the safest place. You know where they are. They've turned the Britannic Mineral Water Works factory over in Kowloon into a temporary shelter as well. But then you'd have to get over the harbor. Stay on this side, actually. There's some Japanese custom that when they win a battle, the soldiers get three days to run wild and do whatever they wish, so that's the most dangerous time, obviously. Try to be indoors at all times." Dominick pauses, and looks at Will. "By the way, I've got a Christmas present for you."

He goes back to the car and comes back with a cane, a beautiful one, made of polished walnut, with a brass tip.

"I'm afraid I didn't have time to wrap it. But I thought you might find it useful." He smiles crookedly and hands it to Will. "There you go, old chap."

"Thank you," Will says. He takes it and hangs it on the arm of the chair he's sitting on.

"What about me?" Trudy says. "Nothing for me?"

"This just fell into my lap." Dominick says. "I saw it on the black market and I had just enough money for it. Didn't ask for much. I guess the market for canes is not so good in wartime."

"Funny, that. I would have thought they would be popular, what with the war creating all those cripples and everything," Will says.

"One might think, yes."

Trudy stops the exchange. "But the doctor says that Will is going to be as good as new, so he won't need it in a few weeks, will you, Will? We'll use it as a poker for the fire, then."

After Dominick leaves, they sit, the air somehow gone from the room. It feels colder, the evening approaching.

"Turn on the phonograph," Angeline says. "I want to hear music and dance, and feel normal."

"And drinks!" Trudy cries. "It's Christmas and we should be having drinks."

She fetches new glasses, lights candles, and puts the duck and bread and jam out on the table, and it tastes marvelous, their Christmas supper, with the liquor warming their cheeks and stomachs.

They carry on in this way, Trudy and Angeline dancing, carols playing, Will applauding, pouring more drinks. They drink and dance in the chilly drawing room of Angeline's grand old house, the twilight encroaching, glasses in hand, tippling until they are all quite drunk and they stumble up to their rooms and collapse. Trudy is sweet to Will in bed, her hands and mouth moving over him until he forgets the dull throb of his knee and the spinning of the ceiling. That is the Christmas of 1941, a wistful, melancholy, waiting kind of day he will remember forever.

In the morning, Angeline knocks on their door. Will opens it, groggy, his mouth feeling like cloth. For some reason, she leaves her hand suspended in the air, frozen in midknock.

"Morning," he says. She looks at him, her face pale and hung over.

"Happy Boxing Day," she says. "It's finished. I just heard on the radio. We've surrendered."

December 26, 1941

TRUDY IS FRANTIC to find Dominick. "He will know what to do," she says over and over.

"We will just stay here until we can't anymore," Will says, trying to calm her. "It will be fine in the long run. The Japanese cannot win against England, and America, and Holland and China. It's just going to take a little while."

"Would you mind if I went into town and tried to find him? Or maybe I should try to find Victor," she says, ignoring him. "I don't think you should go."

"I would slow you down, I know." He cannot calm her. "How are you going to find them? It will be impossible. Just stay and see. It will all be fine, you will see."

She whirls on him, her face unrecognizable.

"And in the meantime?" She almost spits it out. "What do you suggest we do in the meantime while the Japs are swarming over the town, doing whatever they like, to whomever they like? They're going to be all over the place, like filthy little ants. What do you think America and Holland and jolly old England are going to do then? Are you going to help me? With your leg the way it is? We have to."

He hesitates, then takes her shoulder with one hand and slaps her face with the other. "You need to settle down," he says. "You are hysterical."

She sinks to the floor, weeping.

"Will," she says through her hands. "Oh, Will. What are we going to do?"

He gets up with difficulty and kneels down on the floor with her.

"Darling Trudy," he says. "I will take care of you, even with my terrible, gimpy leg. I swear."

Later, after he has put her in a bath, and gotten her a drink, there is a knock at the door. With the women upstairs, he goes to answer it, first looking outside to see who it is. A sandy-haired man in uniform is standing by the door.

"Who is it?" he shouts.

"Please, sir, it's Ned Young, from Canada. With the Winnipeg Grenadiers."

He opens the door.

"Come in. Are you all right? Are you alone? What the devil are you doing all the way out here?"

"Yes, sir. I was on a van being transported with the others, as POWs, you know, and I managed to jump off and just walked and knocked on doors that looked safe."

Inside, the man is revealed to be a boy, so young acne still pocks his skin. His trousers are soiled and he smells to high heaven.

"Have you had anything to eat?"

"Not in the past few days, sir." He looks ravenous and polite at the same time.

"Here, sit down here in the dining room. I'll get you some things to eat." He gets a plate and puts out some bread and the remaining duck from last night. There's a beer and he opens it, pours a glass of water as well. The boy falls upon it, shoving the food in his mouth.

"There's more. Don't worry," Will says. "You'll get your fill."

"It was awful out there," the boy says. His mouth is full and he begins to weep. "It was awful. We were in the mountains, in trenches."

"Don't talk. Just eat and try to relax."

The boy goes on, as if Will hadn't spoken. "I saw my buddy's guts come out. He was alive. He was talking to me, and his guts were outside. Then I smelled him, he was cooking, his guts were cooking and it smelled like food. I saw a woman with her head blown off and her child sitting next to her, naked, with shit running down his backside, with flies buzzing. We had to leave him. They wouldn't let us take the child. I've never seen such things. We were in Jamaica just a month ago, training, eating bananas. They told us we wouldn't see any action here." He weeps and weeps but keeps eating. "And I didn't have water for days, it seems. I just wanted to die, but I jumped off that truck 'cause I seen what those Japs do. They're not human, what they do to other people. They're not human. I saw them rip a baby out of a pregnant woman. I saw them chop off heads and put them on fence posts."

Angeline walks into the room.

"What on earth?"

The boy stands up, still crying, still eating.

"Hello, ma'am. I'm Ned, Ned Young, from Winnipeg."

"I see," Angeline says, and sits down. Will appreciates for once her cut-and-dried sophistication, so needling in peacetime. "Ned Young, where were you? Did you see any of the Volunteers?"

"We've lost. We've surrendered. I haven't seen anyone but Japs. They're so well equipped. They have mountain shoes, and belts with food concentrate, and maps. We didn't have any of that. They gave us rum for breakfast. They just dropped us here weeks ago and told us we'd have time to train."

"What did you see in town?" They want information. He wants balm.

"There're riots, and dead people. Everything smells so bad, you want to die too. It's thick out there, the smell, and people are scared, but the scoundrels are out, stealing, burning. They're taking advantage, before the Japs get everything."

"Why don't you rest, Ned," Will says, realizing he is not able to give them anything. "You bathe and rest. There's a bed upstairs and we'll wake you if anything happens."

Angeline brings him up. When she comes back down, Will feels the need to be outside and get some air. The young boy has brought a tantalizing glimpse of the outside world with him.

"I'm going out," he says. "My leg feels better and I need to know what's going on. It's driving me mad being cooped up in here all this time."

"Fine," Angeline says. "Just don't go too far. When Trudy wakes up, she'll be wanting you."

Outside, the sky is still blue, and there are birds singing faintly. Save the occasional plume of smoke, it is quiet and lovely up here on the wide, well-paved roads and green manicured hedges of the Peak. From a cliff-side fence, he can see Hong Kong spread out before him, the harbor glistening, the sky gleaming. It is so still outside, he can hear himself breathing.

"One of those moments," he says, before realizing he has said it out loud.

He comes back to Trudy and Angeline in the kitchen pouring all the bottles of scotch down the sink.

"Don't worry," Angeline says. "We got blotto first. And we saved some for you, and our new friend, young Ned Young."

"Only thing worse than a Jap is a drunk Jap, right?" he says. "Keep the empty bottles. They might come in useful."

"We've been thinking, Will," Trudy says, "and we think the best thing to do now is stay here since we don't know that anywhere else will be any better, but we think that you and Ned should stay hidden. Since it's so very obvious you are not Chinese, you know. Unless, of course, you are needed to rescue us, but Angeline and I could pretend to be the servants in the house and they might leave us alone."

Will cocks his head.

"Really? That has rich comic possibility, certainly, but I don't know if that's the thing to do."

"I know it sounds mad, but where would we go? What do you think we should do?"

"We could go into town and see what other people are doing."

"But we might not have a place to sleep or anything to eat."

"Well," Will says. "Let's do this. Let's take the car early tomorrow morning and we'll go down to Central and see what's going on there and we can come back up."

"All of us?"

"Ned should stay, since he's had a rough time, but you and Angeline can come if you want."

The next morning, they pile into the car, Ned as well, as he had not wanted to be left alone. He is freshly bathed and absurdly attired in some of Frederick's clothes, the sumptuous weave of the shirt cloth glowing up underneath his childish face, his torso swimming in tropical-weight wool trousers cut to house Frederick's not inconsiderable girth, cinched inefficiently by an alligator belt.

The road winds down the mountain, and as they round this curve or that, they catch a glimpse of the harbor and Central, looking eerily similar, just without cars. As they enter town, they quiet, looking at the empty buildings, the barren streets.

"Let's go to the Gloucester," Trudy says. "There should be people there."

They park and walk down Connaught Road. Ned touches Will's hand and motions to the side. Between two buildings, a man's body lies, crumpled, blood streaked over his clothes. They pass silently.

"It's so quiet," Trudy whispers.

"No cars or people anywhere," Will says.

But inside the Gloucester, it is bustling, with more people than they've ever seen in the lobby of that elegant hotel. They are sleeping on sofas, on the marble floor, the potted plants all moved tidily to one side, forming a verdant fringe to this strange refugee camp. Uniformed hotel boys are scurrying around with cups of coffee on silver trays, trying to serve the unorthodox guests as best as they are able.

"There's Delia Ho!" Trudy cries. "I thought she had gone to

China. And there's Anson and Carol. And Edwina Storch with Mary. The whole world's here!"

People throng around the new arrivals, asking where they've been, what they've seen.

"Can't help you," Angeline says. "We've been hiding out at home."

"Undisturbed?" asks an American.

"Quite," says Trudy. "But eating like dogs. Is there any food here?"

There isn't much, unfortunately, the hotel trying their best to supply their guests with what remains in their cellar. Trudy sits down to share a rice pudding with Delia, spooning some into Will's mouth, and then, seeing Ned off in a corner, gesturing him over to have some as well.

"The coffee is atrocious," she says. "They've gone to well water."

"What's going on?" Will asks Dick Gubbins, an American businessman who, even before all this, always knew what was going on.

"I've been at the American Club, came here to see if I could find out anything. They're starting to rampage through town, celebrating their victory. Mitzy, that old bird with the antiques store on Carnavon Road, was stabbed by a drunk soldier for nothing at all, for not handing over her purse fast enough, or something." His voice drops. "And you know what happened at the hospital."

"I don't."

"Awful stuff. They're just animals, sometimes. The nuns were violated, the other nurses too, doctors bayoneted while trying to defend them. They're not supposed to touch hospital workers, obviously, but tell that to a bloodthirsty mob. Drew McNamara's over there trying to clean the whole mess up and see that those responsible are apprehended but everything's so chaotic now. Under the Hague Convention, police are supposed to be able to keep order, the old Hong Kong police, but I haven't seen much of them. It's complete madness out there, I tell you. The Japanese are using some of the British constables to stand guard outside their consulate. I don't think they understand the concept of irony.

"The Chinese and Indians should be able to move freely. Trudy's cousin, that Victor Chen, is doing a good job acting as a go-between, trying to lessen the violence and looting. The neutral Europeans should be all right, but it's touchy there. The Japs have asked for prostitutes, in addition to swarming all over the Wanchai brothels. Hopefully that'll get some of their energy out. If you get a drunk or crazy one, they'll swing at your head with a sword and not care if they've cut your head off. They're demanding money and watches and jewelry from anyone they meet on the street. There's supposed to be a victory parade on the twenty-ninth."

"Any word on what they're planning to do with us?"

"No. But if you can get to China, I would. I'm trying to arrange passage now for me and some of my men."

"I don't know why Trudy doesn't go."

"And you should as well, big guy. Nothing for you here, right? Listen, best of luck, and we'll have a drink when this is all over, okay? Call me if you're ever in New York." They shake hands and Gubbins leaves, trailing palpable clouds of American prosperity and assurance.

Trudy comes over.

"You remember Sophie Biggs and her husband; we just saw them at Manley's party," she tells him. "Well, her husband knows some Japanese and so he spoke some to a few soldiers in the street and they thought he was being disrespectful and they shot him in the knee. And he was lucky, Sophie says. He's not in good shape because the hospitals have been bombed and are operating on the barest of levels. Delia says they're setting up checkpoints soon, so we're not going to be able to get around without passes. Should we go back up and get our things? Should we stay up there or come back down here? It is rather more convivial down here in town. I was going a bit stir crazy up there."

"I think it would be nice if we moved into town, yes. But there's no room here. We shouldn't sleep on the floor here when we have perfectly good beds at home. We should conserve our strength to prepare for whatever might be ahead. Who knows when we'll get to sleep well again."

"So you think we should stay at Angeline's?"

"I just don't know where we would stay in town. I'm not going to stay here." He gestures around. "This is a riot waiting to happen. I think it's going to get ugly here, and I don't mean with the Japanese."

"So cynical. Isn't that my job?" But she doesn't disagree. "Isn't it funny," she says. "We're at war but most of what we've done is wait around for something to happen."

"You don't want anything to happen, Trudy. We want everything to remain boring and uneventful."

"But you know what I mean. We just sit at home and look at each other. Is that what war is? I wonder what Vivien Leigh is doing right at this very moment."

He slaps her lightly on the bottom. "She's fast asleep," he says.

Edwina Storch comes over with Mary, her partner.

"How are you, my dear," she says to Trudy.

"All right, darling. How are you all faring?"

"Can't complain, but trying to figure out the new order and how to go about things."

"It's like quicksand, isn't it?" Trudy says.

"You're a survivor, though," says Edwina, with an odd cast in her voice.

Trudy pauses.

"As are you," she says lightly. "I'm sure we'll all be raising a glass of champagne to each other after this is all over."

"I certainly hope so," says Edwina. "You're at home?"

"No, at Angeline's," says Trudy. "Don't know if that's the best place, but that's where we are for now."

"Well, be well," Edwina says. "I'm sure we will see each other soon."

"I certainly hope so," says Trudy. When the women leave, Trudy makes a face at Will, sticking out her tongue.

They gather up Ned and Angeline, Trudy kissing everyone in sight, and stop by a newly sprung market to buy rice, *choi sam,* and rambutans at an exorbitant price, then drive home carefully, avoiding the main roads, feeling like some strange, newly orphaned family.

The electricity finally goes out on New Year's Eve. Will has been making quick, urgent drives to town to get information and supplies, trying to avoid running into any Japs. He's been successful for the most part, with the exception of one day when he was in the car with Ned, leaving town with a sack of rice, melon seeds, and some tins of bully beef, feeling rather victorious at his successful scavenging. A Japanese soldier appeared suddenly on the road ahead of them and waved down their car. Will's stomach had plummeted into the seat.

"Don't say anything," he warned Ned. The soldier had them open the trunk. He looked at the rice and looked at them, and then had them get out of the car. Gesturing with his rifle, he had them empty their pockets and take off their wristwatches.

"American?" he asked.

"English."

The man laughed. He looked to be around twenty-two, with a wide, naïve face.

"We win!" He pushed up his sleeve to reveal five wristwatches, lined up on his pale arm.

There was no reply for that, so when the man took their money and their watches and the rice and beef, Will and Ned got into the car silently and went back home. They had felt lucky.

And then New Year's Eve, Will wakes up and turns on the switch, only to find the electricity is gone. The telephone works intermittently.

Trudy rallies against the silence that greets these announcements.

"Who needs all those gadgets," she says. "They're more work

anyway. And everyone looks better by candlelight." She pauses. "I think we should have a party. A real bang-up New Year's party, and invite all our fellow campers who are up here with us on the Peak. I'll see what we have and we can do a potluck-style evening."

The Millers live down the road, a fashionable American family of six who are hunkering down with their six or seven servants—two or three amahs, a baby amah, a cook, a houseboy, and a gardener. They come by every once in a while to share information and for human contact. Trudy goes with Will to invite them and insists they bring everyone, including the servants and the baby.

"They can hang out in the kitchen and be part of it, a bit. You don't want to leave them alone—they might not be there when you come back!"

The bemused Millers agree to come and bring whatever they can spare, and to spread the word.

On the way home, Trudy says, "There's that story of the village with the soup. Do you know it?"

"No," Will says. "Village?"

"There was a village with a chief who wanted to throw a big party with a communal soup. He asked everyone to bring something for the soup—a meat or a vegetable or something good, you know. But everyone thought that everyone else would bring something so they just brought a stone, figuring no one would notice. And in the end, tragic as it is, the soup was not delicious, or something like that." She stops. "I don't know why I told you that just now. Except that the people in that village were definitely not Chinese, having so little respect for food."

"You're afraid the Millers will bring rocks to our party?"

"No, idiot," she says. "I'm afraid people aren't honorable."

But of course the party is a wild success. Though no dress is specified, people come in their finest, a sort of last gasp to the world as they know it. They gather together at Angeline's house, like moths to a flame, bringing surprising delicacies brought up from secret cellars—a case of champagne ("Why not?" the giver reasons. "Just figured it was now or some Jap would be bathing in it later"), five freshly slaughtered chickens, sardines, a small sack of rice, watercress, cheese, bananas. And this still being Hong Kong, people have brought their servants to prepare and serve it all.

"A veritable feast," Trudy says, looking at the table.

"The proverbial groaning table," says Will.

"I wouldn't go that far, darling." She kisses him on the cheek. "Doesn't it feel like we're on school holiday? You don't need to go to work, I don't need to pretend to do anything with my time. Anything goes."

Young Ned Young, a little more comfortable in his situation now, pulls Will aside. "That Trudy is something else," he says. "Where'd you find her? I never met anyone like her, for sure."

Men in dinner jackets and women in evening gowns are lounging in chairs, on the floor, drinking beer and tea out of odd containers—jam jars and tins—eating crackers and sardines. There's no music so people offer to sing and play the piano. The instrument's terribly out of tune, but the music is sweet and the voices lovely.

Close to midnight, they gather around the biggest candle in the living room and count down.

"Ten, nine," they start, before Trudy interrupts.

"Let's prolong this. Let's count down from fifty instead. Do we really have anything better to do?" People are agreeable and start over.

"Fifty, forty-nine, forty-eight..." And then something odd happens. Somewhere between thirty-four and thirty-three, the mood changes and it seems as if they are counting toward something that is rather important. They are chanting and their voices gather force and purpose, so that as they count down into the twenties and into the teens and the single digits, they become louder and braver, until they get to "five, four, three, two...one" and they burst into cheers and hug one another and feel, for a moment, as if something has been salvaged. Women wipe away tears and men clap one another on the back.

"Happy New Year, my darling," Trudy says, kissing Will. "May this be the worst Eve we ever experience."

To the room she lifts her glass. "It's time," she says, "to bury the silver and put away the sheets in the hot room. It will be over, but we don't know when."

At the end, guests leave in the wee hours, or stay, strewn among the many sofas and chairs, scared to go back outside, but wanting to get home. Trudy ministers to them, providing water and soothing words, until they muster up the courage to pull themselves together, expel the effects of drink, and lurch into the night, one eye cocked toward the sky for enemy aircraft.

January 4, 1942

ON THE FOURTH DAY of the new year, Trudy comes in with a leaflet in her hand.

"They're collecting people," she announces, and reads from it.

" 'Since the Japanese occupation of Hong Kong on Christmas Day, enemy aliens have been allowed free movement in practically all urban districts of the colony'—very generous of them isn't it? Then there's something about generals and army orders, and then it says, 'All enemy civilians'—that does make you sound dangerous, Will—'all enemy civilians shall assemble at the Murray Parade Ground on January fifth.' You are allowed to carry personal effects, and the care of your house is your own personal responsibility. Enemies include British, Americans, Dutch, Panamanians and whoever else has been disagreeable enough to war with our conquerors." She looks up. "I think I'm off scot-free."

"Are you?"

"Well, I'm none of those categories, certainly. And I've secreted my British passport away somewhere very safe so no one need know about it. And I don't think a dislike of origami qualifies me as warring with the Japanese. But we'll have to get you there, I suppose, unless you want to go elsewhere?" She wrinkles her brow. "China? Some people are arranging passage."

"No, I think staying in Hong Kong will be better. They will have to do things in a way that is accountable. If they gather us together, they have to register us and let our governments know, I would imagine." He shrugs his shoulders. "But we should decide what to do with Ned."

Over a sparse lunch of rice and salted cabbage, they decide to clean the Canadian up and register him as English.

"Pretend you lost your passport—a fire when a bomb hit your home or something. Your accent is a problem though," Trudy says. "Do you think the Japanese will notice?"

"I could pretend to be American," he says earnestly.

"But we don't know any Americans to take you under their wing. Better you stick with Will and keep your mouth shut."

Trudy says again she will not register.

"Angeline, you could go with Will and Ned, since Frederick is English. You're counted as English, then. You have your marriage certificate somewhere, don't you? I'll be fine out here without you. So many family friends have offered to take me in, I won't be alone." Trudy strokes her friend's arm.

"I'll stay here with you, I think. Don't you?"

"Why can't you pretend you're in government and not go?" Trudy asks Will. "Colonial staff are exempt from the order."

"Darling," he says. "There are ways of verifying these things. It would be worse if I lied and were to be found out."

"But you won't be allowed to come back, then, do you think? They're not going to write down your name, give you a pat on the back, and send you on your way?"

"Realistically, they're going to keep us all in a group. So I assume there will be some sort of collective living for a while, as they figure out what they're going to do with us. I've heard of mass exchanges between governments, so they might exchange us for Japanese who are living in our countries. But it might take a rather long time to get all that sorted out, so we should really have a plan of how to keep in contact."

After lunch, Will and Trudy go upstairs to pack a suitcase.

"What will you need? A toothbrush." She hands him a new one. "Tooth powder. Surely those are necessities. A comb—can't have you looking disheveled. On the other hand, perhaps we don't want you looking too handsome and getting yourself and all the ladies in trouble."

"Will you come with me?" he says. This is what he has wanted to ask all morning. The thought of leaving her makes him short of breath. He has seen her every day for months, not gone more than a few hours without smelling her skin, her hair. He finds other women grotesque now—they are too large, too loud, too slow. One afternoon, a short while after he had first arrived in Hong Kong, he and Simonds had sat at their desks and watched, mesmerized, as one is by the mundane, as their office lady, Miss Tsai, boiled water and poured it into a thermos. Miss Tsai was thin and wore metal spectacles. Her shoulders, which she covered with the same gray cardigan every day, were so small they looked as brittle as a bird's bones. Her hair was cropped short and often shined with grease. Simonds had turned to him—this was before Trudy—and said, "I don't understand how some find Chinese women attractive. They have no sex, so spindly." Will wishes Simonds had met Trudy, the languorous slip of her. He had shipped out a little after the time Will had first met Trudy at the party, still professing his desire to find a buxom young Englishwoman with whom to form a family. He's probably found her by now. But Will suspects he would find his English lass too rosy, too exuberant, next to the rapier-sharp silhouette that is Trudy.

She stops at his question, but only for a moment, then continues packing. "Why on earth would I cage myself up if I had a choice?"

"You don't know what it's going to be like out here," he says. "At least in there, you'll get three squares a day and a bed." He cannot bring himself to simply ask her to come to be with him. Instead he sells it like some low-cost holiday.

Finished with her package, she begins to pack some of her own clothes in a suitcase.

"I'd rather take my chances out here," she says. "You don't know what it's going to be like in the camps. The Japs can be brutal. And it will be good for you to have someone on the outside. I'll come and give you packages and news of the outside. The Lusitano Club is taking all Portuguese, half-breeds like me too, and they have decent sleeping quarters. If things get bad, I'll just go there. And Dommie will take care of me."

"We could marry," he says. "I'll take care of you better."

She looks up. He is frightened of her face, willfully blank.

"You don't know what will happen out here," he repeats. "At least we will be together."

She goes on folding her sweaters. Her hands are quick and sure.

"Do you know what the Chinese think of the English?" she says a moment later, as if he hadn't said anything of importance.

"Not really, but I hope Dominick isn't representative."

Trudy laughs.

"Well, a bit, although there's more to that situation than meets the eye. Don't be too harsh about him. He has his reasons. But many Chinese think English are rude and arrogant and think so much of their own heritage when ours is so much older and richer. And they're terribly stingy. I've never seen an Englishman pick up the bill for dinner, when even the poorest Chinese would be ashamed to let someone else pay if it were his invitation. It's odd, don't you think? I like our way so much better. We Chinese are not stupid. We know that most of the Englishmen here live in a way they could never afford in their own country, and they're living here like kings because their money happens to buy a lot more of our labor than our own money does. So they think they're the lords here and we're the serfs. But it doesn't change the fact that back at home they could never have the lavish life they have here. They're living on borrowed money, under assumed identities. You're not very English, Will. You're generous to a fault and very gracious and humble. I'm so glad you're not like most of your countrymen."

"I say," he says. "I don't know if this is the thing we should be talking about. I mean, this is quite a moment, right?"

"I know, I know," she says impatiently, as if he's missing the point. "I just meant that a lot of the locals don't really care what happens to the British. But at the same time, they don't really care about the Japanese either. Everyone just wants to live their lives, undisturbed, make a little money, make a little love, die with some food in their stomach. That's all."

Trudy's points always take a while to sink in because they're unexpected, as if spoken from the mouth of a child, and then Will always realizes how very shrewd she is. And how practical. He watches her pack an evening dress and, after a moment's hesitation, a matching shawl.

"Have you seen my silver evening shoes?" she asks.

"Never knew you had any," he says. He doesn't ask why she might think she would need evening clothes in a time of war.

"I always look forward," Trudy says suddenly. "Never backward. I hate photographs, diaries, clippings. What's the point? I don't understand how people can keep diaries—horrid things." He is surprised at her vehemence.

"I've always kept a journal of my travels."

"That's different, more of a travelogue, I would think."

"Well, my impressions, certainly. And the people I meet."

"I certainly hope I am not in this journal of yours."

"You would be disappointed," he says after a pause.

"People can be so loathsome, don't you think?" she says. "If we aren't together in the future, please don't think of me with hatred. Think of me kindly or forget me. I always try to do that. Think with kindness and don't judge. And know the entire situation."

"What on earth are you saying? Don't take such absurd leaps." He feels like she's punched him in the stomach, cannot feign the nonchalance, but cannot say too, don't leave me.

"If you love me, you know exactly who I am."

"Trudy, you are not this person. You are not."

"And you are not stupid, my love." She hands him his bag. "There. All set for your grand adventure."

At the parade ground, he notes with chagrin that others seem to have brought all of their belongings, stuffed into enormous suitcases that are filled to bursting and tied shut with heavy twine. Some practical joker has brought his golf clubs. There are people sitting on their luggage, drinking from thermoses, looking lost. There are also, curiously, Chinese people with all their belongings tied up in pink and red cloths, slung over their shoulders, squatting in the shade.

Will has money tucked into his trousers, and a few gold rings and bracelets Trudy has forced on him. "Gold is good; people will always take gold," her voice rings in his ears. He has only his small satchel, with the few essential items she had packed. Ned has some of Frederick's clothes Angeline gave him, ill-fitting as they are—the young Canadian bringing out the maternal side of both the women.

Trudy had stopped just long enough for them to get out of the car and to give him a light kiss, and then she had spun away quickly. A good-bye made of nothing. He stands there for a moment, Ned shuffling awkwardly near him, then picks up his bag, feeling slightly embarrassed that the young man has seen their bloodless good-bye. He spots the Trotters, the Arbogasts. He goes over to Hugh Trotter and introduces him to Ned, explaining his situation.

"This is quite bad," Hugh says, not caring about the travails of the young Canadian. "I hear that over at the bank, they're burning unsigned notes so they don't get into the wrong hands."

"Yes," Will says. "This is not good at all."

"You know, two days ago, they declared a new government for Chinese civilians—they're calling it the Civil Department of the Japanese Army and they're trying to sort things out, get the gas, water, and electric rolling smoothly again. They want everyone to get back into the flow, open their shops, resume their jobs. All except us, of course. We're enemy prisoners now."

"Then why are the Chinese here?" Will looks around at all the locals. "Surely they can't be registering everyone in the colony."

"No, it's a mix-up. The Japanese didn't realize that the Chinese here regard themselves as British nationals, so a lot of them have shown up, and there's a lot of confusion as to what to do with them. I think they only want the *gweilos,* to put it bluntly. I would imagine the Chinese people will go home today."

Will notices children playing—what are they doing here? They should have been sent away months ago. Hugh follows his gaze.

"Yes, and of course, the children. Damn fools, the parents," he says. "Sentimental. Didn't want to send their families away to safety. Like ostriches, they were. I hope the conditions are decent."

"Well, one hopes, yes."

"And you heard Millicent Potter went blind from shock?"

"No, I hadn't heard," Will said.

"Her child died in her arms, shrapnel from a bomb, and she was holding him, and her husband said all of a sudden she couldn't see. It comes and goes apparently, but it's been gone for a while."

"Awful."

"And Trudy?" Hugh asks. "I assume she's not involved in all this?"

"Yes, she's Portuguese and Chinese, so both good things to be at the moment."

"It'll be good to have someone on the outside. She can help you get things and messages. We have our amah and houseboy tailing us at the moment. I've given them more money than they'll see in a lifetime so I hope they don't run off with it. But what could we do?" Hugh gives a wintry smile. "Ironic, isn't it?"

Reggie Arbogast joins them.

"The situation is bad right now. They're winning in the Philippines and all over Malay and Burma. They're gaining too much momentum."

A Japanese soldier rides up on a horse.

"Line!" he shouts. "One line. No Chinese."

The crowd hesitates, moves in an amorphous mass, like a jellyfish, Will thinks, if he were watching from the sky. They ripple and lap, an uncertain sea creature.

"One line! No Chinese!" shouts the soldier again, this time more loudly. He canters the horse around, waving a sword in the air. The Orientals in the mix pick themselves up and move to one side, a gradual sifting of the races.

"It's like he's herding us," Hugh says to Will. "We're the cattle."

Will takes account of the clothes he is wearing—a sturdy pair of cotton trousers, two shirts, a sweater, and a jacket. He's suddenly aware that they might have to last him for a long time. He's glad he wore a heavy belt. Somehow, he thinks the strong leather and metal will come in useful.

The soldier swings around and leaves. The crowd is silent. A woman sits down on her suitcase and begins to cry. "Buck up," her husband says. "This is just the beginning."

They divide them into nationalities and march them in single file. Will watches the Americans walk away, along with the Dutch and the Belgians. The British are made to wait until the end. The Japanese seem to have some special prejudice against them.

They walk for hours, on almost unrecognizable roads with burning piles of rubbish outside charred buildings and the overpowering stench of rotting bodies and human waste. The mothers and children march with the men, babies crying. The roads are lined with locals, silently watching the unlikely spectacle of Western people being led away under the rule of the Oriental. Some spit in their path but most just look. Will sees relief in their faces, relief that they are not the victims, at least this time. There is also pity in some of the older faces. One brave soul in the procession tries to strike up a rendition of "Hail Britannia," but his melody fades away under the implacable gaze of a soldier who slows his steps until he is menacingly abreast of the singer. And there is the silence again, broken only by the tramping of feet and the heavy breathing of the conquered.

They are herded into the Nam Ping Hotel, which has clearly been used as a brothel in the recent past. The lobby is dingy and smudgy-looking, with peeling red paint and garish gold Chinese characters painted onto signs.

First, they are told to take off all their watches and jewelry and place them into a large sack. Then, a Japanese soldier jerks his gun toward the stairs to indicate they should go up.

The rooms are tiny, and things get ugly, with people rushing to claim their space until they realize that no matter how quick they are, they will have to squeeze four or five into a room. The stucco walls are bubbled with moisture and decay and flakes of ceiling fall down at the slightest tremor. There are iron beds with wafer-thin mattresses and *mintoi,* the Chinese quilt, with large, copper-colored stains. Large cockroaches scurry around, alarmed at the sudden invasion, and the floor is wet and unpleasant. It is chaos, with people demanding toilet paper, towels, clean water, not knowing that no one is there to supply them. Some don't seem to realize the days of amahs and chauffeurs are gone. The toilets stop up almost immediately and the hallways are filled with an unspeakable odor. Will and Hugh organize teams to clean. Some refuse, or don't show up. Will tells the others not to worry, that there will be plenty of work to go around soon, and that everyone will do their share. The Japanese provide no guidance—some look amused at the chaos, and others are simply oblivious, putting their feet up and having Chinese children run errands for them, fetching them beer and cuttlefish.

There is no food the first night. They go to bed hungry, rooms alive with the sound of whimpering children and the labored breath of their parents. Will tucks his hands into his armpits, hears young

Ned's snore—a strange, interrupted, barking sound—and wonders what Trudy is doing.

And so he finds out. Not tooth powder but food. Food is the luxury. The Japanese hand out a watery vat of rice in the evening, with not enough chipped bowls and spoons. There is some putrid boiled meat, a few rotting vegetables swimming in brown water. The first evening, some women refuse to eat it. By the next, everyone takes their share. They find Chinese willing to go fetch food for coins tossed from the balcony, but this is an iffy proposition at best as some disappear with the money, never to be seen again. Those lucky enough to have their amahs or houseboys on their tail throw down money and get fish and vegetables tossed back in return.

There is a lieutenant in charge of the hotel, Ueki, a small man with round glasses and a mustache. He is impossible to read as Will finds out when he is elected to meet with a supervisor about the living conditions and the food. It is an odd meeting, tense and excessively polite.

Ueki has commandeered the hotel manager's office behind the reception desk and is sitting behind a metal desk with an open bottle of whiskey and a lit cigarette smoldering in an ashtray. Smoke hangs thick in the air, unmoved by the fan that circles slowly overhead.

Will bows because it seems the right thing to do. Ueki inclines his head slightly.

"I have a few issues I'd like to bring to your attention," Will says.

"Speak," says the man.

"The toilets need to be cleaned, and we need supplies to clean them with. Can you provide us with some toilet brushes and cleaning powders? Also, a plunger would be helpful."

"I will see what I can do."

"And Mrs. Aitken is eight months pregnant and quite uncomfortable. Could we find a bed for her? She's in a bed with two other people right now. Everyone else is doubled or tripled up as well."

Except the corpulent secretary from Australia who refuses to give up her bed, but that's another matter.

"Fine."

Ueki waves off the request, so Will is not sure if he means yes or no.

"And the food..." Will hesitates.

"Yes?"

"The food is inadequate."

The short lieutenant studies Will.

"Do you want smoke?" He offers a slim silver case, probably freshly looted from some friend of Trudy's.

Will takes one and leans over so that Ueki can light it.

"Do you know where I learned the English?"

"No, but it's very good." Will tells himself he's not currying favor, not being obsequious, just honest.

"English missionary came to Japan, taught me for three years."

"There are lots of missionaries doing good works out there," Will says, it seems to him, idiotically.

"He was good man. For him, I will try to help you."

Will says thank you, and then sits for a moment before he realizes he has been dismissed. Getting up, he says thank you again.

Nothing ever comes of the meeting.

It is in this unlikely place, this old brothel, that the detainees find themselves pooling information and tales of what had happened in the days prior. Since they have nothing but time, they gather around, exchanging stories, trying to piece together a coherent history of the final, chaotic days before the surrender.

Regina Arbogast, a delicate-faced socialite who arrived at the parade ground in a rickshaw and seven trunks, six of which she was forced to let her servants bring back home, is full of stories of atrocity that happened not to her but to friends of friends of people she knew. She is full of opinions and appropriated outrage.

"The Chinese got the brunt of it really. They're defenseless, without a proper government to help protect them. They've been under our protection for so long, they don't know what to do. All the girls have been raped, but the Japanese are afraid to touch the English. They know it will come around in the end."

Regina had been staying at her friend May Gibbons's house, where they were living in fairly high style until some Chinese gangsters came in and tied them up while they looted the house. She talks incessantly about the jewelry she lost and how she'll never be able to replace it. Her husband, a successful importer and businessman, finally blows up after she has gone on for a particularly long time.

"For God's sake, Regina, just shut up and give us some peace. I'll buy you all the jewels in China after all this is over."

She looks at her husband balefully and whispers to her friend, Patricia Watson, about how beleaguered she has been and how Reggie has been just impossible throughout. Patricia smiles and looks satisfied. She had, quite by accident, been spared her valuables at the hotel as she had placed them on the floor in front of her, and the Japanese had refused to bend down to pick them up, and had not bothered to ask her to do it.

A young woman, Mary Cox, says her husband was grabbed by Japanese soldiers and made to clean up after bodies had been dragged along the street, shedding body parts like animals. They had to clear all the bodies before they got in the water supply and spread disease. He came home soaked in blood and bits of decaying flesh and wept before falling on the sofa, exhausted. He was gone the next morning. She hasn't seen him since. She has a two-year-old boy, Tobias, who trails her, one hand always on some part of his mother, the other holding a toy airplane. He hasn't spoken since Christmas, she says. Another man, gaunt with worry, says he had been walking with his wife down Carnavon Street, and some soldiers had come and seized her. They held him at gunpoint while they took her away. He hasn't seen her either. "And yet," he says, "I used to think the Japanese were the most peaceful, serene people, with their cherry blossom paintings and the elaborate tea ceremony. How can they be so brutal?"

"A soldier is only one part of a country," Hugh says. "Certainly not representative of an entire people. And wartime makes different animals of us all."

"How can you say that?" Regina Arbogast cries. "They are each one as brutal as the other, as far as I'm concerned. You would never see a British soldier behave the way these animals have behaved to us."

"You are, of course, right, my dear," Hugh says, ending the conversation.

The next day, Mickey Wallace comes into the lobby where some of them are sitting listlessly. He is bleeding from the ears, his eyes already starting to swell blue and shut. He had been on the roof, looking down, when some Japanese soldiers saw him. They stormed up to him and beat him bloody because nobody is to look down on the Japanese. Only they are allowed to look down on others. This, their enemies' peculiar preoccupation with placement and particularly with height, because of their generally smaller stature, becomes ingrained in all of the prisoners until many years after the war is over, when they automatically check who is standing where, on what step or from what position.

And the random cruelty makes them all wary. A soldier, drunk and angry about his gambling losses, strikes a small child on the way to his post. The little boy has a fractured nose and loses three teeth. A higher-up Jap spirits him away with his mother, and they are never seen again. Evidence gone. On his way up the stairs, Will looks down at the alley between the hotel and the adjacent building. He sees a body covered by a blanket, a shock of fair hair, too high up to see who it is. When he goes down, the body is gone. He wonders if he imagined it, knows he did not. Another day Trotter comes to him, says *sotto voce,* "I wonder if I'm going mad. I was on the balcony having a smoke, and in an alley between buildings, I could have sworn I saw a man beheaded by two others." His voice trembles but his face is calm. "I saw the spurt of blood, the man falling down from his knees, hands tied behind his back. I could have sworn I saw it." How can one stand it? "And then I left. I didn't want to see the cleanup." How does one stay sane?

There are small insults in addition to the large. A plague of the most enormous mosquitoes Will has ever seen, caused by inadequate drainage. His body is spotted with their bites, red, raised, and angry. When he swats at them, they explode into red bursts of blood, gorged on their many victims. Pests crawl into their thin mattresses, which they try, unsuccessfully, to combat by immersing the iron bed legs in bowls filled with camphor and water. Weevils in the rice. Stinky, warm water they have to hold their noses to drink. The attendant diarrhea that comes from drinking the water, until they gather together some tins and boil it first. Then the burned tongues from drinking the newly sterilized water as fast as it comes off the flame, because they are so thirsty a burned tongue seems small penance.

And then they can look outside the dirty windows to the sight of Japanese soldiers, drunk and vomiting on the sidewalks, being held up by Chinese prostitutes, as they celebrate their victory. Sometimes an unfortunate coolie is dragged in to clean up the mess, but more often it is left to rot in the street. Will thanks God it is not high summer, when the odor would intensify ten times as quickly.

He does not remember what it is like to smell fresh air. Instead, urine, feces, the thick, cloying smell of human waste, clings to the very insides of his nostrils. His skin, his hair, his fingers, they are all infused with the smell of shit, no matter how hard he washes. His hands have known the slick inside of a toilet bowl, trying to get the foul mixture of vomit, urine, and shit to flush through its own thickness. The drainage systems are no match for five hundred rapidly sickening refugees—and that is what they are, regardless of whether they were bankers or barristers before—fed with pest-ridden rice and tainted water. The guards are cruel, save one. He is a young boy dressed in a soldier's uniform with a wide, placid face, and he smiles constantly, apologetically. He turns down his eyes when his colleagues hit the prisoners or poke at them with their bayonets. He speaks a halting English, but only when there are none of his compatriots nearby.

Trudy never comes, although others' loved ones find a way to come, leave messages. He finds himself mentioning her to everyone, including her in the conversations, as if the mere incantation of her name will keep her real, keep her alive. Her jasmine scent becomes further and further away, a mere memory; the olfactory sense doesn't keep well. He shifts constantly in bed, unused to the tight, narrow quarters of a space without a companion, her slight warmth. He is not angry with her, yet. Who knows what is going on outside.

Ned is going mad. The young soldier is far from home, far from any love or comfort he might know, and he has stopped talking and eats very little. His face is wan and swollen. Will tries to get him to move around a bit every day but he withdraws a little more every day.

And yet for most, life settles down amazingly quickly. Human beings tend toward routine. It is as if they have been displaced refugees for months, although it has only been a week. Businessmen shuffle around with undershirts falling out of their trousers, their natty suits packed away. Socialites do the wash alongside schoolteachers and shop proprietors. A black market springs up. As some have a lot of money, Arbogast and Trotter arrange a fund so that everyone will get some food. People contribute what they want and then they arrange to buy Russian black bread for six Hong Kong dollars a half-pound, powdered milk, soybeans, carrots, sometimes butter, which they spread sparingly on their bread and eat slowly, savoring the precious fat in their mouths. Young Chinese boys smuggle in the food, but must get past the Japanese guards, who know what's going on, but take what they want from the meager supplies. "Tax," says one every time, laughing at his inane joke. That guard takes almost half.

"I do think," Trotter's wife says fretfully to Will, "that it is so spread out that no one gets to enjoy it. Don't you think it would be a better idea to have a lottery of some sort so that one person could enjoy a full stomach for once?"

Will shrugs. He's not about to get into it with her. He does note, though, that she is as plump as ever. Some women volunteer to do the cooking—one is Mary, the woman with Tobias, the mute child, who hasn't seen her husband. She is sweet and quiet, and does not take the opportunity of being in the kitchen to take more food for herself and her son, although Will would not have blamed her if she had. The cook girls, as they call themselves, come up with startling dishes: broccoli black bread sandwiches with oyster sauce, watered-down condensed milk stews with plums bobbing about, eggy greens. They have managed to get a cooker from the outside, and in the evenings, they huddle around the blue flame, where their dinner is cooking.

Surprisingly, it settles into normal. If they steer clear of the guards, they are generally left alone, as the guards are too busy drinking and finding women or things to steal. There are always rumors about where they are to be relocated. Some think they will be repatriated immediately. Others, more realistic, hope for a more comfortable place to wait out the war. But they too think it will be over in a matter of weeks or days.

January 21, 1942

FINALLY, after two and a half weeks, the order comes. Dr. Selwyn-Clarke, the director of Medical Services, has persuaded the Japanese to move the civilians to the empty Stanley Prison on the southern tip of the island, where he believes the fresh air and proximity to the ocean will lessen the outbreak of infectious diseases. Excited, the women gather their belongings and make the beds, filthy as they are—habits die hard even in wartime. Men try to get more information from the guards and are rebuffed. Will gets Ned out of bed and makes sure he is counted.

Lined up outside the hotel, they are packed into large lorries that rumble into life and the children peek through the slats in the back and shout as they pass various landmarks. The children have come to be a blessing, although it is hard on them. They make games out of nothing, play jacks with pebbles, and run around shrieking. Women sit on their bags in the back of the lorry, flesh trembling with the uneven road, society matrons looking as haggard as the governesses and nurses next to them.

Soon, buildings give way to trees as they drive through Aberdeen and into the South Side, where the sea meets the mountains and a lone winding road takes them to Stanley Peninsula. It is quiet here, and seemingly untouched by the violence of the past few weeks.

The vehicles drive through a large gate and into a compound with squat three-story concrete buildings, hastily spray-painted with large *A, B, C* marks. Soldiers jerk their guns to indicate that everyone should disembark. They are grouped by nationality, lined up to be counted and registered—name, age, nationality, family or single, etc.—an exercise that will grow all too numbingly familiar over the coming weeks and months.

The total: 60 Dutch; 290 Americans; 2,325 British; the rest odds and ends—Belgians, White Russians, foreign wives, even Akiko Maartens, a Japanese woman who married a Dutchman and refuses to leave him for the outside. The guards spit at her and leer, knowing she's one of them, saying what Will can only assume are outrageous vulgarities, but she ignores them as she waits in line with her husband for their room assignment. She never speaks a word of Japanese, but her bowing and mannerisms give her away immediately. All the enemy nationals have been assembled at Stanley for internment. Will sees faces from that day at the Murray Parade Ground. Everyone says to one another, "I heard you were dead," smiling and relieved that they are not. Will spots Mary Winkle, the smaller partner of Edwina Storch, looking bewildered. Her constant companion seems not to be with her. The Americans and Dutch have been sequestered in different hotels from the British, the Belgians in their consular office since they are so few in number. From what Will can glean from hurried asides, their experience has been much the same: they are all dirty and hungry. He asks after Dick Gubbins, the American businessman he saw at the Gloucester, and no one has heard anything about him. Hopefully he's made it across the border into free China.

The Americans have somehow been assigned the best building and, as they are dispatched to their new home, pull together rapidly to organize everything to a fault, arranging to have furniture delivered, sorting out rooming and distribution of supplies, building a store. They are cheerful and productive, as if at a picnic. They seem to have already gotten a government of sorts running, from when they were in the hotels. The first evening, they are seen sitting outside in the twilight, in languorous poses on makeshift chairs, laughing, talking, drinking glasses of weak tea made from smuggled-in tea bags.

The Americans may have the best building, a man he recognizes vaguely says, ushering people through the door of the building he's been directed to, D Block, but there's not a lot we can do about it. They all have private bathrooms in their quarters. They seem to have some favor with the Japanese, maybe the governments have some understanding with each other. And our police have the next best one but they won't give it up for the women or children. They got here a few days ago to get things ready and they've taken all the good spots. In my opinion, they should be in the POW internment camp in Sham Shui Po, but they've ended up here with us civilians, but what can you do. Will just nods. He is too tired to care. He and Ned go up the stairs and in through a door. You can't sleep here, it's our room, someone says from a corner, snarling. Fine, he says, and they keep going until they find an empty room and put down their satchels.

They are divided up, and the fractions get smaller the more people stream in. It ends up with thirty-five people per former prison guard flat, fifty in the bungalows, six or seven people to a room. Many rooms have no furniture at all. Some people rush to mark out the prison guard flats because they are larger and a mite better furnished, but it turns out they are more crowded in the end. There are two or sometimes three married couples per room, and a lot of families in the administrative buildings. The singles in the cells have actually fared better, excepting the bathroom situation, which is a hundred people to a stall, and quite filthy. Will finds himself in an old prison cell, two meters square, with Ned and one other, Johnnie Sandler, a playboy who was always at the Gripps in a dinner jacket, with a blonde and a Chinese beauty on either arm. Amazingly, he still radiates style through his soiled trousers and already-fraying shirt. Unselfish, he's the first to help, rearranging beds, moving bags. It's surprising how true personalities shine through after a few weeks of hardship. The missionaries are the worst. They steal food, don't pull their weight with the chores, and complain all the time.

The first day, after people have established their places, everyone congregates in the large central yard, sitting in the dirt. All are paranoid that they are missing something, a meal, a handout, information. Hugh Trotter gathers the British together and explains the need for a more formal government and some sort of order. Will has talked to him about it, and found Hugh thinking the same thing.

"Why don't we nominate Hugh as the head of things?" Will says. After a pause, people murmur their assent. "All in favor say 'aye.'" Will looks around. A loud round of *ayes*. "Any *nays?*" Silence. At least in this, their first foray into group politics, there is harmony. That is something.

Hugh elects other people to head up subcommittees. They settle on housing and sanitation, work detail, food, health, and grievances, with others to come as needed. Will is selected to head up housing, to mediate any disagreements stemming from their accommodations.

Sleep is elusive the first night, as they try to get used to the new surroundings; those lucky enough to have beds shift around, unused to the strange creaks. Will is on the floor, which is filthy, with his satchel as a pillow and various articles of clothing as blankets. The stone is cold, even after he puts more clothing down as a mat; he is unable to doze for more than ten minutes at a time. It is a relief when the sun begins to stream through the window and he can stop the charade of sleep.

They come down to posted signs that say all rooms will be inspected for contraband in the afternoon. Most scamper back upstairs to squirrel away their belongings, hoping they will not catch the eye of any of the inspectors.

"I don't have anything worth taking," Will tells Ned, "and I don't think you do either," and they continue to the dining hall. And at the appointed hour, Will, Ned, and Johnnie watch as a chubby soldier rifles through their things. He holds up a particularly fine cotton shirt, Johnnie's, of course, and shakes it insolently, while rattling off something in Japanese to his companion.

"He's going to the ball in that," Johnnie says. The soldier whirls around and barks out something, clearly that they are to remain quiet while they finish up. He then flings the shirt on the dirty floor.

In the end, they come out better than most. They have given up a few gold cuff links ("Thought they might come in handy for bartering." Johnnie shrugs), a little box of tools that Johnnie had smuggled in, with pliers, a hammer, and scissors; and a wool hat.

"You did such an atrocious job of packing, they didn't want anything of yours," Johnnie observes to his roommates after the men are gone. "Congratulations!"

"It's lucky few of us are their size," Will says. "I think we'd be going around starkers."

"They can take the women's clothes. They'd look quite fetching in a nice poplin garden dress, I think."

They gather in the hallways and compare what's been lost. Some are beside themselves at the loss of family heirlooms, others happy that they managed to hide their valuables away.

"Did you hide them in your bum, then?" asks Harry Overbye to the group, an unpleasant sort who is smug because he has a Chinese girl on the outside who he is sure will provide for him. He has a wife he sent back to England some months before, and then he acquired the girlfriend. He is ignored.

"While we're here," Will says, "I'm organizing a cleaning detail to make our conditions more pleasant. I'll have a sheet up when I can acquire cleaning supplies, and I expect everyone will want to pitch in and help keep our temporary home as clean as possible."

Overbye snorts, but there are general noises of assent from the others.

"Good," he says. "It's not the Ritz but it will have to do for now."

"That's an understatement if I ever heard one," Johnnie says.

Will is getting very worried about Ned. He speaks only when spoken to, and then only in one- or two-word replies. He says he feels all right, but he is wasting away, hair thin and matted, eyes dull. He sleeps all day and shows little interest in food.

"Shock," says Dr. McAllister, when Will asks him. "He's had such a shock, he can't process anything. Who knows if he'll come out of it. This is certainly not the ideal situation for convalescence." Asked for a tonic, or anything, he throws up his hands. "I have nothing! Not even an aspirin! I've put in a request with Selwyn-Clarke and the authorities here for some basic medicines and supplies, but they've yet to reply. Just keep an eye on him. Unfortunately, that's about all we can do right now."

At dinnertime, they gather in the dining hall, where the separation of countries is again evident. A tall, rangy American businessman, Bill Schott, has been elected camp representative to the Japanese, by the Japanese, and he stands up to address the whole camp.

"The Japanese have decided that we are to man the kitchens and cook our own meals. These will be coveted jobs, so we are going to rotate them so that everyone gets a chance to serve." He doesn't say why the jobs will be so desirable, but everyone can see that proximity to food is only a positive thing. "We will also be assigned what I'll call housekeeping duties, not only our private rooms, which should be kept clean and which will be inspected on a regular basis, but also sweeping the courtyard and other duties as they see fit. I have been assured that these tasks and our conditions will be in keeping with the Geneva Convention, although, technically, Japan is not under its auspices, as they signed the agreement but never ratified it. They say they are agreeing to it for goodwill. We will be given adequate food, as per the Convention, which I believe is some twenty-four hundred calories a day. I have inquired as to mail and contact with the outside world and we are to receive letters and packages on set days of the week. Obviously we will not know whether that is reliable, but they have said they are willing to do it. Our governments are to be notified of our presence here and of the living conditions and we are to have Red Cross representatives come periodically and make inspections. In the best case, of course, there will be arrangements for repatriation and there will be some sort of swap of citizens between countries." He pauses. "Obviously it is unclear when all this will come to pass. We are, it is important to remember, in a war that is still very much going on. It could be weeks, it could be months. In the meantime, I hope we can all live together in harmony and try to help each other as much as possible while the situation is like this. If anyone has any complaints or comments, please come to me and I will try to make our views known to the camp supervisors, but I'm afraid we are not operating from a position of great power. At any rate, I wish everyone well as we go forth from here. Let's make our countries proud."

He sits down. There is an exhalation of air, as everyone digests what he has said. And then hands pop up in the air. Schott stands up again to take questions.

"Do we have any idea how long we're to stay here?"

"None at all, unfortunately."

"Are we allowed to have money? Or can we get money from the outside?" asks a Dutchman.

Schott laughs. He is very rich himself and has already acquired a great many comforts for the American faction, which have all been diligently and enviously noted by the other groups.

"I imagine you're allowed to have whatever you want, if you can keep it a secret, or if you want to share it with them. I don't know. This is one of those murky areas you don't really want to get into officially. Just use your common sense."

"Can we write letters to the outside?" Hugh Trotter asks.

"I don't think so. Or if we did, I think the people we wrote them to would never receive them or get such censored letters that they would be rendered useless—an exercise in futility, I suspect. I will certainly ask, but it seems unlikely. I'll try to get Ohta, that's the head of the camp, in a good mood, and ask him then."

The questions fly fast and furious, mostly routine matters, prisoners worried about their daily comforts. Will starts to eat.

"What about me?" Ned says suddenly to the table. It's the first time he's spoken all day.

"What do you mean?"

"I'm registered as British, but there's no British Ned Young. It's going to be all messed up. No one at home is going to know I'm here. Where are all the Canadians?"

"I think your compatriots are at the POW internment camp at Sham Shui Po. It is odd there are no other Canadian civilians, but perhaps they went home before all this erupted. I think you're better off here than with the troops. And I'm sure Britain has enough Ned Youngs or Edward Youngs—it's a common enough name—that they'll take you in first, and then you can sort it out when you're in. It will be asking for trouble to get you back with your colleagues."

"No, no," he says. "It's all messed up. It's all messed up now. I've done it for myself, haven't I? No one knows I'm here. Nobody. My mum won't know I'm alive or anything."

"It's all right. You're here and you're alive. That's the important thing. Don't worry too much about registration and things like that."

"That's easy for you to say," the young Canadian snaps. "You're all proper and accounted for. I'm alone here." He stands up and walks out.

"He needs to have a moment," Johnnie says. "Leave him alone. He'll be all right."

Will looks after Ned's receding body. "It's hard for him. I don't think he's eighteen yet. He's here, halfway across the world, all by himself, with no hope."

"Join the club," Johnnie says. "It's misery all around here at Camp Stanley. And it's only the second day."

After dinner, he and Johnnie go back to their room. On Will's bed is a neatly wrapped package, with a note. It's unsigned but it's apparent that it's from Ned.

"I wish you the best. Don't worry and thank you for everything." He has left the majority of his borrowed clothing.

"How on earth does he think he's going to get out of here?" Johnnie sits down on the bed.

"Lord knows. He didn't want to incriminate himself or us, I suppose, with this rather cryptic note. I'm thinking the worst. He has no idea of the terrain out here, or even in town, no friends, no Chinese language, nothing. Even if he gets out of the camp boundaries, he's a blind man. And he's left all his clothes . . ." His voice trails off.

"Not the sign of a sane man, certainly," Johnnie offers.

"No." Will crumples up the note and puts it in his pocket.

In the morning, some internees are talking over breakfast about how they heard gunshots in the middle of the night, toward the southern wall of the camp.

February dawns the next week and it is cold. Hong Kong has a subtropical clime so there is no heating infrastructure and the winter is always an insidious, creeping cold that surprises you in the middle of the night or when outside too long. No sign of Trudy. It's now been more than three weeks since he's seen her. It's getting to be more than disheartening—it's embarrassing now as people inquire as to how she's doing. Amahs, houseboys, local girlfriends, and spouses who are still on the outside for one reason or another come to try to see the internees, but the camp is still working out the visitation rules and they are turned away with their packages. Still, their visitors are allowed to leave word that they've been there.

Will concentrates instead on winterizing the buildings as much as he can. Beds have been provided, with some semblance of bed linens, but the temperature plummets at night. He's never thought of the cold in Hong Kong as anything more than brisk, but he realizes now that that was with a proper winter coat and well-insulated walls. Everyone is hunched over, trying to conserve body heat, sleeping with all their clothes on, shivering in the bathrooms, not taking baths. When Will brushes his teeth, the silver water feels like ice. He puts in an official request for more blankets and winter coats, especially for the children, who are running around in their parents' extra clothing, hems and sleeves trailing the floor. He organizes a patching team that goes around plugging any holes in the wall with a crude mix of mud and leaves. All this does little to alleviate the creeping misery of unrelenting discomfort that clouds their days.

Trudy, when she comes, is unexpected. A guard plucks Will from the lunch queue and takes him to the office of Ohta, the head of the camp.

Expecting a response to his blankets-and-coats request, Will is taken aback when he is told he has a visitor. They have not been allowed yet. But, of course, rules have never really applied to Trudy.

Ohta, a portly man with greasy skin and smudged wire spectacles, gestures that Will is to sit down. He is attired in a Japanese version of a safari suit, but one with long sleeves and pant legs.

"You have a visitor."

"Is that so?"

"We have not yet allowed any visitors."

"I'm aware of that. But I don't know anything about it."

Ohta eyes Will over his desk.

"You want drink?"

"Please." Will knows to accept.

He gestures to the soldier by the door and barks out something in Japanese. Whiskey is poured into small, dusty glasses.

"Kampai!" He lifts up his glass with one pink, porcine hand, and

drains it, tossing his head back with a grunt. Will follows suit, with less vigor. Ohta shakes his head as if to throw off cobwebs. "Good!" He pours another.

"Your visitor, your wife?"

"I have no idea who my visitor is."

"Woman, Chinese?"

"Trudy Liang?"

"Yes. Miss Liang is here to see you."

"Oh, good." Will's heart is beating fast. "Thank you very much."

"I told her only one time she can come on no visitors' day. Special for her."

"Well, she is special, isn't she?"

Ohta stares at him.

"No one special now. Everyone same, prisoner or not Japanese. Same!"

"Yes, of course." Mercurial, he thinks. "Well, I think she's special because she is to me." Lame finish.

Ohta gets up. "Wait in room here."

After a few minutes, during which Will sips at his whiskey, enjoying the warm burn in his throat, trying to calm his nerves, the guard gestures for him to come. They go into a small room with a table and five chairs, where Trudy is sitting, looking uncomfortable. She is thin, her clothes serviceable. Her hair is pulled back into a chignon, face colorless without any sort of makeup. Still, somehow, she radiates privilege.

"Darling," she says. "I've missed you so much."

He doesn't say anything about her absence, just asks her what she's been doing, forfeiting the right to rebuke her for her neglect.

"Frederick is dead, so I've been with Angeline, but she hasn't really spoken for weeks. I keep telling her she has to cope for Giles's sake, but she doesn't seem to listen. She wants to bring him back here but what kind of place is this to be responsible for a child? She doesn't want to go to England where she doesn't have any family but Frederick's, not that she could go right now, and his family was against the marriage in the first place, so it's a rather difficult situation. So that's what I've been doing. Besides trying to get a foothold in the new world out there."

"You're all right for food and all that? Dominick is taking care of you?"

"The Japanese are so odd," she says, ignoring him. "They have this extraordinary custom of defecating in every room of every house they loot. Isn't that awful? Marjorie Winter's house was completely soiled—she found it when she went up to get some supplies. The odor! The whole city smells of waste. That's one Japanese custom I'm not too enthralled by. So extraordinary. They have that beautiful tea ceremony and all that lovely gardening, and then they go and do something like that. And of course, all the women are in a tizzy about rape. You're not supposed to go anywhere alone. I brought a driver."

"Ned is gone. I think he tried to escape but I'm quite sure he was shot in the attempt. He was going rather mad."

Trudy's face falls. "Don't tell me such awful things, darling. I can't stand it as it is. Can we talk about something else? Something else entirely, something quite trivial in comparison. Like how I'm scrabbling all the time. It's terribly unbecoming. At least here, you don't have to do that. You just stand in a line and get food handed to you."

"You have quite a good idea of what goes on here, have you?" It's the first time he's been sharp with her and she takes note.

"Is there anything you need that you think I might be able to procure outside?"

"It's scant hunting out there too, isn't it?"

"Yes, but I could get Dommie on it. We have food but it's rather dear. I could weep when I think of the Japanese bombing the godowns. There was so much food in there, and they just incinerated it all. They said you could smell the food burning miles away.

Makes me ravenous just thinking of it. At least there's no chance I'll get plump if this goes on. You don't like plump women, do you, Will? No chance of me getting that way." She chatters on. "Conditions in Sham Shui Po and Argyle are supposed to be hideous," she says. "They're coming down very hard on the uniformed. You're lucky you're here. That Jane woman at the hospital really saved you, I think. Very clever of her."

"Do you think I should be there?" he asks, hard. "Do you think I'm a coward for being here?"

"Are you mad?" she says with genuine astonishment. "Of course I don't."

How quickly he has lost the ability to gauge what she thinks, he realizes. She is off to something else entirely.

"Do you remember what it was like just three months ago?" she asks. "Conder's Bar, the Gloucester, the Gripps, the parties. Can you believe it was just a few lousy months ago?"

"No," he says. "Have you any news of what's going on out there? We've no way of getting any reliable information and it's driving us mad."

"Carole Lombard died in a plane crash, that's the biggest news." She winces at his reaction. "Sorry, irreverence not appropriate? All right, reality, then. It's grim all around, darling. I don't know much but I'll try to find out for you. The paper now is all Japanese propaganda and says everything is going swimmingly. We can get rice at one of fourteen depots, so that's usually our main task, getting food. We send the maids to one, and we go to another, and hope one of us gets lucky. But that's not so grand in the way of news, is it? What else. In the days right after you left, they were in a democratic mood so they were encouraging one and all to go to the old colonial bastions, so you would walk into the Pen and see laborers squatting on the chairs, having tea! They came with the cash they made from looting, to try to see how the other half lived. It was just beyond! It's difficult to get reliable information—the paper just says that the Japanese are conquering everything in sight and it's hard to read between the lines." She pauses. "Dommie's doing fine, fraternizing with the Japanese. He seems to think he's one of them. He's in business with Victor now, a bit shady, but what isn't these days? When I go to visit him in his offices—he has offices in Central—he always opens up a bottle of champagne. The whole thing makes me quite ill but I drink it anyway. And I see some of Victor. He's the one who got me in here. Had a word with someone he does some business with."

"Dommie's never had a job before and now he's a businessman?"

"War does strange things to people. I think this might be the best thing to happen to him. He's rather found himself." She laughs, an odd laugh.

"He should be careful. At the end of all this, he's going to have to account for himself. And Victor too."

"Dommie doesn't think that way. He's always lived in the present—you know him. Victor is another story. I'm sure he's covering his tracks well."

"But you should warn Dommie that he should think ahead this time. And tell him to be careful of Victor."

She waves her hand impatiently. "So I've been summoned by a Japanese," she says. "A man named Otsubo who lives in the Regent Suite and is in the gendarmerie, which I'm told is a good thing to have on your side. They're the military police. He wears a special chrysanthemum pin on his collar, which signifies gendarme-ness. I think he might want me to teach him English. Do you think I should do it?"

"Not you too," Will says. "Are you going to be best friends with the enemy?"

"I resent that," she says. "You know me."

"I do, darling, and I love you despite it."

"Very funny, my idiot."

How are they back to this already? This needling, their sophisticated parrying, from a time when such things mattered.

"Do you think it's safe?" he says after a moment.

"Well, I'm bringing Angeline with me. She'll be a chaperone, so don't worry." She pauses. "It's the funniest thing... I've had a phrase running through my head all week—plutocrats and oligarchs—and I haven't the slightest idea what it means. It must have been something I heard somewhere. You're clever—what does it mean exactly?"

"Plutocrats are the ruling class," he says. "And oligarchs are governments ruled by a few. I suppose they mean the same thing, really. Why do you think you've had that on your mind?"

"Haven't a clue," she says, dismissing it as quickly as she brought it up. "So I'll be a tutor. He's very important, apparently, head of the gendarmerie. And he lives at the Matsubara—I mean the Hong Kong Hotel. They've renamed everything, you know. The Peninsula's the Toa now. Maybe I'll get some special privileges and then we'll be on easy street."

"Yes, maybe," he says. He notices, but is not suitably appreciative of, the "we." He wishes she would go. He is tired. But when she gets up to leave, he feels bereft.

"I'll see you again?"

"Of course. I'll bring things too, what I'm able to scrape together, if you think it would be helpful. Maybe next week if they're less irritating about the visiting hours." And she's out the door, elegant even in her reduced circumstances. He smells her jasmine perfume in the sweep of air she's left behind.

There are five guards assigned to their building. They patrol the adjacent grounds, do random inspections, and make their presence felt. Most leave the prisoners alone, but one, Fujimoto, a skinny fellow who smells like rancid fish, is particularly cruel and delights in making the men sweep the yard or do one hundred jumping jacks when they are so tired and weak they can barely stand up. Fujimoto has it in for Johnnie, for some reason, and whenever he sees him, he will stop him and have him clean the latrines or dig up holes in the garden—senseless tasks that just reveal the hardness of the man. But he is mild compared with the men who are assigned to investigate covert activities. Word of a shortwave radio gets out and the three men who are supposed to have the components are dragged off to a distant room. Only one comes back, and he is barely alive, bones broken and one eye almost gouged out. He dies later in the makeshift infirmary. "They let him come back alive as a warning," says Trotter. "That much is clear."

Lack of food makes them tired. The promised twenty-four hundred calories turn out to be more like five hundred per person—a large bowl of rice is supposed to feed a roomful of adults for the whole day. Sometimes, there is a protein, conger eel or red mullet, but it is often spoiled and melts away to oil when cooked. Still, they eat it hungrily, their bodies ravenous for any fat or taste. People are sick constantly—pellagra, dysentery; wounds never heal, teeth rot, fingernails don't grow. Will's lids are hooded and his limbs leadlike. All he wants to do is lie in bed, especially in the late afternoon when everything is dragging. He forces himself to get up and find tasks to do. Many sleep the days away but he can't abide that. "Doesn't it seem as if we should be getting something out of this time?" he asks Johnnie. "When people ask what we did during this time, I don't think the answer should be slumber."

"Such a good man," Johnnie says. "Industrious little bee." But he is also the first to help Will, and never complains.

The next week, Trudy is allowed to visit again, and others are allowed in as well. She is ebullient. The head of the gendarmerie says she is to come twice a week to teach him English at the hotel where he is quartered.

"The food there! You wouldn't believe it!" Her voice lowers to a whisper. "I eat enough to last me until the next visit. And he's had me up to the house he's requisitioned in the Peak, the old Baylor place. He has it as a sort of weekend place. The old staff are still all there and were so thrilled to see me! An odd scene, though. When I went up, he was practicing archery on the lawn and had someone bring me a glass of champagne. It's as if he were mimicking the life of an English lord. One can almost believe life's back to normal when it's like that. And he just wants to chat, get his conversational English up to par. Of course, he's pumping me for information too, thinks I'm an idiot, but who cares when you're eating bananas and fresh fish and all the rice you can finish! Can you believe I've become such a peasant about food? Anyway, Otsubo is obsessed with lining his pockets. He thinks I will help him, unknowingly, or knowingly. It's a time-honored tradition of war, I suppose, the officers getting rich off the conquered."

"And you and Angeline go to teach this man?"

"He told me to drop her, says he doesn't need two teachers, but I bring her back loads of food. Told him I'm staying with her and I'm obliged. He wants me to teach him Western table manners. Isn't that a scream? He wants to know the whole thing, fish knives, dessert spoons. He can't pronounce the word *etiquette* since I've brought it into his life, but he means to be a master of it. We had lobster the other night and he wanted to know the proper way to eat it. I just smashed away at it merrily and he thought I was joking."

"So now you're having lobster dinners with this man?"

"Oh, it's not what you think—Dommie was there too. They're best friends. It's really quite sickening. I'm just along for the free food. I brought you some too, darling, look." She looks behind her to make sure the guard isn't watching, and spills out a duffel sack of fruit and some tins of meat and a small bag of rice. "I slipped the guard who checks the bag some cigarettes at the door so he didn't bother me but I don't want this one to go getting any ideas. Don't go being noble and share this with everyone. I want you to have it, not little Oliver or Priscilla, no matter how gaunt and adorable their wee faces are. It's for you, and I wouldn't give it to you if I thought it was going elsewhere. You have to develop a thick skin, Will, it's wartime."

"What makes you think I don't have one?"

"You're too good, that's your problem. People like you have trouble surviving in times like these."

"But you're having dinners with this man," he says again.

"Yes," she says patiently, as if he's mentally impaired. "It's not the sort of situation where I can tell him to bugger off. I have to keep on his good side."

"But surely you can do that without having these inappropriate..."

She cuts him off. "You've no idea what it's like outside. It's quite the norm. We have to get along with these beastly people until we prevail. Have a plum and shut up."

When he doesn't take it immediately, she snatches it back petulantly and takes a bite. Juice comes out of her mouth and Will thinks suddenly that she looks like an animal.

When it rains, it is difficult to rouse oneself. On a cold, damp Tuesday, Will lies in his bed, thin mattress hard against his body, and listens to the rain splatter rhythmically on the roof. He's not sad, just immobile. The gray wall opposite is trickled with water leaking in, and there is a pool forming on the concrete floor. It's become a routine faster than he would have thought, internees shuffling around, arguing about food distribution, pilfering, work duties.

There is no damn color here in camp. Their clothes have long faded to gray, the food is all one color—an indistinct muddy brown on the plate, the buildings concrete. He longs for red, magenta, sunflower yellow, a vibrant green. The only relief from gray and brown is the sky, sometimes a glorious bell-clear blue, and the sea, a choppy turquoise. Sometimes he sits at the fence and just stares out. It is absurdly beautiful still, the horizon and the water and the clouds. Dr. Selwyn-Clarke chose the site because he thought the seaside location would reduce cholera outbreaks and other infectious diseases. Unfortunately, it is not the infectious diseases that are the issue, but the lack of vitamins and proper nutrition.

Johnnie walks in, soaked from the rain.

"Lovely day." He sits down heavily on his bed.

"Can you believe we're here?" An inane response is all Will is capable of.

"Rather be home, that's for sure." He brightens. "There's a rumor that Red Cross packages have arrived. They might distribute them after dinner."

"What's in a Red Cross package?"

"Food, man! Chocolate sometimes. Diversions. The children have been talking about it all day. I might have to wrestle a little girl for her package."

In the afternoon, Will hears little Willie Endicott shouting as he runs through the camp as fast as his spindly legs will let him.

"The packages are here! The packages are here!"

Looking out the window, Will can see little Willie's arms are covered in mosquito bites, which he has scratched until they are red and runny, making his mother worry herself to death because of the malaria. She has covered his welts with valuable toothpaste. He runs, the white-toothpaste-speckled boy, shouting his message, delirious with the notion of food.

The line is tense as everyone waits. When it comes to their turn, the guard hands them a soft brown paper package wrapped in twine. They retire to their room in high excitement to open it.

"Feels like Christmas!"

Will is finding the package hard to open. His fingernails are as soft as the paper. Finally he is able to undo the knots. They store the string away carefully—nothing is ever discarded these days—and gaze in grateful wonder at what is inside.

"It looks like a scientist packed this!" Johnnie exclaims.

There are six chocolate bars, slightly moldy, but no matter, a large tin of McVities biscuits, coffee, tea, a good amount of sugar and powdered milk, and some knitted socks and a muffler. These ordinary items look as valuable as gold coins. There is also a bonus: a tiny chess set and, hidden discreetly within, a small piece of paper with rounded, girlish writing.

Johnnie reads it aloud, the muffler tied comically around his head like a turban:

" 'Our thoughts and prayers are with you. Keep your spirits up and good WILL prevail. My name is Sharon and I would love to correspond with you if you are able. I have blond hair, blue eyes, and, people say, a ready smile.' "

"Lovely penmanship," says Johnnie, sniffing the paper. "Nice sense of balance, just enough so that the censors wouldn't get her, yet still unambiguous. And look, here she's written her address."

"Delightful," says Will drily. "Sharon from Sussex, our savior."

"I'm going to look Sharon up when I get home," says Johnnie, tucking her note into his shirt pocket. "She seems like the kind of girl I should settle down with."

"What about me?"

"You already have a sweetheart. Don't be piggy. Sharon's mine." Johnnie shoves an entire bar of chocolate into his mouth.

"Do you know how to play chess?" Will begins to assemble the pieces.

"Is there any money in it?"

"No, but there is your mental well-being to consider. Our brains are beginning to rot in here." Johnnie is his first friend, Will realizes. He hasn't made any in the colony, didn't have to, with Trudy. It feels good.

The next morning, Will sees the little boy from the hotel, Tobias, squatting alone outside the bathroom with his airplane.

"Did you enjoy your chocolate?" he asks.

There's no answer.

"Where's your mother?"

The boy just stares at him, his face pale, his fair hair lanky and matted. He works the ragged airplane around his hand, smoothly. It's become a part of his anatomy.

"Is your mother not feeling well?"

The boy starts to cry.

"It's all right. If she's in there she'll be out in a minute."

Just then the door bangs open with a crash. Fujimoto steps out, buttoning his trousers. Will steps back instinctively but the man ignores him and walks away.

"I guess she's not. Do you want to come find your mother with me?" Will extends a hand. The boy looks down at the floor and shakes his head vigorously.

"Listen," and then the door opens again and Mary Cox comes out. He blinks. Her hand goes to her mouth when she sees Will. She turns away.

"Come on, darling," she says to Tobias. "Let's go get supper." She brushes past Will and scuttles down the hall, dragging the child with her. Then she turns around and stares at him, her face hardening into something unapologetic, fierce.

So that's how it goes, he thinks. That's the beginning of how it all changes. We become survivors or not.

He tells Johnnie about Mary Cox.

"That was only a matter of time, though, wasn't it? Market economy springs up everywhere. People figure out what they have to sell and what they want to buy."

"Bloodless of you."

"This war has been bloody enough without me getting all sentimental. And you too, old man. Don't get all soft on us. It won't do anyone any good."

But Will is unable to get the image of Tobias waiting outside the bathroom out of his mind.

At dinnertime, they walk outside to find a scandal of another sort has erupted. Regina Arbogast has accused one of the mothers of stealing chocolate and biscuits from her Red Cross package and is demanding a trial. Hugh Trotter is trying to explain to her that the legal system they have set up is meant for more serious matters, such as mistreatment by the guards, or stealing from the communal kitchen, but she refuses to listen.

"You and your filthy children are eating more than their share! They should have been sent home to England months ago. They shouldn't be here at all, taking food from others! They shouldn't be here at all."

The woman looks ambushed.

"Regina," she starts. "I didn't take your food but you have a family too. How can you talk about children like that?"

"My children were raised right, not like yours. They're like animals! And mine are in England where they belong!"

"But yours are grown. I couldn't send Sandy and Margaret away. They're too young to be separated from their mother."

"You should have gone with them!"

"You shouldn't be here either, then," the mother says finally. "It should be just the men. All the women and children are supposed to be gone. So you're draining us of resources as well."

"What rubbish!" Regina looks as if she is ready to strike the woman. "Your family has always taken advantage of situations. Reggie's done business with your husband and always said he was a common man, a slippery sort, always getting around things."

"Just a minute there," Hugh Trotter interjects. He has wisely tried to keep on the sidelines, but this venture into the personal cannot be ignored. "Let's keep to the matter at hand."

"The *matter* at *hand*, Hugh," Regina says slowly, as if he is mentally challenged, "is that this *woman* has taken some of my personal belongings and you are refusing to treat it in a serious matter."

"For God's sake, Regina." Hugh throws up his hands. "We are

bloody refugees here. None of us owns anything at the moment. They were packages for war refugees. Can't you be a little more generous? We're all in the same boat."

"Don't you dare swear at me!" Her voice goes high-pitched. "We are not in the same boat! I will never be in the same boat as that woman. She is something else quite entirely."

The Americans are watching from afar, aghast. Sometimes Will feels traitorous, the way he admires the Americans, or not really admires them but feels like he is more one of them. Despite her professed love for Americans, Trudy never really liked them—Will thinks they're too democratic for her tastes. She likes a little delineation between the classes. Here, though, their system is so clearly superior to anything any other group has. Even in these surroundings, they radiate plenty and wealth. Bill Schott is autocratic, to be sure, but he gets things done efficiently and quickly and has managed to acquire a great many things for his people, mostly at his own expense, it is surmised, but still. Those in the British camp who have the wherewithal to help others rarely do, preferring to hoard what they have for fear of darker days ahead. The Americans have a system for sharing what they do have, although because they are fewer and not so strapped, it must be easier.

Regina Arbogast stomps her foot like a child and cries out.

"This is just impossible! There are no standards at all! Nothing is to be done here. I'll have to take matters into my own hands." She walks off in a huff.

"A little diversion is always welcome," observes Johnnie. "She's quite a pistol, that one. We're going to have to watch her."

Rice, rice, rice. After some two months, it's all anyone talks about. They have become absurdly creative with it—grinding it for flour, boiling it for gruel and water, trying to stretch it out as much as possible. Food is the main topic. For one glorious week, there is pork on the ration lorry every day, until the story gets out that a pig farm had been shut down for disease and they are being fed the carcasses. Still, most just boil it well and continue to eat it. Beggars can't be choosers.

The internees steep tea out of dried bark and dry grass on sheets, which they then shred and roll for cigarettes. They have lost so much weight, men's faces are gaunt, women look decades older. Some suffer excruciating pain in their feet, the result of malnutrition, and cannot walk.

Some people are cracking under the pressure. Reggie Arbogast comes to Will to ask him to talk to his wife, who has stopped talking to anyone, but apparently she has always had a soft spot for Will, a feeling that he had certainly not known existed, and did not reciprocate to any degree. Still, he agrees to go visit with her.

Knocking on the door, he goes in to find a surreal picture—Regina Arbogast sitting on her bed dressed in a crimson evening gown, her hair put up in a messy chignon, some wisps escaping. Her eyes are smudged with black. Looking closer, he realizes it is charcoal. Her lips are messily slathered with lipstick, the crimson bleeding past her lips and onto the skin.

"Mrs. Arbogast," he starts.

She continues to sit, looking like a grotesque marionette.

"Regina," he says. "You must get out. The sun is glorious today." She looks at him.

"Will," she says finally. There is lipstick on her teeth.

"Yes, Regina? The fresh air will do you good if you go outside."

"Will. You have always been a good man. I have admired you. You came to Hong Kong and were not polluted by it like so many others."

"Thank you, Regina. I don't know . . ."

"But others are poisoned by it. It's too easy here, life. As many servants as you want, lives subsidized by the government or your company. Everything is provided. You become weak."

"Regina, these are not good things to dwell on. Keep your mind exercised. I think some of the women are talking about putting on a show, a play. You should get involved with them..."

"Paaah!" She expectorates onto the floor. "Stupid cows!"

He sits, not wanting to provoke her further.

"They are stupid, absurd women, who think a few clever lines will make us forget we're here, in this tragedy of a situation. I despise them."

And they, you, Will thinks, but doesn't say.

"What would you like to do?"

She looks at him incredulously.

"What the bloody hell do you think I'd like to do? Get out of here and go home to England!" Regina Arbogast seems to have been transformed into a dockworker.

"Language, Regina," says Reggie, who's just come through the door. His eyes are dull and sunken. The doctor has told him he needs vitamin C but there is no citrus to be had anywhere.

"Oh, shut up, Reggie."

Will stands to leave.

"No, you stay," Regina orders. "Reggie can do whatever he wants. I really don't give a fig anymore. I have things I want to tell you, Will, because I think you deserve to know."

"Regina, I don't think Will..."

"Reggie!"

Reggie Arbogast looks at Will helplessly as if to say, See what I am dealing with? and then leaves. Will looks longingly at the door.

"Regina?"

"Will, you were one of the ones I had high hopes for when you arrived," she said, like the high priestess of society she had always styled herself to be. "Reggie knew about you from work and always spoke so highly of you. I wanted to have you to dinner many times." Regina Arbogast's dinner parties had been sought-after invitations in Hong Kong for their lavish style, elaborate themes, and restrictive guest lists, for those who had cared about such things.

Trudy had laughed at everything Regina did. "So fussy! So pretentious!" she said. "You know, she was a Manchester shopgirl before she married Reggie. All of her airs are very recent indeed. I heard he used to be a very nice man before he met her."

"That's very good of you, Regina."

"But then you took up with that Liang woman. Did you know about her past? I felt she got her claws into you right away. She knows what she's doing, that's for sure, that one. She took you off the market before anyone else even knew you had arrived. You know what they call her, don't you? The queen of Hong Kong!" She laughs. "It's so preposterous! With her queer half-breed customs and way of thinking she is above everything. Forgive me but she is insufferable. I suppose love makes you blind."

Will doesn't know why Regina is talking to him as if he were one of her fellow society matrons and they were gossiping over tea at the Peninsula.

"I don't know that this is the right time or place for this," he starts.

"Listen. I have a point. You think I don't but I do." Regina Arbogast leans forward. "Reggie met with the governor when he arrived. Governor Young had a secret meeting the first week. The day of the Tin Hat Ball. He wanted to get to know some key people in the colony and ask their advice. He was new to the colony and didn't know a thing about how it ran. He knew the war was getting close to Hong Kong but he didn't want it to get out and alarm the general public, the nincompoop. So, at this meeting..." Regina sits back. "Do I have your attention now?"

Will looks at her, exasperated and compelled at the same time. "Regina."

Satisfied, she leans over again. "At this meeting it was discussed, among other things, what was to happen to the Crown art collection at the governor's mansion, which, as you might know, contains some priceless pieces, mostly Chinese antiquities that are sensitive because the Chinese think they were stolen, ancient texts and vases and things like that that were excavated. Reggie said they were centuries old, some of them. It was decided that the collection would be hidden away and the location would be divulged to three people in three very different situations so that no matter what happened, at least one would...survive."

Despite himself, Will is listening, intrigued.

"And, of course, Reggie was one of the three." Regina permits herself a smile of congratulations. "And he told me about it. But he hasn't told me where. Or who the others were." Her smile disappears. "He's always been irritatingly honorable about that sort of stuff. He values country over anything, something bred into him by his family. I really think he would give me up if it came to that. Maybe even the children. I suppose he was a good choice, then."

She gets up off the bed and shuffles toward the door.

"I don't have any proper shoes here, and no one has been able to procure any for me. Do you know anyone? All I have are these terrible slippers that look like they belong in a fish market."

"Regina, why did you tell me this?"

She smiles coyly. It is a grotesque thing.

"I have a feeling, Will. I know things are going on outside, and I know that many secrets and plots are in motion. I just wanted you to know." She reaches over and clasps his hand in hers. They are dry and reptilian. "Consider it a gift from me."

Trudy turns up the next week in a well-tailored suit and a hat, carrying the most enormous package Will has ever seen.

"The outside is so queer," she says, pulling off her gloves and sitting down. "There is the oddest society of people you've ever seen, a motley crew if I ever saw one. All the Russians who we loathed before are everywhere, and they are even more unbearable. They think they're somebody now that everybody is gone. They're worse than the Swiss with their self-righteousness. I was at a dinner with the doctor—you know Dr. Selwyn-Clarke, he's the official medical adviser to the new Japanese governor who's arrived, Isogai—and Sir Vandeleur Grayburn, who's still delicious as ever, although terribly down about everything that's going on, and this Russian girl, I don't know if you remember her but her name was Tatiana, always out and about town before, but out in that bad way, drinking a little too much, a little too forward, you know, and she just said the rudest thing to him, the doctor, and she is married now to a Chinese man who is in bed with the Kempeitei and so now she's bulletproof, or so she thinks.... Of course she didn't bring him to dinner. I think she just married him as an insurance policy. I'm going to shoot her myself when this is all over."

"Where was the dinner?"

"At the Selwyn-Clarkes', but you know they have to do it so hush-hush. He had to pretend it was a planning meeting, for supplies and things, which it partly was, but they had guards outside, listening, so it was hardly a casual event. And do you know who's dead? Crumley, the American who was always at the Grill? I remember the day he came in and told us how he had opened his mouth while he was at a picnic in Shek O and a butterfly flew in and he swallowed it, and now he's dead. Swallowed butterfly or not. That's what I think about sometimes, you know." She speeds up, talking about this and that, nonsense about people.

"Otsubo adores me now and gives me anything I ask for. Look at all I was able to bring you! Ham and coffee, sugar and powdered milk. I've unearthed more of that strawberry jam that seems to be everywhere. Honey, even. You do have cause to be jealous now, darling." But she looks worse than ever, gaunt, with cracked, dry lips and hair scraped back into an untidy bun. Her blouse is very large on her, the collar gaping up behind her neck, as if she's sinking into it.

"I've been trying to think what kind of man he is, and I think I've got it. He's the kind of person who, when you say something, and he doesn't understand, he will ask you to repeat it, and then again and again, until he understands, whereas most people would politely pretend to get it after the second or third explanation. He's unrelenting and has no interest in social graces. I suppose that's why he's done so well for himself in his career—meticulous and all that."

"Are you eating? You look like you're eating nothing."

"I took Otsubo to Macau and fed him those 'beans,' you know, the baby mice that the uninitiated think are beans? He loved them. And they say the Chinese will eat anything."

"I don't care about that...you look like death warmed over." He grabs her hand. "I don't care if he's mad about you and you have to do things you don't want to do....I just want you to be all right."

She laughs abruptly.

"And how do you know I don't want to do them?" she asks. "What if I'm a willing participant?"

She thrusts a package toward him. "Here," she says. "More food."

"Come into the camp," he says. "I'll take care of you."

"Will, darling." She cups his face in her hands. "It's too late. I like it on the outside. I've finally got a foothold on the situation, however tenuous."

The door opens and Edwina Storch comes in with a large package.

"Hullo," Trudy says. "Are you here to see Mary?"

"Yes," says Edwina. "Hello, Will. How are you doing?"

"I'm fine, thank you. Mary is as well as can be expected in here. Her good spirits and courage are a boon to the community."

"Yes, she's very good," Edwina says. "What a horrid situation." She takes in Trudy's package with a discerning eye. "You've gotten a large ration of the jam, Trudy. And coffee! You must know someone very important indeed."

Mary Winkle enters and the two women embrace, one large, one small. They go into another room.

Trudy looks at the closing door.

"I see her around all the time now," she says. "She's quite in evidence in the postwar world." She pauses. "But I think I like her."

Will takes her hand. She looks so lost.

"Do you know my best quality?" she asks.

"Of your many, I could not say, my darling."

"I see the best in people. I fall in love with people when I see a window into their beings, their shining moments. I've fallen in love with so many people but the trouble is I fall out of love so quickly too. I see the worst in them just as easily.

"Do you know I fell in love with you right away? That day at the Trotters' I had noted you because you were new, of course, and then you sat down at the piano, and you played a few notes, but you played them so well, with no self-consciousness, and no idea that anyone might be listening. It was in that room off the garden and you were the only one there. I was passing through on the way to the ladies' room and saw you there. I fell in love with you right then, and so I spilled my drink all over myself so I could meet you."

"Darling Trudy," he says.

She stands up.

"I can't bear it," she says in a rush. "I just can't." And then she turns around and leaves. "Eat what I've brought you," she calls out behind her as the door swings shut behind her with a clang. "You need to be strong." Her voice fades as she walks away.

"Johnnie, I have to get out of here."

He says it that night, after they have gone to bed, and he can hear his companion's breath just deepening into sleep. It stops, then starts again.

"You do?"

"Yes. I'm losing her."

"I see."

"Will you help me?"

"Of course."

But he didn't need to ask. Of course, Trudy had another way.

"I've gotten you a week's furlough. Otsubo got me a pass that says you're to do some work for him. Isn't that wonderful?"

"What kind of work am I to do?"

She looks at him as if he's completely missed the point.

"No idea. Some kind of clerical work which you and only you, the inimitable Will Truesdale, are qualified to do. Proper accounting. Plant watering. Japanese flattering. Does it matter? You get to get out of here! Aren't you thrilled? That's gratitude for you!"

"What do I have to do?"

"Are you a complete moron? Nothing!" she cries. "Absolutely nothing. I thought it would be nice for you to get out and see what's going on outside. No one else has this kind of opportunity, you know."

"Well, thank you," he says. "I do appreciate it."

"You'll get to see what life outside is like, what my life has become."

"Perhaps you'll do an exchange," he says. "Come in here for a fortnight."

"*Peut-être*," she says. She always reverts to French when she wants to change the subject.

So the next Monday, Will is waiting by the sentry's bungalow. He has been treated rather well for the past week. Ohta came to see him with a copy of the furlough order, trying to fish some information from him.

"Otsubo has sent for you," he had said.

"Yes," Will nodded.

"He is head of gendarmerie."

"Yes."

"You have important skill?"

"Yes."

Ohta stood for a moment, trying to see if Will would give him anything. When he didn't, he threw the order on the floor and said he should wait by the gate on Monday. But then Will noticed that all the guards were more polite and that he was not subject to taunts and searches anymore.

Trudy pulls up in a convertible and insists on driving although she is alarmingly bad, screeching the gears and turning far too wide. "What happens when you have a driver all your life," she says with a shrug when Will finally demands she pull over so he can take the wheel.

"You look well," he says, glancing over. She's in a spring dress, now that the weather has gotten warmer, and a wide-brimmed yellow straw hat.

"I found my old tailor, and he whipped up a few things for me. He desperately needs the work and I have events I'm supposed to look nice for."

He doesn't ask.

She takes him to the Peninsula.

"It's the Toa now, remember," she says.

Trudy is greeted with smiles and bows as she sweeps through the formerly grand lobby, which is now filled with soldiers, steel tables, and other grim army-issue furniture.

"Otsubo has a suite of rooms here so Dommie and I stay in them. He's requisitioned a place up on Barker Road for himself. It's better here than the rat hole we have outside. We're lucky. You wouldn't believe how people are living outside, two or three families in a flat. Rather appalling, but I suppose it's wartime. My old place has been requisitioned for some midlevel soldier. Insulting, isn't it? I thought it was quite nice, myself."

"How's your father?"

"Fine," she says abruptly. "He's fine."

"What are you doing for funds?" Now that he is outside, he is thinking of matters he has not had to worry about in weeks.

"We're allowed to withdraw a little money every week, but it's touchy. Not large amounts, obviously, but nonetheless it's odd for them to know you have accounts that you're drawing against. You don't want to make them wonder too much. Everything's fluid, in a bad way. There are no rules, and even if there were, they could be changed at any moment."

"Do you have to look out for yourself? Isn't Otsubo the magic trump card?"

Trudy considers. Her mouth draws into a bow. Will resists the urge to kiss her small, self-preserving face.

"Mmmmm...I wouldn't say a trump card because he's rather mercurial. He does favors and then regrets them. He gives and wants to take away. And he has to be persuaded rather strongly not to. Not a generous man. Powerful men usually aren't. Here we are." She opens a door into a room that is a veritable palace compared with his quarters back at Stanley. A suite with large windows overlooking the blue sea dotted with boats, plush carpet, thick silk draperies, and fans that swing lazily around and around.

"Welcome to the Pen!" Trudy curtsies.

"Look at this," he says, sitting on the bed. "A bed made up with actual linens! Curtains to draw against the sun! And I wager there's even toilet paper in the bathroom."

"You would be right. And now, do you want to thank me, you ingrate? It's been complaint and suspicion ever since I cooked this up. Thank me."

The reunion is sweet, the late afternoon sun slanting through the window, the flat horizon of the sea and the boats floating in the harbor, and Trudy, right here, right next to him. He has thought of her for so long, missed the feel of her skin and the smell of her breath, that he moves as if he's in a dream. She is quiet, more than usual, and seems skittish. They are both too sapped, too thirsty, to ever be quenched by something as mundane as the physical.

"Tell me the truth," she says, sitting up afterward, clutching the sheet, "is there a hussy you have in Stanley? Some American vixen who's stolen your heart? Surely you can't have been celibate all this time, someone as voracious as you. What else do you have to amuse you in that dreary camp?"

"I'm only voracious around you, you know." He doesn't ask her the same question, feels any answer would be unbearable. If he can keep some small part of her for himself, it might be all right. "Don't mind about those things, and I won't either." He extends this olive branch so that their time together might be enjoyed.

She relaxes and curls into him.

"It's been horrible," Trudy says. "The Japanese are rounding up Chinese who are sympathetic, shall we say, or pretend that they are, for business purposes, and holding these absurd dinners where their policies are toasted with champagne and they're lionized as if they've made enormous contributions to society. All quite surreal. Victor Chen is hot and heavy with the Japanese, of course, and trying to do business with them every which way. I'm worried about Dommie. Victor is just using him.

"We went to one of these dinners, and an old family friend of ours, David Ho, stood up and offered a toast to Pan-Asian superiority. Now, mind you, he was married to an Australian woman, and devoted to her, but she died a few years back, and he remarried, lucky for him, to a Chinese. He's such a coward. I wouldn't have believed it if I hadn't seen it with my own eyes. He has children in school in Australia. Don't know how he'll be able to look them in the eye now. They are the funniest dinners. They have them in the ballroom of the Gloucester and try to make them fancy but they are just the worst functions you've ever seen. Propaganda films, bad alcohol, and hypocrites. Nothing worse."

"So why do you go to these things?"

She gets out of bed, her body a long rebuke.

"I had forgotten what it was like to have my conscience with me always. Sometimes, Will, you have to do things you don't want to. We can't all live in perfect harmony with our integrity."

He hears her turn on the water. She has always loved baths and used to spend so much time in them she would emerge with her glossy skin pruny and her face glowing with the absorbed heat.

"How's the water here?" he calls out, by way of apology. Their time is too short to be beset by old complaints.

"Not bad, as these things go. Nothing worse than a lukewarm bath, don't you think? Do you want to join me?"

She pours in Badedas, bubbling the water hot and steamy. The green, limy smell rises in the heat. Together, they slip and slide, washing each other while careful not to prod too deeply, keeping everything on the surface, their mood as fragile as the bubbles in the bath.

Outside is strange—an odd approximation of free society. Pinched faces, suspicious shoulders, everyone trying to blend in and look inconspicuous. The opposite of normal—Americans speaking softly, British acting humble, Chinese acting shy. Everything is hushed, except for Trudy and Dominick, who's joining them for lunch. He meets them in the lobby of the hotel and kisses Trudy on both cheeks and nods slightly to Will.

"Hello, darling," he says to Trudy, handing her a large envelope filled with papers. "This is from Victor. He sends his love." Trudy blanches.

"Love, is it?"

As they leave the hotel, Trudy and Dominick walk down the street as if they own it, laughing loudly and wearing flamboyant, obviously expensive clothes.

"If you act as if you're bulletproof, most people will assume you are, darling," Trudy assures Will. "Believe me, I've tested this theory extensively." She pulls out a worn blue booklet covered in stamps. "And this helps enormously, of course. It's from Otsubo and it tells whatever foot soldier stops me that he better treat me with kid gloves or there'll be hell to pay. Usually, when they see his stamp, they sort of freeze, then shove it back toward me as if it's on fire, and they bow and scrape to an embarrassing extent. I'm quite addicted to it."

"And Dommie?"

"He has one with his patron's stamp. All the best people have one, you know." Her laughter is brittle.

"And what does Otsubo think of you springing me from the camp? Does he know?"

"Well, he arranged it for me. I don't think he's the jealous type, to be honest. I don't think you will be spending much time together. Do you want Cantonese food? I'm in the mood for noodles, actually."

"Chinese?"

"Yes, the other food is unbearable these days since there's no one proper to cook it."

"Have you ever missed a meal?"

"Darling, if you miss a meal, the light quite goes out of the day. All Chinese know that. I wouldn't unless things were absolutely desperate. Dommie knows this little place where they serve the most amazing rice noodles with broth they steep all day long. Of course, it's better at two in the morning since it's been cooking all day, but nowadays you're viewed suspiciously if you're out late without one of our great leaders."

"How is the Grill? Still operating?"

"Oh, we still go. It's pretty jolly, actually. And not all Japanese. There are groups of Americans and British on the outside, and it's not done to ask why, and the Japanese don't seem to bother them, and all sorts of other people, you know, Swiss Red Cross, the occasional German. I tell you, Hong Kong right now is the most *interesting* mix of people. The war just shook out all the people and what remained behind in the sieve is diverse, should we say. There's this woman, Jinx Beckett, who's an American, and I can't quite figure out what her story is and why she's not in Stanley with you as I'm sure she's not an important banker or government official. I'm sure you'll meet her. She is absolutely everywhere, and poky too, nosing around in all sorts of things. And there are still parties. We still go to the Gripps for dancing but they'll stop the music every once in a while and project these hilarious propaganda films onto the ballroom walls. It's all about Pan-Asiatic superiority, don't you know? They don't seem to understand that they're screening for a bunch of non-Asiatics. Screaming irony."

Will sees a newsstand, for him a startling sight.

"I'd love a newspaper. How is the English broadsheet these days?"

"Run by a Swede under the careful watch of the Japanese," says Dominick. "Result as you would expect. Piffle. I expect you'd like one."

"I would," Will says and takes the *Standard* and the *News*. Trudy pays.

"It is propaganda," whispers Trudy. "They print whatever they're told to."

"Subtlety, my darling," Dominick says, shushing her. Suddenly he relaxes and turns to Will. "So, how is it being on the outside?" They have exchanged only the barest of civil greetings. "And is it as atrocious on the inside as they say? Of course, the paper claims that you are being treated as if you were honored guests at the Ritz."

"Certainly not ideal. But it seems rather fraught out here as well. Everyone tiptoeing around."

"Is it true that Asbury is in there, doing his own wash like a common rickshaw boy?" A famously haughty banker, whom Will has indeed seen poking around in the dirt, trying to establish a garden, and hanging up his undershirts to dry, as his wife is abed most days.

"He is, but he's holding his own. Surprising, the dignity that still holds in any circumstance."

"Yes, we're not our own men anymore, are we?" Dominick looks around. "But some are more so than others."

Will says nothing.

"It's better to be a free person, though, isn't it?" asks Trudy. "We have to mind our manners out here but there's no one telling us what to do or when to eat. Services are all getting back. Food prices were going up and down but they seem to have stabilized. We can withdraw small amounts of money. Public transport is working, as is the mail, in a way, and people are starting to settle, although it's still a hard life. You do still run across the occasional corpse in the street, which is unpleasant. And the Japanese do work the coolies quite hard, harder than any Chinese I've seen, and they are having a hard time of it. They're sending them back to China in droves as well. I think they aim to reduce the population by half."

"Nothing is easy these days, is it?" Dominick says. "Aaah, here's the noodle shop."

After lunch, Dominick goes to work, "such as it is," he remarks, languid as always, and Trudy and Will go shopping. Trudy frequents the markets in search of treasures.

"I've seen things that I recognize from friends' houses!" she says, rifling through a table of pilfered goods. "The ormolu clock from the Hos', and that extraordinary dagger that was hanging above the mantel at the Chens'. I wanted to buy them but didn't have enough money. Those," her voice drops, "filthy rats just took away everything they could carry, and then the locals came after, and picked every house clean. Enough to make you weep, seeing those ships set out for Japan filled to the brim with all the lovely things our friends had collected. Cars and furniture and jewelry! Many a soldier's wife is playing tea party with someone else's Wedgwood these days."

"Is there food we can buy so I could bring it back to camp?"

"Depends on the day and what they've been able to find. Sometimes there's powdered milk, sometimes there's crates of mustard.

We'll see." She pauses. "It's sort of freeing, this paring down to the necessities. It seems so frivolous to have thought about dresses and picnics."

"You and Dominick seem to have your meals and lodging pretty well figured out." He says this striving for a tone without judgment.

"Yes, we do," she replies carelessly. "But it could all be taken away tomorrow so we must enjoy it while we can, no?"

She cuts down Pottinger Street and into a small alley.

"There's a small shop here where you can get some amazing things."

"What's in demand?"

"Food, mostly. Some people have started speculating in gold and such. We'll go to the market after this."

A bell jingles as Trudy pushes open the door. Inside, it is dark and pungent with the smell of teakwood and the waxy oil used to polish it. A curio shop, with scratched, smudgy glass counters filled with Oriental peculiarities. Trudy speaks in Cantonese to the woman behind the counter, who scurries to the back, cloth slippers swishing on the floor.

"What are we looking for here?"

"Oh, I'm just doing an errand for my master. You know."

"How mysterious," he says.

The woman comes back with a man, small, with a bent back, dressed in black silk. He seems irritated. Trudy speaks rapidly again, her small hands outlining a large rectangle in the air. The man shrugs and shakes his head. Trudy's voice turns shrill. She ends with a sharp outburst and turns to leave.

Outside, the sun is shining, an abrupt change from the dark gloom of the shop.

"So, food?" he asks. She will tell him when she's ready.

"Yes, food," she says, taking his arm, an implicit gesture of thanks. "Sometimes, I think you could be Chinese too."

• • •

The wet market seems the same as ever—wizened old ladies with wide-brimmed coolie hats, dressed in black smocks, bent over their wares, calling out to potential customers. Here, a basket of greens; there, soybean curds resting in a container of milky water, with yellow sprouts. He remembers the smell, the green, slightly brackish scent of dirt and water still clinging to the vegetables. He used to come with Trudy on weekends, her mother having told her that she was never to become too grand to go to the market for her own food. "At least, every once in a while," she says. "Not all the time, of course. And you won't catch anyone we know here. But I don't mind. It's kind of elemental, isn't it? Deciding which exact onion you want, or what fish you're going to eat and have them clean it for you."

"How is it that there isn't a shortage?" he asks, as she bends over to inspect some radishes.

"There is, but these are available for exorbitant prices. All the peasants from the outlying territories make the trip into town now because they know they'll get five or six times what they could get out there, so it's all concentrated here. They come out with ten watermelons or a bag of watercress. It's good for the soul to see how basic life can be. Grow something on the land, dig it up, sell it for some money, buy something you need."

Afterward, when they have procured some tinned foods, vegetables, and cigarettes for Will to take back to Stanley, Trudy takes him for a drive around the Peak, to see all the bombed-out houses and ruined roads. Every wall is crumbling, bricks falling to the road.

"Can you believe what all the bombs did? They're starting to rebuild, though. They have the slave labor or Volunteer Corps from China, as they call it, and they're patching up the roads and trying to salvage the homes. Some have been taken over by Japanese military, and they look quite nice."

They pass a house where some dozen coolies are painting the exterior white.

"The king of Thailand has an elephant that they trained to paint."

"That is one of your outlandish stories."

"No, I'm serious. Father said he saw it himself."

"They had the elephant paint the palace?"

"Certainly not! I'm sure he just painted the rough outbuildings and barns and things like that."

"Of course, darling." They've stopped at an overlook where tourists used to come to look over Hong Kong harbor.

"Should we get out?"

There is a wobbly iron fence, pebbles and dirt underneath, wind with the metallic smell of lingering winter. She leans into him, hair blowing wild, as they look out onto the green sea, the white, stocky buildings crowding the shore and the harbor.

"It looks so peaceful now, doesn't it?" Trudy says musingly. "The water in Hong Kong is a different color from anywhere else in the world—kind of a bottle green. I think it's the mountains reflected in it." She pauses. "It was quite red with blood just these few months ago. There are boats and bodies on the bottom of the sea, thick on it, I'm sure. It was shocking how quickly things looked normal again, how nature swallows up the aberrations."

"What happened to Angeline's house?"

"She's managed to hang on to it, although I don't know why she doesn't come into town. This place is filled with Japanese army officials who have taken over the houses and I don't see how it's safe for her here. We have lunch every once in a while, Dominick, Angeline, and I. Try to pretend things are normal."

"She's all right, though?"

"Not really. None of us are."

They return to the hotel, where Trudy starts to pack his newly accumulated things into his suitcase.

"You'll be popular when you get back."

"We have to figure out a way to get supplies into the camps. The children need vitamins and protein."

The phone rings.

"Victor," says Trudy when she picks it up. Her voice is even.

"Yes, I did get it. Dommie gave it to me." She pauses. "I know. I'm trying." Another pause. "I'll be in touch when I can, but please don't call me about this again." She hangs up the phone with a bang.

"Everything all right?" Will asks.

"Watch me be frugal, Will," Trudy says instead, ignoring his question. She starts to brew coffee on a small cooking plate. "This is my third go-around with these grounds. Have you ever seen anything so industrious? Aren't you proud of me?"

They sip the hot, bitter drink without milk or sugar.

"Oh, I forgot. There's something I wanted you to see." She goes to the bedside table and pulls out a folded-up newspaper.

"This editorial was in that ridiculous paper on Valentine's Day. Dommie wants me to frame it." She reads, " 'The Eurasian is a problem in all British colonies. The term is applied loosely to the offspring of all mixed marriages and to their children, et cetera, et cetera. That Britain and some other of the Occidental powers chose to victimize the Eurasian rather than accept him and make use of his qualities is astonishing to students of the question. The Eurasian could be of great help to these powers, contributing valuable liaison between the ruling nation and the native population.' " She looks up. "Want to hear more?"

"Can I see that?" She gives it to him. He scans it. A column of coarse intelligence.

"The funny thing is, I was talking about being Eurasian to Otsubo about a week before it came out."

"Really?"

"Yes, really. Isn't that interesting? I was telling him how when I was young, the other children would laugh and point at me, and on the streets, some Europeans would take my photograph as if I were some animal at the zoo."

"It must have been difficult, but those people are just ignorant."

"Turn the page," she orders, gesturing to the paper.

"More of your influence?"

"No, just another example of the absurdities we are subjected to every day. Do you see that piece about the houseflies, there? Where if you catch two taels of houseflies, you are entitled to a catty of rice if you bring it to a district bureau. And I've seen people carrying around these bundles of flies. It's beyond. The Japanese are even more bizarre than the English. I've never imagined such a thing."

Suddenly, she turns to him.

"Did you know I was eight when my mother disappeared? And eight is supposed to be such a lucky number for the Chinese. I've always wondered if it was because I was only half Chinese. And half of eight is four, which is a terrible number. You know, it means death."

"What do you remember of her?"

"Bits and pieces. She didn't go out much, because she didn't fit in. She wasn't English, so the English wouldn't have anything to do with her, and the Chinese *taitais* certainly didn't like her. And she wasn't strong enough or confident enough to do anything about it. So she had very few friends and she was at home a lot, dressed beautifully with nothing to do but gossip with the servants. I suspect even they looked down on her. My father loved her, married her despite family disapproval, but he was so busy he didn't have much time for her. She took me to the botanical gardens every once in a while, and to tea at the Gloucester. She wore gloves and a pillbox hat, and the straight skirts. She wanted me to be dressed properly as well. She was very beautiful. But I think she was sad."

"You've never talked about her before."

"I don't remember that much." She pauses. "I remember she told me about her childhood. She was very poor. She was funny about it too. She refused to eat soup, because to her that meant poverty.

She had grown up in a house where they threw whatever little they had into a pot of water, sprinkled it liberally with salt, and called it a meal. She didn't want me to grow up oblivious to our good fortune, but at the same time, I think she liked how the rich felt bulletproof—not her, obviously, but I think she liked that I might feel that way, but worried at the same time that it wouldn't last. And she was right, wasn't she? I'm not bulletproof. I've come a long way in the world, but the world has changed and I'm not sure anymore of what I am or what I can do."

After love, they lie on the bed. She shifts away, suddenly shy, and stares at the ceiling. Words burst forth from her, as if unbidden, a confessional fountain she cannot stopper.

"I've always known, my love, that I was a chameleon. I was a terrible daughter because my father let me be one. He didn't know what else to do with me, feeling so guilty I didn't have a mother. And I was a good daughter when my mother was around. Because she couldn't imagine anything else. And then when I was older, I was a different person every year, depending on who I was with. If I was with a scoundrel, then I became the type of woman that would be with a scoundrel. If I was with an artist, then I became a muse. And when I was with you, I was, for the first time, I'm sure people have told you, a decent human being. All Hong Kong wondered why someone like you would bother with someone like me. You know that, don't you?"

She props herself up on an elbow, bronze hair falling across her shoulders.

"But now circumstances have changed, and I have reverted back to form and become a woman who is with somebody because it suits her situation and for no other reason than that simple and venal one. I'm no different from that Russian girl Tatiana, the one I pretend to despise. We're more sisters than anything else. We recognize each other. I'm sure no one is surprised. Do you understand?"

"Melodrama," he says. "You're being absurd." She is quiet, one hand nervously pulling her hair back from her face, the other fluttering around her mouth.

"Don't ever say I didn't tell you. I told you. You must know that I told you."

The phone rings in the room.

Trudy picks it up and her mouth draws into a tense line.

"Yes, of course. Of course. I'll see to it."

She hangs up and turns to him, face unreadable.

"As it turns out, Otsubo is interested in meeting you. *Intéressant, non?*"

"Is it?"

"I don't know what his intentions are. But we have to do what we're told, don't we? You don't mind? It's not as if we have much choice in the matter. Dommie will be there too."

So that evening, after another silent, hot, soaking bath and having got dressed in silence—Trudy had brought some of Will's old clothes and they had laughed to see how they hung loose on him, one spot of forced gaiety in a tense afternoon—they are seated in a small room of a restaurant in Tsim Sha Tsui, contemplating nuts in a small porcelain dish embellished with red dragons, as Trudy quaffs champagne at a rapid clip. Will lights a cigarette.

"This place any good?"

"Not much to look at but currently the best seafood in town." They had seen the tin buckets in front upon arriving, large, lazy fish swimming inside, oblivious to their fate.

"He likes Chinese food?"

"Seems to be acquiring a taste." Her nails clatter on the table as she drums her fingers. "Dommie is late, the fool. Why does he do this all the time?"

"You eat with Dominick often?"

"Every night."

"Why are there so many seats? Who else is coming?"

"They travel in packs, darling. He wouldn't dream of being seen without his entire coterie of yes-men and sycophants."

"And he is, of course, late."

Just then, the door opens and a string of men is ushered in. It is immediately clear who Otsubo is as the others wait inside the room until he has entered, and wait for him to choose his seat.

"Otsubo-san," Trudy says gaily, standing up. "You're late as always." She looks lovely tonight, dressed in a sleek tomato-red silk tunic dress, her hair swept back into a chignon.

Time to sing for supper. Will stands up.

"Very nice to meet you. I'm Will Truesdale."

"Otsubo," the man says gruffly, and gestures that they are all to sit. "Mr. Chan not here?"

"He'll be here soon. It's a difficult time to get around." Trudy sits between Otsubo and Will.

The man is stocky and short, in a finely cut suit of tropical-weight wool. His hair is cut close, military-style, a centimeter long so the oily surface of his scalp shines through. His eyes, porcine and bulbous, sunken in a puffy, smooth face. In short, an unattractive man. Next to him, Trudy looks like a gaudy, gorgeous flamingo.

His men sit down at the table, anonymous in their multitude. They talk among themselves, but quietly, so that Otsubo needn't talk above them. He orders Cognac.

"Otsubo's acquiring Chinese tastes," Trudy says. "He loves XO now."

"Some things Chinese are good," Otsubo says. "At least they are Asiatic."

There is a silence.

"What should we eat?" Trudy asks into the void. "Abalone? Shark's fin? Would you like me to do the honors?"

Otsubo nods and she orders rapidly in Cantonese. She speaks everything well—Cantonese, Shanghainese, Mandarin, French,

English. Some of the men look at her as she is ordering, their faces unreadable. She must be a complete mystery to them, probably straight from the countrysides of Japan, pressed into service for their country to come to this place, where the language and customs are different, where a woman like Trudy flits around like a flamboyant butterfly. They drink beer straight from the bottles, and smoke without ceasing. They are not offered Cognac.

Dominick enters hastily.

"Otsubo-san." He bows. "So sorry to be impolite. Urgent matters held my attention." Will has never seen Dominick in this ruffled state.

"You are late again," Otsubo says. "Bad manner for business and society too."

"I know, I know. My masters at Harrow were always on me for tardiness."

Trudy will tell him later, the Japanese love that Dominick was at the best schools in England, they want to know all the details, and that Dominick indulges them at every chance. "They hate it but they love it too. Isn't that always the case?"

He presents a box to Otsubo. "A gesture of my appreciation for everything you've done for me, and for Hong Kong."

Otsubo grunts thanks but does not receive the box. Dominick, so obviously unused to gruffness, takes a step back, recovers, and slides smoothly into a chair.

"Maybe later, then," he says to Will, a collusive greeting that implies they are made of finer stuff than this Japanese man.

Will turns away, unwilling to be allies with Dominick, unwilling to be as stupid as he. Trudy pours more tea.

"Mr. Truesdale," says Otsubo in English. Then he speaks through his translator.

"How are you finding the camps?" The translator is a young, slender man with spectacles. His accent is almost unnoticeable.

Will hesitates. How honest to be? "It's livable but, unfortunately, despite the best efforts of the camp officers, there are often shortages of food and medicines and, as there are also women and children in the camp, we feel this need acutely."

Otsubo listens and nods. He replies, "That is a shame. We will look into the matter." The translator looks nervous.

The first dish is served. Chinese-style, it is a cold jellyfish appetizer. Will has learned from Trudy that a proper Chinese meal unfolds in a certain way. First, a cold appetizer like pig's feet over jellyfish vermicelli; then a warm one, perhaps sesame-crusted shrimp, a shark's fin or winter melon soup; a signature dish such as Peking duck, a meat—sweet-and-sour pork or braised beef with *choi sam,* a fish, a vegetable, finishing always with noodles or fried rice, depending on the region. Chinese don't take to heavy desserts—enjoying a cold coconut-milk dish or, if especially peckish, apple dumplings fried in hot oil and then immediately crisped in ice water.

Otsubo takes the first portion, then spins the lazy Susan around to his men. Trudy pretends not to notice the slight. She serves Will and Dominick before taking her share, a minute serving of amber tentacles covered in mustard sauce.

After chewing laboriously, Otsubo speaks again.

"There are many illustrious people in the camps, are there not? Leaders of society and business?"

"I suppose there are. But we're all reduced to the same circumstances now, really. Nobody has more than anyone else."

"It must be curious for them to be in such a place. Quite difficult to come down so much in life."

"I imagine it is."

Trudy has been uncharacteristically quiet.

"Like poor Hugh," she interjects finally. "I can't believe that lovely man has to wash his own socks. I don't think he'd ever made himself a ham sandwich before this."

They eat the jellyfish. It is cold and rubbery.

Otsubo speaks again.

"And there is a man named Reggie Arbogast?" asks the translator. "A businessman? With ties to government?"

"Yes, Reggie is one of the interned."

Otsubo looks at Will thoughtfully.

"Is he a friend of yours?" he asks through the translator.

"*Friend* is too strong a word. We are acquaintances but our mutual experience has made us more intimate, no doubt about it."

"Have more drink." The translator fills Will's glass with whiskey.

"Thank you." He raises his glass to Otsubo.

"Whiskey good." The man speaks for himself, pronouncing *whiskey* "whysky."

"Yes, very good."

"Drink. Tonight you are free."

"Not so bad." Will holds the door open for Trudy. The evening air is crisp and clean after the smoky, warm room.

"Yes," Trudy says. She seems happy, relieved the evening is over and her pass has not been revoked. "Better than expected."

"He's an interesting..."

A car stops in front of them, and a window rolls down. A pudgy hand emerges and waves Trudy in. She looks sick, then gives him a quick kiss and climbs into the car.

"I'll see you later, darling," she says. "Don't wait up."

Early in the morning, around three a.m., while he is sleeping restlessly, the door opens quietly and Trudy stealthily pads her way to the powder room. He turns on the bedside light, listens to the water running, and waits for her to come out from her ablutions. When she slides into bed, he sees the enormous yellow bruise starting to form around her left eye. Something about her demeanor warns him not to fuss.

"That's quite a shiner you have there," he says.

"He's surprising, that one," she says, and reaches to turn off the lamp, plunging them into gray, a wakeful twilight where they listen to each other's breath.

After a few long minutes, just when he is about to drift into sleep despite himself, seduced by the utter luxury of the soft bedding and the now unfamiliar warmth of another, she murmurs, "You know, when I said surprising, I meant a surprising lover. You knew that, right? He's not a bad man. Really." At that moment, lying there with the moonlight glinting off her shiny hair and smooth, glossy skin, he thinks she looks like a scorpion.

He cannot let it go. He sits up. She looks at him, quizzical.

"Trudy." He stops, to think how to say this. "I need you to know there is a limit." He raises her chin toward him. "There is a limit to how sophisticated I can be."

"Oh."

"I'm not the person you want me to be. Not right now."

"I should be careful. I should take care." She says it penitently. "I'm sorry, darling. I'm drunk. Don't let's quarrel."

"Yes."

She sits up and turns on the light.

"Sleep is not something I can do right now. Should we talk? Should we try to become who we were before all this happened, just for a moment?"

"That's impossible." He brings her to him, her head nestled in his shoulder. She smells of cigarettes and liquor. He tells her so.

"I smell like a whore." She moves closer to him. "I told you Frederick died but I didn't tell you how."

"No," he agrees. "You didn't."

"Well, he was able to get back to Hong Kong. His whole regiment had been slaughtered, and since he was the head, or whatever his title was, they allowed him his life and let him walk back, escorted. They let him come back, but they made him carry..." Her voice falters. "They made him collect the ears of all of his fellow soldiers, and he had to put them in a little bag and carry it. They said his hands were soaked in blood and the bag was drenched. And the smell...I keep thinking about it, over and over, and how it must have smelled awful and how it must have been slippery and how he must have been so tired...

"And then, the hunger and the famine right after, before they could reestablish some of the markets. The rumors, the horrible, horrible rumors. Pets disappeared. Even..." A hiccup. "Even babies, they said."

"Trudy, there's no end to the misery if you keep thinking about it."

"And that dinner I told you about, the one where the local swells were trying to get on with the new order, where my family friend who had married an Australian denounced the white races, you remember that one? The one Victor organized?"

"Yes, I do."

"I didn't tell you but at that dinner, we were all sitting, all trying to sit in our fancy clothes without feeling too hypocritical, without feeling like we were giving up too much of ourselves and hoping we could still look at ourselves in the mirror at the end of it all, and then at some point in the evening—there had been quite a lot of drinking—Dominick said something stupid. I don't even remember what he said, but it was silly and clever, you know, like him."

"I do know," he says.

"And then the man who had arranged the dinner, Ito, the head of the economic department of the Gunseicho, whose table it was, he just stood up, walked over, and he walked very deliberately, and the crowd sort of hushed because he had this sense of, I don't know, I suppose you'd call it purpose, and he walked right up to Dommie—we had been seated at one of the best tables, his table—and he stood in front of Dommie and he slapped him across the face. He slapped him really hard."

She works the sheet through her hands over and over.

"And that sound, you know, it sounded like a gunshot, because everyone had been watching, and it got very quiet, there might have even been a gasp from everybody, I don't remember, and Dommie sat there, with his cheek getting red, and then he tried to gather himself, he just sort of looked away, and then he picked up his champagne glass, and took a sip. And then the whole room took a collective sigh, and we tried to pick up where things had stopped. And Victor, that bloodless leech, didn't do a thing about it.

"But it was as if the whole room had been slapped. And Dommie, you know, he tries to be a cool customer, but his hands shook the whole night after. I know you think he's dreadful and soulless, but you do not know him. You do not know him. I've known him all my life and he's fragile, and can break at any minute, and I want to protect him and save him from himself if that is at all possible. He is my only family out here. We are looking out for each other. He can be a terrible person, but there are reasons for that, you know. Not like Victor, who's hateful because he only thinks of himself and money. Dommie hates himself, and so he can be awful." She pauses. "I've never told anyone this, but Dominick was never quite right. There was a scandal when he was younger, around twelve, something about him and the maids. He made them . . . do things, and he did things to them, and they were found out. Someone walked in on them. So his parents were dreadfully embarrassed and they got rid of the maids, young girls from China, paid them off, and sent him to England when he was really too young. They were never really cut out to be parents. I think he was a mistake. And although he had done these terrible things, he was still so young. And he went, and he didn't speak very good English at the time, and he stuck out with his odd clothes and his funny accent. And then somehow, it got out at the school what he had done, and the older boys . . . they made him do the same things. They made him . . . you know. You know what it's like in those schools. He told me this one night when he was dreadfully drunk. I don't know that he even remembers telling me. But we've always been like brother and sister. So, after that, I don't think he was ever quite the same. How could you be? And that's why he hates the English, for the most part, although he is so damn English in so many ways. It's very complicated. And in the end, I think, we're all just trying to survive, aren't we?"

"Sometimes there are things more important than survival." It sounds self-important but he cannot help himself. He wants to warn her, not for himself but for her own sake. And to defend a horror like Dominick! She was blinded by misguided loyalty.

"Tell that to someone who's about to go under the guillotine," she retorts hotly. "Tell that to someone who is about to get shot. I'm sure all they're thinking about is how to get out of the situation. I'm sure survival is quite important to them at that moment. You might even say, the only thing. You might have the luxury of pondering the dignity of the soul, but...never mind." She stops. "I can't explain it to you, or justify to you, or anything, so what's the point?"

"I'm sorry you feel like you have to justify yourself to me."

She waves her hands above her slowly, like small satellites.

"This night feels like forever. I feel like Scheherazade trying to prolong the night."

"Do you think I'm going to kill you come morning?"

"Everything changes when the light comes, doesn't it?"

Later, he will wonder what exactly she meant.

They go to sleep, or their approximations of it, each careful not to disturb the other.

In the morning, over coffee, she offers her feet to him to be rubbed.

"Everything seems better in the morning, don't you think?" Her implicit peace offering. She pours cream into her cup and spills some into the saucer. Her hands are shaking a little.

"*Mon amour*," she begins.

"Yes?"

"*Une question pour toi.*"

"Yes?"

"The good general is interested in me for many reasons," she begins. "One of which is that I'm rather pretty. But, as you know, Hong Kong is filled with pretty women, and so his interest in me has lasted the time it has because he is also very interested in assuring his future while he's here. An ambitious man, Otsubo. And he thinks I should be able to help him. And being a man of large appetite, he is not content with the occasional wristwatch and woman's trinket—his sights are set much higher. He'd take land if his government would let him, but it won't, and he's getting rather frustrated." She pauses. "There are those in Tokyo who are particularly interested in the Crown Collection of Hong Kong. It's supposed to have many priceless Chinese pieces, centuries old, inestimable in their value, politically sensitive, of course. And those have not been found. It's thought they were secreted away before the war began here. And the Chinese want their heritage back, the Japanese want them for their value, and the English think it all belongs to them. It's very confusing.

"To make a long story short, Otsubo thinks that a few of the men in Stanley are privy to information that would help him locate these pieces. In particular, he has an idea that Reggie Arbogast knows where it is. I think Otsubo would be handsomely rewarded for locating these items and getting them back to Japan. You know, it's been a complete madhouse over here with the looting and the ransacking and things turning up in the market places, museum pieces selling for two cents or worthless twaddle being shipped off to the homeland like it's worth something. No one really knows what's going on, but he's determined to find these pieces. He's had me look through the pawnshops and talk to people, but nothing. So, that is why he furloughed you and wanted to have dinner with you and talk to you."

"But why would he think I would know anything about it?"

"He's heard that you are well liked in camp. You've been elected head of something or other, haven't you?"

"What's that got to do with it?"

"Do you know anything?"

The abrupt question takes him by surprise.

"Do you wish I did?"

"Does that mean you do?"

He stands up. The parrying is sickening to him.

"Trudy, we're not at war with each other."

"No, but we might be at cross-purposes. Will, I need something from you now."

"Everything I have is yours." It sounds false, even to him, metallic in his mouth, as he watches her desperate, dissembling face. What does she inspire in him now? Still love? Or pity?

"So, you'll help us?"

What could he do? She didn't ask for herself. She asked for them. She was lost already.

Part III

May 2, 1953

MISS EDWINA STORCH, an institution in Hong Kong, hosted occasional ladies' lunches at her home in the New Territories. She was the headmistress emeritus of a well-regarded primary school in Pokfulam and a renowned expert on Chinese porcelains—an old China hand who had retired to the New Territories. She lived famously in an old house with Alsatians, chickens, an elderly married Chinese couple in service, and another English spinster—her lifelong partner, Miss Winkle. They sometimes came for lunch at the Ladies' Recreation Club, where Claire had seen them holding court among the other expatriate women, and she had seen Miss Winkle wrestling carnations into submission at Mrs. Beazley's flower-arranging class at the Duddell St. YWCA. Miss Winkle was small and slight, with frail bird bones, and Miss Storch was large and heavy, with thick calves that ended in a straight line at her feet. They both wore knee-length skirts and white cotton buttoned blouses with Peter Pan collars and often took slow constitutionals around the countryside with their sensible shoes and large dogs. Her invitations were rarely turned down, for some reason that Claire had not been able to glean. So when her invitation arrived in the mail, heavy cream bond with a gold crest—rather much for a retired schoolmistress, she thought—she accepted with curiosity.

Claire drove up to a white wooden gate. She had to get out of the car to open the gate, drive through, and then get out to close it again, with a little hook that had been haphazardly screwed into the wood. Somehow, she didn't dare leave it open, although she knew some twenty people had been invited for lunch. She drove up a dusty road, past gracious old trees, one with a wooden swing attached to a large branch, to the house itself, a rambling stone structure that seemed on the verge of falling down. There was a porch, with a screen door slightly ajar, but she walked around the house to the back garden, where she could hear music and voices.

Alongside the house there was a drinks table set up with a bucket of ice and various mismatched glasses, a large punch bowl, and small egg salad sandwiches that were already attracting flies. Five other people had already arrived, none of whom Claire recognized. Then Miss Storch came over to greet her, walking slowly with a cane.

Miss Storch was one of those people so comfortable with herself that everything she did seemed unsurprising. If she served you wine in a teacup, it would seem the most natural thing in the world, and that anyone thought otherwise was hopelessly bourgeois. Her lunch was, Claire would discover, rabbit pie, tomato soup white bread tomato sandwiches, and ice cream on a stained cotton tablecloth in a weathered old tent outside in the garden. At each chipped place setting was a carved camphor wood fan to stir up the hot and humid air. Women stood around fanning themselves as they sipped warm lemonade and ate cocktail sausages and pineapple speared onto toothpicks.

"So nice to meet you," Miss Storch said. "I've been meaning to have you over."

"The pleasure's mine, Miss Storch," Claire said. "I've heard wonderful things about you."

"Edwina, please, and call Miss Winkle Mary. I'm giving you permission right now."

"That's very kind." Claire was very aware of Miss Storch's intelligent, razor-sharp gaze. Beads of perspiration trickled in her décolletage. "Do you have these lunches often? I've heard of them, of course, but didn't know if they were…" She trailed off, unable to come up with the words to complete the sentence.

"Mary and I live so far out, although this is the way we choose to live. We like people, and it's hard to see them out here, so we came upon this idea, to have regular lunches, and people seem to like them, luckily, so they make the effort to come. We've had most everyone out here, a few governors, the occasional lord and lady, many travelers in from England. You know."

"And you've been in Hong Kong long?"

"Longer than you would believe, child."

"Oh!" A large Doberman had come up and nosed her hand.

"That's Marmaduke, the dear," said Miss Storch affectionately. "He keeps us safe and eats his weight in scraps every day."

"Do you have more dogs?"

"We have seven, but most of them are out roaming around right now. They'll come home for dinner. We adopted them after the war when there were so many animals looking for homes. We couldn't bear to say no, and we ended up with far too many. There are eight budgerigars in the house, with three cats who would love to eat them, and I think there's a terrapin somewhere in the kitchen as well."

"Were you here during the war?"

"Of course, through all the madness and its aftermath." Miss Storch adjusted her spectacles. They were steaming up in the heat. Her eyes bulged behind them, her skin red and fleshy.

"A friend of mine . . ." Claire stopped.

"Yes?" Miss Storch prompted.

"A friend was here as well. But I've just realized how stupid that must sound. There must be thousands of people who went through that experience. I'm sorry." Claire ducked, a sort of apologetic curtsy, and left abruptly. Marmaduke trailed behind her hopefully, then went off to find better prospects. Her heart was beating so hard, it felt as if it might burst through her chest. She walked in a daze until she came to a chair and sat down heavily. She had no idea what had come over her, what strange combination of the heat, Miss Storch's intent gaze, and her own preoccupation with Will had conspired to make this moment into something that felt so momentous.

She got up to get a fan from one of the place settings and fanned herself. When she peeked over, Miss Storch was busy with someone else and didn't look at all put out by Claire's strange reaction.

She sat and cooled off. Gradually she started to take in her surroundings. It was lovely out here. There was a large, graceful oak tree and an expansive lawn rolling down to a view of the mountains.

"Doesn't feel like Hong Kong, does it?" said a voice behind her. Claire jumped.

"So sorry, didn't mean to startle you." She turned around to see a little woman with spectacles hung around her neck. "Mary Winkle."

"Yes, of course. I'm Claire Pendleton. Thank you for having me today."

"It's our pleasure. We like to see people so we try to entice them out with a good meal."

A small Chinese woman came by and waited expectantly.

"Would you like a drink? You can tell Ah Chau what you'd like."

"Some of that lemonade would be lovely."

"Lemonade, please," Miss Winkle said loudly. Ah Chau nodded and left.

"She's a bit deaf since the war. The Japanese knocked her about a bit."

"So sad," Claire said. "Very good of you to keep her on."

"She's like family. When I was at Stanley, she came with provisions every single week, and I know her own family didn't have enough to eat. And she stayed with Edwina, who was on the outside."

"All these stories I keep hearing about. It's extraordinary."

"Well, it wasn't comfortable back in England either, I'd imagine."

"We were quite sheltered. The food was a bit short but otherwise, not too bad. I remember the air sirens and running to the shelter with my mum."

"Of course. And the dropping feeling in your stomach when you heard them."

"Yes. Like a bad dream, as they say."

A bell tinkled.

"It looks like it's time to eat."

They walked over to the tent.

At lunch, Claire watched as Edwina Storch took one of the tomatoes that were piled in the center of the table like a centerpiece. She was sitting on her right. The woman ate it as if it were an apple, with utter disregard for the red, staining juice as it dribbled onto her white linen blouse.

Miss Storch noticed Claire's stare.

"Delicious, child. Have one. They're as sweet as sugar, grown in my garden. We made the soup with them too, to get the last of them."

"No, thank you," she said. "But how wonderful to think you can grow your own vegetables in Hong Kong."

"Oh, I couldn't live anywhere else. I've been utterly spoiled. If I went back to England, they'd say I'd gone native, and they'd be absolutely right."

"Do you think you will never return?" There was something about the older lady that invited intimacy.

"I don't know what I'd return to. I haven't any real family anymore, and the family I've made is here."

Claire sipped the cold tomato soup. She grew bold.

"Can I ask you something impertinent?"

"If I can choose not to answer it," Miss Storch said.

"How do you decide who to invite to your luncheons? We've never met before, and although I was so pleased to come, I don't know how you even knew who I was to extend the invitation."

Miss Storch laughed, pleased.

"A good hostess always thinks of the whole. What a bore to see the same people over and over again. You need a mix of nationalities, professions, personalities. As you know, Hong Kong grows very tiresome as the community is so small. And one must amuse oneself as one gets old, don't you think?"

A Chinese woman with an American accent spoke to Miss Storch.

"I've heard you have a museum-quality collection of Song porcelain from Shanxi. Do you ever show people?"

"Sometimes," Miss Storch said with a smile. The Chinese woman waited expectantly. Miss Storch's smile grew wider.

The red-haired woman on the left of Miss Storch spoke up in the pause. She had been speaking importantly on women's suffrage and rights and immigrants' plights throughout the lunch.

"Have you heard? The government is forming a commission to rout out all the Japanese sympathizers once and for all. They're sick of those scoundrels trying to blend in and pretend they weren't part of the evil."

"Well," said Miss Storch. "That's a strong word. There were certainly those who were opportunistic. But most were people simply trying to find any sort of work and get some food on the table. I think the ones who most need to be prosecuted are those who had no such worries but simply wanted to profit enormously and didn't care about who they hurt along the way. Greed and dishonesty are always around, whether there is war or not."

"They'll have to answer to a higher authority," said the redhead, with a certain pleasure.

"It's difficult to prove anything, what with the lack of documentation during that time," said another woman, plumpish. "They never did find out what happened to the Crown Collection."

"I suppose they will rely on witnesses and first-person accounts," Miss Storch said.

"Why now?" Claire asked. "It's been ages since the surrender."

"Well, it's not anything official, but there have been a few events that make this particularly timely. The obvious people, Sakai, the Japanese commander-in-chief, and Colonel Tanaka, have been executed or imprisoned, but I think there's an emphasis on finding the local civilians who were a little too enthusiastic in befriending their new masters and who are pretending that nothing of the sort happened. I do think old grudges are being dredged up."

"So you've heard of this?" said the red-haired woman.

"I have been told that something like this may come along, as I may be of some help to those in charge." Miss Storch stood up. "Who wants to come and see my new Crosley?" she said. "They delivered it last week. It doesn't spoil the butter and defrosts automatically." It was clear the conversation was over.

Women were lingering over lemon tea and Tcachenko's cold cream cake when Miss Winkle was suddenly standing over Claire's shoulder.

"Claire, would you do us the honor of playing some music. We've heard what a talented pianist you are."

She flushed. "Hardly talented," she demurred. "I teach, but rarely play for myself anymore."

"You are teaching Locket Chen, are you not?"

"Yes, she's been studying with me for a few months."

"How do you like it? And her parents, Victor and Melody?"

"I haven't had the pleasure of getting to know them more intimately as they're rarely home when I go to teach."

"Yes, they're busy, I'd imagine."

"You know them?" Claire asked.

"Know them?" Miss Winkle said with an odd cast in her voice. "Yes, I should say we know them. And Edwina knows Mr. Chen very well indeed."

"Well," Claire said. "I'll give them your regards if you wish." She sipped her tea. Thankfully, the idea of her playing for the party was not resurrected. Miss Winkle was called away on some issue with the biscuits and she was free to gather up her scarf and pocketbook and say her farewells.

May 5, 1953

"People have always expected me to be bad and thoughtless and shallow, and I do my best to accommodate their expectations. I sink to their expectations, one might say. I think it's the ultimate suggestibility of most of us. We are social beings. We live in a social world with other people and so we wish to be as they see us, even if it is detrimental to ourselves." She laughs, lifting her face toward his. Her eyes, her skin, they glow, distracting him. "What do you think?"

HE WOKE with a startle, then exhaled heavily in the hot air, slowly noticed the fan moving sluggishly overhead as consciousness surfaced. Perspiration covered his body and the bed linens were soaked. Her voice was as clear as a bell in his head, her sharp, vivid outline moving against a dark background. He had forgotten how much she loved her own pronouncements, how she would philosophize over a cold drink, how she was startlingly insightful at the oddest times.

She was waiting for him, expecting him to save her.

What would become his story now? he wondered. And there was Claire, who had grown important to him despite himself, in whom he saw his undeveloped self, nascent, with her silly prejudices, her cherished ignorance, and, surprisingly, her moments of clarity. Her naïveté was a salve to his battered expectations. Wasn't love always some form of narcissism after all? She came unbidden to his dreams too, battling with the other woman, the one who haunted him day and night. Claire, with her blond and familiar femininity, English rose to Trudy's exotic scorpion.

The black night beyond the window was velvet and welcome in its anonymity. He got up and opened the windows. Hong Kong's warm, intimate smell came into the room, redolent of human bodies and the ever-present sea, even at this elevation. It was never crisp here, just moist and close, though not always unpleasant. The darkness enveloped him. A lone light winked in the distance—a boat? A fellow insomniac?

He heard her voice again. It sounded more desperate now, more shrill.

He knew it was time to act.

CORONATION FEVER had hit Hong Kong. The imperially slim Princess Elizabeth and her handsome prince had seized the imagination of expatriates and locals alike, and all through town there were placards declaring coronation sales, tailors advertised coronation gown specials, and special coins and stamps were being processed to mark the occasion. Society matrons were planning their coronation parties and teas and all the hotels were booked up for balls. Claire found herself waiting for the newspaper delivery every morning so she could read about all the details and preparations.

She had always been fascinated with the princesses, had read the scandalous book by their nanny, Marion Crawford, and devoured the details of their private lives. And now the princess was becoming the queen!

In Hong Kong itself there would be grand parades and decorations. Both the *South China Morning Post* and the *Standard* devoted much of their front pages to the impending event. There was to be an illuminated fountain in Statue Square with a royal blue Maypole topped by a crown, and four lions to symbolize the United Kingdom and four braziers to represent the flame of Commonwealth unity. It was to be guarded day and night by Her Majesty's personal representatives. There was also a Coronation Garden in Kowloon planted with blue hydrangeas and red and white water lilies, in the pattern of the English flag. The newspapers also dealt with the mundane. The Building Authority had warned that verandas and balconies should be sufficiently buttressed if property owners felt that they might be filled to capacity with revelers.

Claire read carefully about the arrangements the post office was making so that the high demand for commemorative coronation stamps would be adequately handled. There would be dedicated counters for selling the stamps, and more counters would be added. She planned to go to the Des Voeux Road branch to get hers. She had also put aside money for commemorative plates with the image of Princess Elizabeth stamped on them.

Will laughed at her when she told him of her excitement.

"Why on earth do you care about a silly woman getting a crown because she happened to be born into a certain family? And also because her uncle fell in love with someone that others find objectionable?"

Claire was shocked.

"You sound Communist, Will," she warned. "I wouldn't go around town airing those kinds of views."

"Sometimes you are such a ninny," he said, but his voice was kind. "You are the silliest woman I care to know." And he kissed her forehead gently.

They had been together for some eight months. Long enough to have a rhythm, but new enough that her palms still tingled, new enough to still check her reflection in any available surface before she was to meet him. Martin's steady hours gave them time together, but it was Will's work that confounded Claire.

"They never use you," she said. "They have two others, local Chinese. Why did they hire you?"

"I'm useful in my own way," he said. And refused to elaborate further.

But his lack of work meant they could spend afternoons together, in his small flat, having sent Ah Yik on one of many endless errands. How to deal with the small woman was one of Claire's regular ordeals. Her illicit status ate at her, making it difficult to look Ah Yik in the eye. She worried unceasingly about what to say, or what not to say, or whether to even acknowledge her presence. When asked his opinion, Will claimed not to care, even more maddening than usual.

"It doesn't matter," he said. "She is the soul of discretion and loyal to a fault."

"That's not what I'm worried about," Claire said.

"You're worried about her opinion?" he needled.

"I find it uncomfortable, Will," she said. "That is all."

"I understand. But she doesn't care at all what we do. She's seen much worse."

"And how is that?"

"She's been with me for years."

"Are you saying…" She stopped. "Never mind." She didn't want to know what he meant.

"Why do you care about the queen?" he asked suddenly.

"She is our queen," she said. "What do you mean, why do I care? Why would I not care?"

"You believe in empire?"

"Of course," she said, although she didn't know exactly what he was talking about.

He propped himself up on an elbow, interested now.

"Now, what about this. Do you think the queen cares for you?"

"What? You are asking such queer questions, Will. Sometimes I don't understand you at all."

"I just want to know if you think the queen, or rather, the queen to be, takes an interest in your well-being."

"She has many subjects but I'm sure she wishes the best for all of us."

"And you owe her your loyalty, and regard yourself as her subject."

"I do, yes." She shook her head. "Why are you being so obstinate? These are the things that we hold dear as British subjects, and it is not so uncommon to think this way."

Will smiled, a lazy smile.

"I just think that lovely little Lizzie doesn't care for you as much as you seem to think she does."

"You're incorrigible," she said. "Let's not talk about it anymore. It's putting me in a bad mood. You're a terrible person and you make me angry."

He laughed. He liked it when she scolded him.

But Will was erratic. His temper flared at the oddest things.

She had locked the door after them once, and having heard the click, he had turned around with real anger in his face.

"I told you," he said. "I never lock my door. Please unlock it."

She had, feeling chastised, her face blooming with embarrassment.

Later, she tried to bring it up.

"Why do you get so angry about locking your door? It seems so silly."

"It's a long story," he said. "But please don't ever do it again." He offered no apology or further explanation.

She tiptoed around him, but then he would pull her into bed or kiss her, and she would feel like it was all enough—that all the uncertainty and humiliation and guilt was worth it.

And there was this too. Claire wanted a baby.

It had happened all of a sudden. After years of regarding the mewling creatures as nothing more than nuisances, something had shifted inside her, and every particle of her yearned for a child, an infant to hold and smell and embrace. She longed for her belly to swell and expand, to feel the mysterious knocks from within, to walk around knowing that she was nurturing a child inside her.

She saw babies everywhere, strapped to the backs of Chinese women in their cloth sacks, towheaded infants playing on the lawn at the Ladies' Recreation Club. She felt bereft, unwomanly, as if something vital had been torn from her. She recorded her menstrual cycles and wept when blood stained her undergarments. When acquaintances told her they were expecting, her stomach dropped, as if from the want.

And, of course, it would be Will's baby. The thought of having Martin's child was, while not entirely repulsive, foreign to her, as if it were hardly a possibility. Martin had in fact receded so far from her life as she lived it that she was always faintly surprised when she woke up next to him. His smell seemed strange, his skin too clammy and corporeal. She resisted his advances, and he good-naturedly acquiesced, which made her despise him, which in turn made her despise herself. Had she always been this cruel? What had made her this way? Martin simply worked harder, spent more time at the office, and made it easy for her. What had made him like that? What had made her like this?

May 8, 1953

A CHANCE to get to know the Chens better arose. Not that Claire felt she wanted to.

It had been an odd circumstance. Locket's mother had come into the room after the lesson, looking rather harried. There was something about her that was different these days. She spent most of the time locked up in her room, it seemed, as she was now almost always home when Claire came for Locket's lesson. And she had lost so much weight she was gaunt.

She started when she saw Claire.

"Oh, Mrs. Pendleton," she said. "How are you?"

"Fine, thank you." Claire started to put away her things. It was the end of the hour. Locket had scampered off as soon as Claire had leaned back from the piano.

"I say," Mrs. Chen began. "You wouldn't be free for dinner tonight, would you? You and your husband? I know it's terribly short notice."

Claire didn't know what to say. Her mouth opened but nothing came out.

"It would be lovely to have you. Victor and I are having a dinner party, you see..."

And then Claire did see. It was a last-minute invitation. Someone had dropped out and they needed two people without other obligations.

"I'm afraid..."

"Oh, please say you'll come," Mrs. Chen cried. "It's a nice group of people. Government officials as well, so I would think Mr. Pendleton would be interested." She dangled this before Claire.

"Well..." she said. She knew Martin would want to go.

"It's settled, then. It's at The Golden Lotus, a Cantonese restaurant in Central at eight. We have a private room."

"Thank you so much for the invitation," Claire had said.

"Do you think they'll expect us to eat caterpillars or chicken's feet?" Martin asked at home when told about their sudden plans.

"Who knows what they do," Claire said. "I won't eat anything like that." She watched Martin wet his comb and draw it through his hair.

"What shirt should I wear?" he asked.

"I don't know why we're going to this dinner, I really don't," she said, but Martin had already left the room to rummage through his shirts. She stared at her face in the mirror. She looked drawn. She powdered her nose and pinched her cheeks for color.

The dinner did not go well. It was difficult to have a conversation with people who talked on a scale Claire was unused to. And they talked about themselves so much!

They had arrived on time, so they were the first other than the Chens, who were standing in a corner having a drink.

"Oh, I'm so glad you could make it," Melody said, coming toward them. Her gaunt body was enclosed in a fantastic outfit of green silk chiffon with bell sleeves, and she had on emerald chandelier earrings and the most enormous emerald ring Claire had ever seen. She couldn't take her eyes off the stone.

"Melody," Claire said, feeling the unfamiliar name on her tongue. She had thought about what she was going to call Mrs. Chen and decided on the way to the restaurant it would be appropriate for her to call Mrs. Chen by her first name since it was a social occasion. "Melody, this is my husband, Martin Pendleton. We met briefly at the beach club."

Martin and Mr. Chen shook hands.

"I understand you're in water," Mr. Chen said. He took Martin over to get a drink from the bartender.

"Your dress is lovely," Mrs. Chen said of the simple shift Claire had also worn to the Arbogasts' party on the Peak that day ages ago, when she first met Will. "I adore white, so fresh." She seemed sincere. Her once-pretty face reminded Claire of a bony chicken, the flesh thin but sagging.

They were perfectly pleasant—ideal hosts, entertaining and engaging, introducing them to every single person who arrived, and yet Claire felt more and more uncomfortable as the night progressed.

She was seated next to a Mr. Anson Ho, who operated textile factories in Shanghai and was setting up new ones in Hong Kong. He made it very clear that the scale was large, and that the British had nothing to do with his success.

"Chinese are very entrepreneurial," he kept saying. "We will find a way to make money anywhere. The old government did not give enough chances to the local population. The British are very arrogant but they need to realize it is a new age now. The Chinese in Hong Kong need to govern themselves." He had a red, bulbous nose that suggested too many nights of Cognac. He drank his wine roughly, swirling it around in large circles, gulping it down. She nodded and smiled.

Martin was seated away from her, and was talking to an attractive Brazilian woman. He had drunk a fair amount and his gestures were becoming more animated. Around the table they spoke of Red China, the Koreas, "Rhee is playing with fire," and what was going on in Myanmar. Opposite Claire was Belle, a woman from America, a journalist, she said, and she declared the harbor in Hong Kong to be inferior to the ones in Sydney and Rio. Belle smoked theatrically and asked Claire's opinion about the harbor matter and Claire wiped her mouth with her napkin and excused herself to go to the powder room.

There, she found Melody Chen washing her hands nervously, wringing them again and again in the water, looking at herself in the mirror. She jumped when Claire came in. The ring rested on the basin.

"That's a beautiful stone," Claire said. "I've never seen anything like it."

"I have to take it off before I wash my hands," Melody said, drying her hands. "Emeralds are very fragile and I'm afraid I'll do something to it. It keeps slipping off my finger too." She picked it up gingerly and slipped it back on. "Such a bother!"

"You've lost such a lot of weight," Claire said. "Are you all right?"

"Fine, yes, fine," Melody said, not meeting her eye. "I must take better care of myself. Victor says I run around too much."

Claire didn't move although she was blocking the way to the door.

"Are you having a good time?" The Chinese woman stepped around her. "Victor and I were so glad you could join us on such short notice. We're delighted with Locket's progress—you've been a real boon to her musical education." She held the door open for a moment. "It's a nice evening, isn't it?" The door closed behind her.

Claire took one of the cloths carefully folded on the restroom shelf and wiped all the moisture off the basin. It looked pristine again.

When she returned to the table, people were reminiscing about the war and the aftermath.

"What I found extraordinary," Melody was saying, "was how, after the war, Hong Kong was so friendly then, and there was so much good feeling toward all and sundry, and then when everyone started coming across the border, that lasted awhile. But now, of course, if someone manages to come over, they're no longer greeted with such enthusiasm. There are just too many of them, and too many sad stories. Our sympathy has a time limit. You know Betty

Liu had some six relatives staying with her for a year. She finally managed to pack them off to Canada but it took some doing. She had to hire three more maids!"

"That must have made for a busy 'Arrivals and Departures' column," Belle said, speaking of the much-read column in the *Post* that marked those leaving Hong Kong by aircraft, and those who had arrived and were staying at the Gloucester.

"It's like the tide, the Chinese come and go from China to Hong Kong depending on what turns history takes," said Victor. "But nothing ever changes too much."

"Where were you?" Belle asked Melody. "Were you here when the Japanese were?"

"Oh, no," she said. "Victor saw what was coming far before it did, and he packed me off to California to stay with my college roommate, who lives in Bel Air. I was pregnant at the time."

"Very clever of him," Belle said. "But he's always been clever."

Everyone seemed to have history, as if they had all grown up together, although they hailed from all corners of the world. Their language was the same.

"Yes, I'm very lucky," Melody said. "Victor has always thought ahead." Her face was still as she said it. There was a slight pause.

"Well!" said Victor. "My prescient self thinks we should play games. Isn't that what you English love to do at dinner parties?" He directed this question to Claire. "I'm always being forced to play charades and act like a horse. For some reason, that's viewed as entertainment by your countrymen."

Claire opened her mouth but nothing came out. Everyone waited for her rejoinder. All she could think of, absurdly, was the phrase "The Communists are coming, the Communists are coming." It ran through her mind like a jaunty little ditty.

"You should be one to talk, Victor," Belle said finally, rescuing her. "I've seen you crack a monkey's head open and eat the brains, and think that's a fine way to spend the evening."

"Well said!" said a Frenchman. "Good defense is always a good offense!"

As the conversation drifted on, successfully defused by the others, Claire sat quietly, trying to tamp down the flush of pure panic that had enveloped her when everyone's attention had been mercilessly focused on her for that brief moment. She wished desperately for the evening to be over, even as she felt Melody Chen's eyes, not unsympathetic, on her, and managed a wan smile.

When she and Martin returned home, he garrulous with wine, she silent, they went to bed upon washing up and changing into their nightclothes.

"Did you find there were a lot of awkward moments tonight?" she asked.

"I didn't notice, no," he said.

She wanted to beat him then, for his dumb, unknowing nature, beat him with her fists against his stolid, ignorant chest.

He laid a questioning hand on her shoulder. She turned away and he fell quiet.

"Claire," he started.

"Martin, I'm exhausted." She cut him off. "Please."

He was silent. Then he settled into the sheets and pulled up the blanket. After a pause, a gentle "Good night, dear."

She didn't know whom she hated more at that instant: Martin or herself.

The next day she told Will about the ring, how beautiful it was. A strange look came over his face. "It is unforgettable," he said. "I've seen it before."

"Are emeralds very costly?"

"Some might say that one is without price," he said.

"You know that particular ring? Has she had it long?"

He laughed, a short, violent laugh.

"You women and your baubles. All the same."

And he refused to be drawn out further.

"I was at Edwina Storch's for lunch the other day," she told him finally. "Do you know her?"

A shadow passed over his face. They were lying in bed together.

"I've known her for a while. She's been in the colony just about longer than anybody else. She's pleasant enough, I suppose, although she managed to keep herself out of Stanley during the war under very murky circumstances. A survivor, to be sure." He paused. "Did you enjoy yourself? The din at these hen parties must be as loud as blazes what with everyone chattering away about their latest frock."

"Is that what you think we do? Talk about dresses and how to make preserves?"

"Isn't it?"

"I'll have you know," she said, "we have very serious discussions about politics and reparations for war."

"And amahs," he said, biting her shoulder. "And where to find the best leg of lamb, and how to entertain your . . ."

She covered his mouth with hers.

"Do shut up, darling," she said, thrilling to the notion of being a woman who would say such a thing.

Afterward, she turned to him.

"There was something interesting. Someone said they were going to be digging up all the people who had collaborated with the Japanese during the war and prosecuting them. Do you know anyone who did such a thing?"

"What is it with you today?" he asked. "I feel like I'm being interrogated. Where does this sudden curiosity about everything come from?"

"Don't be silly," she said. "I just want to know. They say war does awful things to people, and I wanted to know if you knew anyone who had really done terrible things and got away with it."

"No," he said. "I don't, and I'm glad of it."

"Must be awful to live with secrets like that."

"It must be," he said. "I imagine you'd want to die sometimes." He paused. "I say, I don't know if you would agree but I need to go to Macau to take care of a few matters. Would you think about going with me? Do you think you could make up an excuse to get out for a night?"

This Will, suddenly shy, touched her. It was so rare he asked something of her. He was usually not very kind to her.

Claire couldn't rest the night before the trip to Macau. She had coasted on the edge of sleep for most of the night, and when she finally got out of bed, she felt light-headed and silvery with exhaustion. She had told Martin the Ladies' Auxiliary was going bird-watching in the New Territories and making a trip out of it at a member's weekend house out in Sai Kung.

When she met Will at the terminus, she felt him look at her and imagined he found her sallow. When he wasn't looking, she pinched her cheeks and bit her lips to bring the color back.

They walked to the pier where the ferry would take them to Macau. There was a crowd forming around the entrance. Policemen were standing around, preventing people from entering. Will went to ask what was going on. He came back while Claire waited by the ticket office, nervous that she would see someone she knew.

"Very unfortunate. A man has jumped off the pier. Apparently he had just lost his job as a cook. He's being taken to the hospital now, but he's dead."

"How awful."

"Yes. It's all getting cleared up now, and they'll be resuming the service."

The sea was green and brackish. When she stepped onto the gangplank, she could see rubbish floating on the water below. Someone died there today, she thought, and could not reconcile the momentous thought with the dirty surface that had paper wrappers and orange peel floating on it.

Once on the boat, her motion sickness and nervous apprehension merged and made her unable to speak. She sat, trying to focus on one spot on the faraway horizon. Two weathered men in singlets and grimy trousers clambered around the deck, winding and unwinding the thick sea rope around various posts, and pushed the boat off the dock, chattering loudly all the while. Their skin had the texture of brown leather and their teeth were yellow and cracked as they spoke.

Around them were locals, a couple with a baby, the woman exhausted-looking, the baby wailing. Claire's stomach flipped and she looked away. The baby cried on and on, sickened by the waves. A man dressed in an undershirt read a newspaper. The front page carried a photo of two English sappers who had been lately much in the news for murdering a local woman. They had been sentenced to death yesterday, the first Europeans since the war to get such a punishment.

"Their faces are so young," she said to Will.

"They're getting what they deserve," he said. "Too much the old attitude. They think they can treat the locals like animals. It's a different world now."

"The woman was an amah at the barracks." Claire was not sure if she meant it as innocently as she said it. She had been around Will enough to know it was throwing something down.

"And?" Will said. It was the first time he had been sharp with her.

Later, he told her a story. A family had had their amah follow them while they were being interned during the war. She was to bring them extra food and supplies whenever she could to Stanley camp, which she did, in a large picnic basket. She had been with them for sixteen years, from when she was a young girl, and the family had been very kind to her, so, when they were interned she was determined to show them her loyalty. The amah brought food faithfully, every week, until one week she had not appeared. The day after she was to have come, the family received the same picnic basket. Inside was a small hand, wrapped in dirty towels. "They thought it a funny joke. Of course," he said, "the truly sadistic Japanese were the exception, but they were all we could think about and all we ever remember. We never knew what happened, whether she had offended someone or done something wrong or was just in the wrong place at the wrong time."

The story was his apology. She knew he didn't owe her one. This was how she knew his affection.

At Macau Station there was a portrait of the governor, Commodore Esparteiro, with mustache and white hat, waiting to greet the visitors.

"He looks very distinguished," Claire said.

They stepped outside passport control to instant chaos. Clamoring men pressed up against the steel fences, waving their hands, shouting.

"Taxi, taxi." "Car, car, drive you."

Will went off to the side and negotiated with one quickly in Cantonese. When he spoke the language of the locals, the unfamiliar sounds coming from his familiar mouth, she felt her insides tighten, something more than desire. The driver looked at her, understood instantly. He leered, showing brown, chipped teeth. She looked away and let Will put his arm over her, he instinctively knowing what had just transpired.

"Let's go now," she said, grateful for his protection.

"Almost done," he said, and finished up the bargaining.

In the taxi, the air was thick and it was unbearably hot. Will rolled down the windows. As the car picked up speed, the wind was filled with particles that hit her face, but it seemed churlish to complain at this, the beginning of their romantic escapade.

Here I am, she thought, a woman on an illicit holiday in the Far

East with her lover. She looked out at the people on the street. They didn't know. Her secret was safe with them, their blank Oriental faces, their busy lives unencumbered with her transgressions.

They got out of the taxi at the Hotel Lusitania, off the Largo do Senado.

"This is the center of town," Will said. "And that over there is Sao Paolo, the white stone façade of an old Jesuit church. It's just the front that's left."

"Was it the war?"

"No, a fire in the 1800s. We'll go there later. You can still see all the reliefs and carvings. Quite beautiful."

The lobby was shabby but grand. Will seemed to know his way around.

"Have you been here often?"

"I used to come a fair amount," he said. "But not in the recent past."

They were shown up to their room by a Chinese bellboy, and when the door closed behind him, they looked at each other, shy once again.

"You look different here," she said.

"Yes," he said.

In the waning light of the day, sun streaking through the dusty window, they reacquainted themselves with each other, their displaced bodies somehow new, somehow more thrilling.

Afterward he said, "It's almost like we're an old married couple, coming away to a new place together."

"It's nice," she said. His tenderness was new and it unnerved her.

"It is."

"What is it you have to do here?" she asked.

"I have to pay my respects to someone," he said.

"Am I to come?"

"If you wish." He twirled her hair around his fingers. "It doesn't matter."

• • •

They took a taxi to a cemetery. Will paid the driver and got out. Paint peeled off a dilapidated, vacant guardhouse. A large tin sign with garish red Chinese characters teetered precariously above it.

"A cemetery!" she said. "You know how to treat a girl on holiday."

"Do you know anything about how the Chinese bury their dead?" he said, ignoring her.

"No," she said. "Is it very different from our way?"

"Yes." He consulted a map on the wall and traced his finger along a route. "Here we go."

The air seemed thicker here. Claire didn't want to breathe in, for fear that the essences of the dead would enter into her. She had grown more superstitious despite herself during her time in Hong Kong. In the cemetery, there were tombstones—smallish gray stones with English and Chinese characters interspersed—and paths intricately intercut among the graves, with rough stone steps leading up a hill.

She read the tombstones as they passed.

" 'Here lies William Walpole, brother of Henry.' No other family, I suppose. He died in 1936 at the age of forty-three. And this one, 'Margaret Potter, beloved.' I like that one. I think I would want something simple on my tombstone, don't you?"

Will spoke as if she had not said anything.

"It was very difficult after the war, you know, to catalog the dead. For the most part, they did mass graves. But it was very hard on the families. Not having the body of their loved ones to bury."

"The ceremony is what comforts, a little, at least, I would think."

"Yes, these rituals came about for a reason. People need something to focus on, to focus their grief on, and to keep busy. All over the world, rituals are part of death. It makes you hopeful for humans, that they have something in common."

"In civilized times," Claire said. "People are different when lives are at stake, not death."

Will looked up, surprised.

"Yes," he said. "In civilized times. At other times, all bets are off."
He grinned.

"My savage mistress," he said. "You are magnificent today."

"Can I ask what we're looking for?"

"An old friend," he said.

They stopped at the top.

"Chinese like their graveyards to be built on hills. They think it's more auspicious, and being the class-conscious society they are, they are consistent even in death: the top of the heap is still the top of the heap, as it were."

The gravestones had given way to small structures, some quite elaborate, with turrets and gates and carved doors, resembling small residences or temples. Some had porcelain urns underneath.

"Do those contain ashes or bones?" she asked.

"Bones," Will said. "The skull is laid on top."

He was looking carefully at each little house as he passed. Suddenly he stopped.

"Here we go," he said.

It was whitewashed stucco, with a wooden door that had an iron knocker in the shape of a dragon. Above the door was a sign with gold Chinese characters.

"We didn't bring anything," Claire said.

"We're not here to give," Will said. "We're here to take."

He pushed the door open and stood outside. He seemed to be waiting for something.

"Will!" Claire said, scandalized. "You're disturbing the dead!"

"I'm quieting them," he said, and went inside.

WHAT SHE REMEMBERED later of Macau was vague. The heat, of course, a good Portuguese restaurant with wooden benches and crumbling plaster walls, hot, crusty bread, carafes of red wine, something called African chicken, and the *dan taat,* the glossy yellow egg tarts. "You say pataca, I say potato," he sang to her, changed in this little colony. The cemetery, coming back to the hotel, and Will on edge throughout. The interior of the little shrine had been cool and dark, but with the pungent odor of incense. They had knocked up flurries of dust when they entered.

"This is where Dominick is," he had said.

"Who is Dominick?"

"A man who was, I think, misunderstood. Not least of all by me. At least, that's what I think when I am being my most charitable self. But a sad story. In the end, his family didn't want anything to do with him, and so he is buried here by himself, not with his family in Hong Kong. He wasn't from Macau but this is where he ended up. An unwilling exile."

"Did he die during the war?"

"Something like that. Maybe because of the war?" Will raised his voice in a question. "Who knows. It wasn't that simple." He ran his fingers along the dusty altar.

"In the end, it doesn't matter though, does it. Here he lies, and all he's done and all he did is forgotten by most."

Then he spat on the coffin.

He had taken something from the little mausoleum, something he put in his pocket so casually she dared not ask what it was. But after that, they did nothing else unusual: they ate good meals, napped after tiffin, had champagne at the hotel bar, walked around and looked at Macau, so she assumed that was what he had come for. He reverted to his old sarcastic self. They came back to Hong Kong and he did not mention what had happened at the cemetery again.

May 13, 1953

SHE WENT to the Chens' the next week and found Locket missing.

"She gone somewhere!" cried one of the servants. "Don't know!" But the girl didn't seem very concerned.

She sat in the room for half an hour before going to the powder room. As she washed her hands, she saw Melody Chen through the sheer curtain. She was sitting outside in the garden, writing a letter and weeping. Quietly, Claire gathered her things and left.

The next week, Yu Ling brought the newspaper to the breakfast table. The main story of the day was the queen's list. Victor Tsing Yee Chen.

"Look, Martin," she said. "Victor Chen's got himself an OBE."

"Really?" Martin said, impressed. "They're not handing those out by the boatload."

"Yes, and it has his history." She scanned the column. "Did you know his grandfather was instrumental in opening up trade between China and the world?"

"Well, you'll have to give him my congratulations when you go to their house. Is today your lesson day?"

"It is but I rarely see him," she said. "There's usually no one in the house except the child and the servants."

"Well, I'm sure it's a proud day for him."

"I never knew they gave such things to foreigners," she said.

But when she went to the Chens', she ended up losing her temper with Locket. It had been a terrible lesson.

"Locket, if you don't practice, you will never improve," she said as she stood up and put on her jacket. Her head was throbbing from the atonal pounding Locket had produced. There had been long silences as Locket strained to read the notes she had clearly not looked at since the last lesson.

"Yes, Mrs. Pendleton," Locket said as she pushed back from the piano.

"And it's a waste of my time and yours for you to have a lesson and then not touch the piano until the next lesson."

Locket giggled and covered her mouth. She had the irritating Oriental habit of laughing nervously when in uncomfortable situations.

"I don't know if it's worth it to teach you." Claire was getting more and more agitated. The girl had stumbled over the simplest exercises and had no instinctive ability to read music. And she with a Steinway!

"I'm sorry, Mrs. Pendleton." Locket was already by the door.

"And it's extremely rude for you to stand by the door as if you are waiting for me to leave."

Victor Chen poked his head in.

"What's going on here?" His voice was not friendly.

"I haven't been practicing, Baba," said Locket. "And Mrs. Pendleton was telling me I should."

"But what was the talk about manners?"

Claire's mouth opened but nothing came out.

"Mrs. Pendleton said it is rude for me to stand by the door," Locket said.

"She did, did she?" He looked at Claire. "You think it's rude for Locket to stand by the door?"

"I do," she said finally. "I feel as if I'm being rushed out the door."

"Locket, you can go to your room now. I'm sure you have studying to do," he said without looking at the girl. She ducked out gratefully.

"Did you enjoy yourself at dinner the other night?" he said from the doorway, apropos of nothing. "The company was good?"

She nodded. Then she remembered.

"Congratulations," she said. "On the OBE. Your family must be very proud."

Victor Chen walked right into the room and up next to Claire as if he hadn't heard her. He put his head close to Claire's, as if he were about to tell her a secret. She flinched even before he spoke.

"I hear you're spending time with Truesdale," he whispered. He put his hand behind her head and drew it closer, gently, intimately. "Is it love?"

The violence in his voice was palpable. She started back, stumbling a little on the edge of the carpet, and then grabbed blindly at her bag.

"Do give him my regards," Victor called, as she backed out of the room. "And be sure to ask him if he's going to come back to work anytime soon. We haven't seen him lately."

She ran out of the room and out the door, into the sudden heat.

"And ask him about Trudy!" Victor Chen's voice filled the hallways of his house. "I'm sure you should know about that." He laughed, a loud, bitter gasp.

She walked quickly down the path, past her bus stop, past the other buildings, in a panic. Her head was filled with a hot, white sound that slowly diminished as she got farther away. Almost imperceptibly, the sounds of the day, cars passing by, the occasional bird cry, began to filter through again and she slowed her pace. She was drenched in perspiration and her blouse was stuck to her back. She pulled it loose and tried to air out her body. The heat roared up her back and exploded in her head.

"Claire?"

The voice came from a distance.

"Claire?"

"Will?" she said, struggling through the dark.

"It's Martin," said her husband. "Who's Will?"

"Martin," she said. "Where am I?" It was now too bright to see. Her head throbbed from the sudden change from black to white.

"You're home now. The Chens' amah found you on the street and brought you home. Yu Ling called me at the office. You woke up, had some water, and went back to sleep."

"Did I faint?"

"Must have. How do you feel? You're white as a ghost."

She shut her eyes. "Awful." She remembered. "Oh! Victor..." she started, then shut her mouth.

"Victor Chen?" asked Martin.

"...was so kind," she said. "I saw him at the end of the lesson."

"Well, that's good, then," Martin said. Then he remembered. "Did you congratulate him?"

"I forgot," she said. "I just saw him a moment."

"Oh." He paused. "Well, I'll let you get some rest. Do you want anything?"

"No, I should be fine. Just need a moment."

"The thing is..." He lingered. "There's this project..."

"Go," she said. "No good you hanging around here. I'm feeling better already."

He pressed his lips on her forehead.

"Darling," he said, and left.

The next day, Melody Chen rang as Claire was about to leave the house.

"I heard you fainted outside our house," she said. "I just wanted to call to make sure you're all right."

"That's very kind," Claire said. Then she didn't know what else to say.

"So, is everything all right?" Melody repeated.

"Oh, yes," she said. "Sorry. I didn't..." she trailed off. She remembered Victor Chen's breath hot on her face. She remembered seeing Melody weeping through the window of the powder room.

"And you're feeling better now?" Melody asked into the silence.

"Yes." Claire remembered the dinner. "And thank you so much for inviting us to the dinner. We had a very nice time."

"Oh, of course." Melody Chen clearly had no idea what she was talking about. She had already forgotten about the dinner. "I'm so pleased."

The conversation had started and stopped so many times Claire felt disoriented.

"Well, thank you very much for calling. It's very kind. I was just on my way out the door...."

"Of course," Melody said. "I'm glad you're feeling better."

She was meeting Will at the botanical gardens above Central, a steep, winding maze of tropical flora and animals. She had called him for an emergency rendezvous, but he had sounded quite unconcerned with her urgency.

"I just had a call from Melody Chen," she said when she saw him waiting for her on the corner.

"Hello to you too." He snaked an arm around her and kissed her hard on the mouth. Possessive. She looked around instinctively. The animals lazed inside their cages, too hot to move.

"The monkeys don't know you're married," he said.

Sometimes she hated his nonchalance.

"Melody Chen called me," she repeated.

"Something with little Locket? A situation with the Steinway?" he asked, not really interested.

"Something like that," she said. Suddenly, she was afraid of what Will would do if he found out what Victor Chen had said to her. Or maybe she was afraid of what he would not do.

"Let's go back to my place," he said lazily, turning away, sure she would follow. And her insides folded, like always, as she did exactly that.

• • •

The sound of water splashing, Will humming a song in the tub, the door slightly ajar, a humid milky-sweet fragrance escaping the bathroom. Claire sat at his desk, heart pounding. She opened the drawer to his desk quietly. A bank book. She opened it—a modest balance. Some letters, tied together with red postal string, with names and addresses she did not recognize. London postmarks, scribbly writing. Some stamps, a pen, a book of matches from the Gripps. And then, a photograph. Four people, in evening dress, laughing, with cigarettes and drinks in hand, at a party: a picture of privilege. Will, Melody Chen, and another man and woman, both Asian or Eurasian, Will the only European. The woman who was not Melody (Trudy?) was very striking; she dominated the photograph, although she was slight, in a slim, short dress, with her vivid face and short, simple hair that somehow emphasized her femininity. It was hard to tell who was with whom; they all were linked together familiarly. Claire traced Will's face with her finger. He looked so boyish, so innocent, his face all smooth cheek and bright eyes above his dinner jacket, bow tie loosened and hanging.

Will came into the room, wrapped in a towel, rubbing his head with another. He stopped when he saw her in front of the open drawer.

"What are you doing rummaging through my things?" he said.

She couldn't read his tone. She decided to be unapologetic.

"What's this?" She held up the photograph.

"A picture," he said.

"I can see that. It's of you and Melody and some other people."

"Yes," he said. "It is."

"Did you used to see her socially? Who are the others?" She tried hard to make her tone conversational.

"Sometimes, Claire, you can be so provincial." He let out an exasperated whistle. "But yes, I'll say it for you. I used to see Melody at parties, not just in the backseat of the car I drive."

"But it's so strange," Claire said. "What happened?"

"Do you feel my fall in social status? Does it bother you?" he said. He was mocking her, mean.

"I just want to know about you!" she cried. "Why must you make everything so ugly?"

"There's a lot there, Claire," he said. "You don't want to know."

"How can you be so sure?"

"Claire," he said. "Just stick to pilfering from the Chens and leave the larger stuff be."

She felt immolated from within. Her face stung with a blush that rose so quickly she felt almost faint. She hadn't been sure he had known. She had stopped the stealing long ago but he knew how to turn the knife. She slapped him, hard. He didn't move. As she got her clothes on and left, he stood still, watching her. The silence between them was so long it waxed and waned in its intensity, and then felt ridiculous. The other questions—Who is the other woman? Why does Victor Chen care?—so big she could not bring herself to ask them. She closed the door behind her quietly. Slamming it would have seemed childish. She hated him, did she not?

On the street, she didn't know where to go. She hailed a taxi to go into town. It was still bright daylight, and in Central, everyone seemed to have a purpose to their walk. She got out on Queen's Road and wandered among the frame shops and jewelry stores. She stopped in front of a window. The display glittered out at her, necklaces and rings and bracelets, even a small diamond tiara. The Chinese were quite showy with their jewels. In the reflection from the glass, her face floated in front of her, an Englishwoman, attractive but wan. Someone whose lover had just been cruel, someone who didn't know what to do about it. She tried to position her face so that a diamond necklace would be reflected around her neck. She crouched, to make it the right height.

Then she stood up, straightened her blouse, and walked to the Star Ferry, where she would wait for the bus that would take her home to Martin.

May 20, 1953

When Claire went to the Chens' the next Thursday, she noted a driver sleeping on a bench in the garden, newspaper over his head, the maids chattering gaily as they washed the windows, and breathed a sigh of relief that Victor Chen was apparently not at home.

"Missee all right? Fall down!" the maid who had answered the door asked.

"Yes, thank you very much." She noticed for the first time how this servant had a generous face, with bright, wide eyes and a pleasant mouth. "It's very kind of you to ask."

The woman smiled uncertainly and led her to the piano room, where Locket was waiting.

"I heard you had an accident last week, Mrs. Pendleton. Are you all right?" Locket was leaning over a tray of biscuits, crumbling one into her mouth. "Would you like some lemonade?"

"That's very kind of you, Locket. I am feeling much better, thank you." The little girl was finally learning some manners, she thought.

"Mummy said you must be expecting!" Locket giggled. "And Daddy laughed and laughed."

Claire's back stiffened.

"Locket, have you practiced?" she said, with frost in her voice.

Locket looked up, startled at the sudden change.

"I had a rehearsal on Monday for *The Mikado* . . ." she started.

"Never mind," Claire said. "Let's just begin."

After the lesson, Melody Chen came by the room and asked Claire to stay for a cup of tea to talk about Locket's progress. She walked Claire to the living room and excused herself to go see about the maids.

The Chens had a mantel full of photographs, in silver frames. Very English, Claire had thought when she first saw them, except the photographs were filled with Orientals. She got up to look at them more closely. Mostly Victor and Melody, with various family members and older people, a few of Locket by herself, and then a woman, in a swimsuit at the beach, holding a cigarette and sticking her tongue out at the camera. It looked like a picture out of a fashion magazine, and as Claire peered closer she got a shock as she realized it was the same woman in the photograph with Will and Melody at his house. She was Eurasian, whippet-thin, very glamorous, with a flowered bathing cap. Her face stuck out, angular and attractive.

"That's my cousin Trudy," said Melody, coming up from behind with a small glass of water.

"She's very beautiful," said Claire, careful not to sound too eager.

"Not beautiful," Melody said immediately. "Not beautiful. She was half-Portuguese, so Eurasian, you know, and the Europeans always found her attractive. But Chinese don't like half-breeds, really." Claire noted the casual slur, was surprised by it. Melody was usually so refined.

"But everyone, absolutely everyone, noticed her. She was very famous in Hong Kong during her day. Some might say infamous. She brought her terrier to a dinner party once as her companion. Had him in a bow tie. She sat him at a seat and everything, until he urinated on it. Livy Wong was livid!"

"Well, she looks like she knows how to have a good time."

"Yes, I always think that if she were still around, she'd be the first woman in the colony to wear a bikini, and she'd wear it to a picnic at the governor's house or something wildly inappropriate like that. She was that type of girl. Scandalous, but she got away with it usually. Fearless."

"Is she not?" Claire asked delicately. "Around anymore, I mean."

Melody looked away, sipped at her glass, made a grimace.

"No, not anymore. She was a casualty of war, I guess you would say."

"It's difficult to believe," Claire said, looking at the photograph. "She looks like she was full of life."

"Almost to bursting," Melody said. "Her father was my father's cousin, so she was my second cousin."

"Were you close?"

"Oh, in a way," Melody said. "I think she probably found me quite boring. We were very different. And we had a lot of cousins running around Hong Kong. We're a big family. She was close to another cousin of ours—Dominick—but he died during the war too. I would say they were like best friends. They were quite well known, the two of them. The Terrible Two."

"And..." Claire didn't know where to begin. But it didn't matter. Melody Chen was in the mood to talk.

"And she gave me this beautiful emerald ring, one that I always wear on special occasions because it's so spectacular." She stretched out her hand as if she had it on.

"I saw it, at the dinner party you had. It's really something. That was very generous of her."

"I like to have something to remember her by," said Melody. "Isn't that what family's all about?" The servants came in with a silver salver of drinks.

"Tea?"

"Yes, please, with lots of milk."

Melody made her a cup, but didn't have any herself. She sipped at her small glass.

"Victor treats me like some fragile flower," she said suddenly. "But I'm not as weak as he thinks I am. You know, he shipped me off to California. I kept asking him questions. I think I was irritating to him."

"I'm sure you were no such thing," said Claire.

"And I came back, and everything had changed," she said faintly.

The afternoon stretched on, with Melody Chen talking in circles, seeming as if she had all the time in the world to chat with her daughter's piano teacher. She had not mentioned Locket or her progress, even once.

"Have you ever thought back about someone who died?" Melody asked. "How it was when they were alive. Sometimes, when I think about Trudy and Dominick, I feel like I saw a black spot hanging over their heads, as if they were marked and I just couldn't fully see it at the time. I feel like they were doomed from the beginning, that they had this specter hanging over them." Melody stopped, and her eyes became glossy, wet.

"I still can't believe Trudy's dead. Her father married a Portuguese woman, and she was so peculiar. Do you know she disappeared when Trudy was a child? They put it out that it was an abduction but my mother always thought she got tired of the whole thing and just got on a boat for America.

"Her father was related to my family. Who knew he would have such a head for business? I think he did better than anyone, actually."

"Is he still alive?" Claire asked.

"Of course not," Melody said. "He died along with all the other wretched detritus of the war, those who were not on the right side of things, who refused to play along."

Claire nodded.

"So you do have someone close who died?" Melody asked again. "I know it's a silly question after the war, but still, some haven't been touched. Some were lucky."

"Yes," said Claire. "Not anybody close though." An uncle, met once, a picture of him at her eighth birthday party. Various acquaintances during the war. The closest had been a girl from primary school, who had gone on holiday to Wales and drowned. The school had given everyone the day off, and when the students came back, many had black ribbons tied around their arms. Claire had not known to do that, and she had felt excluded, as if everyone had known something she had not been privy to.

"Do you know Reggie and Regina Arbogast?" asked Melody, switching subjects again.

"I've been to their house but I wouldn't say I know them," said Claire. She was just trying to keep up with the odd, meandering conversation.

"They're having a coronation party. They're having two actually. The first is a bit smaller, more intimate, and they're listening to the coronation on the radio. Then they're having the reels flown in from England, and they're going to have a television-watching party for a larger group. I think that one is more of a cocktail party. It should be fun. Do you have plans for the coronation?"

"Not as of yet," Claire said.

"I'm putting something together so you and Will must come," Melody said suddenly.

"You mean Martin," said Claire, taken aback.

"Of course," Melody said smoothly. "So sorry."

"Of course," repeated Claire.

Melody seemed to be waiting for something else. The afternoon light had dissipated and Claire could no longer see the motes of dust floating on the rays of sunlight that had streamed through the window.

"I think it's late," she said. It had been the oddest, most disjointed afternoon she had ever experienced. "I should be going."

At that moment, Will came through the door.

"You!" Melody called to him in a wavering voice. "You're stirring everything up!" Her tone was light, but for the first time, Claire understood, the knowledge blooming in her head like a rapidly spreading ink stain: The Chens were afraid of Will. They had taken him on to keep him close, had paid him money for a job he didn't do, because they had no choice. She saw her lover through a new lens. He was the benevolent one. He was the dispenser of their destiny.

"I need to see Victor," he said, without acknowledging Claire.

"He's not here," Melody said.

"Is he expected back soon?"

"Don't patronize me, Will," Melody said abruptly. "We've known each other long enough."

"You have nothing to do with this, Mrs. Chen."

"Oh, stop the charade, Will," Melody cried. "The *Mrs.* and the *Mr.* and the *Sir,* and the 'Where would you like to go today?' Were you laughing at us the entire time? And what you've done. And poor, poor Trudy."

Claire grasped that Melody was quite drunk, and that she had been drinking a kind of spirit, not what Claire had assumed was water.

"Don't mention her, Melody. You have no right to ever say her name again."

"And you! You have one?" The Chinese woman's voice grew shrill. "As if you have any right at all. The woman you pretended to love!"

Will grew white with anger.

"Melody," he said. "That is utter rubbish." He controlled himself with difficulty. "This is not for you to do. You stay out of it."

"Will," Melody said. "This is all spinning out of control. Victor is furious. You have to stop what you're doing. I'm telling you as someone who was once your friend. You have to stop it."

"It's too late, Melody," Will said. "There's nothing I can do now."

While they spoke, Claire let herself out, quietly, and stood in the corner of the driveway, heart pounding, waiting.

When Will walked out, he looked angry, his hands shoved deep into his pockets.

"Who is Trudy?" she asked, stepping forward.

He started.

"Not now," he said. "Not now, Claire. Come with me. Let's go for a bathe."

May 20, 1953

THE SHARKS WERE BACK. They had been sighted off Stanley Beach and Shek O as well. A local man had been dipping his hands in the water while on a diving platform in South Bay, and had a finger nipped off. He had sat in blind panic waving his hand about while screaming until a woman on the beach had heard his cries and they sent a boat out to get him.

Claire and Will liked to bathe at Shek O but they could only go in the early morning or in the late afternoon during the week, when it was unlikely that anyone they knew would see them. On this day, they drove in silence to Will's flat and picked up some bathing clothes, drove to the beach, and parked the car. They were in luck. The beach was empty.

The sand in Hong Kong was gritty. Will had told her of beaches in India where the sand was like sifted flour, so fine you could almost inhale it. But at Shek O, when the tide went out, there were tidal pools filled with hermit crabs, and in the past they had caught them and Claire had brought them back home and put them in a bowl with seawater until they had started to smell fetid.

"You are a mermaid," Will said, finally breaking the silence. He was sitting on the straw blanket they had unfurled on the beach, watching her as she undressed.

She still got tongue-tied around him, unable to respond to his teasing. She folded her clothes and put them in her basket. He stood up.

"Let's swim to the dock," she said, then remembered. "Do you think there are sharks around?"

"The unfortunate man from last week would say it is a certainty," he said, getting up.

"Should we bathe, then? I've been longing to all day."

"How adventurous are you feeling?" he asked. They were both facing the water, she slightly behind him.

"Never very, but it's so hot." She put her hands flat on his back. He had taken off his shirt and his back was already slick with perspiration. "Do you ever get used to it? The heat?"

"No, you just live in it." He reached behind and took her hands off his back. He did things like that a lot, gestures that felt like rebukes, ways to keep a distance between them. She pretended not to notice and moved away, walked into the water up to her knees.

"And the water's never cold here either, is it?" she called back to him. "More like a bath."

"Yes, Claire," he said. "Hong Kong is not England."

She looked toward the horizon. This day had had a jerky quality—things happening that were out of control, that she didn't know how to react to or how to feel about.

"Why so rude?" she said, but he didn't hear her, or pretended not to.

He plunged into the water.

"Last one there loses."

"Wait," she called. "I don't . . ." But he was already in the waves, swimming a fast crawl toward the diving platform. She hesitated but, watching him grow smaller and smaller, knew she would have to follow.

"Damn you, Will Truesdale," she said.

The water had two levels—the warm layer above, heated by the sun, and, somewhere below waist level, the frigid water of the deep. She tried to swim in the warm part, frightened by the cold, but her legs sometimes sank into it.

She did a leisurely breaststroke and tried not to think of sharks.

Ahead of her Will pulled up onto the diving platform. His body glistened in the sun. His was an older body, but still lean. He evoked desire in her, so strange when her body was surrounded by water. She swam on, pushing away the panic, the desire.

By the time she got to the platform, she was furious.

"I told you I didn't want to swim out here."

"You didn't."

"Only because you were so far out already you couldn't hear me." She sat away from him, on the bobbing disk. "You gave me no choice."

"Don't be angry, kitten."

She didn't answer, just twisted her hair into a ponytail and squeezed the water out. The drops puddled onto the wood and disappeared into a large dark stain.

"Do you remember the first time we were on a platform?" He was trying to make amends. "Doesn't it seem so long ago?"

On the beach, a local couple appeared, set up a blanket and an umbrella.

"It does, yes," she allowed. Then, "You should know I can go. You could lose me."

He nodded, understanding, capitulating for the moment.

"You don't need me anymore, Claire, if you ever did."

"Yes," she said.

They sat together peaceably now, the pressure let out. The weather was perfect, the sun slowly sinking toward the horizon, a cool breeze coming off the water.

"Will," she said. "What is going on?"

When he didn't answer, she said, "You know what I'm talking about. Everyone is behaving in such a queer manner, and you're at the heart of it."

He lay down and shut his eyes.

"You know, the most absurd things happened during the war," he said. "Do you know that while we were interned, the Japanese administration presented us with a bill for accommodation and food? Can you imagine? And we couldn't very well throw it back in their face, so we had to tell them we would write promissory notes that would be honored by our government when everything had been worked out. They wanted us to pay for the rotten vegetables and cup of rice we got every week."

"But now?" she asked.

"I'm getting there," he said with an edge to his voice. "Just listen." He began again.

"And so we danced with them, our captors, although it was always a fine line between being good and being proud. We always hoped. There were small things like growing the vegetables in the garden in a V so that when it sprouted up, it would be a nice surprise and an encouragement. Childish, you know. One never gets used to being a prisoner, although we got used to our daily routine.

"And people were petty, of course. And others were unbelievably kind and generous. You had all sorts of behavior. The Japs too. There were good ones and bad ones."

"There was a woman," Claire said. "Trudy."

"Yes, Trudy." He stopped. "Trudy. I think you would have liked her."

"We are different," Claire said. She didn't know why, as she said it, she felt that she was being kind to Will.

Will snorted. "Yes, you are. That's an understatement. But you would have liked her, I know."

"You were with her."

He hesitated. "Yes."

"And..."

"No longer. She's gone," he said.

"How?"

"I failed her," he said. "She wanted me to come out and live on the outside with her. She was on the outside because she wasn't British. She got me a pass. But I refused."

"You didn't want to leave the people inside the camp?" Claire asked.

"Yes," he said. "That was part of it. I was helpful inside the camp and could get things done. Certainly no one wanted me to leave. But—" He stopped.

"Yes?" Claire prompted.

"But I think I was afraid too," he said softly. "If I went outside, it was a whole new world and I'd have to learn the new rules. I would have to start as a beginner, disadvantaged, get my bearings all over again.

"I was tired," he said simply. "And I didn't want more change. It was hard in the camp but if you obeyed the rules, you weren't bothered. Outside it was chaos. Trudy had things snatched from her hands as she walked down the street. Once it was food and the boy crammed some bread in his mouth as he ran. He was starving and couldn't run properly. He had no shoes and no shirt. I think all he had was the trousers he had on. There was starvation and desperation and misery. She told me about it. There was no filter. It was real."

He looked at Claire.

"And she died," Claire said, almost without knowing it.

"Yes, she died."

"How?"

"Some would say by the hand of her benefactor," he said. "A man who gave her many things, and took them away when he wanted. If I had been outside with her, he would have controlled me too."

A mosquito buzzed between them, floating in the damp air.

"He made her do awful things. He found out she was smuggling messages into the camp along with the food, so he made her bring tainted food the next time. Not enough to kill, just sicken, and there was nothing in the way of medical supplies, so people suffered. That's the kind of bastard he was. I had to tell her the next time she came, and her face just crumpled. She hadn't known. I believe that still. She hadn't known but she couldn't do anything. She didn't know if he would do it again, or if the food would be all right the next time, and we were in such desperate need that we just took it and ate it."

"How do you know he did it?" Claire asked. "Maybe it was just a mistake."

"Oh, yes," Will said. "We knew. He asked her after she returned how her friends were doing, and he laughed in her face. She only told me that afterward."

"And Victor?"

"Victor Chen." He laughed. "Oh, yes, my esteemed employer."

"But what?" she asked. "What of him?"

"What of Victor Chen?" Will said. "What of Victor Chen? How to begin?"

He slapped Claire suddenly on the arm.

"Got it," he said, lifting up his hand to show a bloodied black spot, a tangle of tiny insect legs and antennae. "Damn bloodsuckers."

He leaned over and rinsed his hands in the sea. He lifted them up. Drops of water sparkled and dripped from his fingers. He looked at them contemplatively.

"Victor Chen murdered Trudy," he said.

April 10, 1943

"A GRATEFUL OTSUBO is what I want," Trudy is saying. "If he's grateful, who knows what he'll do. Maybe he'll get you repatriated! But you can't leave. I don't want to live in England."

She never asks him again, not directly. She whispers, implies, ingratiates. She dangles rewards before him and then, finally, hatefully, hints at what may befall her if she does not come through for the man.

"He wants one big payday, you know," she says. "He is a simple man. He wants to go back to his country, buy some land in the country, and build a cottage for himself and his family. He wants to bring his parents out, take care of them. He's really a family man."

As she outlines this outlandish idea, he nods, pretends to listen, possibly agree.

"And he's getting a wee bit impatient, but I think he's getting close. He's found out that Reggie Arbogast is indeed one of the people who was entrusted with the location. So you should know that. He has eyes and ears everywhere and I think they're making progress. But he does get frustrated..." she trails off. "And when he's frustrated..."

Three weeks later, another furlough.

"I'm working on getting it weekly for you. Do you like it?" she says when she picks him up. "All the bankers are outside, I don't see why you shouldn't be. They're putting them up at the Luk Kwok and they escort them down to the office every day. I don't think they're getting better rations than us, but who knows."

He gets in the driver's seat.

"Have you seen Angeline? How is she doing?"

Trudy looks up at the sky.

"Angeline," she starts. "Angeline seems to have suffered a crisis of conscience, is that what you call it?"

"What happened?" He starts up the car.

"She has gotten all up on herself and has decided that I am not a person that she wishes to associate with. Can you imagine?" She smiles tightly. "The godmother of her child!"

"Did she give you a reason?"

"No," she says. "I went to visit her in Kowloon and her maid told me she wasn't home. She was funny about it, though, and when I walked away I looked up and saw Angeline at the window. She wasn't even trying to hide. She looked at me straight and then drew the curtains. Very grim."

"You are presuming..."

"Oh, no, darling," she says. "I know Angeline very well and she doesn't need to say anything to me for me to know exactly what she is thinking. I'm just hoping you won't come to the same conclusion. I'm going to become a pariah; I can just see it now."

He bursts with his own confession.

"Trudy, I haven't asked."

She knows immediately what he is talking about.

"Maybe the right time hasn't come up," she says.

He cannot lie to her.

"I will not ask," he says. "It just seems wrong."

"Oh! You won't even try!" A choked sound comes from her throat. "Wrong! Well, I can see that."

"And why would Arbogast tell me anyway?" he finishes lamely. "We aren't friends."

She doesn't speak again until they're at the Toa.

"Here we are," she says. "Are you hungry?"

Always the Chinese with their damn food, he thinks.

"No," he says, getting out of the car. "Are you?"

"Otsubo wants us to meet him for lunch," she says. "He's waiting upstairs."

"And you were going to tell me this when?" he says. "When I sit myself down on his lap?"

"Will!" she cries. "This is serious. Dominick has promised Otsubo he will get the information and that I will help him to get it. I wouldn't ask you if it weren't important, but ..." she trails off.

"Trudy, I can't help you," he says. "I cannot."

"Will," she says. "If you really knew what was at stake ..."

But her mouth is set. She knows this man. The question is how much she can manage the other one.

By the time they get to the room, she has shaken off her bad temper. Her moodiness is like a cloak she can take on and off at will.

"If I lose my pass because of this, you'll be the first to pay," she says lightly. She pushes the door open. "Otsubo-san! The valiant Will Truesdale is here to tell us of the wonderful resortlike conditions in Stanley. Was it coq au vin at dinner last night? And I heard you have entertainment now. The Stanley Players?" And she's off, bubbling with vivacious energy, going around the room, dispensing kisses and quixotic pronouncements, clinking ice in highballs, as if she hasn't a care in the world, as if she hadn't fixed him with a long, pleading look right before they entered.

Dominick joins them for lunch, and Will notices the way Otsubo looks at him with barely disguised contempt, and yet, now his hand lingers on Dominick's shoulder longer than necessary, he allows Dominick to serve him food, and Dominick treats him with a servile facility that sickens Will. So that's how it goes, he thinks. The sophisticate becomes the dog and the soldier becomes the master. Brute force trumps all in the end, doesn't it.

Still, this is not what concerns him. What's been eating at him since they alighted from the car and made their way to Trudy's suite is something else entirely.

What is making him uneasy is his own unwillingness to compromise and where it might be coming from—the niggling feeling that he cannot shake: that he is calling his reluctance integrity, but what it might be is simply cowardice.

May 2, 1943

ARBOGAST IS SCREAMING. Will cannot stand to hear it, cannot stand not to hear it. He is frozen, wants to clap his hands over his ears, wants to scream himself. Around Will, the adults are pale and silent, mothers rushing the children away.

Usually the guards take the unfortunate suspects away to a far-off house where they are made to sign their confessions, written long before they start to talk. But Arbogast! They had come silently, grimly, filled with purpose—two men—and seized him under his arms and dragged him to Ohta's office, just next to the officers' mess. He had gone quietly, but then the screaming started.

It has been three days since Will returned from his furlough and he has made it a point to avoid Arbogast, as if even coming close to the man will transmit his secret to him—a secret he has no intention of learning if he can help it.

He doesn't want to know anything about Arbogast. If he is the type of man to keep a secret to the end, if he is the kind of man who will value his family more than his country, or if he is the kind of man who will take a deal to better his circumstances. He wants to know nothing. Instead, he tries to ignore him—the once proud man with his swollen beriberi feet, dragging around the camp, complaining about his wife and his dysentery.

The door opens and Arbogast is brought out, bucking. Strange how violence is not as vivid in real life. There are only a few streaks of blood. Mostly the impression is that he is wet. The water torture. They take him to the outskirts now. He is still screaming but his voice is starting to fray from the exertion. Will's own throat hurts from the tearing sounds coming from Arbogast's mouth.

So this is the man he reveals himself to be, Will thinks suddenly, inappropriately, bloodlessly—a man who screams when he is in danger. He hopes he himself will be silent. But one never knows.

Johnnie is at his side suddenly. They watch the man being dragged off again.

"That poor devil," he says. "I wonder what they think he's done."

"Does it matter?" Will says.

"Not at all," Johnnie says. He glances at Will. "What a cynic you've become."

The next day, Arbogast is brought by two soldiers to his room and dumped unceremoniously on his bed, where Regina has a fit, falling and having hysterics on the floor while her husband lies, nearly unconscious, above her. His right hand is gone, the stump of his wrist wrapped in bloody rags.

Some sensible women drag Regina away and ply her with tea while the doctor is summoned. He shakes his head, powerless without any equipment, any medicine.

"What can I do?" he says. "He will live or die. That is all."

They leave him there, with the powerless doctor, his face swollen blue beyond recognition, blood from the wound soaking through layers of ripped sheets. In the morning, the other residents of D Block will complain they could get no sleep because of the old man's moaning. Arbogast, the rich businessman, has been reduced to this, and the others have been reduced to that.

The secret must be out now, Will thinks. And that should be that.

VICTOR CHEN was in a panic. Even Claire could see that, hidden away in the piano room. He was streaming from room to room, shouting at the servants, shouting at Melody, picking up the phone and banging it down again.

For the sake of the child, she tried to keep the lesson going but it was almost impossible. After a door slammed for the third time, she reached over and shut the instruction book.

"Well, Locket, what do you say?" she said.

"About what, Mrs. Pendleton?"

For the first time, Claire felt sorry for Locket. What must it be like to live in a house like this with parents like Melody and Victor? The child's face was heartbreakingly smooth, the Oriental skin almost glossy, her eyes curious hazel orbs. Claire reached over and tucked a loose strand behind Locket's ear. The maternal gesture surprised her almost as much as it did the girl herself, who gave a quick, shy smile.

"How about we finish a little early?"

"All right, Mrs. Pendleton." Locket got up quickly, bumping the piano, and spilled the glass of water that had been sitting on top. "Oops," she giggled. "Mummy says I'm very clumsy."

"You just have to be more careful," Claire said. "All children are careless."

"Mummy says I give her a headache," Locket said more somberly. "I'm not to disturb her in the afternoons anymore so that's why she's got me signed up for so many lessons."

"I'm sure she wants you to grow up to be an accomplished lady with many interests." Claire patted her head.

"We're having a party!" Locket brightened. "For the queen's coronation. Daddy got a big honor from the queen, you know."

"Yes, I heard. You must be very proud."

"I'm getting a new dress. It's a tangerine silk taffeta with guipure lace," the girl recited carefully. "Mummy had the lace flown in from France and it's the only one of its kind in Hong Kong."

"That sounds lovely, Locket." The girl beamed, then looked uncertain.

"Of course," Locket faltered, confessed, "it's just the leftover from Mummy's dress. She had some extra so she gave it to me so I could have it put on mine."

"I'm sure you'll both look a treat," Claire said.

The reason Victor Chen was in such a state, Claire surmised, was what had appeared in the paper today. It had been relegated to page 7, pushed back by the relentless, breathless coverage of Princess Elizabeth and the latest details of her procession to Westminster Abbey, but it was still there—a small column about the formation of a War Crimes Committee, to be headed by a Sir Reginald Lythgoe, based on new information that had come to light. Will had pointed it out to her earlier in the afternoon.

"It's bloody unfathomable!" she heard Victor shout into the phone. "It's a witch hunt. The war's been over for a decade and they want to dredge up this rubbish. You tell Davies I won't forget this. It's pure anti-Chinese sentiment. They can't stand to see someone do well, and the OBE was just the last... That wretched old woman was playing Chopin on the Government House piano the entire war, drinking scotch and dining on veal, under my protection! She has no right..."

Someone shut a door so his voice was muffled.

Locket smiled.

"So I can go?"

"Yes," Claire said. "Run along."

Claire let herself out quietly, without running into Melody or Victor. She had an appointment with Edwina Storch.

• • •

The old woman had rung her up last week, asking to get together for a cup of tea. They decided on the Librarians' Auxiliary in Mid-Levels, and Claire had arranged to meet her on the next Thursday, today.

The bus stopped outside the building on Tregunter Path and Claire got out. Miss Storch was just entering the clubhouse. Claire stopped to watch her. She had on a pink hat, under which her salt-and-pepper bun peeked. Her bottom was wide and encased in a matching pink cotton skirt that went to the knee. Varicose veins trailed down her thick calves, and as she walked with her cane, she swayed ever so slightly from side to side. She stopped to catch her breath outside the door, then stepped up and went inside.

Behind her, Claire waited, then walked to the door and pushed it open herself. Inside, it was dark and cool, fans swaying as they turned, and heavy damask curtains shielding the furniture against the bright sun outside. Claire squinted, trying to make out the shapes in the room.

"Hullo," said Edwina Storch. Claire jumped. Edwina Storch had taken off her spectacles and was rubbing them with the hem of her jacket. "They steam up in this humidity, you know."

"Hello, Miss Storch," she said. "I was right behind you on the path but it was just too hot to rush."

The old woman did not reiterate her past desire to be addressed by her first name.

"Yes, it's terrible out there, isn't it," she said, pulling out a white handkerchief and wiping her forehead. "Does something to the character but I haven't pinned it down yet. It's something that people who live here over twenty years develop but I can't put a name to it."

"The heat?" Claire said.

"Yes. Most of your day is spent trying to avoid it. And the endlessness of it. Always at war with the elements, instead of in harmony with them. That's us, the British colonials, battling against our circumstances, always." Miss Storch peered at Claire. She was reminded of the first time she had met her and the gaze that had almost made her faint. "Shall we sit?"

"Certainly."

Claire was unsure as to why Edwina Storch had rung her up. The old woman moved slowly, and was treated with great respect by the staff.

"Lovely to see you again, Miss Storch," said the manageress, who had come out to greet them. "So nice that you can come into town and see us."

"Do you know Mrs. Maxwell?" Edwina asked Claire. "She's been around almost as long as I have."

They shook hands and were escorted into the dining room—more of the heavy damask curtains, a mix of old, good tables and new chairs, too shiny.

"We have your favorite currant scones today," Mrs. Maxwell said. "And the good Chinese oolong."

"Splendid," Edwina said as she lowered herself carefully into a chair. "You're too kind, Harriet. We'll both have the high tea, please."

"It's very pleasant here," Claire said. "It's my first time."

"Not too bad," Edwina said. "During the war, I spent a few nights here."

"Yes," Claire said.

The waitress came over and poured water for them into faded, scratched glasses.

"There's something sad about the Eurasian, isn't there?" Edwina Storch said, looking after the girl as she left. "Something incomplete, something wanting in them. I always feel they are searching for something to make them whole."

"Do you think so?" Claire said politely. "I find them very attractive, actually, with their beautiful skin and golden eyes and hair. When I first was in Hong Kong, I did find them odd-looking, but now I think they are just splendid."

"Hmph," snorted the old woman. "You're young and romantic. The children feel dreadful because they are not accepted by either race."

Claire had not thought Miss Storch to be so narrow-minded when her own lifestyle was not at all conventional.

As if she could sense what Claire was thinking, Miss Storch drew herself up slightly. "Mary and I have always led our lives with good Christian values!" she said. "We love all of God's creatures, even the less fortunate."

"Of course," said Claire.

The Eurasian girl came over again with a pot of tea. She set down the cups and put a strainer on each of them. Her eyes were downcast, steady on the table.

"I'll pour," said Miss Storch, dismissing her.

"You don't think she's attractive?" Claire asked. She felt an obstinate urge to pursue the matter.

"Claire," Miss Storch said. "I do not. She is unfortunate. She is lucky to have a respectable job because I am sure that her father left her mother after he had his fun with her. You know, that's how most of these situations are." She poured the hot tea into Claire's cup. Claire lifted up the milk pitcher.

"You don't pour milk into this sort of tea!" Miss Storch barked. Claire's hand hung suspended in the air, frozen. "The whole point of this tea is to have it unadulterated. Put that milk down. I don't know why they even give us milk."

Claire paused and then poured the milk into her tea.

"I prefer my tea with milk," she said.

Miss Storch stared at her, then took off her spectacles and started rubbing them again.

"So you've got some spunk," she said, inspecting her glasses. "Glad to see that."

Claire was silent.

"You're going to need it," Edwina Storch said. "There's a pretty kettle of fish going on, and from what I understand, you are in the middle of it."

"I don't understand," she said.

"Oh, I think you understand more than you let on." Miss Storch sipped her tea, made a grimace. "Too strong. They let it steep too long."

"I'll call for hot water," Claire said, and raised her hand.

"Don't bother. I've better things to talk about." She sighed. "You have a fondness for the Eurasian race."

"Hardly," Claire protested. "I just..."

"And I am sure you know of Trudy Liang, then." She peered intently at Claire over her glasses. "She was one of the better-known Eurasians in Hong Kong when she was alive. She was from a very wealthy family and so escaped much of the prejudice that comes from being mixed." Edwina Storch said this with a complete lack of irony. "You know who I'm talking about?"

"Yes," Claire allowed. "I have heard of her."

"And that whole business during the war. She was out of the camps because she was Portuguese and Chinese, and I was out of the camps because I thought it better, and I had a Finnish mother and I was able to work it out. If you were persuasive in the early days, these things could happen. It was very confusing and the rules changed every day." Her eyes shifted, became wistful. "Of course, I couldn't get Mary out, but I was able to provide for her when I was outside, and brought her packages and all that. It was for the best.

"You know, Claire," she said suddenly. "You have a face for listening. People must always confide in you. Do you find that to be the case?"

"Not really," Claire demurred. She thought to herself that

Edwina Storch's face resembled a large, fleshy reptile now. It had shrewd opportunism and greed written all over it.

"You know about Trudy and Will Truesdale, then?"

"I've just heard stories, like everyone else," Claire said. "But it has nothing to do with me."

"It doesn't!" Miss Storch laughed, a harsh chuckle. "Oh, I imagine you would like everyone to believe that. But yes, the two of them were thick as thieves. Everyone thought they would marry. If you ask me, he got the short end of the stick. He could have done much better. But no, he was with her, and then the war happened, and a lot more." She paused. "I'm sure you're wondering why I asked you here today, or why I asked you to lunch the other week. I wanted to get a good look at you, at your face. But it is a long story. You should eat while I talk."

The woman looked suddenly very serious.

"You must be different now," she said. "You must rise to the occasion. And you must be strong. Now is the time for you to make a difference."

In the late afternoon light, the door to the Librarian's Auxiliary opened. Claire stood, blinking even in the fading light. She was saying good-bye to Edwina Storch.

"Thank you very much for the tea," she said.

"You're quite welcome, my dear," said Miss Storch. "I hope I have been enlightening."

"Yes," Claire started. Then, "No. Actually ... I don't know." She stumbled over her words.

"Not the way, dear," Miss Storch said. There was exasperation in her voice.

"But Miss Storch," Claire said hurriedly. "Miss Storch, I do feel ... There is something that I would like to say. When I met you at your garden party some weeks ago, you said that I reminded you of a young you. I just want to tell you that I think that is not at all correct. You and I are as different as can be." Then she turned and walked away quickly, not looking back.

The sun was setting and Claire could not imagine that it had been an ordinary day outside, before she had entered the dark rooms and into an afternoon of storytelling by a vicious old woman with an ax to wield.

1943

THERE WAS A BABY.

There was a man with eleven fingers. Now ten. Now eleven again. The finger always grew back, taking one year, exactly. A good measure of time.

There were good men.

There were bad men.

There were dead men.

There was a woman, disappeared.

There was a baby.

Trudy, her slim figure enveloped in looser and looser tunics. Her face growing rounder, her skin mottled with the mask of pregnancy. When had he noticed? It came upon him, like so many revelations, when he was about to drift off to sleep, after another furloughed weekend. He jerked, realized: *a baby*. He could not sleep after that, turning on his thin mattress, restless and wild, his mind aflame.

She had not told him. He had not noticed. It had been so gradual.

His thoughts like an old woman's. What sort of world is this to bring a child into. How was she going to have a baby during a war. And then the other thought, the one he pushed down, but kept surfacing into his consciousness.

Did those things even matter anymore at a time like this?

Then one day, another weekend, Trudy saying abruptly, "I always knew I'd be one of those women who grew enormous during pregnancy." The first time she had acknowledged her condition. She said it gamely, over a breakfast of noodles and roast pork, shoveling the long noodles into her mouth like a street hawker, not caring what she looked like. If she had told him a few weeks earlier, before he had noticed himself, he would have been more generous, said it suited her, but he kept quiet. His small, petty revenge. But against what, whom? Not the woman. The war. The unfairness of it all.

And then it grew obvious, suddenly, in that way women look pregnant overnight. Her growth accelerated. She was still small, but her belly swelled and spilled out of whatever loose dress she was wearing. It looked like a tumor to him. He was ashamed he felt that way.

She never said anything else about it.

There was a man with eleven fingers.

Dominick. His face grown sharp with his newly acquired cunning, his body gone soft with indulgence. Trudy, saying, sotto voce, "Dominick has changed. He's with that odious Victor Chen all the time. They're trying to get my father to go in on some Macau company they're setting up that's doing a lot of trading with the Japanese. I don't want my father involved in any of that—he's not well—but Dommie won't listen. He's gone over to Victor's side." And in that statement, her profound disappointment. Her best friend, gone. A loneliness. Will was inside. Dominick was changed. Trudy didn't have anyone anymore.

There were good men.

When Will went back to camp, after the first furlough, eager faces greeted him, hungry for news and hope. He distributed what he had brought back—the guards left him alone now, as news had spread that he had a connection outside—and went back to his room.

Johnnie Sandler appeared at the doorway.

"You prefer to be alone?"

"No, it's all right." He waved him in.

"So, how was your furlough? Lots of jealous people back here at home base, you know. The news spread like wildfire. You're either a scoundrel or a hero. Lots of divided opinion."

"Johnnie..." he started. He didn't know where to begin.

"Anyone still out there that we know?"

"Yes, but... They say that two hundred Chinese die every day on the streets. Brutally. Anonymously. Half the hospitals are still closed."

Johnnie studied his face.

"You look a bit shell-shocked. Is there anything else going on?"

"Too much, my friend. Too much."

"Trudy doing all right out there?"

Will nodded.

"You don't know her that well, do you?"

"Just from around," Johnnie said. "As well as I knew you, I suppose."

"And what did you think of her?"

Johnnie hesitated.

"That's a rum thing to ask. She's your girl."

"No, really. I want to know."

"I liked her. What I knew of her. There was always the noise about her, I know, but I've learned that most of that is just that— noise. She seems a good sort, just had a lot of attention on her all the time, and I thought that must be hard."

"Very diplomatic," Will said.

Johnnie grinned. "What do you expect, old man?"

"Why did you never find someone? I always saw you around with a few girls, never one, never for a long time."

"Never found anyone who'd have me," Johnnie said lightly. "Once they'd spent enough time with me, they'd be off like a rocket."

They sat together for a while. Johnnie brought out some home-made cigarettes.

"The good stuff, rolled from native Stanley grass." He offered one to Will.

Will shook his head.

"What am I thinking?" He produced two packs of Red Sun cigarettes from his bag under the bed. "I brought these back for you.

Japanese, of course, but the real thing, nonetheless. I don't know if your scruples will allow it."

Johnnie laughed with delight.

"That's very good of you, sir!"

They smoked for a while, enjoying the small pleasure of nicotine.

"There's a few men in C Block who've rigged up another short-wave," Johnnie said. "They haven't gotten anything interesting, but they're trying."

"Trudy's got in with a bad sort," Will said.

Johnnie looked at him. "I'd figured as much."

"She's in over her head, although of course she doesn't think so. She thinks she's doing well, surviving, getting in with those she thinks will be helpful."

"What does she need?"

"It's not what she needs. They're asking her for things. Asking her for things that could compromise others."

"That is dangerous," Johnnie said simply. "She should watch out, and you too."

"Yes," Will said. "We will."

"It's almost time for supper," Johnnie said, standing up. "Our brilliant cooks have invented a new dish that is startlingly good. Banana peel fried in peanut oil. If you close your eyes, it tastes like mushrooms. I can't get enough of it."

"Sounds good," Will said. He was glad to stop talking about Trudy.

There were bad men.

Victor Chen, embracing Reggie Arbogast, both in the Western dress, the blue tropical wool suit, red tie. He had thrown a cocktail party for select Stanley survivors after the release. Not the riffraff, of course, but the doctors and the barristers and the company heads. He commiserated with them about what the war had done to them and their countries and plied them with champagne.

And imagine this. Governor Mark Young returning from his Malaya arrest to the site of his humiliation and that of his country. The war is over. Every effort is made to glorify the triumphant return. An RAF Dakota, escorted by Beaufighters and Corsairs of 721 Squadron. A dramatic landing at Kai Tak. Motorcycle escort back to the Pen, and then the ceremony. Guns, uniforms, pomp. He shakes the hand of community leaders, is welcomed back with speeches. And see Victor Chen there, reading a speech of his own, about Hong Kong's fortitude and greatness of spirit.

Otsubo, reading documents in the dark, a table lamp illuminating only a small circle on the desk. His lips moving as he reads, Trudy and Dominick sitting next to each other on a bench in the office. They do not talk or look at each other. They wait for his signal.

There were dead men.

Was it his imagination? The sound of a man screaming. Will sat up in bed and tried to listen. The sound of the sea came in through the open window, but he did not hear anything else. A child cried out in his sleep. A mother shushed, drowsy.

In the morning, passing by, he discovered Johnnie gone from his room. The room was ripped apart, although the man was fastidious. The mattress lay half off the bed, sheets hanging off.

They brought Will to the interrogation rooms on the east side.

Johnnie, his eyes open, his shirt ripped and dirty. He lay on the floor of the room, a blanket thrown carelessly over him, with only a stool and a bare electric bulb. They had let Will in to see him, a warning, he supposed.

"He didn't talk," they said. "So this."

"He didn't know anything," Will said.

"You say," they said.

"He didn't," Will said.

"Do you?" they asked.

• • •

Dominick.

He screamed and begged and wheedled. Was prodded with the tip of a bayonet. His cheek scratched so blood beaded up. Then a pinkie finger broken with a mallet. Then all of the others. A week in the hole.

Denied everything. Confessed to everything.

Scratch the surface of a man. See what appears.

Wan Kee Liang, Trudy's father.

Dead in his mansion on the Praia Grande, body wasted away, smell of urine soaking the sheets. A neglected corpse, not found for days.

There was a woman, disappeared.

Trudy clattering up the stairs of the gendarmerie headquarters on Des Voeux Road, stomach swollen, about to give birth.

Looking back to blow a kiss to Edwina Storch, who had accompanied her. Her look wistful, not condemning. We are condemned to repeat the past. Trudy's mother, gone. Trudy, gone.

May 10, 1943

EDWINA STORCH was outside by suspect means, people whispered. She had parlayed a dead Finnish mother into a Free National passport and revoked her English citizenship. Mary Winkle had been corralled and sent to Stanley and Edwina sent her provisions as often as she could.

Spotting her on the street, Trudy went over to say hello. She had always had a soft spot for the idea of Edwina, although she had heard odd stories about her tenure at Morris Primary. She had apparently wielded her authority with a bit too much enthusiasm and not enough oversight. There had also been a story about a boy who had ended up in the hospital after a too vigorous disciplinary action, but that had been hushed up. He had been Eurasian, the father an English civil servant, the mother a local Chinese mistress, preferred but not legitimate. He hadn't returned to the school.

"You're out too?"

"Yes, thanks to my dear, departed mother. Finland."

"Any way you can. It's dreadful everywhere though, isn't it?"

"Yes, but your relative Victor Chen has been very helpful to me. He has the magic touch and can procure anything!"

Trudy's face darkened.

"For the right price, I'm sure. I'm glad he's been helpful to someone."

"You're cousins, aren't you?"

"Not exactly. I'm related to his wife, Melody. She's in California right now. She's going to have the baby there."

Edwina's eyes flickered down to Trudy's own swollen belly.

"That works out well, I suppose." Miss Storch lowered her voice. "Until everything here gets worked out, I mean."

"Yes, well," Trudy said. "I suppose it will all work out, won't it?"

"Of course," said the headmistress.

"Well," Trudy said. "I hope I will see you around in this strange new world of ours. I'm just on my way to meet Dominick for lunch."

"Give him my best," the old lady said. "Yes, we will all get by."

Trudy watched Edwina Storch walk away, with an odd look on her lovely face.

May 28, 1953

IN THE LATE AFTERNOON SUN, Will grunted and moved in bed, his sleep disturbed. His head was damp, perspiring in the midday heat. Claire clapped her hands, to see if she could rouse him, but Will just shifted again, whimpered.

She looked at his face, damp with sweat, his mouth moving almost imperceptibly in his sleep, and felt pity for him, for the first time.

*   *   *

"TOUCH ME," she says. Her voice is desperate. "I want to feel real again."

He embraces her, holding her as tightly as he can.

"You don't know what he made me do," she says, muffled, into his shoulder. "You don't know."

"It's all right," he says. "Don't worry."

"It's not all right!" she cries. "It's not. You don't know. If you knew, you'd never want to see me again, never touch me again. You could never look at me straight in the face." She draws back and looks at him, searches his face.

He is quiet. She winces.

"I knew it," she says. "I knew it. What did I expect?"

"I don't know what you need from me," he says.

"This is why I loved you so much," she says. "Not only because you were so good and you didn't need anyone and I thought I might be able to make you need me, but because..." and she's crying, this Trudy he's never seen, this Trudy who's as fragile as gossamer and doesn't care who sees it. "Because no one has ever loved me. They loved my money or the way I looked, or even the way I talked, because it made them think I was a certain way. Or my father, he loved me because he had to. My mother loved me but then she left. No one loved me for me, or thought I was more than a good distraction at a party. It's the tritest thing in the world, isn't it? But you loved me. You liked the person I was. I really felt that. And it was a revelation to me. But then, after Otsubo and after I asked you to get me the information, I saw that you changed. Or that your feelings changed. You didn't love me in the same way anymore. I was changed in your eyes. I wasn't that person you loved no matter what." She wipes her eyes. They are red and swollen.

"Oh, I must look like a troll," she says suddenly, the old Trudy surfacing for a moment. "So when that happened"—she takes a deep breath—"when that happened, Will, it all snapped into place.

"I had been playing at being this person I am when I'm with you, and all it took was a few weeks' separation from you . . ."

"And a war," he says. He doesn't know where the words are coming from, where this mechanically speaking person has sprung from.

"Yes, a few weeks' separation and a few well-equipped, menacing Japanese, and *poof*, I was back to being the old Trudy, who cared only about herself and her very malleable morals. And it felt right. It felt awful, but it felt right. I'm not who you think I am. I told you that before you left to go to the parade ground, and I wanted you to understand what I was saying. Did you? Did you?"

"I can't be the one to absolve you, Trudy."

She slaps him.

His hand goes up to his cheek, like a woman.

"I want to kill you, sometimes," she says slowly. "You and your so-called morals."

She turns around and tries to leave. He catches her elbow.

"Even that," she says, "is so false. It's not worthy of you. Be a man and show what you really feel for me." She stares at him. He cannot move. "I thought so."

She turns back to the door.

"Thank you, Will," she says quietly, with the back of her head to him. "I know where I stand. Thank you for releasing me."

She has always been too strong for him.

The way we hurt the ones we love.

THE NIGHTMARES. The visions.

Men with their tongues burned, knees crushed, eyes gouged out, piled in heaps on the side of the road to Stanley, mothers covering their children's eyes.

Girls in rooms with blank faces, torn dresses, bloody chunks of hair torn from their scalps, bruised legs slick with men's fluids.

A door opened, a girl found tied to a desk, almost mute.

A body, sewn in Hessian, arms crossed, tipped into the sea, making barely a splash as it sinks down into the dark.

Ah Lok brushing Trudy's hair in front of her dressing table. Methodical strokes, the glossy strands, the sound of bombs outside. Trudy applying lipstick. Her jasmine scent.

Dominick's refined head, in front of Otsubo's legs. His eyes meeting Will's, opening wide in panic, then deadening to gray. He didn't stop, he just closed his eyes. Will, leaping back instinctively, yet knowing not to slam the door, having the presence of mind to conceal his intrusion.

A baby, born in the middle of the night, given away to an indifferent nurse, never seen by its sedated mother.

A young woman, just back from California, still puffy from childbirth, with empty eyes, arms filled with another's child.

June 2, 1953

A GOOD EVENING PARTY always gave off a glow. Drinks were refilled quickly, the food was abundant, the servants silent and efficient, and the guests all secure in the knowledge that they had been chosen to attend, that many others had been excluded and might wish to be here in their place.

The Chens' coronation party gave off such a glow, even as Claire and Martin approached the front door.

Candles set in sand in small pots lit the driveway up to the house. Uniformed men whisked away the cars. Music tinkled in the background; the Chens had hired a string quartet, installed in the foyer, three sweaty Chinese men in dinner jackets and a tiny woman with a violin tucked under her birdlike chin. Their arms sawed back and forth, making the music seem more labor than art.

The hostess at the door, holding a glass of champagne, an apparition in a dress seemingly made out of silver.

"Hello, hello," trilled Melody. "How lovely to see you all. Scepters for everyone." She gestured to a bowl filled with wands. "We're all queen today."

"You're so wicked!" rasped a rapier-thin blonde. "Another day, another party. I've seen you, what, three times already this week? At the Garden Park, at Maisie's lunch, and at that little Italian in Causeway Bay? Who were you with, you minx? That was a very handsome man."

"A cousin, of course." Melody winked. "Family's very important to me."

"What nonsense we all talk!" said the blonde and swept on inside.

Martin and Claire stood together, waiting.

"Claire!" Melody said. "I'm so glad you could come."

"Thank you so very much for having us," Martin said. Claire could see he was uncomfortable and she was suddenly irritated with him for it.

"Nice to see you, Melody," she said. "What a lovely party."

Martin got them drinks and Claire stood in the living room she had been in so often before. It was alive, different, filled with people talking, laughing, leaning toward one another confidentially.

"I don't know a soul," Martin said when he returned. "Makes you wonder why they invited the piano teacher and her husband."

"Martin!" Claire said. "You don't need to feel that way."

But Martin was right. The other guests at the party all knew one another and were not receptive to newcomers. Claire and Martin smiled and sipped their drinks in the corner, wholly ignored.

Martin gave up and went out to the garden to look at the flowers and the view of the harbor. Claire stood by herself for a moment and then went to inspect the photographs on the mantel that she had seen before.

Trudy was still there, in her swimsuit, laughing at the camera.

There was a group of four, talking about their last trip to London, the types with feathered hats and silk suits. Claire listened to their conversation, nursing her drink.

"But it was beastly. Service there is horrible after you've been in the Far East. You can't imagine what they serve you for dinner, cold and awful, and they're not in the least apologetic about it. The idea of service is dead in England. Grim, grim, grim. Much prefer it here where they take some pride in it."

"And Poppy's in London now, isn't she? I wouldn't be surprised if she were at Westminster Abbey now."

"Oh, she's horrible. I'm sure she's tried everything to get herself in. I suppose we'll have to hear about it when she comes back."

Claire cleared her throat. One of the women, a buxom redhead, glanced over her shoulder, and continued talking.

From her position, Claire could see the two men facing her, and the two women with their backs to her. They were all English. She would have thought the Chens would have invited more locals.

"Is Su May coming today?" the redhead asked the other woman, a younger blonde with a bob. The men left to refresh their drinks.

"I don't think so. I think she and Melody had a falling out."

"Really? Do tell!"

"The usual. You know"—the blonde's voice dropped—"Melody is just impossible these days, so forgetful and rude. I had a lunch for the Garden Club on Thursday, and she didn't let me know if she was able to come, never showed up, and then never said anything about it! I don't know what's going on with her these days."

"The OBE's gone to her head!"

Even lower. "Isn't it funny how the most local people are the most Anglophilic?"

"I know, darling. Look around! We could be in Mayfair!"

"But you know, it's unusual for locals to host anything at their house. I think this is the first Chinese house I've been in since I've been here."

"Victor is good at hedging his bets. He's having another party tomorrow, for an entirely different crew, but not at his house, at the club, with mah-jongg afterward and everything."

"His own kind."

"I don't know how Melody puts up with that man. He's the most obvious, venal person Charles has ever dealt with, he says."

"But, you know, I've wondered. They say, *opium* . . ."

The two women stopped talking as another woman passed by and said hello. They swooped and rustled and pecked at one another like birds.

"Lavinia!"

"Maude!"

"Harriet!"

Claire slipped away.

Later, she found herself talking to Annabel, a frosted champagne-blond American from Atlanta, Georgia, who was in Hong Kong with her husband, Peter, who was with the State Department.

"What's your story, darlin'?" Annabel asked. Her eyes were bright with alcohol, her hair in a beehive.

"I am here with my husband, who's with the Water Department," Claire said.

"All these departments!" Annabel hooted. "The State! Water! Make sure it's in the pipes!"

"Er, yes," Claire said. She never knew how to talk to Americans, who were so informal, or what to say to their odd exclamations.

"And you, what do you do to pass the time? Do you have children?"

"No," Claire said. "Do you?"

"I have four, all under five. I keep popping them out and Peter's ready to strangle me. I tell him, I wasn't the only one involved here, you know? At least here, we have all the amahs. Back home, it's not like this."

"Have you been long in Hong Kong?" Claire asked politely.

"Three years. Had Jack here, thank God he was a Cesarean..." The woman chattered on and on, buoyed by her own effervescence, and Claire listened, glad to have an excuse to stand quietly and not look awkward.

Martin found her later, waiting by the powder room.

"Hullo," he said. "Ready to leave soon?"

She nodded.

"I'll be right out." She ducked into the bathroom and splashed water on her face. She felt as if she were waiting for something to happen.

Later, she heard the redhead and the blonde, Maude and Lavinia, discuss her.

"Who was that woman lurking around?"

"I think I heard Melody say she's the piano teacher."

"Really?"

"Pretty, though, don't you think?"

"In a wan, blond sort of way, I suppose."

The sound of a light slap. "You are such a bitch!" Laughter.

"It's that skin, you know. Drives men wild."

"Yes, it just goes, though. It's wasted on the young."

A sudden commotion near the door. A maid had fainted in the heat. The houseboy was summoned and carried her out.

"Bloody hot," a man in a boater said.

"Always," rejoined another. "Haven't you heard?"

Into this senseless conversation, Will strode, unexpected. He stopped in front of them, the first people he saw.

"Did you hear?" he said, with shock on his face. His voice was not loud but everyone heard him. "Reggie Arbogast's gone and shot himself."

The two men gaped.

"The man who had the parties on the Peak?" Claire cried, before she could help it. In her simple mind, Claire still imagined that money might buy happiness. A few people turned to stare at her; most were still in shock.

The buzz rose audibly, immediate.

"His poor wife."

Sotto voce. "Regina? I wonder he didn't shoot her instead."

"The children?"

"All back in England. They'll send a telegram, of course. What a tragedy."

"When I saw him at Fanling, he seemed rather down. He went straight to the clubhouse for drinks. Rather the worse for wear by the time I'd finished up."

But Will was there for a reason. He looked around the room for Victor and walked over to him.

"You bastard," he said, and swung at the man. "You let him think all this time he was the one who broke." The room quieted immediately.

Victor Chen staggered back but did not fall. He came up, holding his jaw, and tried to smile.

"Now, Will, you come here after not having shown up for days and then take a swing at me? You've been quite the absent driver."

"Shut up. You are despicable."

Around them, people were spellbound, unable to move, even though manners dictated they should leave. A few, more decorous than the others, inched toward the door.

"You are behind all of this. You brokered the damn Crown Collection back to the Chinese government under the guise of patriotism, didn't you? You didn't care who suffered, just that you enriched yourself and got in good with the new people. And you know what your Chinese government did with it? They probably smashed it into shards, as representative of bourgeois values!" His voice rose.

"The Chinese have the right to their own history," Victor said stiffly. "It should never have been taken from them in the first place."

"You are such a hypocrite," Will continued, as if he hadn't heard. "When you were reading history at Cambridge, you were all about jolly old England, punting and strawberries and cream, and then when it suited your purpose here, you became the model China man, currying favor with the Nationalists, the Communists, whoever would receive you. You don't know whether you're coming or going, old man." He stepped closer to Victor, menacing.

"I wouldn't expect you to understand, Will," Victor said, adjusting his shirt. "You least of all. You come to Hong Kong and find your little nest of cronies, and your half-breed filly, and all is right with the world. Bloody British on their moral high horse, while they poisoned half of China with opium for their own gain."

"It doesn't matter anymore, Victor. You are doomed."

"You've always been dramatic, Will," Victor said. "Just like Trudy. Sentimental too. Those qualities are luxuries, I assure you."

Will stood still for a moment.

"You aren't worth it," he said finally. "You will never be worth anything."

Suddenly Melody was next to Will.

"Will," she pleaded. "We are not enemies here. We loved the same people. We all had tragedies during the war. Can't you forgive, just a little?"

She looked at him, but he didn't move. She shifted, then for some reason changed direction toward Claire, and appealed to her.

"Surely you must understand, Claire. Life is so complicated and we make decisions that are difficult."

Claire, caught unguarded, was exposed. Martin was there. The whole world was there. The women who had been talking about her stared; she was reborn in their eyes—someone worth seeing.

Now she was being unveiled in front of the world as somehow connected to their hosts, and to Will, a part of this puzzle. She was unused to the attention. She remembered the moment at the Chens' dinner party where everyone had stared at her, waiting for her witty rejoinder, a sign that she belonged with them—a response that had never come. She thought of the feeling she often had around Will— that she was someone else entirely, the other Claire who had never gotten a chance to surface, a Claire who had opinions and said things that people listened to, someone who was visible. She thought of all these things, and looked back at the sea of faces as they waited for her to answer Melody.

First, she nodded, as unobtrusively as possible. She blushed, looked down. Edwina Storch's pale, sweaty face rose in her mind. *You must rise to the occasion.* Yes, but in a different way from what Edwina imagined.

Claire looked up from the floor, raised her eyes.

"Melody, we all make choices but we have to stand by them and acknowledge responsibility if we find ourselves on the wrong end." Her voice quavered but the attention of every person in the room was on her.

She felt Martin staring at her, bewildered. She couldn't look at him. She focused instead on what she was doing.

"I don't know what's going on here, but I do know that Will is telling you something important."

She wanted to be generous, she wanted to understand. The queen, being crowned in England on this very day, surely would expect it of her. She wanted so badly to be merciful and kind, and to touch Melody gently on the shoulder and tell her it would be all right, that things would work out, that she herself would make sure of it.

Claire was thinking of all of these things, feeling the warm glow of benevolence.

But then Melody's face twitched.

It was quick, and then it was over, but Claire saw it nonetheless. This woman, Melody was thinking, is my daughter's piano teacher! She is someone I hired to teach Locket how to strike some black and white keys on a musical instrument. She is simple, English, not anyone I need to ask a favor of.

And then it was gone, erased by the woman's innate practicality. But it was too late. Claire had seen it already. The heat rose from her chest to her head. She was the one who didn't need anything of anyone. She turned to her lover.

"Will," she said, emboldened. "I know you don't..."

"This doesn't concern you, Claire," he interrupted. He barely saw her.

But she knew him well now.

"I know," she said. "But Melody has a point." She knew this would inflame him further.

"Don't be absurd. You have no idea what's going on."

"But..."

"Out," he said, pointing to the door.

Part of her thrilled to Will's command of the situation. He was owning her, finally. She heard a faint "I say" that sounded like it came from her husband. She closed her eyes. She couldn't see Martin now, couldn't see his bewildered, humiliated face, and have to sort out how that made her feel. So she closed her eyes and felt the dull throb of the blood coursing through her head and the weight of all those eyes on her and she opened her own, looked around at the blurry sea of faces, and then she thought about what she should do and everything seemed to be going in slow motion, as if she were under water. She blinked, and everything was still blurry. A maid cried out from the kitchen, unaware of the drama going on at the party, she heard glasses clink as they were assembled on a tray by another unsuspecting servant, a fly buzzed terribly near her ear, and she saw a redheaded woman slowly, slowly sweep her hand through her hair, all the while looking at her. All this happened as if it were in a room far away from her, enclosed in glass. In the end, she stood up a little straighter, took a deep breath, and then she did the only thing she could think of doing at that moment, that particular instant: she just walked away. It was cowardly and messy and left much to be dealt with later but her heart felt full and tender and she didn't see that she had any choice. She walked away from the gaping women and the perplexed men, and went directly to the door and put her hand on the knob. She hesitated, she didn't know why, and then she turned the door handle—she remembered always the cool metal in her palm—and she walked out. She didn't look at Martin. She couldn't. She didn't even look at Will. She walked outside, to a new and unknown life.

LATER, SHE HEARD what had happened. Women who had never acknowledged her presence called her or stopped her in town, ostensibly to ask her how she was doing or tell her what had happened after she left, but really to find out her connection to the situation.

"They said he went out on the tennis court and put the gun in his mouth. Very messy. And you know, he only had the one hand. The hook, of course. Quite tricky. The amah found him. Had to be hospitalized herself with the shock. The servants always want to be a part of it, don't they?"

"Poor Regina," said Claire. She remembered the party she had been to, the one where she had met Will, with the Pimms' and the boy and his father hitting the ball back and forth in their tennis whites. She tried to imagine Reggie Arbogast sprawled out on the grass, blood running out of his mouth. "Does anyone know why? Other than what was said..."

"He'd not been himself," they would say. "Blamed himself for letting the collection disappear. And couldn't stand to see all the fuss around the coronation, and all the patriotism. Made him feel awful. And I think he felt he was in some way responsible for the death of Trudy Liang." A pause. "And did you *know* Trudy? Or Dominick?"

"No," she would say. "They were gone before I even arrived. I just found out who they were recently."

"Dominick was just terrible. He went through women like they were used handkerchiefs, although they say he liked both sides, if you know what I mean..."

Claire would wait patiently.

"And the Chens? They were just livid about how Will came in

and ruined their party. I can't believe you just left, darling, it was so dramatic! Melody was in hysterics, Victor tried to be cool, and Will, well, he controlled himself and left not long after you, leaving all of us gaping like fools. I've never seen anything like it. What a scandal! Were you close?"

"I don't know much about that," Claire would say. "You see, I was teaching Locket but didn't have much contact with the Chens so I didn't know them very well. They'd always been very kind to me."

"Oh ..." A sigh, down the telephone line, disappointed. "Well, they are really something." A pause. "And are you ... all right?"

"As well as can be expected," she would say, or something of the sort.

"And ..." And only a few of them could bring themselves to say it. "And Martin?"

And she would not answer, and the deepening silence would embarrass them into hurriedly filling it with small talk and fervent wishes to see her soon, to have tea, or to go for a walk.

They rang off shortly afterward and never called again. She wondered at their transparency.

The government wrapped up its investigation into the disappearance of the Crown Collection. Reggie Arbogast was posthumously honored with a commendation from the queen for his services to the English empire. Regina Arbogast sold the big house on the Peak to a Shanghainese merchant looking to relocate to Hong Kong and set sail for England. Victor Chen was not officially mentioned.

July 5, 1953

FROM A DISTANCE she saw him approaching, a spindly figure with a cane. Hard to imagine this man was the enigma who had ignited such desire in her a mere two weeks ago.

But then he came close, his pale, narrow face, his untidy hair, and he spoke, and she felt his pull all over again.

"Claire," he said, kissing her on the cheek. "Sit down." Almost avuncular. She felt rebuffed. He always set the tone of their meetings.

They sat on a bench looking over the harbor. They were on the Peak, where they had arranged to meet, thinking they would not run into anyone they knew, for different reasons than before, and they had been right. They were alone in the twilight hour. The warm wind blew, not unpleasantly.

"I came here with Trudy sometimes," he said. "That is the same iron rail that was here when I was here with her. I touched it then and I can touch it now, but the circumstances are so different. I'm so different. Do you ever think about that?"

He was a different man, as if a great weight had been lifted off his shoulders. She could feel his lightness.

"Will," she started.

"And what will you do?" he said as if she had not said anything.

"I don't know," she said. "I've been in touch with my parents but they don't seem too eager to take me back in. Something about the cost and his pension. I don't have a job, or any means of getting one, I think. So I don't know." She said this simply, without meaning to cause obligation.

"I see," he said.

"And you?" she asked.

"I don't know either," he said. "It seems impossible to stay here, and it seems impossible to leave."

"Yes," she said.

"So here we are," he said. "Two people without places to go."

"Do you think I should continue with Locket?"

"They haven't said anything?"

"No, we haven't spoken since the party."

"Well," he considered. "If they haven't told you to stop, I would go. But then"—he grinned—"I'm sort of perverse."

"What was it you took from the grave in Macau?" She had been wondering.

"Oh, that," he said. "Trudy had a deposit box at the bank and she had always told me that Dominick or I could access it. And I got a posthumous letter from her solicitors telling me I could pick up the key after the war when she had been declared legally deceased. She had told me about another key to the same box before the war but I had never tried to find it. And when I received it from the solicitors, I didn't know where to put it. So I hid it in Dominick's grave. Thought no one would ever go there. And it felt right. A little dramatic, but right. And I was always looking for what felt right."

"What was in the box?"

"Some bank books, financial papers. But what she wanted me to have were the documents, the letters, the things that showed what she had done for Otsubo during the war, and what others had done."

"Others including Victor Chen?"

"Yes," he said simply.

"And what did you do with the contents of the box?"

"I just had them sent to the right people. Anonymously."

"But Victor knew it was you."

"He knew I was the only one who might have access to that sort of information."

"Are you in any trouble?"

"I don't think so," he said. "But I've been wrong before."

They sat together, strangely comfortable.

"The thing is," he said, "Victor Chen was not wrong in some way. The British government didn't, doesn't, have the right to own all those irreplaceable Chinese artifacts. They stole them from them in the first place, although they would dispute the verb. But the way he went about it . . . ." He shook his head. "That man only knows one way to do things.

"And I didn't abandon Trudy, not totally. Otsubo stopped signing the furloughs when he realized I wasn't giving him anything. But there was never one time, or one big reason, that I couldn't get out. I had a year of furloughs. Trudy would have got me out if I had wanted. That's one of my deepest regrets. That it just kind of . . . fizzled. She deserved better than that. And I don't know, really, what happened to her. I don't know. I suppose I could find out. There are only too many people who would be delighted to tell me all about it. Including Victor."

"But what could you have done?"

"Anything but what I did," he said. "Anything but the nonsense I did in camp: form committees, campaign for hot water or more sheets!" His voice rose, grew violent. "I was a coward, a coward. And didn't do anything to help her. The woman I loved. I did nothing. Hid behind what I pretended was honor."

"Did Trudy ever . . ." Claire couldn't finish the question.

"She never said anything. She never reproached me or challenged me. She was always who she said she was. She never pretended to be anything else. That was the beauty of her."

He straightened his back.

"She behaved as if she believed me when I said I couldn't help her. But she was so clever—she saw the real situation. But she didn't say anything; she forgave me."

He stood up, walked over to a tree, and absently snapped off a leaf. He split it in half, then half again, then scattered the pieces on the ground.

"Hong Kong is always so damn green," he said. "Don't you wish for some absence of color sometimes? Some English gray, a little fog?"

Claire nodded. He was unraveling, slowly, and she wanted to give him some room.

He continued. "Sometimes, I hate her for that. That she didn't call me out on it. That she let me be a coward. It was cruel, in the end."

Trudy would despise a man who wept, he knew.

"I have this image," he said slowly. "This image of Trudy running around outside, frantic, like a chicken with its head cut off, not knowing what to do, not having a center, just desperate. I feel like she was desperate. But she didn't come to me for help. Not after the first time. When I said no, she never asked again."

Claire reached for his hand, resting on top of his cane. He didn't yield and she settled for placing her hand on top of his.

"And she wouldn't have had anyone to confide in. She was totally alone. And I made her that way."

The air was damp still with the ever-present Hong Kong humidity. A drop of perspiration slowly wended its way down Claire's back.

She willed him to look at her, to acknowledge she was there, a part of this, but he stared out at the harbor, his eyes blank. Slowly, she realized: His new lightness was not just relief at the passing of his burden. There was emptiness there too.

*   *   *

HE SEES TRUDY, waving on the steps of the Toa, as he gets in the car that will drive him back to Stanley. She has a wistful look on her face, her amber hair lit from behind, the setting sun sinking into the Hong Kong horizon. Pregnant Madonna. She blows him a kiss, suddenly winks. He hates how she does that—always turns a serious moment into a joke. But this is how she lives, how she survives. This is the animal she is. She had never told him anything different. She had warned him.

Arbogast broke, she had told him during this furlough, and he had nodded. "Yes, I saw him afterward," he said.

"But you know," she said, her voice slightly panicked, "it wasn't the correct information. Otsubo is furious. But there was evidence that it was there. An old storage building in Mong Kok. Someone else got to it first."

"How did Otsubo know that Arbogast might know where it was?" he asked.

She hesitated.

"I think, Victor," she said finally. "Although I have nothing to back that up. He has his finger in every pie, that man."

"Be careful," he said.

"I know." She nodded. "Otsubo's tired of me now, anyway. I think we've run our course."

"What does that mean for you?" he asked, careful to mask his relief.

She laughed.

"Oh, nothing good, I'm afraid. Just means I'm under his thumb just as much as always but I no longer have the means to coddle him out of his bad moods."

"Do you want to come into camp now?"

"Again, with the camp! You cannot cage this bird, my love. I've grown used to dark, dangerous freedom and all its attendant humiliations."

"But you could..."

"I am in the process of lining up another... sponsor," she said slowly. "Or one is being lined up for me. So don't you worry."

Tears sprang to his eyes, hot, unexpected. He felt as if he might die if she saw them.

"I should go," he said.

"Yes."

He turned to go. She caught his arm, studied his face.

"Every time I say good-bye to you, I wonder if it's au revoir or adieu. You know what I mean?"

He nodded.

"You've too much power over me," she said lightly. "I have to pretend like it doesn't matter, like you don't matter. How did that happen?"

He looks at her, his love, her face ruddy with pregnancy, birdlike ankles swollen, this woman, a survivor, six months pregnant with an unwanted child, and finds he cannot forgive her this last transgression. It is easier to brand her a villain and go back to camp, play the victim, lick his wounds. This is what he does. There is no glory in it, but there is survival. And he realizes that is what they are playing at now.

May 27, 1953

EDWINA STORCH had told her everything, sure that she would pass on the information to Will.

Edwina's voice in her head, the old woman pouring tea in the dark club.

"Trudy redoubled her efforts to be indispensable to Otsubo. She knew what kind of asset she had in him. I knew Otsubo because he had been of some help to me in getting my pass, and I kept in touch and tried to help him in whatever small matters I might be of assistance." She had peered at Claire over her spectacles. "You understand, I was not collaborating with the enemy. I thought I would be of better use to England and everyone if I kept abreast of the situation, and there was no reason to alienate the man." She took off her glasses and rubbed them again.

"And when Trudy started to prove herself really indispensable to Otsubo—you know, the girl knew everything about Hong Kong and all the skeletons in the closet—her cousin, Dominick, who I never liked, started to get jealous. It was as if they were both vying for his favor, and there was only room for one. Dominick was a terrible person. I don't know if you know anything about him but he was just awful. A sadistic, small man who always felt that life owed him everything. They were both Otsubo's flunkies and ran around getting him meetings with Chinese leaders and keeping him informed about everything that went on in the Chinese community, and even in the small European community that was still outside. Dominick made some money buying and selling necessities. He would buy it cheap through his sources and charge exorbitant rates to the local market. Very distasteful. He'd also try to get information on who was helping whom and report back to Otsubo. Needless to say, this made him less than popular with their old crowd, but he was certainly the best fed. Dominick was more out in the open about it than Trudy. People stopped talking to him."

Claire interrupted.

"Did you have to do any work? How did you survive?"

Edwina pursed her lips.

"I've always preferred not to dwell on the unpleasantness of the past."

Claire almost laughed aloud, but saw that Edwina Storch was unaware of the enormous irony of what she was saying.

"There was all this business of the Japanese in Hong Kong trying to enrich themselves. It's quite common in a victory but there was a lot of chatter about the Crown Collection, which had some extremely rare and priceless porcelain pieces. Otsubo found out I knew a bit about the subject and called me in to get some information. I told him what little I knew."

Edwina's eyes sparkled.

"Actually, I knew quite a bit more than I let on but didn't think it was an opportune time." She paused.

"What if I were to tell you, Claire, that the governor had just flown into Hong Kong on the eve of the war." She sat very still, as if in a trance. "He was stepping into a very tricky situation and he knew it. He had just been sworn in and was taking over a colony that was, from most intelligence reports, going to be conquered in short order. He had orders from London, one of which was to secure the Crown Collection which was in Government House. His strategy..."

She laughed, interrupting herself. "Interesting story, isn't it? Politicians are so stupid. No sense at all. His strategy was to tell three different people about the location he was going to have it sent so that it would survive the war. Communications to London were already compromised so he had to think of another way." She looked at Claire. "I was one of the three."

"That must have been a great honor," Claire murmured. She imagined the scene: Edwina Storch summoned to Government House, given tea, scones, a cordial reception from a man who had little knowledge of his new territory, still settling into his private quarters, getting to know the servants, his enormous task, Edwina condescending, as only a woman of her age and experience could be. How did she get away with it for so long and without challenge?

"They knew I had been a long time in Hong Kong and knew a great deal about the people, the history, the place, which I do, of course," Edwina mused. "And the other two. Well, I found out who they were as well. We weren't supposed to know, but this kind of information gets around. The governor was nervous and confided in a few people, not the location but our identities. As chatter grew, it all came to light. One was Reggie Arbogast. Do you know him?"

Claire nodded. "Slightly."

"He turned a bit queer after the war." Her mouth grew set, grim. An unforgiving expression settled on her face. "And a silly cow of a wife, Regina."

"And the third?" Claire couldn't help asking.

Edwina looked surprised.

"I thought you would guess. The third was Victor Chen."

April 1942

WHEN IT RAINS in Hong Kong, the world stops. The deluge is so overwhelming, so strong, that the city disappears under a sheet of gray water and people vanish like panicked rats, scurrying into doorways, shops, restaurants. Inside, they shake off the water, ordering coffee or browsing through dresses while they wait for the rain to stop.

Trudy and Victor Chen sit inside Chez Sophie, a small French restaurant in Causeway Bay, and watch the rain fall outside.

"It never seems clean here, even after the rain," Trudy says. "The water washes the grime off the streets but it's back two instants later. Hong Kong is just *dirty*. Always has been. Can't live anywhere else, though. This filthy city is home." She rubs the arm of her chair, red velvet, the fabric starting to shine from constant use. "I've always loved this restaurant," she says. "As a child, Father used to take me to the Sunday brunch here every week, and I'd buy a new dress to wear."

Victor harrumphs.

"Every week?" he says. "You were spoiled, weren't you?"

"Spoiled?" she asks. "Don't worry, Victor. I'm sure this war will beat every last shred of privilege out of me."

"People will show their true colors."

"They already are, Victor, dear cousin, and people are already commenting on it. I've heard people call us collaborators. Isn't that what you call those who get too close to the conquerors?"

"*Collaborator* is a dirty word, Trudy. I'd be careful how you use it." Victor sips Cognac, his face reddening. Trudy lounges in her chair, sleek in a tan wool skirt and ivory blouse. A half-empty coffee cup sits in front of her.

"But that's what we are, aren't we, Victor?" Trudy asks, needling him. "Isn't that what they call people like us?"

"Don't be naïve," he snaps. "You are providing English lessons and etiquette. You're basically a governess to the good general, educating him in the ways of the Western world that he is so interested in, despite himself. And I am merely doing my best to provide a smooth transition so that our people do not have to suffer. Never say something so stupid again. Not everything is so black and white. Should we spite ourselves and alienate the very people who might help us through this difficult time? Trudy, you are no longer a child."

"But Otsubo is so . . ."

"You do not have to concern yourself with him other than to give him English lessons and try to fulfill his requests." His face turns shrewd. "I would say you should comply with every request, no matter what it is or how veiled it is."

"He is a pig," she says quietly. The waiter comes and silently refills her cup. She puts sugar and milk in, takes a sip.

Victor studies her face.

"You've changed," he says. "Is it the Englishman? Has he inculcated you with his timeless values, the right way to do things, honor and all that rubbish the English are so good at spewing? And yet, when it comes to their responsibilities, they always find a reason why they can't fulfill them, and they always sound so good when they do. They've refined it to an art. They sound good and do nothing."

"Who don't you hate, Victor?" She thinks privately that his speech is undermined by his Oxford accent.

"You are more Chinese than anything else, Trudy. You will always be viewed as foreign in any other country. You belong in Hong Kong."

He lights a cigarette, doesn't offer her one. She knows he's always disapproved of her smoking in public. He thinks women should be demure and quiet when out.

"These are going to be currency too now, you know," he says, inspecting the lit tip. "Things are going to be different, and getting a foothold in the new world is going to be like building a foundation on quicksand. You have to be adaptable."

Trudy puts her hands on the table and leans forward. If she could, she would bare her teeth and hiss.

"I'm busy, Victor. Why did you want to see me?"

"I just want to be sure we're on the same side," he says. "Being as we're family and all."

Trudy laughs.

"You've never felt so familial before, I'm sure." She hesitates. "Maybe I'll go into Stanley instead. Will said . . ."

"Don't be idiotic, Trudy. You can get a lot more accomplished out here than you can by being in a prison. And make no mistake, that's what it is in there, a prison. Why would you give it up?"

"But Will . . ."

Victor laughs.

"I didn't know you were so sentimental, my dear. And of course, there's the matter of your father."

Trudy tenses. "What of him?"

"I didn't want to say anything but . . . he is not well."

Trudy's face doesn't move. "He's never said anything to me."

Victor looks at her as if she were stupid.

"And you think he would?"

"I don't believe you."

Victor waves his hand. "It doesn't matter to me in the least." He catches himself. "Of course, I am concerned with his welfare and I thought you had a right to know."

In the restaurant, the pianist comes in and sits down. He starts to practice. Trudy and Victor sit across from each other, each unwilling to make the next move.

"Debussy," Trudy says.

"Yes."

They sit, two chess players, looking at anything but each other. Victor smokes his cigarette down to the stub and crushes it in the crystal ashtray. He speaks first, oblique.

"The Players are already hard to get. The Japanese are bringing in their own brands, Rising Sun and rubbish tobacco like that. It's going to be all about transportation and access to imports. The channels are going to get narrower. Goods will be dear."

Trudy looks up. "Goods like, say, medicine, you mean?"

"Well, of course. That's just one example. Good-quality medicine. American and British pharmaceutical companies are certainly not going to be shipping goods to conquered territories. At least not legally. People are going to have to be clever."

"And you've always been clever, Victor. And criminally unsubtle."

He throws up his hands. "I've always been called something. But I'm just trying to make sure you understand the entire situation. *Food* is going to be in very short supply. It's not just a matter of silk stockings and good port."

Trudy stands up. "Excuse me, I just have to powder my nose." She walks gracefully over to the powder room and the door closes silently behind her.

Victor waits, tapping his pack of cigarettes on the tablecloth.

When she emerges, she is fresh-faced, with a new coat of lipstick, woman's armor.

"People will think we're in love, Victor. This illicit meeting in an out-of-the-way restaurant." She smiles at him.

"Having an affair?"

"You don't fancy me?"

Victor considers her teasing more seriously than he should.

"You're like a sister to me, Trudy. Melody has always been very fond of you. She asked me to take care of you while she was gone, make sure you were all right."

"That's funny. She told me to go to Macau, to be with my father."

"He does need someone to help him out, take care of him."

"He has Leung." Her father's devoted houseboy, with him for forty years. "He'll take care of him better than I ever could."

"Didn't you hear?"

Trudy's face falls. "No, what?"

"Leung was knifed in the lung. Seems he was trying to prevent some Japanese private from taking your father's Rolex. It was touch and go for a while, but then he finally succumbed. These soldiers know just where to put the knife."

"Father would have told me," Trudy says. "He would have contacted me."

"You know how it is with your father," Victor says soothingly. "He doesn't want to be a bother to you. But don't worry, Trudy. I took care of it. I have a woman from Shanghai living with your father, cooking and taking care of him. He didn't want you to worry. I didn't want you to worry. I only brought it up because..."

There is a long pause. Trudy looks up and smiles at Victor, brittle. She reaches slowly across the table for the pack of cigarettes and takes one out. Victor does not offer a light so she goes into her handbag and gets a lighter. Her hands are shaking. She inhales deeply and blows the smoke at Victor.

"Otsubo..." she says. "He adores me. Thinks I'm some exotic flower."

"I know," Victor says. "You should make sure that lasts."

He looks at her searchingly with narrowed eyes, then turns away, satisfied.

"I'm having a garden party next week," he says. "You will be the hostess. We are family, so people won't talk. Bring Otsubo and tell him to invite whoever he wants."

Trudy nods, so slight a movement it is almost unnoticeable.

"I think we're finished here," Victor says. "But one more thing, Trudy. When you decide to do something, you should do it all the way. There's nothing worse than indecision, or ambivalence. That's the kind of thing that endangers lives. But you're a smart girl—you know what I'm talking about. Have a good day."

He tosses some bills on the table and walks out.

CLAIRE SAT in the library with the retired headmistress, stunned.

"Victor Chen?" she asked. "He was one of the three? Why didn't he just..."

"Oh," Edwina said. "He didn't want to sell the information too cheap. Nothing if not a good businessman, that fellow. Very misinformed about him, the government was. I could have told them he'd sell his own mother if the price was right. They thought it would be good to have a Chinese person know, in case the English were all imprisoned or killed. And they thought he had loyalties to England because he had been schooled there. He found out that I knew and that Reggie knew, but Reggie was in Stanley and he knew he'd never say anything. Me, he didn't know so well. So he had me over a few times as well. I've never been so lavishly entertained and skillfully interrogated about my intentions. But I knew better. We played cat and mouse for a while and he always kept tabs on me."

"Did Trudy know about this?"

"I don't think so, or else she wouldn't have run around so hard, trying to procure the information. I think Victor got some pleasure out of seeing her work so diligently to get something that he already had. And Dominick too. The two of them were something to see. Victor watched them for a while, and then I think he decided they were getting a little too influential and he decided to do something about it. He was really the one pulling the strings. They were just his puppets."

Edwina paused.

"Do you want some of these scones?" she asked. "They're the best in Hong Kong. Made by a Mr. Wong who I trained myself. He's the best Chinese English baker in the colony."

"No, thank you," Claire said.

Edwina spread jam on a chunk and popped it into her mouth.

"Mmmmm," she said. "I've lived here so long but still can't get by without my tea and scones.

"So, Victor Chen started to get irritated with the way Trudy and Dominick were carrying on. They were being rather conspicuous and too cozy with their relationship with Otsubo. It was quite unseemly. So, he started to sow a little unrest between them. He wanted them more under his thumb than Otsubo's. He also included Dominick in his business, which was flourishing. He was supplying Japanese troops in Guangzhou with petrol and basic supplies and making an absolute fortune. What Dominick had been doing before was small potatoes and he told him that. He had factories and enormous resources backing him up. Then he told Dommie that Trudy was going behind his back and trying to get the information without him, and of course, Dominick believed him. So Dominick started to do things that would undermine Trudy. He told Otsubo that Trudy knew where the Crown Collection was but just wasn't telling him. Victor was only too happy to back this up."

"Did Dominick know that Victor knew?"

"No," scoffed Edwina. "Victor didn't tell anyone. I was the only one who knew. But you know, the funny thing is . . ." Edwina's eyes looked far away. "It was very odd. It was as if Trudy knew what was going on but she didn't do anything about it. She had already given up. It was as if she didn't care anymore and she was just going through the motions."

Someone opened the door and looked inside. Edwina Storch didn't look up. The door closed silently.

"And so, Otsubo decided that Trudy was too much trouble and he'd grown tired of her. He'd moved on to Dominick, at any rate. They were lovers as well. He liked anything and everything, that man. He was insatiable. A real pig. So he used this as an excuse to get rid of her. And he asked me to help. But you know, the odd thing was that nothing he did seemed to faze her. She was untouchable and it made him crazy. After she fell pregnant, he told her he was giving her to his lieutenant, that he was done with her, but she went quietly. She did everything he said and didn't give him any satisfaction. I think he wanted her to suffer. So he passed her around—she was an heiress, you understand, had been given the best of everything from birth, knew everyone. I don't know why she did it. She just did not care anymore." For the first time, Edwina Storch seemed saddened.

"So how did Trudy die?" Claire asked.

"Dominick had told Otsubo that Trudy knew where the Crown Collection was. Trudy denied it. Otsubo thought she might confide in me because I was English so he had me bump into her a few times so that we could rekindle our acquaintance. It was easy because he knew where she was all the time. So Trudy and I bumped into each other regularly."

"Did you feel any scruples about doing this for this man?" Claire asked.

"Not at all," Edwina said instantly. "You have to understand, Claire, that no one was a saint in any of this. Otsubo was the enemy, but Trudy, Dominick, Victor, they were all getting in bed with him, so as far as I was concerned, they were all the enemy. They didn't have anyone's interest at heart except their own."

"It was almost your patriotic duty," Claire said quietly.

"Yes." Edwina seized on this idea. "I thought this was one way I could help our country. I knew Victor Chen was going to give up the Crown Collection at some point. It was just at what price. And I thought if I kept tabs on it, I might be of some help in tracking it down. So, what I did was...I told Otsubo that Trudy did know."

"What?" Claire's mouth hung open. "But..."

Edwina stiffened.

"I thought it was the best approach. The man had to be led down the wrong path so he wouldn't find the right one."

"But you assured her death by telling this to Otsubo." It was out before she could stifle the thought.

"So simple," Edwina said. "So black and white for you, is it? The truth is, dear, Trudy was doomed from the start. The way she was acting. She wouldn't have lasted another month. So, Otsubo had two sources telling him that Trudy knew but was keeping it from him. So then he asked me to escort her to his office. It was very odd the way he wanted to handle it. Must be Japanese. Odd people, you know. She knew something was off because she went there all the time and didn't need me to escort her, but she was very polite. When I showed up at her door, we sat down for tea and had a nice chat. And then we walked over together and she went into the building by herself. I told her he was expecting her. And, that was it. No one ever saw her again."

The room seemed colder. Claire folded her arms in front of her chest.

"So..." The thought hung in the air.

"No, dear," said Edwina. "The Japanese are quite unsentimental about that sort of thing and don't leave witnesses. I think they may have let her have the baby and then I don't know what happened after that."

"And Dominick, her cousin?"

Edwina shook her head.

"That one was never going to come to a good end. He got in over his head. He was used by everyone. Victor installed him at a company he had formed called Macau Supplies. He made sure Dominick's name was on all the legal papers so he could keep his hands clean. But it didn't matter. I think Dominick got greedy and started skimming, and the Japanese found out. It was never clear what happened to him either but at least there was a body. He turned up in a canal in the seedy part of town. All of his fingers had been cut off, save one—an eleventh finger he had, apparently a birth defect."

"Oh." Claire exhaled slowly. It was so much to take in. "And whatever did happen to the Crown Collection?"

"Well, you can never let it be said that Victor Chen is not clever. He had an inkling that the secret might leak, either through me or Arbogast, so he had the collection taken away and stored somewhere else. And then he intimated to Otsubo that he had found out Arbogast knew where it was. So he was masterful at manipulating the situation. He had Otsubo owing him a favor then, you see. And Arbogast never knew. They took his hand. He was lucky they didn't do more. So Arbogast broke, as many men would have under that sort of…duress, and then when Otsubo sent his men, the collection was no longer there. Arbogast had some rough days after that as well, but Victor Chen got off scot-free. Arbogast never knew whether he had given it up or not. I think that was worse than the torture." Edwina's face turned contemplative. "Funny what the mind can do to you. He did very well for himself after the war, and did a lot for the unfortunate, but he was never happy. Felt he had failed his country, you see, and he was the sort of man that the notion would always haunt him.

"Anyway, later, Victor could sense the tide turning in the war and he thought it might be more advantageous to give it back to the Chinese and bank a few favors from them. So he put the collection on a train to China. A gift from a loyal citizen. I didn't know until after the fact."

"And that was the end of it. And you never told anyone?"

"No," Edwina said. "Victor made it abundantly clear it was to my advantage to keep silent."

Claire thought of Edwina's comfortable life, her large estate in the New Territories, all apparently paid for on a headmistress's civil pension.

"Who knew?" she asked.

"I don't know, my dear. Victor plays his cards close to his chest."

"How much of this does Will know?"

Edwina smiled.

"Well, you'd have to ask him, wouldn't you?"

"And why are you telling me this? I have nothing to do with this story." Claire asked.

"You are...close to Will, are you not?" asked Edwina.

"I know him," Claire allowed.

"Don't be coy," Edwina snapped. "He listens to you?"

"Not at all." Of this she was sure.

"Well, I think you'd be surprised. You're the first person in a long time that our Will has deigned to spend time with. I just think he needs a little push to do the right thing. A woman knows the right thing to say. It's our instinct."

"I don't know that I understand what you're saying." Claire was deliberately being obtuse.

Edwina slapped her palms on the table.

"That man," she cried. "That man, Victor Chen, promenades himself around Hong Kong as if he owns it. He hobnobs with everyone who's important—you know he was chosen to host a party for Princess Margaret when she came to town? And who is he? Some trumped-up Chinaman in a Savile Row suit! A collaborator. An opportunist." She said this almost spitting. "He pretends to be better than everyone, even English people! It's nauseating and I won't have it."

Her outburst rang out, incongruous, against the heavy damask curtains.

"He snubbed Mary in town the other week. He's forgotten old friends in his haste to ascend to the top. Well, he'll learn." She looked at Claire. "He is an awful person who doesn't deserve anything of what he has."

"It's hard to say who does deserve the good in life," Claire said. She felt as if she were placating a large, angry animal.

"He thinks the past can be buried. But it has a way of surfacing, again and again."

"And the baby? Trudy's baby?" Claire asked. An innocent, perhaps the only, in all of this.

"I don't know, my dear. I suppose it was taken care of." She paused. "Yes. That was the end. I think about that last afternoon with Trudy quite a lot, how remote she was, how removed. She didn't care if she lived or died after Will abandoned her. I always thought that Will Truesdale broke her heart. And how about that? Who knew that the remarkable Trudy Liang had a heart to break?"

July 5, 1953

"AND NOW," Claire said. "What of us?"

She and Will had sat in silence for long minutes, looking out at the water, the boats streaming silently through the harbor, passing one another smoothly, like toy boats in a child's bathtub. It started to sprinkle slightly. It had taken great effort to ask and she could not bring herself to look at him. She put her hands in her lap and cupped them together primly.

"You don't need me," he said slowly. "I've said it before and it's truer than ever. I'm a liability now."

Her first reaction: automatic withdrawal. Then she realized, with Will's new release came uncertainty: he had lived too long with his secrets and now that they had been poured out, he was likely feeling empty.

"I don't need you," she echoed his words. How porous he seemed, how he always slipped through her grasp. Even in their most intimate moments, in bed, his face hovering over hers, intense with passion, he was never fully there. Now she understood why: he had always been with another.

Another unbidden memory: Will, lifting the strands of her hair as she lay beneath him, letting the fine gold slip through his fingers, his face oddly distant. "Gold," he had said. "I love hair the color of metals: gold, bronze, even silver. The gold and bronze will turn silver eventually, yes?" The closest he ever got to saying the word *love* to her. It stung, suddenly. She had turned away, buried her face in the pillow. In bed, she was always shy around him, afraid that she would say something she would regret later.

"You deserve better, you know," she said, trying to save what, she didn't know. "You can live your life without always regretting."

"You are trying to be kind but you don't understand," he said.

"It's not kindness," she said.

He didn't reply.

"You always tell me to be strong, but you're never strong yourself. When we first met, you told me I should take the opportunity to become something else, to transcend what I had been given. You can't do that yourself. You are mired in the past and determined to be unhappy." She had never seen so clearly before. Anger swept through her—unexpected—clarifying even more. "You cannot let go, and you are sinking. And you pretended to be so strong!" A feeling as if she had been duped, taken under false pretenses. The man she had loved was a mere shell. And she felt something more, unwelcome: a feeling of pity, fatal to passion.

"And I told you to go, don't bother with me," he said, also angry now. He just wanted to be left alone. But she wouldn't leave him without trying to salvage something.

"Why did you come to me?" she asked. "You changed my life. You didn't like me, you said. What was it? Were you bored?" She shot the last word at him, an accusatory arrow.

"You were pure," he said, trying to explain. "You weren't like the others. You had your prejudices and silly ideas, but you were open, willing to change. And I hadn't minded being alone. But you came along..."

"And you were the great opener of my eyes, the wise and..."

"That's not fair," he said. "That is beneath you. I never looked at another woman until you came along. But it felt wrong, as if I were betraying Trudy, who I had betrayed in so many ways already."

"You are wasting your life," she said. Rain had wet his hair so it hung in jagged spikes down his forehead. He made no effort to wipe away the water running down his face. He looked so defeated.

She was cruel, finally. "You are a coward."

How was this the man she had changed her life for? It seemed inconceivable.

"And you are simple," he said fiercely. "And naïve. To think that you can just leave the past behind, like shutting a door."

"You won't even look at me!" she cried. "You won't give me even that. You've always been mean with your attention, so measured." She looked down at herself. She had dressed with care this morning, mindful of the impression she wanted to give: quiet, not reproachful, confident. This had translated into a knee-length navy cotton-voile dress with covered buttons all down the front, a few decorative pleats: tailored, not fussy, freshly washed hair held back with a navy satin headband. She tamped down the word that kept rising to the surface of her consciousness: *fool, fool.*

"I am telling you that it doesn't need to be like this," she said. Her mother's voice suddenly in her head: "Chasing a man, are you? Shame!" Her face turned scarlet despite herself. She waved her hand in the air, almost unconsciously, to dismiss her mother's presence.

"Do you know?" he asked, fiercely. "Do you know what it's like to have your life unravel because of something you failed to do?" He stood up. "It haunts you like nothing else."

"So you give up," she said in a low voice.

"Sometimes," he said, "you don't have a choice in how you lead your life. Please stop before I say more things that I will regret later."

"You should know about regret," she said. "It is what you have made your life about."

They sat, furious now, their anger running clear through them like a solvent. It washed away their short past and allowed them to wipe it clean.

He got up and walked away. She didn't call after him.

July 12, 1953

THE NEXT WEEK, Claire went to the Chens' to resign in person. She went at the usual lesson time and was shown to the drawing room where Melody was by herself.

"Are you all right?" she asked. The Chinese woman was sitting very still on the edge of the sofa with a cup of tea cooling in front of her.

"No," she said. "Something's gone terribly wrong. There's been a misunderstanding. Everyone's got the wrong idea."

"I'm afraid..."

"They cut me," Melody said with a stricken face. "In town today, I walked through the tea room at the Gloucester, and the room fell silent and no one called out to me, not even Lizzie Lam, and I was at primary school with her. We were best friends. She gave me the chicken pox! She pretended she didn't see me."

"I'm sure you are mistaken," Claire said.

"No, it's true," Melody whispered. "People are merciless, you know. In our world, they can be very cruel."

The hypocrisy of the woman was overwhelming. Melody must have seen Claire's ambivalence because then she said impatiently, "Oh, you will never understand.

"And you?" she asked suddenly. "I suppose your life is quite different now, as well."

"Yes," Claire said. "I've telegraphed my parents to let them know my situation. I will probably have to go home."

"It's a pretty kettle of fish, isn't it?" Melody said. "Isn't that what you English say? And you, somehow involved in it. I'd wager you never imagined you would be in this sort of situation."

"No," Claire said. "This is all very foreign to me."

Melody nodded and got up. "I'll let Locket know you're here."

Claire started to explain but Melody interrupted her.

"They say I took her from Trudy, but I didn't, you know. Trudy gave her to me."

Claire opened her mouth, but nothing came out.

Melody went on, in a rush.

"She knew what was coming. She knew she wouldn't live. And she knew I had lost my baby in California. My baby was born dead. I came home after that. I didn't want to stay in America by myself, without family. Trudy wanted me to have hers. It was a gift, from one cousin to another. So many people don't understand, but back in China, it happened all the time, throughout history, particularly during wartime or famine. We are a country used to suffering; our people are practical. Children were given to other members of the family, if they were to be better looked after that way. You Westerners don't understand. It's what Trudy wanted, or would have wanted. She knew that Locket would have a good home. And I think Victor thought Locket would be good insurance as well. She is half Japanese, you know, Locket. Half Japanese, a quarter Chinese, a quarter Portuguese. Although you'd never know it to look at her. You'd never know it. You didn't, did you? And we love her as our own. It was all for the best."

She stopped, looked confused.

"The doctor told me I could never have any more children, that I would die if I did. So I really had no choice." She trailed off. "Oh," she said. "I was going to get Locket."

She wandered out of the room.

Claire sat in the suddenly silent room. A clock ticked loudly. Some long minutes later, Locket showed up in the drawing room.

"I was waiting for you in the music room," she said. "I waited and waited and then Ling told me you were here. You were with Mummy?"

Claire looked at the girl with new eyes. Trudy's child. A girl who had never known her real mother, a child born of violence and deception and desperation. None of this showed on her wide, placid face. The past, her history, had been so easily buried.

"Yes, Locket," she said. "But I've come because I have to let you know something. Why don't you come and sit down next to me?"

Locket sat down. "Do you want some biscuits?" she asked. "I'm feeling a bit hungry." She called for a servant and spoke to her in Cantonese. Claire could now tell the difference between the dialects: Shanghainese, Cantonese, Mandarin. Families like Locket's often spoke all three, as well as English and usually some French. "And will you have a drink, Mrs. Pendleton?"

Suddenly, Claire saw Locket as a miniature Melody, with her assured handling of servants and household matters. But then she blinked. The maid had brought in a plate of jam biscuits with milk, and Locket was a child again, stuffing two in her mouth at once.

"Locket," she said, "I've come to tell you that I cannot teach you any longer."

"Mmmmmm," said Locket, with a mouthful of biscuit.

"And that I've really enjoyed teaching you, although you never practiced as much as you should have."

"Sorry, Mrs. Pendleton."

"But that doesn't matter. I want to tell you that you are a good girl, and that you can do a great many things. You are sweet and have a real goodness about you. Your innocence is special."

Locket nodded, her eyes confused.

"I know you don't understand what I'm talking about, Locket, but I want to tell you. You are a good person. Keep your center. Believe in your instincts. I really wish you the best in life as you go forward." Claire felt the futility of what she was doing, but pressed on. She wanted desperately to leave Locket with something, anything, that would stick. But the very thing that would brand Locket forever, leave an indelible impression, was what she absolutely could not say. She could not take on that mantle of responsibility.

"Mrs. Pendleton, you make it seem as if I'm going to die or something!"

"I just want you to know..." she trailed off. "Just know. That is all." She got up and kissed Locket on the top of her glossy black hair. "Good-bye."

She left Locket in the drawing room with her biscuits and her look of confusion, and a strange, tumultuous feeling in her own stomach.

IN HIS DREAMS, she comes back to him. In his dreams, she forgives him.

"I was always searching for a saint," Trudy says. Her hands are intertwined behind his head, her eyes looking up into his. "I thought you were the one."

"I'm sorry," he says. "I never pretended I was one."

"Oh, I think you did," she says, without anger. "You always had that saintlike aura around you. People always looked to you for guidance. You radiate confidence. Unlike me. I radiate...unreliability. But I'm much more fun."

He touches her hair, the fine, glossy strands of umber and bronze.

"I never locked my door because of you," he tells her. "I thought even if there was the slightest chance you were alive...Stranger things have happened. I couldn't lock my door because I was tormented by the thought that you'd find your way back to me, and that I'd happen to be out, and that you would leave, and then I would have missed my chance. That's why I could never move. People always wondered why I stayed there, stuck in the past."

"Of course I would find you," she says, in her clear, bell voice. "You've forgotten how resourceful I am."

"You made me want to be the worst kind of man," he confesses. "If I had a family, I would have left it for you. If you wanted a bauble, I would have stolen it for you. If you told me to kill somebody, I very well might have done so. There's nothing I wouldn't do for you, and that's the most terrible thing in the world. So I had to get away from it. I had to get away from you, to preserve myself."

"Well," she says, amused. "I don't know if that's the nicest thing anyone's ever said to me, or the nastiest."

She has always told him she is not dependable, that she will leave him in an instant, that she is not to be trusted, but in all her declarations, he has just to look into her eyes, and he doesn't believe her.

"I like to think about when all this is over," she says. "I'm going to have ice cream and champagne at every meal and bathe in honey and wine. I am going to be so profligate, you have no idea! I'm going to act every inch the heiress and demand every extravagance—only soaps and scents from France will touch my skin and fresh, exotic flowers on my bedside table every night. This restraint is just killing me. I've become a dour, wartime matron and I intend to scrub every inch of that loathsome person off as soon as . . ." But she cannot say what will end the war.

He shakes her. He wants to bite her cheek, viciously, until flesh tears off and blood runs down his chin. He wants to devour her whole, until she feels the pain he has been feeling. The pain he has caused her too.

He surfaces, she recedes, he remembers the other one, the one that's still alive. But he goes down again, into the past. Its pull is too strong.

The memory of those days. Sitting on his thin bed, helpless, outraged, angered by the endless monotony around him, the small concerns of the others—whether they were getting their fair ration, that someone had moved surreptitiously into an empty room that had not yet been allocated after the Americans had been repatriated. Ah, yes, the day that the Americans left, their government far more expedient in arranging a prisoner-of-war trade, the indescribable feeling of watching the lorries depart, filled with joyful, bedraggled people, pockets filled with messages from those remaining to loved ones around the world. They promised to get the letters out. The kinder ones had left all their blankets and extra clothes and equipment and even money, but a few took every last scrap, as if they wouldn't throw it out the moment they got home. Funny, the mentality that springs up in such a place. And a few Americans stayed behind: the Catholic priests. They gave up their chance to return home so they could minister to the faithful remaining in the camp, regardless of nationality. Yes, there had been good people.

Another memory, from even before: the first Christmas in camp, a year or so after they had been interned. He remembered the half-dead grass in the center lawn and the dust kicked up by the children as they ran around, shouting excitedly in their ragged shorts—it had been unseasonably warm. The women had set up tables with watery lemonade and Christmas cookies donated from those still on the outside. A program with songs and recitals had been mimeographed and distributed. They had also managed to get ahold of some decorations so the straggly trees on the perimeter boasted tinsel and some garish ornaments. An old gramophone piped Christmas carols as the internees gathered around and chatted, sipping from their cups, a flask surreptitiously passed around. Bill Schott had acquired a Santa Claus costume and came out with a pillow stuffed next to his belly, much to the delight of the children, and handed out a motley but much squealed-over selection of presents: a collection of shiny buttons, a rag doll stuffed with dry grass, a Christmas collage made out of leaves. The mothers had been busy.

The Japanese soldiers watched with bemusement from the side. They had given packets of boiled sweets to the children earlier.

Regina Arbogast appeared before him suddenly, a red muffler wrapped dramatically around her neck. She still had flair.

"Will, Merry Christmas," she said. Her husband was next to her.

It was before the torture. That would happen months later. Will raised a glass to the couple.

"A year passes too quickly, doesn't it? What a difference from last year."

"And here we are," said Reggie.

"You enjoying the furloughs?" Regina asked. Will's fluidity between the inside and outside had been the source of much envy and speculation, although he always tried to bring back supplies to benefit everyone.

"'Enjoy' is a peculiar way of putting it," he said.

"Trudy is tight with the current regime." Regina let the statement hang in the air, a challenge.

"Is that a question or a statement?" Will asked mildly.

"How would you know anything about that, locked up in here?" Reggie said impatiently to his wife. "You presume too much, Regina."

"Well, that's what everyone is saying." Regina winked. "But I suppose the less you know the better, right, Will?"

Reggie rolled his eyes and looked apologetic.

"Oh, look here," he said. "The choir is ready to sing." He took Regina firmly by the arm and led her away to where the older children and women were preparing to perform.

Will remembers this exchange with a sick feeling, and how it all ended up, how they were all playing at something that ended up being all too real.

Then 1945, the recurring sounds of aircraft overhead, whispers of a new kind of bomb. Something extraordinary, beyond imagination, an unthinkable death toll. A giant mushroom cloud of devastation over Japan. Snippets of information smuggled in through the daily vegetable delivery, the spinach suddenly wrapped in the English newspaper.

Guards looking sheepish, being slightly friendlier, allowed more privileges. Their rations grew larger.

Trudy still a daily thought, but now successfully muffled. None of his messages answered, no reported sightings from the people who visited other internees. It was as if she had vanished into thin air. Like her mother, he thought, and pushed that thought out of his head. In war, people die. Later, he would realize that was how a dying man would think.

And the liberation, entering a brave new world outside, still wary of the Japanese, dangerous in their loss. Some lashed out, killed while they could, but most trod the fine line between conquered and conqueror, that undefined space.

As if an old creaky machine were being cranked back into life, Hong Kong sputtered back. The buses and trams started running on their regular schedules, stores started to receive provisions, and prices slowly returned to normal. People ran into one another on the street and clutched each other, remarked on how thin everyone was, happy to have survived and to see each other, even if they hadn't liked each other before. Practicing the normal, trying to get to mundane.

Otsubo was repatriated to Japan. Later, they heard he was hanged at Sugamo Prison. There was no relief in hearing the news.

The strangeness of the first dinner party, and how everyone slipped into it cautiously at first, and then how everyone got comfortable so quickly it was unseemly. They complained about the lack of basic supplies, then the lack of good help, then how hard it was to get good wine, then everything. The amnesia of comfort, soothing, anodyne, too seductive. They were all too soon back to themselves.

How can a woman disappear? How can someone so vivid vanish?

Searching for her in the aftermath, the empty taste in his mouth, the taste of regret. Funny thing: He was always thirsty after liberation. He procured a car and drove the empty roads throughout the island—to her old flat, to Angeline's old house, to her father's house in Sai Kung, all vacant and vandalized, smelling musty and worse. A tour of abandoned houses. Her father dead in Macau, unknown causes during the war. Dominick also gone. Just another sad story.

Without the lightness of Trudy buoying him up, Will became morose, too serious, too dark. He lurked in odd corners of Hong Kong or stayed home, a sparse affair with one glass, one plate, a bare lightbulb. He was no longer invited anywhere. "He's gone odd," whispered around town. He could not define a new self without Trudy.

He sank into anonymity until he caught a glimpse of Victor and Melody getting out of their car in Causeway Bay, with their daughter. Their daughter who looked nothing like them. He remembered hearing something about Melody in the United States, a tragedy, but something that had been whispered once and then never again. He started to think. And then rang up Victor with a hard-luck story and asked for a job, knowing that the man would love to hire an Englishman for what he would consider a menial job, both men knowing there was much more to the request.

Victor loved to show him off to unknowing business associates, particularly those just arrived from Europe or America. Will would pull the car around and get out to open the door. Victor's guests would widen their eyes and step into the car, visibly impressed. An Englishman working as a driver, even for a family such as the Chens, was almost unheard of, especially someone like him, who'd been out and about in society before the war. Still, most were embroiled in their own concerns and many had emerged much changed from the war—the Dutch banker who exited Stanley a schizophrenic and now lived in an alley building in Sheung Wan and came out to beg with a rattan basket, his blond hair matted and dark; or the Miller girl who had been engaged to one of the Hos, the shipping family, but came out of the camp too used, and now lived in Mong Kok and was rumored to be a bar hostess. Will was just another casualty of war, and not the worst off of them. People talked at first, but then it became just another quirky fact of Hong Kong life.

He worked odd hours and tried to get glimpses of Locket, but the Chens always had the other drivers take her to school. Despite himself, he looked at her face, looking for signs of what? Trudy, yes, but also what he could not voice in his own head.

One day, Victor got in the car and directed Will to drive to the Peak. On the way up, he had seemed agitated, fidgeting with papers in the backseat.

"Mistakes were made," he said suddenly, opaquely.

Will had not answered, which had made Victor more jumpy.

"Do you know what I'm talking about?" he had asked.

"No."

"In times of war, there are many decisions that are made, and things that get done without the benefit of reflection."

"Yes, sir," he had replied, his deference more threatening than anything he could have said. He saw Victor's face in the rearview mirror. He was perspiring heavily.

"I've had some news..." Victor started.

"Yes, sir," he repeated.

Victor hesitated, then seemed to get ahold of himself.

"At any rate, Will, the war has changed all of us. We're all in this together now."

Will remained silent.

"I've changed my mind, Will. You can take me home now."

Will swung the car around and took Victor home. They didn't speak on the return journey. His wages were suddenly doubled. Will never found out what had spooked Victor but neither he nor Victor ever mentioned the ride again.

He was waiting for something to happen. And in the meantime, he remembered.

• • •

Trudy and Dominick locked in a terrible embrace.

Funny how so many things seem inevitable, given enough distance. Put a girl and a boy of similar persuasions together in summer and see what evolves. Usually love. Two friends, equally matched, and then one suddenly has an advantage: rarely will they remain friends. This must have been what happened. Trudy and Dominick, alike as two peas in a pod when things were good. When the situation turned fraught, each reverted to form. Trudy essentially good, Dominick an animal. The betrayal sharp.

But his own? Much worse. He knows.

"I forgive you," she says. "I understand."

He clings to this. Hears her say it over and over.

How can he leave her now?

Epilogue

A WOMAN IS SITTING in a chair, reading by a window. A cup of tea has gone cold beside her. Dusk is gathering outside, and when it becomes too difficult to see, she goes to turn on the light. The room is suddenly illuminated.

She lives by herself now, in a small apartment she has found in Wan Chai, amid locals and wet markets. It is furnished simply, with an iron bed and a thin mattress, a wooden fruit crate for a bedside table, a lamp she bought at Dodwell's during the holiday sales. She has a comfortable reading chair as well. She lives very frugally, within her means as a secretary for a shipping company, and she has found that it is possible to live like a local, on almost nothing, bargaining for everything from lightbulbs to tea towels. She buys one orange at a time, or two carrots, or picks her own chicken to be killed, a purchase that will last her three days. She eats at the street stalls: noodles and congee and roasted meats and other dishes she would have found unappealing just a year before. She can wield chopsticks now with the best of them. Sometimes, as she sits on the stools, next to a taxi driver or a shopkeeper, she listens and finds she can understand some of what they are saying; words emerge from the noise, like jewels. In the beginning, she was a curiosity to them, but now they have seen her enough to ignore her. Her Cantonese— still rudimentary—is improving. Now she can order at the *daipai-dong,* and they will not repeat the order loudly, in English; they just grunt and dump the noodles in the broth to boil, same treatment as the locals.

At home, she sometimes wears the black trousers and white tunics—the amah uniform—as night clothes and finds them oddly comfortable. They are made of light cotton and are very inexpensive. The shop owner had assumed she was buying them for her amah and kept asking how tall, gesturing with her hands. Claire held the cloth against her frame and nodded her head. The first day she spent in her flat, she walked down to the local street barber and sat down, much to his surprise, and asked him to cut her hair short all around.

And she knows the streets of the town—Johnston, Harcourt, Connaught—and how to say them in Cantonese. They are like a web of veins emanating out from Central to Repulse Bay, the Peak, Mid-Levels, places she rarely goes now, places filled with English people and the lives they lead. She runs into people she knows now and then, and they always ask how she is doing, in that searching, curious way, and she just nods and says fine, she is doing fine, enjoying the city very much. But are you going home? they ask, and she says no, she has no plans to go home at the moment.

She is talked about less and less. She is becoming a part of some old history that will soon be forgotten, and this suits her well.

Sometimes she is lonely, but she frequents the library at the Auxiliary, taking out three or four books at once. There are so many things to know and learn. She reads about Beethoven, Chinese rice farming, biographies of English prime ministers, and finds comfort in the fact that she will never run out of books. There is also a piano there, and the manageress has told her she can play after hours if she arranges it beforehand. She has been going there in the early evening, when the heat is less, and playing for an hour or so, while the staff cleans up around her. She goes late enough so that all the women she would know have already finished with their tea and gone home to prepare for supper, husbands and children gathering at home, filling the rooms with chatter and noise, so unlike her own.

Martin is still in Hong Kong, as far as she knows. She had stayed at the flat with him for a few days while she was finding her own quarters, a request she had brought up when he had come home, ashen-faced, after the party. He had not said yes but he did not say no. She knew it was more than generous of him. She had poured neat whiskey into two glasses and sipped it with him in silence. She remembered still his posture. He sat heavily at the table, drinking slowly, and fingered the edge of the linen coaster. Yu Ling hovered excitedly near the kitchen door, listening for anything, having already been informed by telephone, before either had arrived home, of the scandalous situation through the lightning-quick amah network.

And he hadn't had the stomach for questions. He wanted her to volunteer the information but she could not bring herself to talk to him. For the first few days, his cold silence when he returned home was welcome; it was when he began to try to talk to her and understand what had happened that she couldn't stand it. She slept on the sofa in the living room, and tried to wake before Yu Ling got up, so that she could put away the pillow and the blankets, but too often she had seen the amah's curious eyes watching her as she woke. She supposes, in Yu Ling's world, such a situation would be settled with a chopper, and that she and Martin seem bloodless, bizarre to her.

Then Martin: "Were you unhappy?" The first sentence he had spoken to her since that night. He had come into the living room from their bedroom; she had been reading.

And what could she have said? She put down her book and tried to think of the answer. She found the question too prosaic, and hated herself for that.

"I needed to believe there was more to life." Said simply. The fanciful notion an affront to good values, and she all too aware of it.

"Where did you go?" His second question. He sat down at the dining room table, far from her. He rubbed at his eyes.

She explained. She had walked outside the Chens' house. It was hot, as usual, and she had no car. So she walked down May Road, the windy, narrow street carved out of the mountain—a snake of a road—until it became Garden Road and she got to Central. By then, she was very hot, so she went into a bakery and drank some cool tea. Her head had been filled with a white noise, similar to when she had fainted outside the Chens' house earlier. Then, not knowing where to go, she had just continued east, found herself in Wan Chai, and found the commotion and bustle soothing. With so much activity around her, the frenzy inside her had quieted. And she had looked around, and thought, I could live here.

"I think I found myself too apparent in the world, after what happened at the party, and I want to be invisible for a little bit," she told Martin. "There was too much going on, and I don't know why I'm a part of it, but I am. And I realize that you must feel the same way, and for that, I apologize."

He stared at her—this unworldly young woman he had brought over from England—and realized he had no idea who she was.

So, she left as soon as she could. She packed up her belongings and got a taxi while he was at work. She hugged Yu Ling, feeling the amah's slight frame under her embrace and an unexpected sadness at leaving her, this life. But she was now finally convinced that people got what they expected from life. Martin had never expected to find love, and so, ultimately, he would be all right. She would not be his great disappointment in life, his tragedy. That would come from somewhere else and she realized with relief she was not responsible for even knowing what that might be. She herself hadn't known what to expect from life, and still didn't. Her life was, is still, a work in progress.

She supposes that she is becoming a cliché, a woman "gone native," someone who eschews her own kind. Amelia, her old acquaintance, had come to see her in her flat and could not quite hide the shock at the circumstances she had found Claire in. She had fluttered around the small space, given her a jar of strawberry preserves and some soaps, and never returned. Claire supposes Amelia dined out on the story for several weeks after. This does not bother her in the least.

Last week she had taken a small bag of costly jewelry, scarves, and trinkets and given it to the local secondhand shop. The woman who had taken the items looked befuddled and at a loss as to what to do with them, amid the dusty, inexpensive sweaters and used pots. Claire hadn't known what else to do with them. As she walked out the door, she felt her mood lift, and she became light.

Now she pauses, looks out the window to the busy streetscape outside. Cars traverse the streets, the red taxis crossing lanes with double-decker trams tethered to their cables, a few men on bicycles. The sky is blue, delineated by the tops of the low buildings with their antennae and rooftop clotheslines. The pungent air from the road rises and enters through her window. A scene she could never have imagined just two years ago.

And a simple knowledge is what sustains her through all of this: that all she needs to do is step out onto that street and she will dissolve into it, be absorbed in its rhythms and become, easily, a part of the world.

Acknowledgments

I want to thank so many people:

My agent, Theresa Park, without whose support and gentle encouragement this novel might still be a jumble of notes on my computer. She has been with me from the first pages of this book.

Abby Koons, Julian Alexander, Rich Green, Sam Edenborough, Nicki Kennedy, and Amanda Cardinale.

Kathryn Court, my wise and elegant editor.
Clare Ferraro for her early and unwavering support.
The amazing team at Viking: Alexis Washam, Carolyn Coleburn, Louise Braverman, Ann Day, Nancy Sheppard, Paul Slovak, Isabel Widdowson, and so many others.
Clare Smith and the wonderful team at Harper Press UK for their enthusiasm and guidance.

Pat Towers, who showed me graciousness, always, while teaching me nuance.
Abigail Thomas, who encouraged me with cake, good judgment, and kind words.
Chang-rae Lee for advice both writerly and practical, always on-point.
Elaina Richardson for the time at Yaddo

For friendship and encouragement, and understanding: Mimi Brown, Deborah Cincotta, Rachael Combe, Kate Gellert, Katie Rosman, Sarah Towers, Daphne Uviller.

I read many books about this period in World War II in both the New York Public Library and the Special Collections Library at Hong Kong

University. In particular, I learned much about the time from Emily Hahn's excellent memoir, *China to Me*, and the colorful *Prisoner of the Turnip Heads* by George Wright-Nooth with Mark Adkin.

I also spent many hours working in various rooms at the New York Public Library, the New York Society Library, and Hong Kong University Library and thank them for being open to the public and providing space for writers to work.

My mother, father, and brother and his family.

The extended Bae family.

My children, who give me joy every day and put everything in perspective.

And most important, my husband, Joe, who is my best friend, my better half, and who supports me with an unstinting love and generosity that I am grateful for every day.

A PENGUIN READERS GUIDE TO

THE
PIANO TEACHER

Janice Y. K. Lee

An Introduction to
The Piano Teacher

Demure and unsophisticated, Claire Pendleton is the
quintessential English rose when she first arrives in Hong
Kong. The year is 1952 and, as the wife of an English engineer
overseeing the construction of a new reservoir, Claire seems
destined to lead an insulated life, socializing with the other
expatriate wives. But when she takes a position giving piano
lessons to Locket Chen, the daughter of a wealthy and powerful
local family, she enters a world of deceit, passion, and dark secrets
that will deeply shock Hong Kong society and change Claire
forever.

At first glance, the British colony seems to have recovered
from the ravages of the Japanese occupation a decade earlier. Yet
memories and reminders of those brutal times are everywhere.
The British themselves are divided into recent arrivals, like Claire,
and those who survived the war, like Will Truesdale, the Chens'
English chauffeur. Will is handsome and darkly charismatic—
everything Claire's husband, the stolid and reliable Martin, is not.
After meeting Will at a cocktail party, Claire begins to see him
everywhere. In Will's company, she finally feels alive, but she is
infuriated by his aloofness. He seems to understand her better
than anyone else, but he reveals little of his own past or emotions.
His gaunt figure and pronounced limp are grim souvenirs from
the Japanese invaders and the time he was imprisoned in Stanley,
the squalid prison camp where most British subjects—including
women and children—spent the war abused, humiliated, and
virtually starved. What little Claire learns is in fragments and often
from gossip rather than from Will himself.

Unexpectedly, Claire receives hints about Will's former lover
from two unlikely sources—Locket's father, Victor, and Edwina
Storch, a matriarch of the expatriate community. Trudy Liang,
it seems, was everything Claire is not—a worldly-wise Eurasian

heiress celebrated for her dazzling beauty and willful personality, who disappeared mysteriously at the end of the war. Claire spies a photograph capturing a night of revelry shared by Will, Trudy, her employers, and an unknown Chinese man. How, she wonders, did Will come to be the Chens' employee after having been so intimate with them socially?

As her affair with Will unfolds, Claire realizes that Trudy's memory is a greater rival for his affections than any flesh-and-blood woman. But the past holds others in its thrall as well and—as the coronation of Britain's young Princess Elizabeth nears—murmurs about the Crown Collection, which had gone missing during the war, grow into angry accusations of collaboration with the Japanese occupiers. Suddenly, Claire finds herself an unwitting pawn in a revenge plot when her affair with Will is manipulated to expose a trove of devastating secrets.

The Piano Teacher is a spellbinding tale of human frailty and passions reminiscent of *The English Patient* and *Empire of the Sun*. In alternating narratives, debut novelist Janice Y. K. Lee brilliantly evokes Trudy, Will, and Claire's tragic love triangle against the relative calm of 1950s Hong Kong and the glittering pre-war era's decline into chaos and ruin.

About Janice Y. K. Lee

Janice Y. K. Lee was born and raised in Hong Kong and graduated from Harvard College. A former features editor at *Elle* and *Mirabella* magazines, she currently lives in Hong Kong with her husband and children.

A Conversation with
Janice Y. K. Lee

What is the inspiration for The Piano Teacher? *Are Trudy's experiences—or those of the other characters—based on those of people you've known personally or on historical characters?*

The Piano Teacher is based in a time and a place that are real, with historical events that did happen, but what happens to my characters—their particular story—is imagined. Of course, people were interned, like Will was, and a few were outside, like Trudy was, but I did not come across anyone who had a similar story. I didn't interview people about their experiences because I didn't want other people's facts to interfere with my fiction. I was very careful about that. I did read books by survivors and so I found out things that happened in the camps—daily life, schedules, activities.

With this book I really started with the characters, developed them until I knew them well. And they started to interact with each other. And that's really where the story came from. The characters led me. In a time of war, there is a wide range of experiences in a short, intense time, so as a novelist it's very freeing in that way to have the liberty to be able to imagine that anything might happen to your characters.

Is there a real Crown Collection? If so, what is it and where is it now?

The Crown Collection is something that I made up. I was looking for something with great stakes, something that would make men lie and betray and kill, and this came to me, and it seemed so natural and right, and it felt authentic. These kinds of fictional details are a gift—you know when they come because they strike the right note.

The novel is beautifully written, yet it also has a cinematic feel. What or who were your influences?

That was one of the most surprising things to me—that the writing was cinematic. I suppose I've been influenced by this visual age more than I knew. I actually haven't had time to watch a lot of movies in the past six years, so I think it must be a repository of images from a long time ago. I have no idea who my influences are, but my favorite writers are, to name a few: Lorrie Moore, Mona Simpson, Michael Cunningham, Jeffrey Eugenides, Shirley Hazzard. These are all writers who, if their newest book comes out, I will rush to get it.

Ned Young and Edwina Storch are relatively minor but wonderfully rendered characters. Aside from the novel's primary players, who is your favorite character and why?

I like Wan Kee Liang; he seemed very real to me. Angeline Biddle is also a character who seemed very true. All of these characters really came to be like real people to me, so much so that I knew how they would react in any given situation. I knew immediately that Trudy's father would never want her to know that he needed her, because that is often how parents are, and that he was not the stereotypical business tycoon, all flamboyance and bravado. Of course, he would be quiet and shy, and outshined by his daughter. Or that Angeline was such a strict person that she would give up her friendship with Trudy because she didn't approve of Trudy's behavior. It was partly self-preservation but largely principles. Their motives and actions are very clear to me.

It's often said that the setting of a novel can be so vivid as to be like a character itself. That's certainly true of Hong Kong in your novel. How did you research what it was like in the 1940s and 1950s?

I am a voracious reader and I came across some books that had been written in those times. I was so interested in the details of the time, and the details that interested me were not the minutiae of the war but all the stuff around it—what types of parties people were having, who they invited, what they wore, what they ate and drank. It's hard to get those sorts of details from history books, so I got them from memoirs, old newspapers, and movies too. I wanted to know how long the trip was from London to Hong Kong, and how many stops and where the stops were, and what they ate on the boat. These are the details that, for me, make a novel come alive. Would an English person invite a Chinese person to a coronation party in the 1950s? How would they talk? Is it a possible that a Chinese person could be more English than the English person? Exploring all of this was great fun.

You were born and raised in Hong Kong and then attended college at Harvard. What struck you as the most jarring differences between life in Hong Kong and the United States?

I think the difference was tempered by the fact that I attended the American school in Hong Kong and so I was already pretty American in culture when I went to the U.S. Still, it was an adjustment. I had never seen a northeastern winter and was amazed by the first few blizzards I experienced and how very cold it could get. I was also struck by how friendly Americans were, how they exchanged pleasantries for even the smallest of transactions, like buying a pack of gum. There's much more distance in Hong Kong. People don't say, "How's it going?" and "Have a great day!" like they do in the U.S. It's a much more formal society. Of course, now I'm very American and often startle people here by accosting them with some overly energetic greeting or too-personal question.

How has Hong Kong changed since it reverted to the Chinese in 1997?

I left Hong Kong in 1987 and did not move back until 2005, so I was not here for the time immediately before and after the handover. When I was a girl, there was definitely a feeling that

Hong Kong was a colony, that Mother England was overseeing everything and that we were her charges. When I moved back, much of the association with England had been erased. "Royal" had been stripped from the name of many services, clubs, and associations. There was much more emphasis on being part of China, being Chinese. However, I will say that the day-to-day part of living for me has not been affected that much. Hong Kong is a large cosmopolitan city and very international in feel and has been that way for a long time.

Is the book being published in Hong Kong and/or Japan? How do you expect it will be received there?

It has not been picked up in Hong Kong or Japan yet, although it has been sold and is being translated in languages as far afield as Hebrew, Catalan, and Romanian. It was explained to me that often people in the countries/cultures that are being written about have less interest in the subject than do people in other places. In a way, it is old news to them. Interestingly, though, it has been sold in Mainland China. The difference is simplified characters versus complex characters in the Chinese written language. Still, I have hope that Hong Kong and Japan will pick it up, as it is a novel first, and I hope that the story will appeal to readers worldwide.

What are you working on now?

I can't say for fear of jinxing it. I am quite superstitious. Suffice to say, it is very preliminary and I have a feeling it will not have to do with Hong Kong and may very well not be historical either.

QUESTIONS FOR DISCUSSION

1. Why does Claire steal from the Chens? Why does she stop doing it?

2. Part of Claire's attraction to Will is that he allows her to be someone different than she had always been. Have you ever been drawn to a person or a situation because it offered you the opportunity to reinvent yourself?

3. The amahs are a steady but silent presence throughout the book. Imagine Trudy and Will's relationship and then Claire and Will's affair from their point of view and discuss.

4. Trudy was initially drawn to Will because of his quiet equanimity and Will to Claire because of her innocence. Yet those are precisely the qualities each loses in the course of their love affairs. What does this say about the nature of these relationships? Would Will have been attracted to a woman like Claire before Trudy?

5. What is the irony behind Claire's adoration of the young Princess Elizabeth?

6. Were Dominick and Trudy guilty of collaboration, or were they simply trying to survive? Do their circumstances absolve them of their actions?

7. Mary, Tobias's mother, and one of Will's fellow prisoners in Stanley, does not take advantage of her job in the kitchen to steal more food for her son. Yet she prostitutes herself to preserve him. Is Tobias's physical survival worth the psychological damage she's inflicting?

8. How do Ned Young's experiences parallel Trudy's?

9. Did Will fail Trudy? Was his decision to remain in Stanley rather than be with her on the outside—as he believes—an act of cowardice?

10. Would Locket be better off knowing the truth about her parentage?

11. What would happen if Trudy somehow survived and came back to Will? Could they find happiness together?

For more information about or to order other Penguin Readers Guides, please e-mail the Penguin Marketing Department at reading@us.penguingroup.com or write to us at:

Penguin Books Marketing Dept.
Readers Guides
375 Hudson Street
New York, NY 10014-3657

Please allow 4–6 weeks for delivery.
To access Penguin Readers Guides online, visit the Penguin Group (USA) Inc. Web sites at www.penguin.com and www.vpbookclub.com.